The Irrelevant Tales

by Othy Jones

The Irrelevant Tales

Copyedited by Kirkus Editorial
Interior design by Timothy J. Jones

www.theirrelevanttales.com

Twitter: @othyjones

First Edition

Printed by CreateSpace, An Amazon.com Company

For Kate, my love

The Irrelevant Tales

"What you do in this world is a matter of no consequence,"...
"The question is, what can you make people believe that you have done?"
~Sherlock Holmes, A Study in Scarlet
by Sir Arthur Conan Doyle

PROLOGUE

I've often wondered: Do we dictate our destiny or are our lives shaped by its experiences? How much of who we are comes from others we've met? I like to think of each person's life as a mosaic of sand. Each time you meet someone else you've left some of your sand behind in their mosaic, shaping something beautiful that's never quite finished: An impression of what would be; an impression of what is. Me own story is just such an impression.

Me name is William O'Brien, Billy to me friends, though the latter will seem irrelevant as me story unfolds. I speak of impressions for I am an Irish Impressionist painter who now lives in England. Never heard of me? I dare say I'm not surprised. Most artists, as I'm sure you know, do not reach their prime of infamy until they've long since been laid to rest. I was born sixty–five years ago on the Ides of March 1854 on the Emerald Isle itself. I was the youngest of four children; two brothers and a girl came before me. Me parents were well into their mid–forties when I was born, so you might say I was the accident of the litter.

Now, me father died when I was a lad of fifteen; something happened when he was lifting a particularly heavy crate down at the shipping docks of Kinsale where he made a living for us. Naturally, in his absence, I took his place at work to help even out the ends with me Mum and sister. Me brothers had lives of their own then, the eldest with an expecting wife at home.

During those laborious days of me youth, I'd often gaze out into the sea dreaming of far off places, hypnotized by the picturesque beauty of the tides foaming up against the shore while the wailing gulls called to each other on an air–wave of their own. One such day, when I was about sixteen or so, I came across an artist from Paris down at the shore. He had been sketching out the sun rising over one of the ships when I came upon him and admired his work with perhaps a bit too much curiosity, though he hadn't seemed to mind.

He introduced himself as Monsieur Pierre de Croismencer (pronounced krə–mwan–sé). He had come to Ireland to paint the Silvermine Mountains and was planning on soon returning to France, since he was anxious to see his family after wandering the Irish countryside for over a year and a half.

Now, I don't know if it was his longing to see his son or that he saw something kindling inside me soul, but from that day on he took me under his wing. He nurtured me potential; taught me about colours and canvases, and all the splendour that can be crafted from the simple length, thickness, and curvature of lines and the stroke of a brush.

I had just turned seventeen when Monsieur de Croismencer left for home. He gave me various art supplies and made me promise to use them at least once a day, in order to keep me craft in tune and to better meself in the future. It was repetitive practise that instilled a thirst for nature within me, a thirst that I continue to this very day to try to quench. So it should come as no surprise that by the time I was nineteen I had honed me skills and was ripe for the world. Against me brothers' wishes,—but not me Mum's, for she had always encouraged me talents,— I made off for France on me own one day in pursuit of an art school I'd caught word of at a local tavern where I'd set up weekend shop to paint quick portraits of random passers–by.

It was the winter of 1873 when I'd arrived in Paris for the first time. The streets where lined with small cafés, bakeries, and the finest shops I'd ever laid eyes on, and still have yet to see! It was a completely different world. The clothing was different. The food was different. Even the godforsaken cats and dogs seemed to be different! Yet, what hadn't hit me until that moment was that the very language itself was different!

The language? Blimey! Had I been so blinded by me hastiness that I'd completely overlooked the single most important thing necessary for a proper education, not to mention mere survival? You bet I had, and when the *L'École des Beaux–Arts* found this out, there was no admittance for a lonely English–speaking Irish lad from the village of Summerstone Cove, no sir. No matter how I tried to convince them that learning was through watching, not through speaking, they simply couldn't understand. That, of course, was no doubt due to the fact that they barely understood any English at all, period. 'Twas then I realized how naive and foolish I'd been, and all I could think about was, What's going to become of me now? Where do I go from here?

I
THE MYSTERIOUS DR. VANT

So there I was—a foreigner in a foreign country—with just enough money to last until I could find a job, which, as I figured, would take about a week or so. Two, if I ate once a day. 'Twas then that I happened upon a cheap little inn where the owner spoke feeble and fragmented English. I suppose money is the universal language and, since I'd be tossin' a coin his way every now and then, he let me stay.

Slowly, I began to learn the lay of the land and I was able to get a job carrying boxes for a grocer delivery company making a few sous a week. It was the bottom of the barrel, it was, but I was a stubborn one, and so I could often be found after work, sitting at *La Maison du Café*, sketching people's portraits under the owner's watch. Though the man didn't speak a lick of me native tongue, he was able to communicate with me through hand gestures and a very expressive face. We had a mutual understanding that I would sketch portraits of the localites, slowly, so that they would, in turn, spend their wages on the owner's fine teas and cakes.

And so, on April the fifteenth, 1874, during the early evening, a strange sort of chap came into the little café. I didn't grasp it at first, but it eventually hit me what was so odd about him. He was an Englishman—a top–of–the–top, bona fide British nobleman—dressed in shades of purple. He stood there in his dark plum–coloured top–coat with a matching top hat that was accented by a lavender band of ribbon wound round the base. You might say he resembled a peacock, having the epitome of posture. He set his walking stick aside and took a seat at a table beside me own.

"Garçon," said he, with a snap of his fingers. "J'ai passé un temps long sur mes pieds et je voudrais du thé, s'il vous plait."

He then turned towards me, and what a sight I must have been, what with me mouth gaping open, astonished at the sight of someone who'd be able to understand the Frenchman's language as well as me own!

"Good heavens, boy, you're liable to catch a cold with your mouth hanging open like that," said the man.

In response, I clamped it shut, amusing him, for he gave a slight chuckle.

"Irish, I presume, in Paris a few months, I'd say, and quite the artist, though you're forced to earn your living the old–fashioned way: hard labour."

"Bless me ears, sir," said I. "How could you be knowing that?"

"Your nationality is easily distinguishable, and I perceive that you've been here long enough to get a job and make a fair living, for how else could I explain your being in a café with a *café au lait* yet still be baffled by the language, since you've not been here long enough to learn it. Therefore, I'd guess three perhaps four months. As for your talent, your canvas gives you away, and yet your hands are bruised and your arms much more greatly defined then the rest of you, which points to the fact that though you'd prefer to paint, you're forced to lift things to make ends meet."

"That's incredible, sir!"

"Such is the power of anthropology."

"Anthro—"

"—pology, the study of people. Perhaps you're more acquainted with ethnology as it's often miscalled. No? Hmmm, what about archaeology?"

"Aye, sir. That's the study of ancient artefacts."

"Correct! It is, in fact, a facet of anthropology on the whole. Coincidentally, so is ethnology, though most Europeans think of them as being one and the same."

"Well," I paused. "Me name's William O'Brien, sir, but you can call me Billy.

He laughed.

"My dear boy, I could never do that."

"Em … why not, sir?" I questioned.

"Because," he explained, "William suits you far better. After all, your own parents saw fit to name you that, and I'd say they chose wisely. Though I've often wondered: Is it the man who makes the name or the name that makes the man?"

I sat perplexed for a moment.

"I'm afraid I don't know, sir."

"It's just as well, for I'm sure science will figure it out one day."

"So, uh, I beg your pardon," I said as I stood, "but may I ask your name?"

He glanced up at me, in his own world for a mere moment. Then he snapped back to life.

"Oh certainly. Good gracious! Where are my manners? I am Dr. Irel E. Vant," said he, as he extended his hand for a shake.

"Surely you're joking, sir."

"I assure you that I am not."

"Irrelevant?"

"Yes, though if you listen to me say it, the 'I' in Irel sounds like the 'eye' on your face."

I shook his hand and couldn't help but feel a bit off guard. Was he, in fact, pulling me leg, or was he being earnest? I couldn't tell.

"Then what's the 'E' for?" I asked.

"E?"

"Aye, sir, your middle name. What's the 'E' stand for?"

"Why, absolutely nothing!"

It was then that the owner brought the gent his cup of tea.

"Merci," replied Dr. Vant.

The owner nodded quietly and returned to his place behind the front counter where he'd been reading his paper.

"So," I blurted out, "you're a doctor of anthropology then?"

Dr. Vant glanced me way while sipping his tea. He then looked down at one of me blank canvases, seeming to take a keen interest, and set his cup down into its saucer.

"I've an appointment with an associate of sorts in about an hour, not far from here. In the meantime, I should like you to paint a picture for me."

I wasn't sure if he was trying to avoid me question or see what me talent was worth, but either way the café was pretty dead that night, save for an elderly woman and her crumpet sitting at the far side of the room, minding her own business.

I knew the owner would appreciate it if I could keep this gentleman around, if only for a bit longer. So I decided to humour this Dr. Vant if, for no other reason, than to pass the time.

"All right, then," said I. "Did you have a specific pose in mind, or shall I just paint you as you are?"

"Oh, my dear boy. I don't wish you to paint me! Lord knows I've never been a worthy subject of art."

"Then who, sir?"

He pointed to the elderly woman across the way.

"Are you serious?" I asked.

"Let us nip this in the bud once and for all. If I do ever intend to jest with you, I shall make it a point of the utmost certainty to let you know well enough ahead of time."

"Right, then. You want to call her over, or shall I?"

"No, you can paint her where she is. Sometimes the best subjects are those who aren't aware they're subjects at all."

I tried to smile, but frankly this gent was a queer one. Still, he had given me a job to do, and I had accepted his challenge. To me, she was just as good a thing to paint as any other. That being said, I flipped one of me canvases up onto me lap, leaned it up against the table while facing the old lady, dabbed me brush in a few colours, and set to work.

While I painted I half paid attention to Dr. Vant, as his gaze fixated on me brush and watched the old woman come to life on the canvas as if she'd always been there. At least now she always would be.

When I finished I sat upright and put forth me attention to Dr. Vant, who stood up from his table and came up behind me so as to get a proper view of me work. In height he had to be six feet or better, lean, yet not sickly thin.

"Remarkable. The wrinkles, the shape, her very essence, all captured for eternity," said he as his sharp speculative grey eyes examined me painting like a bird of prey scouring the countryside. "Well done, William. You make even the most mundane subjects that of true beauty. You add life to the lifeless. Such a talent is far greater than your ability to paint."

"Thank you, doctor."

"Archaeology," he stated.

"I beg your pardon?"

"My doctorate is in the field of archaeology, though I do see myself as more of an anthropologist nowadays." He felt for his pocket watch, which he immediately opened once he'd removed it from his pocket. He then clicked it shut and looked me straight in the eyes. "I'm scheduled to meet a gentleman at an art show that some anonymous society of painters and other artists have put together. Would you be interested in tagging along?"

"I'm not even going to ask you if you're joking again, 'cause if you are, it'd be the cruellest way to learn me not to trust strangers."

"Good, then I hope you'll join me," said he, as he stole the painting off me lap and held it up to get a better view. "We'll bring this along with us. It may prove useful."

With that we were off. We took a hansom cab to the exhibit, which, as I would find out years later, had been housed in what was formerly a photographer's studio. Inside there were paintings of all sorts and each one seemed to explore the life of nature and the modern world in a style very much like me own. They used small brush–strokes that looked as if they were painted very quickly, so as to capture the changing light.

"What do you think?" asked Dr.Vant while gazing around at the people who were gaping at the eye–level artwork.

"Of what?" I asked. "The paintings or the people?"

"Yes, that's how I feel too. Listen, William, I think I see my man over there in the back. Feel free to wander about as you like. I'll just be a moment."

With that he was off, and I could just make out a large, stocky, blond–bearded man in the back. His muscles were quite menacing and his clothing was of a ragged kind that reminded me of the fellows I'd seen down by the docks when I'd pick up goods for me grocery delivery company.

But I made up me mind not to let anything put a damper on me mood. Here I was at an art exhibit, the very first I'd ever attended, and I was mesmerized. The paints, the canvases, the sheer poetic grace of numerous painters' visions wrapped around me attention span like it was a newborn baby nestled in its warm blanket at naptime. I was just about ready to begin me excursion around the room when a moustached Oriental gent in a grey suit, in his mid–sixties, attempted to hand me a glass of some bubbly wine, which today, of course, I know as champagne.

"Och, no, Monsieur," I declined.

"I've always encouraged art to be celebrated," he said, with a sly smile in a calm and even tone.

"You speak English!" He nodded. "Are … are you even allowed to drink in here though?" I whispered.

"What does it matter?" he said, as more of a statement than a question. He then caught the arm of a middle–aged Oriental woman. "I'd like to introduce you to my wife, but I've only just realized I do not know your name."

"Me name is William O'Brien, sir."

"Ah, and the friend you came in with?" He spoke smoothly, almost genially.

"Dr. Vant?"

"Indeed. Do you know him well?"

"Actually, I've only just met him this evening."

"I see."

"But, what about you, sir? Are you a collector or something?"

"Yes … you might say that."

"Well, if you don't mind me asking, what is your—"

It was then that I distinctly heard the calling of me name from behind me.

"Billy? Billy O'Brien!" said the voice.

I turned 'round to greet the familiar voice, which had so often called me name in the past, though I could hardly believe I was hearing it call me again. There, delighted to see me, was Monsieur de Croismencer himself!

"Monsieur!" I said. "Is it really you?"

"Is it really me?" he smiled. "Sacré bleu, is it really you?"

"'Tis sir."

"Incroyable! But how? How did you get to Paris, let alone France?"

"'Tis a long story, Monsieur. But, God blind me, it *is* good to see you."

I reached out me hand but he batted it away and gave me a hearty fatherly hug.

"Oh, Monsieur, allow me to introduce, Mr.—, " but as I turned 'round again, I realized the strange Oriental man and his wife had vanished. "Em, never mind."

"So, I assume it is your love for art which brings you here today."

"That and a man I only met a few hours ago. He's an odd one, he is. But he seems to know the right people in the right places. Afterall, he got *me* in here, didn't he?"

"Better keep close to him then. Sometimes it's very often who you know that gets you what you desire in life."

Just then we heard the sneering words of a disgusted art critic.

"Crikey, what do you suppose his problem is?" I asked.

"He doesn't like these paintings," explained Monsieur de Croismencer. "Something about wallpaper being more finished. 'Impressions', he called them; probably a journalist."

"Sounds to me like he doesn't know art when he sees it."

"Most of the people here do not care for these works. Such radical changes usually take time before they're accepted."

"How do you feel about them?"

"Well, I—"

"Ah, William. There you are. And you've made a new friend I see."

"Dr. Vant, this is Monsieur Pierre de Croismencer. He's the one who taught me the ways of art some years back."

"An old friend then. Pleasure to meet you, Monsieur," replied Dr. Vant. "And I too have someone I'd like you to meet, William. This is Kaleeb Langston. My associate in my most current affairs," he added, as he presented the blond–bearded giant, who, I must admit, appeared more intimidating close up than from the distance at which I'd first seen him.

"Nice to—"

"Unfortunately we've run out of time, and I'm sorry to say that you must bid your friend adieu," said Dr. Vant. "Here, Monsieur, one of William's paintings. Think of it as a parting gift. Now, William, we really should be going."

"But where to?"

"Where indeed. Say your good–byes then, William. Kaleeb and I will be waiting outside. Monsieur, it was an honour to meet you."

So, with a tip of his hat, followed by a tipping of Kaleeb's, they were beyond us and out the door.

"I apologize, Monsieur, for the way in which Dr. Vant acted."

"He definitely has a mysterious air about him."

"Perhaps we can arrange a time to meet," I suggested. "To reminisce, and I can show you what I've been painting since last we met."

"I'm afraid I'm off to America in two days time. I'm eager to paint this 'Wild West' everyone talks about. But do not fret, Billy. I can see from this painting of yours that you've made vast improvements since our last session. Keep with it, and it won't let you down."

"I guess this time it's me leaving you, Monsieur. Take care, and perhaps by some chance we'll meet again."

"I am sure," he said, as he smiled, "that fate will bring our paths together once more. Au revoir, Billy."

When I arrived outside I could find no trace of Dr. Vant or the behemoth, Kaleeb.

"Psst," I heard suddenly. "William, over here!"

It was Dr. Vant, hidden in the shadows on the far left end of the building. I crept over as quickly and quietly as I could and when I got there I could see the immense figure of Kaleeb looming over Dr. Vant from behind.

"What are you hiding for?" I asked.

"I can't explain it here, but we've very good reason to believe that we're being followed."

"Followed? By who?"

"Thieves," spoke Kaleeb. He had a deep, commanding voice even in the midst of a whisper.

"Thieves? Do you have something on you worth stealing? I mean, you don't even have me painting anymore, though I don't see what use it was to you anyway."

"It helped me to explain how we met to Kaleeb, so he would understand that you are just an innocent bystander," Vant explained. "Look, we need a place to go where we can talk privately. Do you know of such a place?"

"There's the inn that I've been living at. But don't you have your own place in town?"

"Indeed, which is likely already compromised. How far to this inn of yours?"

"Let's see," said I, as I looked about to get me barrings from landmarks I'd come across in me deliveries. "About a half hour's walk, I'd say."

"Good, let us try it in half that. Lead on William, and keep us out of the light if you can."

It was a gloomy night to be out, and seemed even more so as we crept through the obscuring shadows, invisible to the public yet among them, moving stealthily. About a third of our journey lay behind us when I felt a hand rest upon me back.

"Be still," ordered Dr. Vant.

I stopped dead with the others. Kaleeb and I looked to Dr. Vant questionably as he raised a single finger to his lips. We listened. If there was anything to be heard, our ears didn't pick up its trace. All was silent within the alley we had come to. We were between two large buildings: a tenement to our right and a building I couldn't make out on our left, for its few windows were boarded.

We remained there until Dr. Vant grasped his walking stick and pointed us onward with the gleaming platinum ball handle. Taking his cue, I gained the scent once more, led us out of the alley, and managed to duck in time to dodge the swing of a beam of wood!

As I stumbled back around I saw me attacker engage in battle with the stick of Dr. Vant. The man was at least six feet tall and had incredible strength. His coat stemmed downward from his neck and fell just below his knees. It was navy blue in colour, though the mask encasing his head was of a black skin–tight stocking sort of material. He even wore a navy–coloured hat, a small square–shaped cap with material covering the sides of his head, much as I've seen worn in sketches of soldiers battling the heat of the Arabian deserts. He was quite Dr. Vant's match and probably would've overtaken him had his next strike not met the quick grip of Kaleeb's massive right hand in mid–swing.

I knew not this man's name, yet his actions convinced me that he must be a cunning detective in some legion of evil. Therefore, I think it fit to refer to him as the Detective.

Try as he did, the Detective could not rip the wooden beam from Kaleeb's mighty grasp, so he abandoned that idea entirely and drew a whistle from 'round his neck, which he gave a blow so piercing to our ear drums that Kaleeb fell backwards and dropped the beam in an effort to cover his ears.

As he quickly recovered his senses and lunged towads the Detective, Kaleeb taunted, "Try that again, why don't you!" Yet even as he did so, a second assailant came to the Detective's aid. It was an agile figure that had back–flipped off an adjacent building and onto the shoulders of the unsuspecting Kaleeb. The form was no doubt female, though the entire body was encased in black tights, including her face, so there'd be no identifying her, either. Hence, I shall refer to her as the Acrobat.

Wasting no time, Dr. Vant flew past me, ordering us to run. Not needing to be told twice, I bolted through the open street and joined Dr. Vant. As I glanced back, I saw that Kaleeb had managed to toss the Acrobat off his shoulders and was headed our way.

"Who are they?" I asked.

"It would not be too hastily judgmental to suggest at this point that, whoever they are, we do not wish to be near them at the moment," commented Dr. Vant. "How far is it to that inn of yours?"

"Not very and at this speed we'll be there in no time."

"Then let us give our foes the slip. We mustn't let them follow us there."

By now Kaleeb had nearly caught up to us and we raced down some French thoroughfare at top speed. When they were just behind Kaleeb, and nearly upon us, the Detective and the Acrobat each darted down separate alleys, the Detective to the right and the Acrobat to the left.

"They've split up," I shouted. "They've each taken a separate passage."

"To ensnare us no doubt," said Dr. Vant. "To where do those alleys lead?"

"I don't really know."

"Then perhaps we'd better take a right at this next intersection!"

As we did so, Dr. Vant nearly slammed into an oncoming carriage, but the driver yanked the horses' reins and pulled it off to the side in the nick of time. But as Dr. Vant regained his composure, and Kaleeb and I rounded the corner, we heard a loud crack, and a lengthy whip snapped out from the darkness and wrapped around the right leg of Dr. Vant tearing him off balance.

He fell backwards slamming against the cobblestone road. There, retracting the whip, was a third assailant, a black–coated figure with a large black–brimmed hat upon his head, like that of an American cowboy. He even had one of those old black kerchiefs covering his nose and mouth. Thus, I think it fit to refer to this man as the Whipslinger.

Shortly thereafter, the man swung his whip towards me, but Kaleeb pushed me out of its path and let it snap and wrap around his immense forearm. He then gave a mighty and vicious tug at the whip and pulled the Whipslinger right up to his face so that he was now staring at the man eye to eye.

Thinking Kaleeb had the situation well under control, I went to tend to Dr. Vant, but me head snapped upright at the sound of a pistol being cocked—aimed at me forehead. It was the Detective.

"Let our man go," commanded the Detective, "or the boy dies."

Kaleeb sent a grim look me way and threw the Whipslinger into a wall a few feet back.

"Very wise," said the Detective, shifting his attention to Kaleeb. "Now I trust that—" his voice broke out into a sudden scream as I jammed a penknife into the lower end of his leg. He stumbled back and Dr. Vant stood up.

"Very nice to meet you," said he as he rose. "This is William, my colleague, but I think you two have already met."

With that, Dr. Vant swung and clubbed the Detective across the chest with his walking stick. The impact had been a powerful one, for Dr. Vant had thrown in every ounce of strength he could muster. The Detective fell backwards, hitting his head on the street kerb, and knocked himself unconscious.

Kaleeb then turned his attention back towards the Whipslinger while Dr. Vant picked up the Detective's pistol and aimed it at the downed man's head.

"Now where have we seen this before?" asked Dr. Vant with a smile.

"Kill him," said the Whipslinger. "Makes no difference to me!"

Suddenly, the Acrobat came plummeting down from the rooftop of a building landed behind Dr. Vant, and pinned each of his arms, forcing him to drop the pistol.

"Here William," said he as he kicked the pistol towards me. "Use it in good health—and show no mercy!"

I grabbed the pistol, cocked it, and aimed at the Acrobat's head.

"Let him go," I ordered.

She hesitated and even tightened her grip at one point.

"You haven't got the nerve to pull that trigger," declared the Whipslinger as he surveyed the scene. "What are you, seventeen? Eighteen? Stabbin' a man's one thing but—"

"Enough is enough!" came the thunderous voice of Kaleeb, as he inflicted an earth–shattering punch into the Whipslinger's gut followed by a second blow to the man's head and a final uppercut that sent the shamed fellow into the air 'til he met the embrace of a not–so–soft brick wall and fell, sprawled out, onto the pavement.

When I glanced back towards Dr. Vant, I saw that the Acrobat had released him and quickly receded into the night.

"Should we follow her?" I asked.

"Whatever for?" asked Dr. Vant, dusting himself off. "We've thrown fear into her heart; she'll be of no threat to us now."

"I beg to differ," blurted Kaleeb. "We may have put a dent into their plans but rest assured, as we found out tonight, where there is one there are two, where there are two there are three and so on. This is far from over."

"Yes, well, obviously! I just prefer to play the optimist once in a while."

"Should we unmask them?" I asked.

Dr. Vant stood silent for a moment, as we loomed over their unconscious bodies. Kaleeb's eyes darted to the doctor's face.

"No," Dr. Vant finally said. "Come, let us get to a safe haven."

"But that doesn't make any sense, suppose you recog—"

"We're running out of time, William, " added Dr. Vant.

"Right. Well, this way then," said I, and I once again led them into the darkness though I couldn't help but wonder why he wouldn't want to unmask them. Something wasn't adding up.

It was well into the night when we finally strolled into the tiny inn at the end of la rue de Foster. We entered, and I led the way, administering a slight nod and a faint smile to the owner as we passed him at the front desk. He was a noble little man, about five foot two in height. I was fond of him because he had always been good to me and if I had realized at that moment it would be the last time I'd see him I would've stopped to tell him so. But I pressed on 'til we came to me room.

Me place was on the ground floor of the two–story inn and scarcely big enough for the bed and a dresser in there, let alone the three of us. Dr. Vant seated himself on the bed, while Kaleeb leaned up against the dresser so as to peer out through a part in the curtains in the room's only window.

"All right," said I as I closed the door behind us. "What's going on here? Why are those people after you? Why did you bring me into all of this? And—most important—what in God's name are we going to do now?" By then I was in hysterics.

"That's quite a lot of questions," said Dr. Vant calmly. "You must've been turning them over in your mind for quite some time."

I gave him a sour look, as me patience in the matter was wearing thin.

"A lot of questions, indeed, all of which you shall learn the answers to. Now then, where to begin? Hmmm, let's see. I've told you that I am an archaeologist, and you know by my appearance that I am British. To be more precise I'm from a very small village on the outskirts of Avebury known as Leocadia. It was named after my great–grandmother some hundred years or so ago. The land was originally apart of the entire Vant estate, which, contrary to documented records, encompassed the whole of Wiltshire for a debated amount of time. And so, in an effort to keep up the great castle, Vant Manor, my great–grandmother sold off half of the land surrounding the property, thus reviving the Vant fortune, which I inherited when I moved into Vant Manor shortly after being married. Know now that I am a widower and have been for twenty years. My wife died shortly after I received my doctorate. So what was I to do? I immersed myself in my work. It has since been my life.

"It is my work that brought me to Paris and consequently to my troubles with such ruffians as we encountered earlier this evening. I am in search of an ancient treasure hidden somewhere in China. Only I know its exact location for only I have seen it once, nine long years ago. It belonged to a great thief hundreds of years ago and contains some of the most sought–after artefacts in the entire world: stolen goods from over fifty different countries worth immeasurable wealth due to their extreme rarity and their age—blue diamonds, red diamonds, black emeralds, pearls of silver, and rare golden coins, some of which came from the tombs of Egypt's greatest dynasties. So you can imagine the archaeological value as well as the monetary wealth. It is because of its location that I sought out Kaleeb here. Kaleeb is the captain of the *Wooden Whale*, a large sailing ship backed by steam–powered engines.

"His ship is said to be one of the fastest and strongest in all of Europe. I had heard of Kaleeb in London from his life there many years ago. His reputation stretches from Iceland to Australia so it wasn't too hard to find out that he had moved to France after meeting a lovely French woman whom he married shortly thereafter. I contacted Kaleeb six months ago and we made arrangements for our quest to China. You, William, were brought into this by me because I needed an outsider I could trust just in case Kaleeb turned out to be someone I could not. No offence to you Mr. Langston."

"None taken," said the mighty Kaleeb, still gazing out the window.

"Now, no doubt someone has learned of our endeavours and wishes to get to that treasure themselves. Still, killing me is no way for them to do it, as the only map to the treasure exists solely within my head. And I dare say I'd rather die than let someone else lay their hands upon that chest! As for what we do now, that is up for negotiation."

"You smell something?" asked Kaleeb.

"No," exclaimed the doctor, as Kaleeb had suddenly interrupted him. "Now where were we?"

Kaleeb left his place by the dresser and knelt down to the bottom of the door. He inhaled deeply, and then felt the door with the back of his hand.

"The way I see it our options are limited, but they need not include you from this point on."

"The building's on fire!" shouted Kaleeb.

"What?" asked Dr. Vant.

"What do you mean the building's on fire?" I echoed.

"Just what I said."

"Preposterous! Are you quite certain?" asked Dr. Vant, rising from his seat on the bed.

"Duck!" cried Kaleeb as he threw himself upon Dr. Vant's body just in time to save him from a flaming arrow, which crashed through the window, flew over the bed and struck the wall where the flames began to multiply.

"Good heavens!" yelled Dr. Vant.

"What do we do?" I asked.

"William," said the doctor while rolling Kaleeb off him. "I do apologize for this, but I'm afraid you'll have to come with us now."

"Come with you? To where? China?!"

"No, look, there's no time to explain, but right now you must to take us to the North Pier 8301. We must get to the *Wooden Whale* if we are to live!"

"Which way do we go? He said there's fire in the hall and there're murderers waiting for us if we head through the window!"

"Leave that to me," stated Kaleeb. He then picked up me mattress and ran towards the window. He leapt up through it, shattering the glass into a million pieces, and landed on the mattress on the other side in the street behind the burning building, where no one was visible.

"Mr. Langston," said I, as we climbed out and helped him to his feet. "How did you know our enemies wouldn't be out here waiting for us?"

"It was an arrow that pierced the window. Arrows are long–distance weapons. So you get the gist of it! Now quickly then, lad, lead on. You've only need to get me within a familiar neighbourhood, then I can take the helm towards the port!"

I nodded and sprang to me feet, leading them, yet again, into the night. But we got no further than a few feet of the scene when another flaming arrow rushed by our heads, thrusting itself into the back wall of the inn. I'd glanced up to the roof of the building across the way and caught a quick glimpse of the Acrobat resuming a hiding place within the shadows cast by a chimney.

Soon multiple arrows, flameless yet deadly, filled the air like a bunch of damned mosquitoes looking to take out their frustration on a bunch of old ninnies like us. We then broke out in a frenzy. I went running with Dr. Vant close behind. Yet somewhere behind me I heard Kaleeb call out.

"Stop! That's exactly what she wants you to do!"

But his words were too late, as we found out the hard way. I slammed straight into the chest of the angered Detective whilst a whip once again lassoed poor Dr. Vant to the ground, this time taking the poor man down by both legs.

The Detective forced both me arms back behind me with one of his arms, and used his other to pull at me hair, thus bringing me head backwards so me eyes met his deadly gaze.

"I hope you weren't leaving on my account," said he. "Not while I owe you this!"

He moved quick, freeing me hair for a second, but only long enough to withdraw me own penknife from his pocket, which he thrust up into me right thigh. I might not tell you how I screamed like a sissy because of that.

"I think this belongs to you!" he said.

"Jaysus–bloody–Christ!" I hollered. "Let me go you filthy bugger!"

It was then that I noticed Dr. Vant lying face down in the street — motionless. The Whipslinger bent down, grabbed the man by the scruff of his coat, and raised him up a few feet, where his face met the right foot of me own attacker. The Detective then threw me aside like the rag doll of some poor lass, bent down to Dr.Vant and raised him completely into the air where he could glare at the man eye to eye, which seemed to be a habit of his.

"And you," said the Detective. "I owe you far more than your little Irish prat!"

I stumbled about and caught me balance, but Dr. Vant, only smiled at the Detective. Then he spat a mess of blood and dirt into the Detective's masked face, the blood no doubt from the cut he had sustained when he'd hit the ground earlier. Furious at this, the Detective slammed Dr. Vant into the side of a building then over to another building several times before finally casting him down upon the kerb.

"Where is Kaleeb?" I heard the Detective ask the Whipslinger, and I wondered how they knew his name. Clearly there was more going on here than I was privy to.

"I don't know, I lost sight of him in the scuffle with these two."

"Find hi—"

But the Detective never got to finish his sentence, for at that moment Kaleeb came riding in on a horse–drawn carriage headed right for the Detective. Narrowly missing his target, Kaleeb brought the carriage to a sudden halt and called out to me.

"Into the carriage, boy, and be quick about it!"

And so, not needing to be told twice, I ran as fast as me bum leg could take me, while Kaleeb sprang from the carriage and scooped up Dr. Vant.

"You won't get far," shouted the Detective as I climbed into the carriage. "Where–ever you go, we'll find you!"

"Here," said Kaleeb, as he tossed Dr. Vant in beside me. "Look after him while I get us out of here."

Kaleeb stirred the pair of horses and we were off like a shot.

"What's … what's?" Dr. Vant was nearly unconscious.

"Rest now, Dr. Vant. We're safe for the moment."

"Which way to the North Pier?" asked Kaleeb.

I darted me head up and gazed out at the cityscape all around, me mind racing to visualize the route before us.

"Hang a right on the next street and take that down to the water's edge, from there follow the Seine and—"

"Say no more. I'll be able to find my way once we get to the Seine!"

So I said no more. Instead, I sat back, took off me coat, and tore a sleeve off me shirt, which I then wrapped around me right thigh, fashioning a makeshift bandage. I then balled me coat into a pillow and rested me head on it while Kaleeb commanded the horses as we met the Seine and began following the banks.

It must've been around four in the morning when we finally arrived at the dock of the *Wooden Whale*. She looked to be a fine ship. She reminded me of pictures I'd seen in me schoolbooks of ships, like those Columbus sailed to the Americas all those years ago. Still, while she resembled the ships from yester–year she had a bit of a modern air about her, and if you ventured to look close enough you'd note that the masts holding the massive sails were actually camouflaged smokestacks. Why? You tell me! I get why they'd want a hybrid ship, but why try to hide that? In addition, the hull of the ship was iron and particularly thick in the front so as to act as a ramrod if ever in a pickle, as I'd learn of days later.

When the carriage was brought to a halt we were met, at once, by some of the *Whale's* crew. One such gent was a short, stout fellow, about mid–fifties, with frayed whiskers of a salt and pepper colour.

"Welcome back, Captain," said he to Kaleeb.

"Thank you, Morton, though I'm afraid we don't have time for pleasantries. Inform the crew of my arrival and get the *Whale* ready for shove–off. Time's no friend of ours this dreary morn!"

"Run into a bit of trouble then?"

"That be so. Now on with ya, and you there, Thatch, help this lad bring out the good doctor, but mind you now, the boy's got a bum leg of his own."

He then turned around to address me as I struggled out of the carriage.

"Now then, William, ol' Thatch here will help you and Dr. Vant inside. I've got much to do in order to get the *Whale* ship–shape, so I'll be seeing you later. We'll meet for breakfast as soon as we've shoved off."

"Aye, sir," said I.

Thatch was a thin, scrawny sailor, with a bit of muscle and a dash of good–looks. He was a fine companion to have alongside you in your hour of desperation, as he cautiously helped me bring Dr. Vant out of the coach.

"Now," I heard Kaleeb say from afar, "where's Isabelle? The doctor's gonna need tending to, and the boy's gonna need some mending of his own!"

"She's out shoppin', Captain. Said she had some errands to tend to before shippin' out!" replied Morton.

"At this time of night? Probably been out since lunch. Just like a woman, always spending my hard–earned money. How's she supposed to cart her crap around town's what I'd like to know!"

"She took Reese and Stanton with her, sir."

"Well, they'd best be back soon, or I've got a good mind to leave 'em behind!"

"But she's your wife, Captain."

"Wife or not, Morton, this ship is leaving when I say she's leaving."

"Yes, sir."

At that time I had taken up Dr. Vant's walking stick, which was just what the doctor ordered, while Thatch had taken ahold of the doctor himself and was leading the way up a ramp and onto the deck of the *Wooden Whale*. Once we'd made it aboard, we saw that dozens of crewmembers were hoisting sails, battening down hatches, and stirring up a contagious bit of enthusiasm. One of them even whistled a merry little tune.

"Cut that out!" I heard Kaleeb call, while I followed Thatch into an enormous cabin, of the likes I'd never seen before. In we strode, me with me limp, him with a sack of dead weight, but still both quite capable of descending the three or four steps downward. The first room we came to, inside the cabin, was an abnormally large room for such a ship as she was. Its dimensions must have been somewhere the likes of around forty feet by seventy. There were four rows of eight wooden tables and benches, which were divided down the centre by the main aisle, and the outermost seats sported a view outside the room's windows.

"This is the mess hall," said Thatch with a grunt.

"I might have imagined," said I. "Are you sure you can manage him all right?"

"I may look petty to the naked eye, Mr. William, but to a trained brawler I'm a virtual bison!"

"Right then," said I with a smile.

We then made our way into the kitchen, passed by the Captain's den—where various maps, charts, and other objects of navigation lay strewn about—and finally came to Captain Langston's own personal quarters. It was a rich, lavishly furnished room complete with its own drinks bar and hookah! There was a table in front of the bar, big enough for two, and a vanity table was set up in the far back corner just across from the massive canopy bed of lush satin red sheets and white lace drapery. The whole room radiated with a woman's touch, and I was suddenly aware at how anxious I was becoming about meeting Mrs. Langston. A true gem amongst a mixture of coal she'd have to be.

Thatch had laid Dr. Vant down upon the bed and I took a seat at the small round table.

"Feel free to help yourself to anything from the Captain's private stash. After all you've been through, I'm sure he'd have no complaints to a few missing bottles of some of his brew."

I glanced down at me wound; the blood had completely saturated the cloth from me shirt.

"Perhaps I'll do that," I said. "Thanks for all of your trouble, Thatch, I'd have been right lost without your assistance."

"'T ain't nothing, Mr. William. Now, I'm off to get a bucket of water and a moist cloth for Vant's head. You'll have to tend to him until the Missus gets in. I've my own work to do if we're to be out to sea when the Captain says."

And so there I stayed the rest of the early morning hours before the sun dared breach the horizon. I'd brought one of the chairs to the bedside and I continually wiped Dr. Vant's forehead clean with a cool compress. Once or twice he stirred, but no more than that, for he'd eventually grow still again.

After a while, when I'd made a good dent in bottle of Kaleeb's whiskey, I heard his familiar voice from the den through the closed door. He was having a conversation with a woman with a gentle—yet stern— voice with a heavy—almost exaggerated—French accent. I presumed it could only have been his wife. It was a little muffled, but surprisingly clear and went something along the lines of this:

"How could you stay out all night shopping until six in the bloody morning's what I'd like to know!" Kaleeb's powerful voice stormed.

"I would tell you if you would let me speak," said she. "We had trouble with ze carriage on ze outskirts of town around midnight or so. We were headed to a particular shop zat was far out of our way. I had wanted get you a special gift, but never mind zat now. For as it turned out, we never made it zere. When ze carriage's wheel broke, Reese and ze driver went out for help while poor John Stanton climbed down beneath ze carriage to mend its broken wheel on his own and somehow ended up stabbing himself in his own leg. I admire his bravado but it just complicated matters. If you like, I can have him explain it to you personally once I see to his wounds."

I remember thinking how peculiar her accent was. Since I'd been in Paris, I'd only encountered a few Parisians who spoke English and none with that type of speech. "Maybe it's a countryside or regional dialect, similar to me own," I thought to meself.

"Go on then, how did you get it all worked out?" her husband asked.

"Yes, well, Reese and ze driver returned with some help, a strong young man, and ze three of zem were able to replace the wheel and put us on ze road again, from which we only now have arrived at ze dock."

"And it's just as well you did, 'cause I was fixing to leave the lot of you! We were attacked tonight. Vant, the boy and I."

"Attacked?" she gasped. "Oh, *mon cheri*, are you hurt?"

"You ought to know me better than that! But the boy's got a leg wound of his own, and Vant's been out cold since the whole ordeal took place. They're in our room now."

"Zen I must tend to zem as well, have one of ze men bring up a bucket of—"

"It's been done, woman, haven't I told you? We've been waiting around here for you for over two hours now!" he shouted.

"You don't have to take zat tone with me. I am a lady and I am your wife."

"You're a woman first, a cook second, then a doctor, then a seamstress, *and then* you're my wife. I don't think lady made the top ten!"

"How rude!" she shrieked and then, all at once, the door flew open and there she stood.

What fine features her face did have, so soft, so —feminine! Her hair was of a blondish brown and her lips were painted a deep wine colour to accent her pastel pink dress and burgundy shawl. She was of average height, slender, and breath–taking. Either that or it was the booze working away at me imagination! Whatever it was doesn't matter now. But take me word for it, she was a looker, she was.

"You must be Mrs. Langston," I quickly blurted out. "I'm William O'Brien, ma'am, but you can call me Billy. If me leg wasn't aching so, I'd follow me manners and give *vous* a proper French welcome, but circumstances being what they are …"

"I'll be out on the deck," said Kaleeb, before heading out the opposite way.

"Billy, you may call me Isabelle —I'd much prefer it to Mrs. Langston, today at least," said she with a huff. She then glanced down at me leg. "Zat must be quite a deep wound you have in your zigh to have lost so much blood. May I?"

I nodded as she slowly untied the makeshift bandage. I forced meself to draw in a deep breath as she removed it and the air set in.

"It *is* deep," she said looking down at it. She then looked up. "But it will heal."

"Bless the Lord for that! But what about Dr. Vant?"

"Ah, yes, Dr. Vant." Her eyes shifted over his way and she felt his wrist. "He has a pulse, zat's a good sign."

I chuckled but hastily contained meself, since the situation really wasn't a funny one. Yet she too burst out into a giggle, and then I started up once again. I don't know if it was the drink or the strain of the long night coming off me shoulders, but a good hearty laugh did me a wonder of good. At sun up,—after we had set sail and Dr. Vant was awake, I began to feel at ease once again. Even me leg didn't seem to ache as much; of course that may very well have been due to the miracles of a woman's touch!

Shortly thereafter I'd fallen asleep and woke a few hours later to the smell of a hearty French breakfast brewing in the galley. Dr. Vant was also alert, but was still feeling a bit weary and we were all too peckish to bother with much idle conversation.

In fact, it wasn't until about an hour or so after we ate that Dr. Vant approached me on the deck. I was savouring the smell of the sea air which, to a boy who grew up near the docks, was like being at home again. Dr. Vant had just finished speaking with Kaleeb when he joined me at the guardrail.

"How is your leg?" he asked.

"Not so bad, really. Just needed some fixin', but Mrs. Langston saw to that. What about you? Feeling like your old self again?"

"Yes, quite. Perhaps more like my old self than I should be feeling."

"Sorry, I don't follow."

"As well you couldn't. There's a great deal about me you don't know, William. Yet all you need to know will be explained in the fullness of time, I've no doubt."

"If you say so," I commented while gazing out into the sea.

"You know, William, I really do apologize for everything that's happened to you. I feel if as though I am to blame."

"Pishaw, doctor, you couldn't have had any idea of what might happen last night."

He stood silent for a moment, an awkward moment, and then spoke once more.

"Even so, I've been thinking these last few hours and I'd like to make it up to you. I'd like to offer you a proposition."

"Oh?" I asked, suddenly interested, as I turned 'round to face him.

"Seeing as to how you've lost your home and no doubt your job, I'd like you to come and live at Vant Manor. I'll need someone to look after things while I'm away and—mind you—I'm away far more than I am actually there. This trip to China for example, I see it being the longest of my endeavours to date. Anyhow, you would live there free of rent, and I will even fully commission your artistic output, so long as you maintain the house and grounds. What you do with the paintings will be completely up to you. Sell them or save them, makes no difference to me. What do you say, William?"

"Sounds grand, sir, but I don't know that I deserve such treatment."

"I have jeopardized your life just by being in your presence. You cared for me when I was unconscious! I owe you a great deal more than that, but it's all I can offer at the moment."

"So you want me to stay all alone in that big old castle of yours? Don't you have any servants who could tend to things while you're away?"

"No, I live alone. Ah, but now that you mention it, there is one person who is in debt to me. She's a delightful old gal teetering on the edge of seventy or so. She'd be just the one to keep you company. Yes, she could fix you your meals and tidy things up. Why now that I think about it, she's even a woman after your own country. Mrs. McGillian's her name, and there never was a finer Scottish lass that I did meet."

"But I'm Irish," said I. "Remember?"

"Oh, yes. That's correct. It's an easy mistake, all Celtic in nature. At any rate, what do you say?"

"You'd commission all of me artwork, and I'd live there free of rent with all meals inclusive?"

"That *is* the proposition."

"Dr. Vant, you've got yourself a deal!"

"Splendid! Just splendid. I'll wire a telegram to Mrs. McGillian just as soon as we reach port." He gave me a pat on the back and went on his way.

And so, as I stood there fantasizing about the twist of fate me own life had taken, I could have never imagined what would be in store for me in the future. For had I realized at the time what was to transpire, it's fair to say that I don't think I'd have given the doctor me word at all. But I'm getting ahead of meself. Now, where was I? Oh, yes, so there we flew—full sail —towards the growing land mass, that lay before us just off the portside bow.

II
VANT MANOR

It was a fog–infested, dreary day with the scent of rain looming as we left the deck of the *Wooden Whale* and stepped out onto the dock in Bournemouth, a city in the south of England. There, the mysterious and respected Dr. Vant joined the behemoth Captain Kaleeb Langston and his lovely wife, Isabelle, meself and the scarred–neck fellow known as Elijah Reese in squeezing into a carriage bound for the local railway.

At first, the conversations revolved mostly around less trivial matters such as the weather, the trip in from Paris and how the *Whale* could be used as a ramrod until we were aboard a local train bound for Avebury, somewhere in the county of Wiltshire. I was seated at the window next to Reese, with the others sitting across from us and Dr. Vant directly in front of me, when he began to speak.

"Leocadia is a very small village, as I think I've mentioned before. Half of the land is made up of Vant Manor itself, though the village is completely self–sufficient. I believe there may even be a place for you to buy your art supplies, William, though I'd steer clear of any social interaction with the localites there."

"Why's that?" I asked.

"It's a very long and complicated story, just trust my judgment. Deal with them only when absolutely necessary, otherwise I've often found it more enlightening to visit some of the other villages outside the local area. That is, when I am at home."

"What's that?" I asked, glancing out the window. "Those stones, they're all arranged vertically in some kind of giant circle."

"Ah, yes," replied Dr. Vant, as he too glanced out the window with a smile forming on his middle–aged face. "That would be Stonehenge."

"*Ze* Stonehenge?" asked Mrs. Langston, with a hint of excited shock.

"The only one I know of, anyway," laughed the doctor, "—at least by that name."

"What is this stone–hedge?" I enquired.

"Only ze most mysterious monumental marvel in all of England!" raved Langston's wife.

"A treasure, to be sure," Dr. Vant agreed. "Stonehenge is a prehistoric archaeological site no doubt dating back to the very first British builders that ever walked these lands. Some believe it to be a religious ceremonial site, some claim it's a pagan temple to worship the cosmos, and others swear we will never know its true significance."

"And what do you believe?" asked Reese.

Dr. Vant sat quiet for a moment, as the small smile faded from his face.

"I believe it's time for us to discuss the next phase of our plan."

"You mean the trip to Eyam?" Kaleeb asked.

"Indeed, and the sooner we get there the better. We'll take William to the house, make our arrangements, and be on our way before nightfall."

"Eyam?" I asked. "Is that somewhere in China?"

Kaleeb and Dr. Vant each let out a quick hearty laugh, before Dr. Vant caught his breath to speak again.

"Eyam is in the north of England. We're going there to pick up one of the last members of our expedition team," he stated.

"Ah," I said, satisfied with the answer but even more curious about their adventure in the making.

"So, when's this Eyam man expecting us?" asked Reese.

"Not *us*, Reese, Dr. Vant and myself only," stated Kaleeb. "You'll be accompanying Isabelle back to the *Whale* with my orders and confirmation of our arrangements."

"Actually," corrected Dr. Vant. "None of us."

"Come again?" Kaleeb questioned.

"The man from Eyam does not expect anyone. In fact, the only way he knows me at all is by an alias name of Nigel Palmer, which I used this past winter during my research of the Eyam people."

"But you said he's the only man capable of getting at that treasure chest!" exclaimed Kaleeb in a fit of disarray.

"Quite so, but I wouldn't let such trivial matters weigh on your mind, Mr. Langston. I've researched and planned everything so perfectly that this man will practically be begging us to bring him along. And now, pray, let us return our attention back towards the window as Leocadia approaches."

Kaleeb hesitated, partly on edge from the discussion about the Eyam man, and also probably from the way Dr. Vant seemed to weave in and out of conversations. Yet eventually the Captain joined us in gazing out the window as the train pressed on past a humble little village just visible in the distance with a large grey castle governing the landscape just beyond it.

"Is that Vant Manor?" I asked.

"It is," answered Dr. Vant. "Unfortunately, this train does not stop in Leocadia, so we'll have to take a carriage in from Avebury, but that leg of the journey should prove to be a fast one."

* * *

It was evening when our carriage finally trudged along the muddy roads leading into Leocadia. The rain had died to a faint mist and an early fog had settled in, preventing a decent view of the village, or anything thirty feet in front of your face. The air was cool and humid and sporadically fragranced by the ghastly stench of our horses' manure as they relieved themselves during our travels. But as we ventured further into the village, where a lively bunch of humble passers–by went about their daily routines, crowding the marketplace and visiting the pubs, the dreariness of the fog seemed to diminish. Just then the setting sun broke through the rain clouds, creating a soft pinkish haze behind Vant Manor further up the road, and evening set in.

"Seems like a friendly lot to me," said I, as our carriage continued on to the edge of town.

"Take it from someone who's lived here for over twenty years, William," said Dr. Vant. "It is not as friendly as it first appears."

"What do you mean?"

"Leocadia is composed of simple, narrow–minded citizens obsessed with gossip, back–stabbing and crafting tall tales to pass the time in an otherwise monotonous existence."

"Right then," I said, not knowing really what else to say.

When our carriage finally came to a standstill, we had come to a black iron gate attached to a fence line surrounding the entire Vant estate. As we emerged from the carriage—Dr. Vant followed by me, then the rest—we could see just how his home was a world apart from the village. Here was a castle—completely in the shadows of evening—imprisoned within an iron fence at the farthest westward edge of a village the size of the very estate the castle itself did sit upon.

Weeds ran rampant as far as the eye could see, while overgrown bushes formed a second line of defence just past the fence, thereby, restricting the view of the estate well up to fifteen feet in height. Even Kaleeb, himself, seemed to be dwarfed by the enormity of the vegetation. In fact, the only view of the estate grounds was visible through the tessellated pattern on the vine–infested iron gate I've already spoken of.

Once up to the gate, Dr. Vant withdrew a bundle of iron skeleton keys, which he used to open three separate locks upon the gate, before finally giving it a good kick open.

The others were in a state of inquisitive awe when the doctor turned around to address us.

"I assure you, Vant Manor is quite safe. Perhaps even safer than where you now stand. That being said, I beg you to follow immediately, for time is one thing we do not have a good deal of."

And so, after shooting each other a few confused expressions, we entered the world beyond the gate, which Dr. Vant immediately closed after us.

"Can't be too careful now, can we?" said he with a smile. "Now then, this way!"

We followed Dr. Vant up the main path of broken cobblestone, past various unidentifiable structures hidden within the tall grass and weeds and, of course, the returning fog. The only thing that I could make out was some sort of dried–up water fountain at the edge of a slime–covered pond and a small well behind it. The fountain was a statue in the shape of what looked as though it were a dual–headed dragon bending down to the pond with each mouth open for the water to trickle from.

We had then come to a halt at the steps of the great arched entrance to the castle. The Gothic citadel before us struck me as more of a cathedral than any castle I'd ever seen. There were two visible towers, one at each end of the manor, and each peaked in a sharp point that seemed to pierce the sky itself. It was all made of stone that had weathered over time, and high above the arched double–doored entrance was a circular stained glass window in the shape of a tree with its branches stemming down into its roots, where the two became one interlocking symbol.

"That would be the Celtic tree of life," said Vant, no doubt seeing me gaze fixed upon it.

"You're Celtic then?" asked Reese.

"My family adopted the Celtic tree of life as a symbol of passing down the estate from one generation to the next," he explained while unlocking the doors. "Unfortunately for them, I am the sole heir and, sadly enough, have fathered no children." The locks gave a clicking sound as he gave the key one last good crank. "Ah, well, do come in."

He opened the mammoth doorway and in we crept.

Until Vant lit a candelabrum, all was dark save for the eerie periwinkle light shining in from the windows, especially from the tree of life.

"Pardon Vant Manor's appearance at first glance," said Dr. Vant. "It's a rare beauty and should not be judged until you've set eyes on it in the full light of day. It's positioned to catch the rising sun, with its back in the west. Here, William, Mr. Langston, please take a candle stick and light the other candelabra around the room."

As we did so, the room slowly began to come to life in the isolated warmth of the candles. We were in a large foyer with a ceiling that reached to the very top of the three–storied castle. You could make out loft–like areas on the two upper floors, which were secured by solid oak guardrails. The railing from the second floor followed a curve to a red–carpeted staircase that descended into the room we had entered.

It was indeed a remarkable jewel, forgotten in dust and wild cobwebs. A deep red colour seemed to surround us, visible at every turn, in velvet red drapes, beautiful monochromatic red tapestries, cushiony red chairs and a sofa, as well as the aforementioned red carpet. And to bring out the red, there was a brilliant gold: golden tassels on the drapes, golden trim accenting the red walls, gold thread in the tapestries, and gold–painted legs on the sofa and chairs. Here was a room unlike any I, and I'm sure the others, had ever seen before. Lastly, I'd like to point out the fireplace, above which hung the portrait of a gorgeous young woman with fair skin and a deep brown head of hair.

"I'm afraid," said Dr. Vant, "that the candles will have to do for now. There's no time to make a fire if we are to make our arrangements in town. Please forgive me in advance, William, for not giving you a proper tour of the manor. However, you will note that there are three entrances into this room, other than that through which we came. To your left, my right, is the dining room, which leads into the kitchen, though I am sorry to inform you that there is no food. On my left, your right, is the parlour with the grand piano and—." He stopped abruptly and headed for the parlour. He then motioned for us to follow, so we did, but stopped short of entering fully.

"That door there, to the North–East tower, must never be opened. It must remain locked at all times. Only I have the key and I can assure you that if you should open *that* door and enter *that* room you forfeit the offer that I have extended to you and infinitely more. Do you understand me, William? The rest of the castle may be your personal playground. I even encourage it. But no good can come from behind this door. Do we have a deal?"

"Aye, sir. You're entitled to your privacy, such as any good man is," said I.

He smiled and seemed fairly relieved.

"Do come along. There's still much to explain."

And so, I didn't bother to give it a second thought. Because, after all, who was I to question a man's wishes in his own home? Besides, I'd later find out more than I'd ever want to about that North–East tower. And if you want me opinion, he was right in what he said about no good coming from behind that door. But again, I'm getting ahead of meself. So, in a few seconds he was off again—like a shot—passing before us to the foot of the staircase.

"On the second and third floors you'll find a series of bedrooms among which you may have your pick. Take one for yourself and one for an art studio, yet leave one for Mrs. McGillian. Please also spare the master bedroom on the second floor, just at the top right of the stairs, as well as the room just beyond it, further up the hall and to the right. That second one is the room I sleep in. You see, I haven't slept in the master bedroom ever since Ristila's death, for it is all rather emotionally draining. Oh, you may visit each room, and if you could give them a firm cleaning I'd appreciate it, but try to leave things the way you find them when you're done."

Once again he broke out into a hasty walk and brought us through the foyer's third entrance leading us deeper into the great manor.

"Note the wine cellar door beside Reese there. And off that way," said he, pointing to the right, "is the library in the North–West tower, and straight on is the West End, which I added on some years ago."

There was a grand map on the doubled–doors to the West End, with Antarctica, Africa, and South America on top, the Dutch East Indies and India in the middle, and Europe on the bottom. It all seemed to be in correct relation to everything else except that, —on the compass, — south pointed up. We all stared at it for a few moments, until Dr. Vant realized what it was we were doing.

"Ah, yes. The world map. Not how you're used to seeing it though, I'd bet. Puts a whole new perspective on things, doesn't it? You cannot judge on what you think you know, but only what you do know, and since, on the whole, we know nothing, we cannot judge. All we can do is question for the sake of informative enlightenment, much like Socrates. The wisest man is he who can admit his ignorance." He smiled, and then clapped his hands together.

"Now, before for we go any further, you simply must meet Victor." He then put his hands around his mouth and began to call out. "Victor? Victor!"

"Victor?" I asked. "But I thought you said you lived alone."

"Oh, yes, well, Victor's not a person, William," he said calmly. But then he began to call out again, only louder this time. "VICTOR! VICTOR!"

"Juzt a moment," cried Mrs. Langston. "You never mentioned zat zere waz a dog prezent in zis houze. I might have told you zat I have a terrible allergy to zem."

Dr. Vant chuckled to himself. "Victor's not a dog," he said.

"Cat?" asked Kaleeb.

"No, … hmmm, perhaps he's in his room."

"His room?" asked Reese.

"Well yes, you can't expect him to … Ah, here he is now!"

There—creeping through the blackness—came a four–foot–tall object with the light from Dr. Vant's candelabrum shining in its eyes and upon its sharp down–curved beak. —It was me first time ever seeing a vulture in person, and he waved his wings broadly as if he too knew this."

"Is that thing legal, sir?" I asked.

"Hmmm, well, I'm not quite sure," said Vant. "Victor, look, I've brought some friends with me. They'd like to meet you."

The bird snorted and cocked his head.

"Look now, that's no way to greet guests. This one is William. He's going to keep you company when I go away on business."

"Why didn't you tell me you had a, a—"

"A vulture?"

"For a pet?" I asked.

"Now be honest. If I had told you, would you have agreed to come?"

"Probably not."

"There, you see? I did the right thing, then."

"Is he safe?" asked Kaleeb. "I'll not have my wife in any kind of danger."

"I hear them things circle 'round you in the desert waiting to pluck out your eyes and strip the hide off ya," Reese blurted out.

"Victor is as safe as any domesticated animal and I can assure you that the only meat he's ever torn into was already dead. Oh, he'll have a randy time chasing some rats here and there, but he just doesn't have the heart to do any killing himself. Few vultures do actually. That's why they circle around animals in the desert. They're hoping the heat will kill them so they don't have to."

"Sound like a bunch of yellow–bellied buzzards to me," said Reese.

"Actually, they help clean up waste. Victor here comes from South America and while he wouldn't kill you to eat you, I don't suggest you get him mad. He can have something of a temper."

With that Victor grunted and gave a deep low hiss, as if to show that he understood what Dr. Vant was saying about him. After that, Dr. Vant seemed satisfied that he had left the impression upon Reese that he had wanted to.

"You'll find Victor to be a rather quiet housemate, William."

"You mean he doesn't have much to say?" I jested.

"That and unlike other birds he has no syrinx. That is, no vocal apparatus at all. Though he makes up for it with the way he can inhale and exhale. You might say the best companions are the silent ones." He let the thought linger. "But enough vulture culture! Time is slipping away from us, and I still want to show you the West End. So, please, follow me. Victor, you may go about your business as usual, or join us if you like."

He then led us through the two sliding doors and into the most magnificent—and I dare say the most eerie—room in the entire place. The West End was actually a three–storey cylinder surrounding an inner courtyard, which was protected from us by a circular glass wall. Above, the dreary evening light shone in and onto the statue of a fair young woman standing in what must have been one of the most elaborate flower gardens in all of England.

"What is it?" asked Kaleeb. "Some sort of greenhouse?"

"It's more than that," whispered Dr. Vant.

"It's a shrine. Ain't it, Dr. Vant?" I interrupted.

Silence encompassed us as the doctor turned to face me. He wasn't cross, but looked rather blissful.

"It is," he answered serenely. "Below that very spot is the burial ground of my beloved. Shortly after she died, I arranged to have this chamber built around her grave so that she would always be with me."

"But you're never here," I pointed out.

"Too true," he said, with a slight crack in his voice. "However, now is not the time to get emotional. We must be off. Kaleeb, you, your wife, Reese, and I will go out into town to make the proper arrangements for the Eyam trip. After which Reese and your wife will head back to the *Wooden Whale*. All while William goes shopping."

"Shopping, sir?" I asked.

"How else do you propose to eat with no food in the kitchen?"

"*Touché*, doctor."

"Hmmm, I see you were able to learn some French, after all. Come, let us be off, then. Here's some money for whatever you may need tonight," said he, as he handed me a small purse. I'll set you up with the rest when we return. I'll see you back here in one hour, William. Meeting adjourned."

And so we departed from the castle, splitting up once we'd entered the village. Gas lamps lit the streets, though I had an oil lantern of me own, which Dr. Vant saw fit to hand me on our way out. The night had crept up on us, and Dr. Vant was behind schedule. But I didn't think about that then. I was too anxious about seeing the happenings of an English village— and besides, it wasn't like I was going with them to Eyam!

As I walked I tried to memorize the landscape, as I'd done in Paris, drawing a mental map with me mind's eye. There were three main arteries: Westbrook, Oakly, and Luxembourg Avenues, and there were a dozen or so streets leading out to numerous lanes where the poor of the village rested their heads. It must have been seven or eight o'clock when I was strolling through the streets, catching the eyes of the localites as they went about on their way. Some looked me over quickly, —kind of hesitantly. A few almost gave me a stare, and yet the majority gave me a harmless glance and went on without a further thought about me. It was a small village, it was, but the population was well into the hundreds.

I had been walking down Oakly, trying to stick to the bigger roads, when I saw a grocer's store open on Rams Street, just slightly down the way. Its sign read "Faulky's", and there were fruit stands set up on the outside. There were apples, bananas, peaches, plums, and mouth–watering grapes, all of which would make excellent still–life subjects, not to mention tasty treats. I was just figuring which mixture would make the perfect composition, when I realized I had no bag to put anything into. There weren't any available in immediate sight, so I entered the store in hopes they'd have a nice canvas bag for sale.

Inside, a warm, friendly feeling was enriched by a lovely bunch of fragrant smells that seemed to beckon to your nose and lure you in to buy something, which must have worked because the little store had about four or five other customers. There was a meat counter, shelves of jams and honey, a few aisles of rice and beans, flour and sugar, and there was even a baker's corner in the far back with fresh pies cooling on the window sill in the nightly breeze. I was in heaven. Yet if I wasn't, I would be in a moment, for it was then that I heard the sweetest voice in all the world call out to me in a way that melted me heart.

"May I help you?" asked the woman's voice.

All right, it wasn't Shakespearean poetry, but still those words sang to me. I then turned to face the most beautiful woman I'd ever set eyes on. Why she even put ol' Captain Kaleeb Langston's French femme to shame! Her eyes were a pale blue, and her skin was as smooth and creamy as buttermilk itself! She had fine features and locks of sienna–brown hair that had been tied back in a sky blue silk ribbon to match her dress and offset her white apron. Little luxuries like a ribbon were practically unheard of among the trades people and even scarcer in such a tiny village!

"May I help you?" she repeated. I had been caught up in her presence but soon regained me senses.

"Em, bag?" said I.

"Bag?" she asked, confused.

"Aye—em—for the fruits and vegetables outside."

"Customer's usually bring their own bags or crates to haul their groceries home in. You must not be from around here."

"What was your first clue?"

"I'd say your accent, but to be honest you have a whole different look about you."

"How's that?" I asked.

"For one thing you're carrying an oil lamp. Most of our customers live within a block or two so wherever you're from it's from someplace beyond the reach of our street lamps."

"Aye, I suppose I am a bit raggedy too. Been on a long journey, I have. Came here all the way from Paris."

"In France?"

"That's the one."

"I wouldn't have figured you French, but I've never heard a French accent before."

"No, no. Me accent's all Irish. I moved to France less than a year ago to study art."

"So what brought you here?"

"A new acquaintance."

"Ah, a young woman, I suppose," she said with a tinge of disappointment on her lips.

"Och, no, such things would be a blessing and a half! I've moved into Vant Manor up the road. I'll be taking care of the place for the doctor while he travels round the world and what not."

"Is that the old castle?"

"'Tis the same, Missus."

"Miss, thank you. I may look older, but I'm only nearing twenty."

"You don't say! I'm barely twenty meself! Just made the change–over 'bout a month ago."

"What a coincidence."

"Yeah," I added, though I really didn't need to. I'm daft that way. Adding "yeahs", "yups", and "you bets" whenever I don't really have anything to say, which, of course, makes things a little more awkward until somebody can break the silence that follows with something worthwhile to talk about.

"So you're looking for a bag?" she asked.

"Bag? Oh … aye! God—er—goodness, where's me head! Would you have one for sale?"

"No, … no I'm afraid we don't. But, I'll tell you what. Since you're going to be here a while, I could loan you a bag and you could promise to bring it back."

"Sounds grand," I said, with a smile.

"I'll just go and fetch it then." And so she was off behind a counter with her sales ledger on top and came back to hand me a perfect little canvas bag. It was then I knew this meeting was meant to be.

"So … uh … when would you like it back?" I asked.

"There's no rush. Whenever you happen back this way, just drop it off. It's my father's bag and lord knows he'd never miss it."

"Well, I mean, I wouldn't feel right about taking a man's bag away from his store. Maybe I could give it back to you tomorrow…"

"Around noon!" she blurted out. "I–I–I could pick it up!"

"You'd do that?" I asked.

"I'd love to."

" 'Tis a date then!"

"Yes … yes I guess it is," she said, blushing.

"I'll be sure to fix you something for lunch, too! 'Tis only proper. By the way, me name's William O'Brien, but I'd like it if you called me Billy."

"Well, Billy, my name is Cara Faulky, I look forward to our lunch date tomorrow."

And so, I was putty in her hands. This whole arrangement with Vant just kept gettin' better! And when I'd arrived back at Vant Manor I told him so.

* * *

"A young lady you say?" asked Dr. Vant while I unpacked groceries in the kitchen. He was seated at the kitchen table with Kaleeb. There were maps, charts, and other odd documents strewn across it.

"Aye, sir. She stole me heart right there on the spot!"

"Ah, love," he said, as he raised his head up and stared off into space, with a glazed look over him. "It's been a long time since I've felt that way: too long. I can still remember the smell of her hair and her skin. Fragrant, soft, … tender. I courted her for three years but only celebrated one anniversary. If only she were here today."

He then turned to me and looked me in the eyes.

"You take this woman, William, and you treasure her. Do you hear me? Treasure her, or you will regret it for eternity!"

"Now, now, Dr. Vant. I don't want to get ahead of meself. I only met Cara Faulky an hour ago."

"Faulky?" he asked, taken aback. "Did you say, Faulky?" He seemed devoid of any emotion as he questioned me, by then his whole demeanour began to change. No longer was he drifting off in some ancient blissful moment; now he was becoming stern, rigid, and leery.

"Aye, sir. Faulky. 'Tis her last name. Her first is Cara."

Even Kaleeb, who had been only partly paying attention to the conversation while reviewing a map, glanced up at the sudden change in the doctor's voice. Dr. Vant slowly rose from his seat and crept near me like a tiger about to pounce. I shot a quick eye over at Kaleeb who was as puzzled as I was.

"You must never speak to this woman again, William," stated Dr. Vant, not once taking his eyes off mine. "No good will come from the family of Faulky."

"But a second ago you were telling me to treasure her!"

"Forget what I said. Hear me now." He got right up near me face. "You are never to speak to this woman again, nor any other member of her family!"

"You're startin' to scare me, doctor. You're like a walking contradiction!"

"I—" he cut himself off mid–sentence, teetering on the verge of anger. But he paused and took a deep breath that he exhaled with a sigh. His face seemed to lighten up, and he stepped back a few paces. "Forgive me, William. I meant no real harm. I've just had years of dark times with that family … years."

"If you don't mind me asking, what'd they do to you?"

"What does it matter now? It's in the past and I've no intention of living in the past."

"There you go again," chuckled Kaleeb from the table.

"I beg your pardon?" asked Dr. Vant, turning to face the seated giant.

"Contradicting yourself! You don't want to live in the past, yet you're an archaeologist! Kind of funny, ain't it?" asked Kaleeb, no doubt trying to further lighten the atmosphere.

"Quiet you," jested the doctor. "Come, let us speak no more of this matter. Pack up the maps Mr. Langston, we've a train to catch!"

* * *

A short time later I was at the front gate seeing them off. Kaleeb tossed some luggage on top of a carriage, while Dr. Vant handed me a set of keys.

"Horses! Carriages! Trains! Give me the sea and a ship to sail her with and you'll never find a happier bloke!" Kaleeb complained.

"Now you're sure you've got them all figured out?" Dr. Vant asked me, in reference to the keys.

"Don't you worry now, doctor, I'm a fast learner."

"Excellent, excellent, all's well then," he said satisfied with the arrangements overall. "Oh, and Mrs. McGillian should be here in time for tea tomorrow."

"Oh but I didn't buy any tea! Christ, I knew I forgot something!"

"No need to worry. I'm sure she'll bring her own anyway. That's the good thing about Mrs. McGillian; she's always prepared. She's an example to learn from."

"Do you want to make this train or don't ya?" called Kaleeb, from inside the carriage.

"And that's what I like about you, Mr. Langston, you're always ready for the next adventure!" he chuckled. "Now then, William, farewell and good luck. Your allowance is in the safe of the master bedroom, for which I gave you a key. Go easy at it. If stretched right it'll last you a year or so. I should be back by then. If not, I'm sure Mrs. McGillian will think of something. I'll write if I've forgotten anything."

"Take care, Dr. Vant. And thank you again for everything!"

He climbed into the carriage and paused while he reached for the door.

"There was once a young man who looked in a mirror and realized his entire life had changed before him in the blink of an eye. But he could never go back to the way things were, because the world had changed around him. He could only look to the future, for what was done could never be reversed." He then shut the door and parted the curtains away from the window.

"Or could it?" he asked, as the carriage tore off. "Adieu, William, adieu," he called out.

I watched until it had gone from me sight and I wondered whether I should've told Dr. Vant that Cara was coming over tomorrow at noon.

"Nah," I said to meself. "He's better off living in ignorance. Besides, what harm could it do?"

Just then I heard something that sounded like a sneeze behind me. When I turned around, there were Victor's inquisitive eyes gazing up at me.

"Here now, don't be sneakin' up on me like that! You'll scare the be–Jaysus out of me! Come on then. Back into the house," I ordered, as I closed the gate and shuffled the ol' buzzard up the walkway. "Are you even allowed to be outside?"

He said nothing. Then again, Dr. Vant did say he was without a vocal apparatus. But birds can't talk anyway, and if they could what worthwhile thing would they have to say? What indeed.

* * *

That night I'd taken a guest room on the second floor, across from the one Dr. Vant told me he now slept in. Mine was fairly large and sparsely furnished. There was a full–sized bed, a dresser, and a wardrobe. It was wallpapered in an autumn leaf pattern and had beautiful hardwood floors that were in desperate need of mopping. But they would have to wait. I was exhausted.

I put fresh linens on the bed and clothed meself in a dressing gown that I'd found in the wardrobe. I'd have to go shopping for clothes in the morning, since all I'd brought with me were literally the clothes on me back!

I'd fallen asleep soon after Dr. Vant left. I'd had a gruelling few days, and the comfort of a nice bed on dry land put me right out. I'm sure I slept soundly, until I felt a nudging at me side. When it finally woke me, I was startled to find Victor's head looming over me from beside the bed.

"Don't tell me I have to let you out to have a squirt!" I blurted out, but then I heard a noise from somewhere else within the castle, and I knew Victor was warning me.

Moving as silently as I could, what with me bum leg and all, I rose from the bed and crept toward the door, which Victor must've opened with his beak. I heard the noise again, and then voices, faint but understandable.

"Try to be a little more quiet," I heard a woman's voice whisper. "We don't want to wake him. Ze less trouble, ze better." There was something familiar about that accent.

"What are you worried about?" asked a man. "This is a castle for God's sake, the wall's are thicker than the clouds in old Vant's head!"

'Twas then that I opened the door a bit more to inch meself out, and the hinges let out a low whine that I was sure the intruders must have heard.

"What was zat?" asked the woman.

"I didn't hear anything."

"Well, I did."

"It's probably that stupid bird strolling about like he owns the damn place!"

"*Zat* is just as bad. Let's get out of here as quick as we can."

Victor and I were now in the hallway on the second floor, overlooking the foyer below. It was empty, but there was a dim glow coming from the parlour to the left of me view of the winding staircase. We slowly crept down as gingerly as I could manage, what with me leg aching from the night before and all, and I peered into the room.

And what did me eyes come upon, but the Acrobat and the Whipslinger trying to pry open the doorway to the North–East tower with some kind of crowbar! Seeing that gave me a burst of inspiration, and I was off to the fireplace where I retrieved a poker. Slowly I entered the room without their knowing it until at last I spoke.

"Just what do you think you're doing?" I asked, as I swung the poker into the air and clubbed the Whipslinger in the forehead, forcing him to drop the crowbar. He hollered in pain and anger, and the Acrobat leapt up into the air in a back flip and was suddenly somehow behind me.

"You come near me, and I'll box your ears you little wench!" I taunted.

From the corner of me eye I caught sight of the Whipslinger yanking the whip from its place at his side and flinging it into the air. As I turned towards him to dodge the blow, the Acrobat sprinted and seized me from behind — but not for long, for there was the demonic hiss of Victor, as he sunk his beak right into her rump. And boy, did she scream!

Once released, I charged the Whipslinger and slammed him up against the door ,which gave way a little, though I didn't have time to really think about it. Behind me, the Acrobat had got a hold of Victor by his neck and swung him around and —through the air —until he too slammed against the door, which caused it to burst open. I fell on top of the Whipslinger, while the Acrobat got a running start and leapt up over us and into the North–East tower where she suddenly began to shriek, which commanded me, and the Whipslinger's, attention.

There, in the middle of the North–East tower floor, was a giant pit, and she had fallen into it! The pit began a few feet into the room and stretched from there to the surrounding circular stonewalls. There was also no sign of Victor, so I presumed he too must have fallen.

"Where'd she go?" demanded the Whipslinger, as he tossed me off him and gazed down into the pit.

She was hanging on to the side of the stonewall a few feet down with a tear in her tights that exposed part of her bum, which I had to thank Victor for. All the while, a strange sound filled the air.

"What is that?" I asked aloud.

'Twas then the Whipslinger hurled a torch into the pit where it fell for three or four storeys until it landed with a thud after having hit the head of the largest snake I'd ever seen in me life!

"Get me out of this!" the Acrobat hollered in horror—her accent suddenly gone.

The Whipslinger reached back into the parlour and grasped his whip.

"Grab hold of it!" he ordered, as his whip cracked against the side of the stone pit.

She reached for it and would've got it too, had it not been for Victor, who had suddenly flown down from overhead, where he must've been surveying the scene, and snatched up the whip with his beak, all too quickly for either the Acrobat or the Whipslinger to realize. And so, as the Acrobat reached out and ultimately missed the whip's promised mercy, she found herself plummeting down into the pit, while the Whipslinger was being yanked off his feet, still holding on to the opposite end of the whip that Victor had seized.

I was on me feet now as I watched the weight of the dangling Whipslinger take its toll on the whip, which was fixed in Victor's razor–sharp beak. So, as you might have guessed, his beak cut through the whip due to the force of the man's weight, and the Whipslinger too fell down into the macabre abyss.

The Whipslinger landed with such a force I was certain he'd shattered a bone or two. I stood there, dazed, not knowing what I should do or indeed *if* I should do anything. Here were two people who had tried to kill me and me friends the night before, and now they were face to face with certain death in a pit four storeys out of me reach before a snake so large I would have thought made up if I'd heard described it to me. It was at least thirty feet long and a foot and a half—maybe two feet—wide. It was olive–green in colour with black oval–shaped spots and a slender tapered head. I was praying that Saint Patrick would come by to drive it away, like the legends say he'd done in Ireland ages ago.

The light was dim but I was fairly sure the snake had been wet, since its skin let off a slight shimmer, and there appeared to be a bit of water on the dirty floor. To me surprise, the snake did not move in haste towards its victims, and I soon found out why. It had a friend.

I squinted me eyes and struggled to get a better view, while Victor returned to me side and also looked down.

"If only there were a way to see what's going on down there!" I complained to Victor.

I heard quick movements, loud hissing, and soon the Acrobat's scream, but the green snake with the oval spots had hardly moved. In fact, its only movement was slow and towards the fallen Whipslinger, who lay entangled in his own limbs.

I looked up for a moment, distraught by the lack of lighting below, and caught sight of a shallow stone trough structure running along the stone wall in a gradual downward spiral, similar to the way a staircase would. As I followed it with me eyes, I discovered that it started right at the very doorway that I was at. It was some sort of tiny internal gutter or channel that smelled rancid with lamp oil. It then struck me that this must be some sort of crude way to light up the entire tower. With this in mind, I bolted back through the parlour and into the foyer, where I took up some matches. I returned to the North–East tower to light one and tossed it into the stone conduit, watching in awe as flames erupted from the dormant liquid, engulfing the tower in a warm, golden light.

I was then able to clearly see the giant green snake as it hissed up at me and the intruding light. That's when I caught sight of its friend. Hunched over the Acrobat stood an eighteen foot long king cobra with the front half of its body raised to a height of six feet and its head reared upright as it too became irritated with the sudden intrusion of light!

The Acrobat had been bitten and was now cowering against the stone wall. The Whipslinger used the diversion to his advantage and forced himself up onto his feet and limped over a foot or so, to where his whip had fallen. The green snake, which I'd later find out was an anaconda, suddenly sprang to attention at the man's movement, but wasn't quick enough to bring him down. Instead, the Whipslinger cracked what was left of the whip at the anaconda's head, forcing it back with an agitated hiss. He then spun 'round to lasso the neck of the upright king cobra and yanked it back the opposite way, slamming the predator's head into the adjacent wall, where it fell limp on top of the angry anaconda's body.

I could see now that there was a three–foot opening in the bottom wall, where traces of water had been smeared by the anaconda's body. It was a water snake that had been beckoned out of its home with the prospect of getting a decent meal, though I hadn't the slightest idea of how it stayed alive down there anyhow.

Yet there it was, hissing madly at the Whipslinger from one end, while its tail began to wrap around the now–unconscious body of the Acrobat at the other side of the pit's floor.

I watched from above, glued to the scene, as the Whipslinger lassoed the anaconda's head, as he'd done to the king cobra, but try as he might, he could not force this snake's head into any one direction. Its neck muscles were too powerful to be detoured, for an anaconda is a constricting snake and uses its body as a tool to squeeze the breath from its victims, rather than poison them with venom from its fangs.

It was at this point that I began to feel sorry for the assassins and feared for their lives; so I took up the poker I'd used earlier and hurled it down towards the anaconda's body, which it missed. But the Whipslinger thought fast and lassoed the poker, brought it to his side, and charged at the anaconda with the makeshift club.

He pelted the snake square in the jaw with such a force I heard two sounds: one of the poker hitting the snake's head, the other of the snake's head thumping against the stone wall. And so it was that the Whipslinger was the victor. But if he was, then the Acrobat was most certainly one of the losers, for there she lay—motionless—on the dirty pit floor with the anaconda's limp tail beside her.

"We've got to get her help!" cried the Whipslinger.

"Aye," I answered. "She needs a doctor, but as I'm new here I don't know where to find one!"

He was then at her side feeling for a pulse.

"She's fading fast! Damn it!" he hollered. "What nut job would keep a snake pit in this day and age?"

I'd be lying if I said that hadn't crossed me mind too, but whatever

Vant's reasoning it was irrelevant at that moment, for the Acrobat's life was at stake.

"There's no way out of this shit–hole!" he cursed.

"If I help you out, you'll have to turn yourself in and call off whatever plans you're weaving against Dr. Vant."

"I'll do whatever you say, just get us out of here!"

Now that that was settled, I had to figure out just how I was going to manage the feat. As I've mentioned, the pit was a good three or four storeys straight down, and there was no sign of a ladder or rope anywhere in sight. The oil lamp trough was simply too tiny to attempt to use, not to mention it was also burning oil, and time was against me. I tried to think. There was the pit, the snakes, the trough, the three–foot opening with water, and...

"That opening down there," I called. "Where does it go?"

"To subterranean river, I think," he shouted. "But what good is it to us if it only runs underground!"

I then remembered the strange dual–headed dragon fountain and small well I'd seen earlier that day. The well had to feed off the underground river!

"Go to it and look for any signs of moonlight. I have a feeling it leads to the well out front. If it does, I can pull you and her up in its bucket! Keep an eye out for me lantern!"

"All right!" he cried. "But let's be quick about it."

Outside it was pitch black and the lantern I'd lit on me way out offered just enough light to find me way to the well harboured in the nightly mist.

"Are you there?" I called down into the well, waving me lantern over the top of it. Me voice echoed into the void and soon I heard a response.

"Send the bucket down!" he commanded. "I'll send her up first."

I nodded me head. Why? I don't know. There was no way he could see me but it made me feel better. So I set me lantern aside and lowered the bucket until I felt the Whipslinger's tug.

"All right. Pull her up!"

I turned that old crank with all me might, straining me muscles as well as the rope, with me bum leg burning from pain, until, at last, there she was. I tied down the rope and steadied meself as I took her out, getting a full view of an exposed buttock in me face and I laid her to the side. I stood there for a second, staring at her wet shapely body with the black suit clung to it in a state of instant awe.

As I thought about unmasking her, I was reminded about Dr. Vant's hesitation to unmask the others in Paris. But why? I thought back to earlier in the night when I overheard them talking. Then it hit me, like a ton of bricks. The Acrobat was Langston's wife! Her accent was a dead giveaway, though I'd been too preoccupied at the time to notice. Vant must have known this too, since he wasn't quite sure he could trust Kaleeb in the first place, but seeing as to how he still needed Kaleeb's ship, it made sense that he'd relinquish his chance to finger them at the time. Them?! I then thought of the Whipslinger and the Detective. If she was Isabelle Langston, then who were they?

"Send it down, send it down! The blasted water snake's got a hold of my leg!"

Hastily I shot over to the well and sent down the bucket as fast as me hands could turn that crank.

"I got it, now pull!"

I began again to crank with what was left of me power, but the weight this time was at least double the weight before and therefore twice, if not three times, as hard to pull up.

"Hurry it up, God damn it!"

I did the best I could and shortly thereafter the bucket came up and he leapt out with the anaconda wrapped around his waist and left leg.

"Get it off! He's crushing me!" he screamed.

I reached for the snake's head, but it lashed out and bit me arm hard. I hollered like a schoolgirl, and fell backwards onto the ground. 'Twas then I saw me oil lamp, right where I'd left it. In a blur, I grasped the lamp and slammed it down onto the head of the anaconda, shattering the glass and pouring burning oil into its eyes. It hissed in anguish, releasing its grip on the Whipslinger's body. With nothing left to hold onto, it fell back into the well where I eventually heard it splash back down into the waters it came from.

I helped the Whipslinger get up and fully out of the well, as best I could, then I fell back and laid there beside the well, heaving me chest for air and surveying the damage done to me bleeding arm.

"You'll live," said the Whipslinger as he stood with the Acrobat slung across his shoulder. "It's only a flesh wound. That kind doesn't have any venom in it. But you'll have to excuse me for not staying here to keep my promise. If I don't get her to a doctor she'll die on me."

And with that, he tore off into the night as fast as he could manage with her on his back and a limp leg to boot. As for me, I must have laid there for another ten minutes before finally getting up and making me way back inside to nurse me latest wound.

For the rest of the night I sat up in bed trying to make sense of those assassins, the snake pit and even Dr. Vant himself. Over the past twenty–four hours he'd proven to be someone much more complex than I'd first given him credit for. There was more to him than met the naked eye, and as Victor rested on the floor beside me bed, I recalled what Dr. Vant had said as he rode off in his carriage earlier that night.

"There was once a young man who looked in a mirror and realized his entire life had changed before him in the blink of an eye. But he could never go back to the way things were because the world had changed around him. He could only look to the future, for what was done could never be reversed—or could it?"

And so, like a creature of the night, I fell asleep in the morning's light.

III
MRS. DIANA MCGILLIAN
PART ONE: THE MORRIGAN

I woke up, startled by the sound of a loudly ringing bell. It came from somewhere outside of me room and beckoned me out of the bed I'd longed for just hours before. Me left arm still ached from the nasty bite of Vant's anaconda, and I rubbed it with me right hand to try to ease the pain. The full light of the day was shining through the westward window, and I suddenly realized I'd overslept!

The lonely image of a disappointed Cara Faulky swept over me mind as I forced meself out of bed and raced out the bedroom door as best as I could manage with me leg. Somehow it had begun to feel better then. So I ran faster down the staircase, out the front doors, down the crumbling cobblestone path, and right up to the vine–infested black iron gate, where Cara had just turned and begun to leave.

"Wait, Cara!" I begged, out of breath, as I fell upon the gate to hold me up. "Don't go!"

"I was beginning to think I was the butt of a cruel jo—"

She had been turning around while she talked and stopped abruptly when she saw me bandaged arm.

"What happened?" she asked.

"You know," said I, "I'm not sure *I* know! It happened so fast and if I didn't have this wound to remind me of it, I'd swear it was a nightmare, but there it is, right there on me arm, and it hurts like a bugger, too!"

"We–well who did it do you?" she asked hesitantly. " Was it a burglar? Was it an accident? Or was it a—"

"A what?" I asked, as I struggled to stand up properly.

"A spirit … a ghost?" she whispered.

"A ghost! Jay–sus, don't tell me the place is haunted on top of everything else!"

"There *are* rumours. But if it wasn't any of those things, what was it? What did that to you?"

"I'll tell you, but first I'd like to change into me own clothes. That, and I've gotta get it all straight in me own head before I can go telling you bits and pieces. Come on," I said, while I opened the front gate. It opened with a rusty squeal, and I offered me hand for hers, which she took, joining me on the cobblestone path.

"This place gives me the chills. But it does have a certain curious quality about it," she said.

"If you think it's frightening now, you should've seen it last night, what with that fog and all!" And with that I closed the gate behind her.

"What if we need to get out in a hurry?"

"Aye, you have a point. But I promised ol' Vant I'd keep the gate closed, and after all the ruckus that went on last night, I wish the whole damned fence line be'd another ten feet taller! But I don't want to scare you too much. Just trust me, all right? Honest, I know what I'm doing."

"All right then, lead on. The sooner we get some proper clothing on you, the sooner you'll tell me your story and I'll judge for myself whether or not you know what you're doing."

"You're feisty one. Ain't ya?" I jested.

She smiled and took up me right arm, which I had extended to her. We walked slowly up the path. It was the first time I'd set eyes on the estate in daylight, and what a sight it was!

To me, it looked like an overgrown forest neglected by years of Vant's personal exile from the estate. The grass grew thick and tall, and the trees were of a varied mix, sporting extra–large oaks, maples, and multiple weeping willows bending down to brush the tips of the high weeds that yearned for the touch of another living entity. It seemed like a lost world at first: forgotten and saddened. But there was an underlying feeling of enchantment in the air around it that seemed kind of calming and tranquil.

"Everything's so green," Cara commented.

"Aye, 'tis. Kind of reminds me of back home, in a way."

"You must miss it something terrible."

"I won't lie to you, Ireland has always been me first love. But I'll be gettin' back to her for the Christmas holiday, and that's at least something to look forward to."

"What's that, over there?" she asked pointing up and off to the left of the path.

"I'm not really sure," said I. "'Tis a fine bit of craftsmanship though!"

There, hidden beneath some weeds and vines, stood a wooden post at least twelve feet in height and a good two or three feet wide. It was carved into various animal shapes; a deer, whose massive antlers stretched out a good three feet on each side, crowned the top, what I guessed was a turtle, a wolf, a bear, and some kind of primitive man in a headdress.

"I'll have to ask Vant about that when I see him again. Either that, or maybe Mrs. McGillian will know."

"McGillian?"

"Aye, she'll be here this afternoon. Vant's got her coming down here all the way from Scotland to keep me company and tend to food and what–not."

"He must think highly of you to go to such lengths."

"I honestly don't know what the man thinks, and just when I think I do, I've had to rethink what I thought, if that makes sense."

"I think so," she giggled and that set me off. After we had some good laughs, I held the door open for her and we entered the castle.

'Twas then that Victor popped up out of nowhere and scared the be–Jaysus out of Cara. She let out a high–pitched shriek that must have been sensitive to Victor's ears too, 'cause he reared back and flapped his wings while letting out a few short snorts.

"Easy, easy, he won't hurt you," I added, as she squeezed me arm tightly. "That's just Victor, one of Vant's unusual pets. I'm actually growing kind of fond of him if you can believe it."

She held me arm tighter, trying to hide behind me, and caught her breath. But she never took her eyes off Victor as he too regained his composure.

"Wait—", she caught her breath. "Did you say *one* of his pets?"

"Och, don't ask. If you think Victor's an eyesore, you dare not think of the others. But you don't have to worry; they're locked away safe and sound. I hope. Ah well, come on. I'll give you the official tour."

We walked through the foyer, the dining room, the kitchen, and eventually the parlour, though I warned her to steer clear of the North–East tower—which I'd boarded up prior to conking out earlier that morning—and then we entered the West End, which immediately grabbed her attention.

"Is it me, or does she look sad to you?" Cara asked, in reference to the statue of the late Mrs. Vant.

"I don't know," I confessed. "I don't suppose I've really thought about it."

"It's like … she's waiting for him. It must be her picture hung above the fireplace in the foyer. She certainly was beautiful. I long for hair so wavy and of such length."

"Don't be knockin' yourself, now. I happen to think you're a right looker!"

"Oh you're just trying to woo me."

"You've got me there. But can you blame me?"

She giggled again. Oh, how I loved that sound!

"I like you, Billy, you make me laugh. I don't think people laugh enough. But when I'm with you, everything seems cheerful. I like that."

"So you're not sad like what's–her–name up there?"

"What *was* her name?" she asked, turning from me and back towards the inner courtyard. I was a bit irritated, I confess. It felt a little like I was competing against Vant's wife for her attention, and I cursed meself for bringing her up again.

"Vant mentioned it, I think, but I'll be darned if I—"

"Ristila," Cara read. "It's written there on that plaque by the base of the statue. Isn't that an odd name?"

"Boggles the mind, it does. Now, why don't we grab a sip of that lemonade I bought from you yesterday?"

"1830 to 1854," she read. "She died young."

"Aye, Vant said she died a year after their wedding, on their anniversary no less."

"She was only twenty–four."

"Oh, that is young," I agreed.

"What do think she died of?"

"Your guess is as good as mine."

"Maybe she's the reason they say this place is haunted."

"Och, there you go again with your ghost stories! How do you expect me to get any sleep tonight if I'm up worrying about spooks?"

"I'm sure you'll figure something out. Besides, you'll have Mrs. McGillian here to protect you," she teased. "I think I'm getting a little thirsty now, so I'll take you up on that lemonade offer, if that's all right."

I smiled and led her out, though she did take one glance back at the shrine as I closed the sliding doors behind us.

After our refreshments I led Cara up to the third floor, where I'd chosen a room for an art studio. 'Twas an old study, with ancient furniture, dust–covered but otherwise left in a tidy fashion.

"It gets lots of light," I pointed out. "And it's got windows on both the east and west sides of the manor, so I'll not have to worry about a lantern 'til well into the evening."

"It *is* a very large room. I wonder whatever possessed him to abandon it for so long."

"Beats me, but look—," said I, as I took her by the hand and led her over to the eastern windows. "I figure I can set up an easel over here, to get the morning sun. And over there, on that old table by the desk, I can spread out all me paints so as to get a real feel for all the colours laid out next to each other. Like … like a rainbow! Oh, 'twill be heaven, Cara! I can't wait to get started."

She smiled and said, "You're like a school boy raving about a new toy!"

"Happier, Cara, happier!"

"Do tell: When you get all these colours, what *will* you paint first?"

"Only the most beautiful sight in all the known world!" I blurted out.

"Go on, what is it?" she asked with a blush.

"The glorious morning sunrise, stretching across a world of inferior beings! Can't you just picture it risin' up over those trees?"

She crept closer until she got right up to me chest and looked me dead in the eyes, as if to calm me down and ease me back into reality.

"Or," said she. "You could paint me."

I swallowed hard and, embarrassingly, a bit loudly too.

"You … you'd sit for me?"

"I would sit for you right now if only you'd ask me."

"But … I've got nothing to paint you with."

"You could draw me," she seemed to almost insist. "Surely there's bound to be some ink in that old desk of his."

"Oh, aye. Probably … probably is," said I, nervous as ever. "But what do I draw you on? Any paper in there's bound to be dust by now."

"I'm sure we could find something."

"Aye," I nodded, stupidly.

"And when you're done with her, I'll be waiting downstairs in the parlour!" chuckled an elderly woman's voice from the doorway, which startled both of us to no end.

She was a chubby old gal, in a worn brown dress and dark black overcoat. Short wisps of white hair poked out from under a shiny black hat that held a silk daisy in its side, and she seemed rather humble in her demeanour.

"Lord, ma'am, please don't be scaring us like that. You've no idea what I've been through in the last twenty–four hours."

"Yes, but one might imagine," she said with a smirk, as her eyes fell upon Cara.

"You must be Mrs. McGillian," said Cara. "Billy told me you'd be arriving today."

"And you must be Cara Faulky! What a lovely child you are, at that."

"Wait," said I. "How could you know who she is?"

"Oh it's right here in Dr. Vant's letter," she said, as she dipped into her coat pocket and removed some sheets of paper.

"Dr. Vant's letter?" I questioned.

"Oh yes," she replied, holding up the papers.

"But I never told him Cara would be coming over!"

"Well no. It doesn't say she was expected. But her name *is* mentioned, and I can draw my own conclusions," she said with a wink. "He left it at the telegraph office in town, along with a box full of goodies and my own set of keys to the estate."

"Your … own keys?"

"And I take it you're William O'Brien?" she asked.

"Oh, yes, of course. There go me manners again. How do you do, Mrs. McGillian?" said I.

"Very well, thank you, William."

"Call me Billy."

"I'm afraid not. Dr. Vant wrote very plainly, and I quote," she said, reading a passage from the letter, "Mr. O'Brien will most likely try to get you to call him by his inferior nickname, but do not give in to this ridiculous request, as his birth given name of William is far more superior, and does him a much greater justice."

"He's off his rocker, he is."

"Well," said Mrs. McGillian, "I for one agree with him. You do look more like a William than a Billy to me."

A silence hung in the air after that, until Cara broke it.

"Uh, I suppose I should be going," she said.

"Going? But what your father's canvas bag?" I asked.

"Keep it. He won't notice. Well goodnight, Mrs. McGillian. Please excuse me. It'll be dark soon, and I work the evening shift over at my father's market."

"Aw, 'tis a real shame, it is," replied the old woman, "having to go to work on such a lovely evening as this. Now, do come by again soon. Perhaps then Master William here can draw that picture for you."

Cara looked back at me a bit unsettled. At that point, we were both trying to feel Mrs. McGillian out.

"Goodnight Billy," said Cara, as she made for the door.

"Aye, goodnight," I repeated, stopping in the doorway. Then I heard a whisper in me right ear.

"Don't just stand around like a mouse caught in a trap! Walk the poor girl to work for God's sake!"

I looked at Mrs. McGillian, astonished, then glanced back at Cara, who had stopped part way down the hall.

"What—else did Vant say in that letter of his?" I quietly asked her.

"Whatever it is, it's for these old eyes to interpret. Now you run along and be back in time for tea."

I smiled, and she must have sensed me elation, for she patted me on the back and began to take off her coat whilst I headed towards Cara.

* * *

When I returned a half an hour later, I found Mrs. McGillian in the kitchen removing a tray of freshly baked scones from the oven.

"You are a wonder, Mrs. McGillian," I stated.

"Well you can't have tea without something to nibble on. And scones are much tastier than biscuits, but not as soggy as muffins can get when you try to dip them in your cup."

"Aye, they are the perfect thing, and they make the kitchen smell heavenly as well."

"Yes, seems things around here need a woman's touch. Or," she said looking at me, "at least the home!"

"Here now, what's that supposed to mean?" I jested.

"Oh no harm, no harm, but what do you say you and I get a little more acquainted?"

"All right then. Where shall we have our tea?"

"It's a lovely evening, as I think I mentioned earlier. Why not have it outside? On … say, the roof!"

"The roof! Why the roof?" I asked.

"It sports a fantastic picturesque view, and I do so love the cool breeze this time of year."

"But where will we sit?"

"Oh, for land's sake! On chairs! There's a deck up there!"

"There is?"

"You, my young friend, need to get out more. If there's one thing I've learned from Dr. Vant after all these years, it's that we can't spend our time wasting away in one spot!"

And so we went to the roof, just like that. I took the tea kettle, cups, and saucers while she brought up the scones on a fine platter of blue and white Ming china she'd found in Vant's cupboards. So we sat down to tea with the sun setting over the horizon.

"Have you ever seen anything more peaceful?" she asked.

"Not yet," said I.

"Hopeful. That's good. Keep that with you, and you'll stay pure forever."

"Hang on now, you seem to know a lot about me. But I don't think it's fair that I know so little about you."

"What do you want to know?" she asked.

"Where do you come from? What do you do? How did you meet Dr. Vant? That kind of thing."

"I thought he told you that I'm a Scot."

"That he did, but from where?"

"Edinburgh, originally, but I first met Dr. Vant down in London, oh about ten years ago. My husband, Albert, had been dead for years, and I'd been laid off as a housemaid, so you can bet it wasn't long before I wound up on the streets, trading a song for tuppence and living out of one of London's shadier alleys. And by shady, I don't mean dark, mind you. I mean shady, in the '–you better watch your back'–kind of way! I'd been on the streets for nearly thirteen months and too ashamed to seek help from my son back up in Edinburgh when I laid eyes upon Dr. Vant for the first time. …"

* * *

It'd been raining —no, pouring—for days, with a bitter wind, the kind that rips into your skin and feeds on your bones. I'd been sitting out, amongst the rest of the rubbish, with a crate full of my belongings soaked down to my un–mentionables, with my swollen ankles, singing myself to sleep and watching the socialites hurry about like ants as they cursed the rain and disappeared into their warm, dry homes.

"Today is the day, the sun slipped away,
Taking my dreams, away on the streams,
How little are we, simpletons indeed,
Hurrying to grow, to learn what we can't know
Just to buy our time back for the life that we've slacked
I just don't understand, the ways of the man.
How little are we, simpletons indeed,
Nothing from nothing into nothing we breathe."

"How absolutely depressing!" I heard a man state as he stepped out of the mists and into the light of the street lamp. He was a handsome lot, he was, clean–shaven, with a slender face, dressed in a long plum–coloured top–coat with a matching top hat hung on his head and an umbrella shielding the rain from his humble, yet sternly formal features.

"Tis depressing to live, sir," said I.

"Life, my dear lady, is what you make of it. Once you step into the puddle of despair, it becomes increasingly difficult to step out again; especially if you're constantly plaguing your own mind with thoughts of stepping into yet another puddle, perhaps even bigger then where you've been."

"How's that?" I asked. He'd gone off on some philosophical tangent, as I soon learned he often does, and lost me back at "dear lady".

"Do you believe in fate, Madame? Destiny?"

"Don't suppose I ever thought about it," I answered.

"I, for one, believe that we are all on paths chosen to take us where our hearts long to go. All you need to do is tap in to your inner compass and follow it to your destiny."

"You'll pardon me for a moment. I feel a sneeze coming o—,"– and then I sneezed, of course. Well, a few times. He then stooped down towards me and handed me a violet satin handkerchief from his inner coat pocket.

"Perhaps you don't know where to look," he said.

"Look?" I asked as I blew my nose. "For what?"

"Your compass."

"Aye, that's it. You've got it, all right."

"Perhaps," he said, as he extended his hand for my own. "But, I'll not sit back and let you lose your way. Come on." He pulled me up to my feet—I come up to his chin, by the way—and he looked into my eyes and probably straight into my soul and said:

"Life is waiting, and you could use a cup of tea."

And then he scooped up my crate and escorted me down the road to a nearby pub.

On the way I introduced myself, and he went on to say that his name was Dr. Vant but that he didn't practise medicine. Once inside, we sat down to a window table, and he called one of the barmaids over.

"'Ere now," she said. "We don't serve 'er kind 'ere."

"Oh, no?" asked Dr. Vant. "Oh, dear, that is a shame, a shame indeed. I suppose, then, that I shall be forced to take all this lovely money elsewhere." He had opened a coin purse and spilled out a fist–full of sovereigns.

"And that, mind you," he said with a grin, "is only one of my purses!"

"Ju—just wait a minute, now," she stuttered greedily. "Maybe I *could* get youse a small somethin' or another."

"Really? How marvellous! How absolutely delightful! The lady and I will take two cups and a pot of tea. Do try to make it a strong brew; it's rather blustery out there. Oh, and we could use a couple of towels, if you could spare them, please."

"As you say sir, and please, take off your coat and relax a bit. Or, or at least 'til the rain dies down."

"Thank you, but I prefer to stay as I am."

She nodded, gave half of a pathetic curtsy, and left us.

"So, Mrs. McGillian—Did I get that right?"

I nodded with a faint smile.

"Splendid! So, Mrs. McGillian, what brings a woman such as yourself to the lonely streets of London?"

"Lack of money, unfortunately; I came here as a housemaid so I wouldn't have to live off my son's charity back home. But circumstances being what they were, the master of the house ran into a bit of bad luck and feel knee deep into debt. So he let me and the rest of the staff go. We all went our separate ways after that. For a while I tried answering advertisements—all kinds, from maid, to cook, to nanny, and there was a time I even tried to get a position as a seamstress."

'Twas then his eyes lit up like wild–fire, and I knew something I said had cranked a rusted gear someplace deep in the far reaches of that head of his.

"A seamstress, you say? My wife once held a position such as that. It can be a good outlet for creativity."

"Oh, you're married? What position is she in now?"

"The eternal position, I'm afraid. She's deceased, has been for ten years now."

"Oh, my dear, I'm so sorry. I know what it's like to lose a mate. I miss my husband something fierce, I do."

"Yes, but we can't let it get the best of us, can we?" he smiled.

It was then the barmaid brought out our tea and linen.

"I suppose not," I said while I began to dry myself off.

"Love is a very strange emotion, Mrs. McGillian. All creatures are susceptible to its unyielding potency," he then pointed out the window. "Take that man there," he said, referring to a chubby gent right outside our window. The man was built like an ox and had a far–off look in his eye, as he seemed transfixed by something across the road.

"What about him," I asked, noting that the rain had passed.

"'Im who?" asked the barmaid, butting into our conversation.

"The love–stricken gentleman outside the bar here," stated Dr. Vant.

"Oh 'im? That's just 'Ugo, my mother's sister's boy. 'E's over thirty but gots the brains of a nine–year–old, says the doctors. They say 'e must 'ave been dropped on 'is 'ead when 'e was a baby, but nobody's ever found any proof of it."

"Love stricken?" I asked. "What makes you so sure?"

"For one thing, he's been staring at that young woman across the way since she came out of that shop with her arms full of parcels. She appears to be waiting for someone, perhaps a coach. This, Hugo, hasn't moved a muscle since, though I don't blame him. He has good taste. She's a rare gem. You can sense her soothing charm all the way from here. And I've no doubt that is what has smittinized our friend, Hugo, here."

"Smittenized?" asked the barmaid. "That even a real word?"

"Does it matter?" asked Dr. Vant. "So long as you know what I meant by it, and you did catch my meaning, did you not?"

"Yeah, I gets what you're saying. But 'Ugo? It just don't make sense, Mister. 'E's too daft to fall in love."

"What does the brain know of love? Such things are the affairs of the human heart. Still, if it were me, I'd offer to help her with some of those packages."

Just then ,a skinny, pompous–looking man with a thin moustache came strolling down the street in front of the young lady across the way. He directed his attention to Hugo, and turned up his nose as if suddenly stricken by a foul odour. To make matters worse, Hugo hadn't moved a muscle and, as such, appeared to be staring straight at the fellow. The man made a comment to Hugo, whom seemed completely indifferent by it. The man then became furious and marched on over to Hugo and got right up in the poor bloke's face, fuming mad, and spitting all the while he talked.

"He must think Hugo was looking to mug him or something," I said. But when I turned back to Dr. Vant, the doctor's seat was empty.

"Where did 'e go?" asked the barmaid.

I glanced back out the window, and there was Dr. Vant, pushing the pompous man back with the blunt end of his umbrella. Suffice to say, neither the barmaid nor myself waited around very long before we too were out the door and on the scene.

"Here now," yelled the man in a nasally voice. "This is none of your business, so be on your way!"

"Who are you to judge my business?" demanded Dr. Vant.

"This beastly man was casing me. No doubt he felt I was an easy target! Or perhaps someone to taunt, but I assure you, sir, that could not be further from the truth!"

The ruckus was now causing a very large gathering and the young lady, who Hugo had been so smitten with gaped inquisitively at the scene, adjusting a parcel for a better look.

"Are you really so self–centred that you could think this man, Hugo, could pose a threat to you in broad daylight, when you only just happened to notice him as you walked by? Tell me, do you pick fights with everyone you encounter, or just those you think you can belittle? I promise you," said Dr. Vant as his temper began to show, "You were the furthest thing from Hugo's modest mind."

"Is that a fact? And how's that?"

"Because he was admiring that young lady over yonder," said Dr. Vant as he pointed to the young woman. "Not you!"

The young woman froze, and silence swept over the crowd.

"Really?" sneered the man. "Then why not let him tell us for himself?"

"Very well," said Vant. "Hugo, you and I have not been formally introduced, but I met your cousin inside—there she is over there—and she told me who you are. We happened to take in all of this from the bar window behind you. Please explain to this arrogant individual what, or should I say who, you were really looking at?"

Hugo stood there for a moment. He had a bewildered look upon his face, and it was next to impossible to imagine what might come out of his mouth when once he did speak.

"I–I–I'm tired now," he stuttered nervously. "I – I'll go home, n – now. Thank you.— Thank you very much. Uh … um … ha–have a nice day." But as he tried to walk away, the lanky man grabbed hold of his sleeve and slammed his fist into poor Hugo's side. Hugo cried out in agony, and that was just a little more than Dr. Vant was going to deal with.

The doctor ripped the man off Hugo by the scruff of his neck and tossed him aside.

"Just who do you think you are?" demanded the man.

"My name is Dr. Irel E. Vant, but you may call me nothing, as I do not give you such pleasures!"

"Irrelevant?" he repeated mockingly. "What kind of fool do you take me for? In any case, this is between me and the ogre there, so I give you one last chance to back out before this becomes more about me and you than him and me!"

"Oh do shut up!" commanded Dr. Vant, and he took the end of his umbrella and slugged the bastard across his face with the handle. The blow seemed to echo into the night and the man stumbled backwards, clenching his cheek and screaming in pain, or perhaps it was the idea that somebody had the audacity to strike him.

"Doesn't feel so good, does it?" asked Dr. Vant. "Maybe next time you'll think twice about the battles you choose to pick. Now be on your way, before I match that blow with one double its strength."

"You'll be sorry!" cursed the man. "I'll get even with you yet! *No one* makes a fool of Payton Von Wildermeier!"

"Then, it pleases me to be the first," sneered Dr. Vant.

After Wildermeier had gone, the crowd clapped before dispersing to go about their own lives once again. When the commotion had ended, the young lady—whom everything had been about—came over towards us while Dr. Vant was addressing Hugo.

"Dr. Vant 'ere just saved your life, 'Ugo," explained his cousin, the barmaid. "Tell 'im thank you and be on your way."

"Thank you!" he stated simply enough.

"You're quite welcome, Hugo, but do be more careful in choosing which sights to view."

"Is it true?" asked the young lady as she approached. "Were you looking at me, sir?"

Hugo's face became flushed, and he seemed even more timid than before, if such a thing were possible.

"I–I–I'm Hugo!" he stuttered, while he buried his head into his right shoulder and reached out with his right arm. Surprising us all, she extended her hand, which he shook bashfully.

"My name is Desiree. I'm sorry that I was the cause of such a feud. I apologize," she said more to us than to him, as she struggled with her packaged goods.

"One need not apologize for being the object of another's affection. You were none–the–wiser, Miss," said Dr. Vant. "Here, allow us to help you with those." Dr. Vant took a few of the parcels and handed some to Hugo to hold, giving the hesitant bachelor a wink. "Would you'd like to join us? You too, Hugo, we've got a pot of tea inside and we could use the help drinking it. Surely on a day like today you cannot turn such an offer down?"

"I was waiting for someone, actually," said Desiree. "My father is picking me up on his way to an auction house tonight."

"Really?" asked the doctor, now quite intrigued.

"Yes, although it doesn't start until nine, everywhere father goes, he goes early."

"It wouldn't be the Menzies/Haviland archaeological auction, would it?"

"Why, the one and same!"

"Excellent, then we shall see you there tonight, for that is the very reason I have come to London this evening."

"Oh, then you're all going? How delightful!"

A hansom drove up then, and she turned around to see her father open up the door.

"I shall look forward to seeing you all again," she stated, handing some of her parcels up to her father. Dr. Vant handed those he held directly up to her father, though Hugo just stood there with his. Finally, it dawned on him to present them back to her. She blushed, handed them to her father, and stepped up into the cab. "Farewell," she offered, and then the cab was gone.

"You don't experience something like that every day," said the barmaid.

"B–bu–bye, bye!" called Hugo.

"You, my dear Hugo, are a man of few words. You are an inspiration to live by," replied Dr. Vant.

"Inspiration?" he questioned. "Nah!"

"Did you really mean what you said?" I asked. "About us going along with you?"

"Unless you have other plans."

I shook my head.

"Not me, I's got work to do," said that barmaid. "But you can take 'Ugo if you want. Just be sure to bring 'im back around these parts so 'e can remember 'ow to get 'ome again."

"What do you say, Hugo?" asked Dr. Vant, "Are you interested in seeing Miss Desiree again?"

"Oh, yes! I'd like that very much, I would. Would like it an awful lot!"

"I thought you might," he replied with a wink, then hastily addressed Hugo's cousin once again. "Would you happen to have any clothing for sale that our friend, Mrs. McGillian might fit into?" he asked.

And so, after I'd changed, the three of us headed out for the auction as the hour struck eight."

* * *

"What was it he was after?" I asked Mrs. McGillian, no doubt breaking her concentration.

"I'm getting to that!

* * *

Now, as we walked, Dr. Vant explained to us that the Menzies/ Haviland auction was renowned for its unusual artefacts and treasures—one of which was a certain violet diamond that he had had his eye on for quite some time. It was rumoured to have come from an ancient Chinese fleet that had set out to explore the world long before Columbus set sail. Apparently these men bartered their spices and such for the treasures of other countries. One such treasure was this diamond, known as the Morrigan, which was thought of as a tool for divination and resurrection, supposedly. Dr. Vant explained that it came originally from a Celtic tribe in which the followers believed the moon held a harnessable power capable of raising the dead. This power could be utilized by the Morrigan, for only it could absorb the moon's power, which when unleashed by the right person, in the right way, could resurrect the fallen.

"Sounds like a fairy tale," I told him.

"Part of Celtic lore—Irish mythology, to be more precise. It is named after a powerful triple goddess with whom death and reincarnation were associated. Thus an artefact with such a magnificent history, even if it were fictional, would become the centrepiece of any archaeologist's collection. And *I* am an archaeologist."

"I like the moon," said Hugo. "It's pretty. It reminds me of the sun, only not as bright. Which is good, because—because you can go blind from staring at the sun. But the moon is just right."

We'd nearly come to the entrance of the fancy brick auction house when Dr. Vant stopped the conversation abruptly.

"You must be very still when we are inside. The slightest move could be interpreted as a bid, and as I'm sure neither of you is in the position to bid on any item, I beg you to remain silent and motionless, like a statue."

"Like a ga–gar–goy–" began Hugo.

"Gargoyle?" asked Dr. Vant as he chuckled to himself. "You are a cultured one, Hugo. It just goes to show, you must never judge one by appearances. I'm sure I never do."

Inside, we made our way through the lobby with its lavish decor and cherry–wood tables to where Dr. Vant signed himself in and paid someone off to get the pair of us through. The main room was a lovely hall where chairs had been arranged and was filled with all sorts of interesting and queer people. Two —in particular —who caught my attention almost at the onset, were some gentlemen roundabout mid–thirties. One of them had a head of hair so light, I'd swear it was white; of course I'm sure it must have been a shade of blond in all actuality. It was long too, slightly longer than shoulder length and nearly as long as his companion's, whose straight black locks would surely have made any young woman envious.

They were both thin and dressed in long black leather coats. The blond man's face was rather ethereal–like, and he sat up taller than the other. It suggested to me that he was probably six feet while his shrewish friend could be no more than a mere five feet tall at best.

Aside from them, the room was broken down into aristocrats, professors, scholars, old crones and young reporters, all awaiting the commencement of the auction that would take place atop a short stage where a podium had been set up alongside an easel and a red–velvet–clothed table. Then it happened. Shortly after we took our seats, clapping filled the air as a small humble man with rounded spectacles took to the stage, joined by a heavier–set nobleman with a thick moustache that blended back into his sideburns, as was the style back then.

"Thank you, thank you," said the smaller man. "Dr. Haviland and myself are pleased to welcome you tonight to our second auction of archaeological artefacts, which we look forward to holding, henceforth, every five years."

"Quite right," said Haviland. "On occasions such as these, we are most pleased to have this large of a turn out. We—that being Dr. Menzies, myself, and our staff of forty—trek the globe to find that which only you could find pleasure in owning."

"Therefore, let the auction begin!" stated Menzies and the room erupted once again into a chorus of clapping.

"Please welcome our auctioneer for the evening, Mr. Payton Von Wildermeier, of the East–Hungarian Wildermeiers!"

"Did he say—" but before I could finish my question, there, taking over the podium from his employers, was the man Dr. Vant had made a public fool of earlier that evening.

"I'm afraid this puts a rather unfortunate stick into my wheel," muttered Dr. Vant. "I've a feeling this is going to be a very long and trying night."

"Thank you, Dr. Menzies and Dr. Haviland!" stated Wildermeier. He gave his slightly bruised mug a firm rub and addressed the audience: "Our first piece comes from—" He stopped mid–sentence as he'd no doubt caught sight of us there in the back.

Some people turned their shoulders trying to figure out what he was looking at. Then I heard the distinctive voice of the young lady, Desiree, among the guests.

"There father, there are Dr. Vant and his friends, whom I told you about earlier. Do let us join them before the auction gets under way."

But all the seats were filled around us, and they must've discovered that, for we heard no more of them during the duration of the auction.

Wildermeier cleared his throat and smiled wickedly. "Our first piece comes to us tonight from an early Nubian tribe, which archaeologists dug up and restored to its original beauty. I give you the Gustavian Zebra Mask, named after the late Dr. Gustav who discovered it three years ago while on an expedition across the African continent."

"Its value is more in decoration than scholarly significance," whispered Dr. Vant, as some men displayed the thing on the easel. "The real gems are the African victory masks, due to their charm and folklore. You simply must see one of my own if you ever visit my home."

"We will start the bidding at four hundred pounds."

And that's how the night began. Strange items were brought out, a bit of their history was given, the bidding started, and then they were sold. Most of the merchandise—as I like to think of it—were dirty old rusting things dug up from various ruined civilizations. Yet, every now and then, something came along that I wouldn't have minded owning myself. One was an exquisitely woven rug from Arabia, blue and gold with fancy tassels in each corner. Another was a silver goblet accented with rubies that had belonged to some king ages ago.

But of course, the thing that took my breath away the most was the Morrigan. When that came out, all hell broke loose. It was one of the last items up for bid and no doubt one of the most–sought after pieces. It had been set into a platinum ring.

I'd never seen a violet diamond before, and was quite taken back by its natural beauty. Dark as a raisin and able to cut glass, as demonstrated, this thing did harness some sort of power—the power of greed.

"Do I hear ten thousand?" asked Wildermeier. "Yes, you ma'am. Eleven thousand?"

"Twenty thousand!" shouted a man.

"Twenty–two!" yelled another.

"Thirty thousand!" called Dr. Vant.

'Twas then Wildermeier grew wilier than ever. He had Dr. Vant where he wanted him, at last, and he was going to have his revenge.

"What's that? Twenty–two thousand?" he asked.

"Thirty thousand!" Dr. Vant shouted louder.

"Forty thousand!" stated the blond haired man in the leather coat.

"Forty–five thousand!" Dr. Vant called.

"Forty thousand?" asked Wildermeier.

"Sixty thousand!" shouted another.

"One hundred thousand!" shouted Dr. Vant.

"One hundred–fifty thousand!" erupted the blond haired fellow as he tried to top Dr. Vant.

"One fifty?" repeated Wildermeier.

"Three hundred thousand!" challenged a particularly astute man with a monocle covering his left eye. The crowd gasped.

"Three hundred thousand? Do I hear three hundred thousand and five?" Wildermeier asked. "No? Very good then, going once, twice—"

"This is ridiculous!" sneered Dr. Vant as he stood up and screamed at the top of his lungs, "Nine hundred thousand!"

The crowd fell silent. Dr. Vant was suddenly the centre of attention. Even the blond haired man and his companion took notice. It was as if Dr. Vant had challenged Wildermeier to a duel, and I could see no way for Wildermeier to win.

"I believe the top bid was three hundred thousand," claimed Wildermeier, trying to restrain his glee.

"What!" someone exclaimed.

"What do you mean?" asked another.

"Going once, going twice—"

"Payton, surely you're joking?" asked Haviland as he took to the stage. "Everyone heard this man say nine hundred thousand."

"Oh, indeed they did, but I assure you, this man hasn't the money to pay such a price. Just look at the common–folk he fraternizes with. I met him earlier on the streets this evening. I'd over–heard him talking about how he planned to con us all, though the fool didn't know who I was at the time. So, as you see, the bid stands firm at three hundred thousand."

"Never was there a larger lie or a bigger disgrace to your fine auction house, Dr. Haviland," said Dr. Vant. "My name is Dr. Irel E. Vant and I am one of the foremost Asian archaeologists, soon to reveal a collection so extraordinarily comprehensive that all concept of the world's greatest societies shall be forced into re–evaluation!"

"Ha, you see, even his name is irrelevant! He's a raving lunatic. Security! Remove this–this *Dr. Vant* from our sight this instant."

"Wildermeier," warned Haviland. "You'd better be right about him, or it's your neck!"

"I assure you," he spoke, as security came for us, "I've never been more right about anything in my life."

And so he smiled and concluded that the final bid was three hundred thousand. The gavel's bang echoed through the air as we were escorted out the back door.

"Intolerable!" screamed Vant. "Absolutely inconceivable!"

"And not very nice either," added Hugo.

Dr. Vant had been defeated, and surely Hugo's dream woman had determined him unfit to be seen with. Everything was against us, but I happen to think that's when Dr. Vant is at his best. No sooner had we reached the street than a plan had formed in that man's conniving mind. Dr. Vant was a crafty lot and he was not one for defeat.

* * *

"Well, go on then, Mrs. McGillian," I begged. "Finish the story."

"Oh, but it is getting rather late, isn't it? And we've talked through supper, though I'm not very hungry myself. It's been a rather long day, Master William. I should be getting to bed."

"You can't do that! You can't cut out right in the middle of the most exciting part!"

She smiled. "Think of what you'll have to look forward to the next time!"

"But I don't—"

"Now then, good night, Master William. I'll finish my tale tomorrow." And with that she picked up her empty scone dish, and left me there on the roof wondering about what happened with her and Dr. Vant and the violet diamond, the Morrigan, those ten years ago.

IV
MRS. DIANA MCGILLIAN
PART TWO: PLAN BETA

I'd been resting comfortably in bed, dreaming about the lovely Cara Faulky, when I felt a stinging sensation coming from me left arm. It came out of nowhere and jolted me out of slumberland, from which I woke in Vant Manor with Mrs. McGillian sitting at me bedside with a saturated rag and some bandages.

"Easy, Master William. I just want to make sure it doesn't get infected."

"The way that felt, I'd swear it already was!"

"Oh, don't be so melodramatic, I've hardly touched you."

"'T ain't being dramatic, just a little sore is all."

"Understood," said she with a wink. "How'd it happen anyway?"

I rubbed me eyes with me right hand to adjust them to the early morning light.

"You know the North–East tower?" I asked.

"The one Dr. Vant left specific instructions for us to stay out of?"

"Aye, the very same."

"What of it?"

"He was right, we shouldn't go in there. That's how I got the wound. The crazy bugger's got a snake pit in there!"

"Snakes?"

"Not your average snakes either, mind you. I'm talking about the kind that can squeeze the life out of a bull and still have enough strength to take out a man!"

"Calm down, you're going into hysterics."

"Hysterics? Look at me arm, one of those damn things bit me! Thank God it wasn't poisonous like the other one!"

"You seem to have gone against a lot of the doctor's orders," said she.

"Things have been complicated."

"Come on, you can explain it to me while we work," she said, as she grabbed me arm and wiped the wound a second time with the alcohol–dipped rag.

"Work?" I asked, wincing from the sting.

"Aye, Master William. Work. Or have you completely forgotten your arrangement with Dr. Vant?

"No, I just … I just haven't had the time, really."

"He cited very clearly in his wire about how you're supposed to be maintaining the grounds and house. I'm only supposed to be cooking for you. But I'm not so cruel. There's no way I'm about to let you clean this place by your lonesome. Now, I've got some supplies already organized at the bottom of the stairs in the foyer. We can start wherever you like, but first I've got to finish with this bandage. So hold still."

She then applied some sort of ointment to me wound and wrapped it with some bandages. Afterwards I dressed and then went downstairs where, true to her word, she had assembled two buckets full of cleaning supplies as well as an assortment of mops, brooms, feather dusters and rags.

The morning light was beaming in from the stained glass tree of life high above, and the brisk morning air seemed to penetrate the castle walls. The foyer was huge and filthy. I ran me finger along the banister, where the dust had caked on it.

"What've I got meself into?" I asked aloud.

"Hopefully something other than a dressing gown!"

Mrs. McGillian entered the foyer from the dining room, that's the South End, wearing an apron and a hairnet, which held her scraggly grey–white hair up and out of her chubby wrinkled face.

"What about breakfast?" I asked.

"The way I see it, I'll start doing my chores when you start doing yours!"

"But I didn't even get a proper supper last night! You went off to bed and left me to fend for meself!"

"You poor thing," she paused. "Oh, come now, did you really think I'd force you to work on an empty stomach? There're eggs and sausage on the table, with some toast and marmalade. You can help yourself."

"You're a piece of work, Mrs. McGillian. But I think we'll make a fine team."

She smiled, half politely, half bashfully, and I could tell she had a good many years left in her. She was a spunky old gal, full of life and integrity. I then followed her into the kitchen where there sat an empty table.

"You're playing with me heart strings," I exclaimed in disappointment.

"Take it easy, your breakfast is in the dining room."

"Oh," I replied, suddenly ashamed of meself.

She shook her head and escorted me into the neighbouring room inside the South–East tower where a magnificently long oak table sliced the room in half. There were eight chairs on each side of it and another two at each end. The closest chair had a plate of sausages and some fried eggs in front of it. Resting next to the plate was a basket of toast with marmalade already spread on each piece and beside that sat a cup of tea.

"Aren't you going to eat something?" I asked.

"I've already eaten. I rise with the sun, Master William. I enjoy making the most out of the few days I have left."

"Aye, 'tis sound advice," I stated, as I took me seat at the head of the table, me mouth watering for a bit of the feast lying before me. "You've certainly lived an eventful life, haven't you? You know, I stayed up a good part of the night thinking about the story you started telling me. You promised you'd tell me the end of it today, mind you!"

"Did I?"

"Aye, and I'm dying to know what happened after Dr. Vant lost the bid on that violet diamond— what was it called? Morgan le Fey? No, the Morrigan? Aye, that's it. That and what became of Hugo the gentle, dense giant who fell in love with the young lady, Desiree, which was the start of all of Vant's troubles in the first place."

"Hmmm, that's quite a memory you have there. You make the whole mess sound like an excerpt from some kind of fantastical novel!"

"It is a good story, I'll give you that much," I added as I bit into one of those delightfully greasy sausages.

She took a seat next to me and seemed to strain through her thoughts as if to sort it all out again.

"Where did I leave off?"

"You'd all been escorted out of the auction house, but ol' Vant already had a plan in his head."

"Ah, yes, he was a crafty lot, he was," she stated, as she stared off through one of the room's many cobwebbed windows. "And he was not one for defeat!"

* * *

"Well that's it, then," I said. "You tried your best, but who would have thought that the man you made a public fool of would turn out to be the auctioneer?"

"Oh, this is far from over, Mrs. McGillian," stated the doctor. "You see, I'm rather stubborn when it comes to getting things I want."

"But, wh–wha–what more can you do?" Hugo asked with a childlike innocence.

"I believe the more pertinent question is, what more can't I do?"

"You have a plan then?" I questioned.

"Actually I—"

"Dr. Vant! Hugo! I just couldn't believe the nerve of that man!" came the voice of Desiree, as she emerged from inside with her father beside her.

"If what my daughter tells me is true, Dr. Vant," declared her stately father, "Then I assure you it will be Wildermeier's job, if not his reputation as well!"

Her father was a man of a proper upbringing, donning a top hat of his own, which was fixated above his thick, bushy grey side–burns. Now the hat, navy in colour, matched his overcoat and no doubt his suit beneath it as well.

"I was just saying," said the doctor, "that I am not yet defeated. My first action shall be to offer my full bid to the winner of the Morrigan. It would be exceedingly unwise for him to turn down my offer of nine hundred thousand, when he himself only paid a mere three hundred thousand for it."

"You wish us to stay out of it then?" asked her father.

"While I do appreciate your concern, I am uninterested in creating more of ruckus than absolutely necessary."

"Take heed then, Dr. Vant, for the man who won rights to the Morrigan—even if they were not legitimately his to win—is none other than Randolph H. Wailling, Earl of Norquecaster."

"Why, I didn't even know Norquecaster had an Earl! But I see your point. It makes the situation a trifle more fragile than I first deduced. However, I am a man of optimism, Mr.—"

"Cronley, Jervis Cronley," replied her father. "Very well then, doctor, we wish you the best of luck. Randolph Wailling can be a rather inhospitable fellow. He is known for his private collections and very often gets what he sets out for."

Dr. Vant smiled in a dastardly sort of way and said, "Then we have something in common!"

"Yes, indeed, forgive me then. The hour grows late and the auction has undoubtedly come to an end. Come, Desiree, I am sure your mother will be waiting up for us."

“You go ahead, father, I wish to stay with our new friends here and do all that I can to aid them after all their troubles this evening.”

Cronley stood silent for a moment.

“Have no qualms, Mr. Cronley,” stated Dr. Vant. “Your daughter will be well looked after. I assure you that no harm shall come to her,” Dr. Vant glanced over to Hugo. “Isn’t that right, Hugo?”

“Ab-abso-solutely!”

“I have your word then?” he asked Dr. Vant, whom nodded in reply. “Very well. I suppose she has been her own woman for some five years now. They do grow fast, do they not?”

“Faster than we care for,” I added.

“Quite right. I shall be on my way, then. Goodnight, all, and in case we do not meet again, the pleasure was all mine. Desiree?”

She turned to him and gave him a hug accompanied by a peck on the cheek.

“Be safe.”

“I will, father. Goodnight.”

And so he left us, and we remained quiet until the sounds of leaving guests filled the air around us, and Dr. Vant sparked to life.

“The time to move is upon us,” he spoke, while digging into his pockets. “Hugo, I need your help. You and Desiree take this money,” he held up two coin bags full of sovereigns. “Offer it to the first coachman you see in return for his carriage. The amount should be enough for him to purchase a new cab and have a good deal left over for personal frivolities.” He handed them each a bag and whisked them off with his hands.

“Bring it to the corner of Arlborough and Kendrek Streets, about a block from here. We’ll meet you there!”

“What about us?” I enquired.

“They are Plan Beta, and we, Mrs. McGillian, are Plan Alpha. Let us be off then; we mustn’t let the Earl get away.”

So I followed Dr. Vant down the alley and out to the front of the auction house, where numerous cabs were filling up with their passengers, and it wasn't long before I recognized the stately figure of Randolph Wailling as he emerged from the house bundled in a black coat with a black scarf and that annoying little monocle covering his left eye. His nose was long and thin, his skin, pale, and his stringy hair had been combed back over his bald spot and fixed there with some form of wax or grease. He took his time as he walked, and beneath his right arm he carried a wooden box with a lock on its latch.

"Hello there," called Dr. Vant. "Lord Wailling! I wonder if you have a moment to spare!"

Wailling glanced around as if suddenly stricken by a foul odour and winced as we approached him.

"We haven't actually met before, but we do share something in common," said the doctor.

"You're that thief, aren't you?" He clenched the box tighter in his grip.

"It's all a misunderstanding, my Lord. I met Wildermeier earlier this evening when the pompous ass openly attacked a friend of mine. I eventually got the upper hand on him, and that is the reason he conceived that distasteful fabrication in the auction house tonight. I assure you that I am who I say and can back myself up with facts and, more important, with funds."

"Assuming that is true. What do you want from me?"

"Dear me," stated the doctor, gazing up at old Wailling's head. "Your head must be freezing. Do take my hat, free of charge. It should keep you quite warm." And with that he took off his top hat and handed it over to Wailling, who merely held it in his hand staring at it distastefully.

"If you're trying to bribe me with a top hat, sir, I would advise you for future reference that a *violet* top hat with a *lavender* ribbon around the base is not very flattering. Nay, culturally inappropriate! And so, again I ask of you, what do you want from me?"

"Why, the Morrigan, of course! I'll give you anything you ask for it. I am the wealthy heir to the great Vant fortune and I am at your mercy."

"Fascinating," mocked Wailling. "But it's not for sale."

"Let us be reasonable and act as noblemen, your Lordship. Afterall, by rights I was the highest bidder and am therefore entitled to the Morrigan."

"First of all, *I* am a nobleman. I've no idea what *you* are, nor do I care. And by rights, *I* won the Morrigan. It will be the crown jewel of my diamond collection. A collection that I am now delighted to say is complete. If you'll excuse me, you're in my way."

Dr. Vant stepped aside, and Wailling continued towards his single–horse hansom cab, where his driver had opened up the front doors.

"Here Roland," chuckled Wailling, handing his driver Dr. Vant's top hat. "A gift!"

"Thank you, sir," said he, as he placed the top hat onto his head.

"I assure you, Mister Wailling, you're making a very large mistake," declared the doctor. "Do not be a fool."

Once inside, Wailling looked through us as if we weren't standing there at all.

"The doors, Roland," he ordered, and the driver closed the doors, shielding the man's legs, and climbed on up to his seat on the back of the cab. He cracked his whip at the horse, and they tore off into the night.

"That didn't go well, did it?" I asked.

"Quickly, to Arlborough and Kendrek Streets!"

He was off like a greyhound, and my poor old legs struggled to keep up. My mind began to wander towards fathoming what exactly the night had in store for us. We turned a quick corner on our right and there—at the very next corner—sat a four–horse carriage with Hugo and Desiree standing out beside it.

"Ha–ha!" declared the doctor. "Four horses to his one! You've outdone yourselves, you have. Now, Mrs. McGillian, you and Miss Cronley must find a way to seal off Sullivan Street, thus forcing Wailling to take Baker Street, where he and I shall face off. Hugo, you must drive me there."

"Drive? Me?"

"Oh for heaven's sake!" I shouted as I hoisted myself up into the driver's seat at the front. "You go with Desiree, I'll take Dr. Vant up Baker Street."

"You're magic, Mrs. McGillian," laughed the doctor. "Pure magic!" He then turned back towards the others. "After you seal off Sullivan, go back to the auction house and wait for us there. When we meet again, I should be in possession of the Morrigan."

"Perhaps it would be better to meet my home," offered Desiree. "I've a feeling the auction house is the last place we should be."

"Agreed," replied the doctor.

"Then we'll see you there. Sixteen Crescent Creek Lane," said Desiree.

Dr. Vant nodded. "Tally ho, Mrs. McGillian!" he yelled, as he hopped inside the carriage.

I gave those horses the best crack of the whip I could manage, and soon we were travelling down Kendrek Street as fast as a hound on a fox hunt!

"Faster," I could hear the doctor chanting. "Faster!"

I cracked the whip again and again, and now we were at top speed, dodging slower vessels and narrowly missing strolling passers–by.

"Your coat," called Dr. Vant. "I need your coat!"

I struggled out of it while still, somehow, managing to control the reins. "Here! Take it!"

I handed the coat down to him and felt him snatch it.

"The next block is Baker Street, you'll make a left there!"

"Aye, left on Baker!"

My old heart was racing, my blood was fired up, and it was as if thirty years had been taken off my life. The wind may have been whipping through my silvery–grey locks, but it also seemed to smooth away the wrinkles of time, and as I made the turn on to Baker Street I found myself in a sea of carriage traffic, which brought us to a much, much slower pace.

"Now what?" I asked.

"You must find Wailling's cab! He too will be required to merge if he expects to return to his inn at a decent hour."

"How do you know where he's staying if you didn't even know he existed until Cronley told you?"

"First rule of thumb, Mrs. McGillian. Only share with people what is necessary for them to know in the moment and be ever ignorant of the rest."

"So you knew who he was the whole time?"

"When going to an auction for a specific item, one must make it one's business to know whom they are up against. Just keep a lookout for Wailling's coach!"

"But there are so many! How will I know his when I see it?"

"Simple! His will be the one with a driver wearing a violet top hat with a lavender ribbon around its base!"

* * *

"The old conniver," I blurted out, interrupting Mrs. McGillian.

"You have no idea!" said she. "Ah, I see you've finished your breakfast. We'd best be getting a start on that cleaning, hmmm?"

"You're pulling me leg, Mrs. McGillian."

"I'll meet you in the foyer, I'll talk while we clean," and with that she took up the empty dishes and disappeared into the kitchen.

Me mind was full of images, like some child dreaming of fanciful fairy–tales, when I entered the foyer and found Mrs. McGillian with a couple of feather dusters.

"We'll do the third floor first, starting at the ceilings and working our way down. This way all the dust falls to the floor, where we can sweep it up easily enough."

"Makes sense, but I never would have thought of it," said I.

"With age comes wisdom. Now, what's your fancy?"

"Since we're starting at the top, best use the long–handled dusters. 'Course we'll have to get a ladder as well if we want to reach the tippy–top of the vaulted ceiling."

"There's a closet under the staircase, let's check there."

As we met by the door, me mind began to wander once again, and I found meself thinking about just how old Hugo and the lady Desiree managed the awesome task of sealing off an entire street. Or even *if* they accomplished the task.

Meanwhile, Mrs. McGillian had opened the closet and disappeared inside.

"I'm afraid there's no ladder in here," said she as she emerged and dusted herself off. She coughed a little and seemed disappointed. Cleaning was obviously very important to her.

"Suppose we try to reach the ceiling from the third floor balcony? The handle's fairly long and I can stretch out me arms a bit."

A flush of cheer seemed to wash over her cheeks and she regained some of her inner bliss—that sort of passion that comes over people when they get the opportunity to interact with what they love—and Mrs. McGillian, as I learned that day, loved to clean.

So upon an affirming nod from the old gal, we grasped the long–handled dusters and took to the staircase.

"So, I have a question," said I.

"Oh? About what?"

"How exactly did Hugo and that woman seal off—. What was it? Sullivan Street?"

"I guess first I should explain that Arlborough ran parallel to Sullivan and Sullivan to Baker. The auction house was on Woollington, which was parallel to Kendrek and thus crossed the others as they ran perpendicular to it."

"So Lord Wailling was travelling down …"

"Woollington, headed for Sullivan, where he'd be making a left."

"And you and Vant?"

"Were headed down Kendrek to Baker, where we took *our* left."

"So since Hugo and Desiree sealed off Sullivan, Wailling had no choice but to make a left at the next street in the same direction," I deduced.

"Exactly. And the next street was Baker, where the doctor and I had planned to intercept him."

"Yes, but that still brings me back to just how Hugo and Desiree managed the feat that Vant laid before them."

"All right," said she, as we reached the third floor balcony. "You start dusting and I'll explain.

"Agreed," I affirmed, as I reached out with the duster.

* * *

Later, when we'd caught back up to them, Desiree explained the whole thing, which happened quite by accident but never–the–less proved our greatest asset. You see, Hugo and Desiree had cut through some back alleys—as they were on foot—and quickly made it to Sullivan's intersection with Woollington.

Once on Sullivan, they began looking for anything to create their diversion with. That's when Desiree suddenly caught sight of a fruit stand, which she thought could be used to their advantage if she could kick out the leg from underneath it, thus dumping all the fruit into the street and, thereby preventing anyone from driving down it, since the owner would be out there clearing the mess.

"Come Hugo," she said, as she began crossing the street. "I've got an idea; we just need to get over to that fruit—"

Suddenly Hugo rushed up and tackled her to the ground as a speeding carriage flew by. The cabbie had tried to halt, but the horses stopped too abruptly, which gave Hugo time to save Desiree but—unfortunately for the driver—forced the carriage to jack-knife and topple over into the street.

Everyone seemed to be all right—the horses were more shaken than anything—though the coach itself had been deemed unfixable. Yet, Sullivan Street was sealed off, and just in the nick of time too, for at that very moment Wailling's cab was about to turn the corner. But upon seeing the accident, he and his driver were forced to continue onward to Baker Street.

* * *

"Where you would surely catch up to them?" I added.

"I'm getting to that."

* * *

"So there we were, myself driving Dr. Vant in a mess of traffic.

"We're coming up on Woollington," announced the doctor. "We can only hope our young friends were indeed successful!"

'Twas then that I caught sight of a coachman with a plum–coloured top hat with that familiar lavender band. I squinted my eyes just to be sure. It's rather hard to see violet on a dark top hat in the dead of night, and I began to wonder why he hadn't chosen a yellow or white band instead. But I didn't have time to think about that then. I had to gain on them or we'd surely lose them.

"Dr. Vant," I called. "I've got them in my sights!"

"Excellent! Don't lose them. Get me as close to them as you can without being noticed. Oh, and don't call me by my name."

"You're the boss!"

It wasn't easy trailing behind, but we were getting closer as some of the hansoms between us turned off Baker and opened up enough space for our horses to catch up. We were making good speed too, until another carriage from the lane beside us pulled out in front of us. Instinctively, I veered right, taking the lane it had left and shouted out to the horses to pick up speed.

The traffic was clearing now, and we were almost upon Wailling's cab, which was but one lane over.

"How's this boss?" I hollered into the night.

"A little closer, he'll be making a turn soon and when he slows down I'll make the jump!"

"Jump?" I asked, turning my head back around to see the shadowy figure that the doctor had become—what with black dubbin smeared all over his face and Hugo's cousin's coat tied round his neck.

"Yes, now do pay attention!"

Sure enough, as the doctor predicted, Wailling's cab lessened its speed as we picked up ours. The corner was in sight, and, like a great cat, the doctor leapt from our carriage and caught on to the back of theirs just in time, for they rounded the corner at that very moment. They were gone from my sight, but I'll tell you the rest as Dr. Vant told it to me.

He was barely clinging to the back of the hansom, for the rounding of the corner threw him off balance. Still, somehow he regained his composure and had no choice but to toss the driver clear off his perch, after reclaiming the top hat. He bellowed all the way down to the road below, where he tumbled a ways before taking to his feet to shake his fist at his runaway hansom cab. Dr. Vant then climbed up to the driver's seat. They weren't going very fast then, as they were nearing the inn, and Dr. Vant knew that if he didn't make his move soon, all would be lost.

"What in God's name is going on up there?" demanded Wailling from inside.

But Dr. Vant didn't answer him; he was commanding the horse to go faster and faster. As they passed by the inn, Wailling no doubt began to feel suspicious. But whatever he felt, it was about to change, for just as they reached top speed, Dr. Vant climbed down from his seat, leapt onto the horse's back, and unfastened it from the hansom. He leapt off as the horse broke free of the cab, which forced the front end to come crashing down, thus flipping the back up through the air some 180 degrees to where it crashed upside down to the street below. The horse had fled the scene, and Dr. Vant had to act quickly. He hurried to the downed cab, pulled the unconscious passenger from its midst—according to Dr. Vant he was otherwise all right—and removed the small wooden box from Wailling's coat pocket.

He then fumbled around in his Lordship's other pockets until he found a set of keys. Finally, he dropped Wailling, gripped the box under his arm, jabbed a couple of keys into the lock on the latch, and proceeded to open the box removing a small silk pouch. It was filled with more silk, and in the middle was the platinum ring containing the Morrigan. He seized the ring, shoved it into his inner coat pocket, and discarded the box. And, as Dr.Vant told us, he left behind the three–hundred thousand pounds Wailling had originally paid in the form of bank notes, adding a generous five thousand extra for the cab, the driver, and Wailling's pain and suffering.

* * *

"Hold up," I interrupted Mrs. McGillian, lowering me duster. "Are you saying he stole the Morrigan from old Wailling?"

"Stole it or paid for it, depends on your point of view," she replied. "Still, he single–handedly destroyed a hansom cab and injured two otherwise innocent people, all for that diamond."

"I'd say he was a criminal, if not for the fact that it was rightfully his in the first place as the highest bidder."

"An unsavoury nature, no doubt. And here I was his accomplice!"

I could only shake me head as Mrs. McGillian finished the tale.

* * *

He caught up with us at young Desiree's house where her father had invited us in for a cup of tea. I sat at the dining room table with Hugo and Desiree holding the Morrigan in my hand while Dr. Vant freshened up in the washroom. Mr. Cronley stood across the way leaning against the wall, shaking his head and staring at the Morrigan.

"So much trouble over nothing more than a rock shaped within the bowels of the earth. I've heard a lot of unfortunate stories surrounding such gems, coloured diamonds in particular, but never could I have imagined the presence of one in my very own home."

"Oh it *is* a rare beauty," I affirmed.

"That's not exactly what I meant," he continued. "Have you never heard of the infamous Hope diamond, for instance?"

"Can't say that I have."

"Wa–was someone hoping for a diamond?" asked Hugo not quite following.

Desiree chuckled at this, though not to make fun of the poor lad; she just couldn't help herself.

"Actually," stated Dr. Vant as he entered the room. "The Hope diamond was said to be cursed and found its way through the hands of many owners, as it was rumoured to be the very thing that killed them."

"Now, that was what I was referring to," added Cronley.

"Well, this one very nearly killed Lord Wailling," I reminded.

"But it didn't! And one never knows which myths to believe," stated Dr. Vant, "such as religion, for example. So many possibilities, many contradicting each other, and yet one has a sense each may be true. So that is how I view the world, Mr. Cronley, a series of myths until proven factual, with the understanding that each may contain some level of truth."

"And who would do the proving, I wonder?" asked Cronley.

"Who indeed?" questioned the doctor, with a faint smile. Yet the smile faded quickly, and then he turned his attention towards us at the table. "I would now like to take a moment to thank you all for your part in tonight's rendition of *true* justice being served."

"Is thievery justice then?" asked Cronley.

"Not thievery, Sir—equity!"

"Equity? We'll see what the morning papers call it."

"Whatever they call it, I am in debt to you all. And to you in particular, Miss Desiree, for putting your life in such jeopardy."

"Dr. Vant please, the error was entirely my own. I should have been watching where I was going. Father's always telling me to be aware of my surroundings, and it was I who let down my own guard. But thank goodness Hugo was there to save me. You really are a godsend, Hugo—so pure, so generous, so very different from the rest of the men in England."

"Aw, 't weren't nothing."

"Don't be modest, Hugo," added the doctor. "You saved her life and still managed to assist me in the process. I am ever at your service."

"No, no, no. We're square, y–you and me."

"Come now, there must be something you need, something you *want*."

"Y–You've given me more than I could have e–ever asked for. Adventure, uh … adventure, and a night out with a b–b–beautiful woman," he giggled nervously. "Maybe, maybe I should still owe you!"

"Oh Hugo," sighed Desiree. "You make me blush. You really are a true gentleman. And if possible, perhaps you and I might make a date sometime."

"Really? You … you'd want to go out wi–wi–with me?" he asked.

"I would consider it an honour," said she.

"Now, you see doctor … Dr. Vant," said Hugo, shaking his head "I–It's really I who owes you!"

"You know, you two really do make a lovely couple," said I. "I just wish I could be around to see your relationship mature."

"That's a marvellous idea," decided the doctor.

"What is?" asked Cronley.

"Perhaps Hugo *can* assist me with one last modest request."

"You just name it!" declared Hugo.

"Mrs. McGillian here, she has no place to stay, no one to turn to. Would you take her into your home and allow her to stay with you if she promised to keep house and cook for you?"

"Boy would I? I'd even p–pay her!"

"But I—," I butted in, but Dr. Vant cut me off very swiftly.

"But nothing. I'd take you into my own home if only I were there more often. You need people to look after, Mrs. McGillian, not just a home. And people need you, even if they don't know it. Besides, maybe with Hugo's help you could earn enough money to finally return home to your children. Consider Hugo's favour to me the washing of my debt with you for all you've accomplished this evening. You've proven that we're only as old as we let ourselves be. You are an inspiration to look up to."

"Oh, good heavens. What can I say?"

"Say you'll stay!" proclaimed Hugo.

"Oh, all right. I'll stay, I'll stay," I cried with tears of happiness. To have a place to stay, to have a home with people who cared about me, such were the greatest of gifts anyone had ever given to me, and as Dr. Vant left that night I told him just that.

We were outside, he and I, as I had walked him to his cab, just outside the Cronley home.

"You know, I am going to miss you, Mrs. McGillian. In some small way you have filled a void in my life. For that, I thank you."

"Me, fill your void? Oh, for God's sake, look at what you've done for me! A home, a job … *Meaning*, that's what you've given me. You've restored meaning to my life. Please, *please*, Dr. Vant, if there's ever anything I can do for you, call upon me. Whenever and wherever I am, I will answer your call, happily!"

"Very well. If ever such a remarkable circumstance should arise, and I need to acquire the assistance of one who's spirit is as energizing as yours, I will call."

I smiled, and my old eyes welled up with tears again. Not because he'd be calling me, but because I would have the chance to see him once again. He had a rare presence, and just being around him made everything work out. At least, that's how you felt. And so with a heavy heart I gave him a genial hug. He said nothing else, but only kissed my hand and took to the hansom cab. When the door had closed, the cab slipped off into the early morning sunlight, and Dr. Vant was gone from our lives as quickly as he'd come into them, having changed us all for the better.

The others came out to check up on me and they shuffled me back inside, but I took one last look into the distance and felt somehow enriched though at the same time saddened.

As the years passed, we wrote to each other periodically, and I eventually raised enough money to return home to Edinburgh, where I've been ever since. I still take holiday in London though, to visit with

Hugo and Desiree. They got married, you know, delightful couple. Anyway, that's how I came to know Dr. Vant.

* * *

"'Twas a fascinating tale, Mrs. McGillian. One that's kept me on pins and needles, not to mention arm rails," said I, as I sat up atop the balcony railing to reach a far corner of the ceiling with the duster.

"Yes, I suppose it is quite remarkable, once you put it all together. Be careful now."

"Aye, I would hate to fall from this height!" I said, as I steadied meself. "So, what did he ever do with it? The Morrigan?"

"Would you believe he's never told me? You know, now that I think about it, he's never brought it up in a single one of his letters, and I've never caught word of his discoveries in any of the papers."

"Maybe he wasn't planning an exhibit afterall. Or maybe he's still searching for some of the missing pieces. That's it! It's got to be. Right now, for example, he's getting together an expedition team to go to China, looking for some ancient treasure."

"If there is an ancient treasure, rest assured, he'll find it."

"Oh, he's already found it, just couldn't get at it. Something about it being cursed, I think."

"A cursed treasure, a purple diamond—"

"Giant snakes, a pet vulture and he's even got some kind of wooden pole outside with animals carved into it."

"Ah, yes, the totem pole, I saw it when I came in yesterday."

"What does it all mean? What's old Dr. Vant got up his sleeves?" I asked.

"Whatever it is, it's taken him a lifetime to amass. That Morrigan incident was ten years ago. I'm sure there's something he's not telling us," said Mrs. McGillian with a glint of curiosity in her eye.

"Aye, but what?"

V
THE EYAM MAN

It had been about a week since me arrival at Vant Manor when Mrs. McGillian and I had finished cleaning the interior of the castle. Well, almost—there was still the wine cellar, but we figured it could wait until some later date. You see, we were eager to get outside, to tend to the estate itself. There was a mystical nature about it; it was like some enchanted forest from the fairy tales me Mum used to tell me as a wee lad.

It was a bright, cheerful day, and we had gotten up early to watch the sunrise from the courtyard on the roof. Vant's estate seemed practically endless from up there, although if you looked close enough, you could just make out the bits of the black iron fence line that peeked out of the overgrown hedges here and there. The hedges, and therefore the fence line, surrounded the property in a giant circle as big as the distant village of Leocadia on its outskirts.

The sun was well into the sky when Mrs. McGillian, me personal sense of motivation incarnate, turned to me as I stared out at the horizon, and said, "What do you say we start at the front gate and work our way clockwise around the estate?"

"Have some mercy, woman! We just finished cleaning the insides last night! I'd like a chance to enjoy the fresh air and sunshine before having to get knee deep in filth and sweat!"

All right, so I wasn't so eager to get outside to tend to the grounds.

But I *was* eager to get out into the open air away from the walls of that damp lonesome castle. The breeze felt heavenly when compared with the stale air of the foyer, and I was still sort of spooked by that statue of Vant's dead wife standing there in the inner courtyard.

Anyway, it was right about then that we heard what had since become a familiar sound, Victor's snorting. He had flown from his window in the South–West tower and accompanied us on the roof.

"Oh, look who's come to join us," observed Mrs. McGillian. "Good morning, Victor!"

He crept forward, and she put out her hand to pet the old buzzard's head.

"Such a handsome vulture, you are," she added.

You could tell he loved the attention, 'cause he'd rub his head back and forth along her hand like some little kitten. He must not have gotten very much, what with Vant travelling all the time. Yet that morning his comfort was short–lived, for suddenly he stopped, leant his head forward, and fixed his gaze towards the front of the estate.

"What is it?" I asked him.

"Look," said Mrs. McGillian. "Up at the gate."

The two of us took to the edge of the rooftop wall to get a better view.

"It's a man," said I. "What do you fancy he wants?"

"To deliver a letter, I'd wager. That's the postman."

"Is it?" I asked, squinting.

"Don't tell me your eyes are worse than mine!" she jested.

"Oh, yeah, I see his pouch. He's putting something just outside the gate. Guess it's too big for the letterbox. So it's a good thing you didn't wager! Doesn't look like he wants to stick around, though."

"Come on, let's go see what it is," she suggested.

It seemed to take us forever to get to the front gate. First we had to go down four flights of stairs and then we had to walk nearly half a mile down the cobblestone path, where Victor soon joined us. Mrs. McGillian unlocked the gate and bent down to inspect the parcel.

"It's a package," she stated.

"Aye, but from whom?"

"From Dr. Vant."

"Which one of us is it addressed to?"

"Doesn't say, just has Vant Manor written on the front of it, along with the address.

"Go on then, let's open it," I suggested.

"Ah, so that's where your eagerness has been hiding. I should put it to work straight away while we're here at the front gate, before it decides to pull one of its disappearing acts again."

"You can be a cruel old gal, you can, Mrs. McGillian."

"Perhaps we should take it inside to open it."

"*Oh, no!* I just got out of there; I'm not going back in until nightfall," said I, as I took up the package.

"I guess we could take a seat on that stone bench over there."

"Stone bench?" I asked, turning around.

There, practically drowned in weeds, sat a little white stone bench.

"Would you look at that," said I.

"Makes you wonder what else is hiding in all these weeds."

"Aye, and that's what scares me," I commented, setting the box down beside the bench.

"Nonsense," she uttered.

"Just the same, I'd feel a lot better with this gate closed," said I as I went to close the gate. 'Twas then that I caught sight of me angel of love, Cara Faulky, headed our way, from up the road.

Mrs. McGillian noticed too and smiled to herself.

"Go on then, close the gate."

"Maybe it can stay open just a bit longer," I added, as Cara came closer.

I had seen Cara only one other time since her first visit to Vant Manor, I had been in town trying to find some painting supplies when I found meself inside her father's shop once again. We had a delightful visit, though I was disappointed to learn that the supplies I'd need weren't to be found in the village of Leocadia. I'd had to put in for an order over a wire.

"Billy!" Cara called merrily as she made her way into me arms.

"A little tawdry for a young lady of your calibre, wouldn't you say?" questioned Mrs. McGillian. Cara dropped her arms from me neck in response and took a step back, blushing.

"What are you doing out here?" she asked me, trying to change the subject.

"Getting the post. What about yourself?"

"I was hoping I might visit with you. I haven't seen you in days! That is, if it's all right." she added, glancing over at Mrs. McGillian.

"Oh, don't leave on my account," Mrs. McGillian replied. "Apparently, he and I could both use some rest."

"Rest?"

"Aye," said I. "We just finished cleaning in there last night."

"Oh, I don't want to intrude in any way."

"Nonsense," I blurted. "Your visits are never an intrusion! Anyway, we're just about to open a package we received from Dr. Vant. You can join us."

"Master William, are you sure that would be wise?" asked Mrs. McGillian in a hushed voice. "After all, we could always open it later."

"What harm could it do?"

"Very well then, come on, let's get over to that bench. I've been standing upright too long."

As Cara entered, I closed the gate, and we soon joined Mrs. McGillian on the stone bench. I helped her tear open the parcel, and we found a thick envelope resting atop Dr. Vant's signature plum–coloured top hat and coat.

"Would you like to read it or shall I?" asked Mrs. McGillian.

"Oh, let Billy read it, I just love his accent," stated Cara.

"Here you are then, Romeo," chuckled Mrs. McGillian as she extended the envelope to me.

"All right, then," said I. I took the envelope and opened it up.

* * *

"My dear William, Mrs. McGillian, I trust that by now you two have become more than adequately acquainted. My apologies to you, Mrs. McGillian, for not being able to greet you in person, but time isn't one of my more favourable friends. I hope that you have both grown accustomed to Vant Manor and perhaps even to Victor. Do give him a good pat on the head for me! I suspect that he may go into a depressed state when I am away and am very grateful that you are both there to keep him company.

You'll note that I've enclosed my top hat and coat. Please see that they find their way into my room, as I'd hate for them to get tattered on what's bound to be a most strenuous journey.

As for myself, I have just come from Eyam. It is a very small and humble village. I'd say roughly a third the size of Leocadia, but most definitely more hospitable. Our journey was brief, but I wish to share it with you. Now, I normally don't speak of my undertakings to others, but I've come to believe that you both have rather exuberant imaginations and a genuine interest in my line of work. So I shall relay the tale, if for no other reason than to pass time on this train ride to port. Kaleeb and our good man, Martin Abbott, the Eyam man, have drifted off to sleep, while I am left to recount our meeting within the boundaries of the human mind and the written word.

It was deep into the night when Kaleeb and I strolled through the streets of Eyam. The village had long since gone to bed, and only a few lampposts lit our way as we wandered through the blackness, which had thickened with a fog that had crept in when we'd arrived. Still, we managed to find our lodgings for the night. We would be staying with an elderly widow who usually had a room to let for a nominal price. I had telegrammed to her ahead of time and instructed her to leave a key for us on a nail beneath one of the windowsills. However, when we arrived, and I felt for the key …

"What's wrong?" Kaleeb asked me.

"The key," I declared, bending down to get a better feel. "It isn't here!"

"Ain't that a fine how–do–you–do! What now?"

"I'm not sure, but keep your voice down. The last thing I want is to call attention to ourselves. Perhaps she's left the door unlocked." Even as I said the words I had turned the knob, but the door was most definitely sealed.

"These are some connections you've got," Kaleeb ridiculed. "A fine mess we're in! What next? Wait 'til sunrise?"

"We have no other choice, we'll have to knock."

"There's a grand idea!" he added condescendingly.

Though he was quite getting on my nerves, I took it to be his over–tiredness and ignored his petty comments. And so I knocked, softly at first, then a good deal harder.

"Maybe she's gone deaf in her old age. You said yourself on the way up that she's in her eighties."

I must admit that I too was feeling a bit anxious. There was even a brief moment when I had wondered if, indeed, I had the right house. I verified the address above the door just to be sure, and it checked out. We were most definitely at the home of Mrs. Bellmore. She had been extraordinarily hospitable to me during my stay in Eyam this past winter, or should I say to Nigel Palmer, the alias by which I am known throughout those parts. I had made arrangements then and telegrammed to her shortly before our arrival, as I've mentioned, and still no answer at her door.

"Her hearing is as good as my own," I explained. "Her nerve is strong. Her heart undoubtedly kind. She'd sooner wait up for you then abandon you. Something is amiss."

"Should we break the door in?"

"I'm afraid we've no other alternative. She could have fallen ill for all we know."

"That's true," he agreed. "We'd be doin' her a service to aid her in her hour of need."

"Then it's settled. Come, we shall do it together. Swiftly and efficiently."

"Stand back," he uttered. "I've got this one." With that, Kaleeb pushed me aside slightly and aimed his shoulder at the door. He gave it a firm shove, as though he were a human battering ram, and then pushed the door open rather quietly. This was of interest to me, as it seems Kaleeb is a man of many talents, many of which I am sure will be put to the test on our great voyage.

However, for the time being, such thoughts would be virtually forgotten, as we discovered the body of Mrs. Bellmore splayed upon the floor when once we had entered.

"My word!" I shouted.

"Quiet," ordered Kaleeb. "We don't know how she died yet, and if foul play be involved the killer could still be at large nearby, or even inside."

I nodded in agreement and then bent down to check the woman's pulse. She was a frail old gal, dressed in her night robe, with her long, white hair flowing loose. She was lying on her stomach, and as I turned her over to inspect her face, I fell back in horror, as the mystery of her death pointed to murder. For there, wound tightly around her neck, was a piece of red satin she used to use to tie her hair back.

"Take a look at this," I insisted and Kaleeb obliged.

"Strangled to death," he observed.

"And her body not yet gone cold," I added whilst feeling her neck.

"I suggest we get out of here, before—"

"Before you get caught?" asked a man's voice from the doorway behind Kaleeb.

It was a constable, joined by two others and a feeble, skittish old woman.

"Look at him, he's strangled her to death!" shouted the old woman in hysterics.

"Yes, it's a good thing you came for us when you did. Run along home now; we'll take care of this."

She did as he advised and was soon out of our sight. The man was lean and had a keen eye, broad shoulders, a slender face, and a thin moustache; I'd put him in his forties.

"You're under arrest, gentlemen. It'll be easier on all of us if you just come quietly."

The others backed up his words by striking their batons against their hands, repeatedly, as if to be menacing, though they really seemed a little foolish to me, and I don't believe they would have instilled very much fear into the heart of a real killer, so perhaps that was why fortune had handed them us instead. Either way, misconception had been laid before us, and I had to set the record straight.

"I assure you, Officer—"

"Inspector," stated their fearless moustached leader.

"Very well, Inspector—"

"Groesbeck," he interrupted again.

"Inspector Groesbeck," I stated. "I assure you that this is not as it would seem. We have only just arrived, as did you. Only we have discovered Mrs. Bellmore's body first. We've also come to believe that she has been strangled to death not very long ago as her body is still warm."

"You don't say?" mocked the Inspector.

I tried to level with them. "Listen, I realize how this may look. My being on the ground near her dead body, having just touched her neck, to feel for a pulse … your finding the door thrashed open and me looming over her … But I give you my word, this is not as it appears."

"I'll decide what went on here tonight and until then, get up. You're coming with us."

"But I—"

"You? Just who are you?"

Kaleeb shot a worried glance my way, and I knew then that we were in for an extended stay in Eyam.

"Nigel Palmer."

"Nigel Palmer," he repeated as he whipped open a pad of paper and grasped a pencil from his ear to take it all down. "And you," said he as he turned towards Kaleeb. "What's your name?"

"Kaleeb Langston."

"How do you spell it?"

"*Kah-leeb,* K–A–L–E–E–B. Langston, L–A–N–G–S–T–O–N."

"Funny, I would've pronounced it *Kay–lebb*."

"Would you now?" asked Kaleeb, once again in no attempt to conceal his sarcasm.

"Yes, but I suppose then it would've had to start with a 'C', as in Caleb."

"My, my" said I. "You certainly do get your facts straight, Inspector. And now that you've solved the mystery of figuring out our names perhaps you'd better spend time solving more pertinent things, like, oh, say … Mrs. Bellmore's murder?"

"That's enough out of you! Grab 'em boys! We've just the place for their kind."

I do admit, it wasn't the best thing to say in the given situation, but they were trying our patience. Especially since whoever did commit the heinous act was still very much at large. Regardless, Kaleeb and I were taken to the Eyam police station where we were questioned and detained for the remainder of the night, short as it was.

I must have been completely exhausted, as I did not wake until sometime after the sun's rise. The rays flooded our tiny cell through the small barred window. I gazed about the cell, which, even in daylight seemed like a ghastly place with its' stone walls and lack of colour, not to mention heat.

Kaleeb was already awake and sat upright on his cot with his back against the damp wall. I too, then sat upright, rubbed my eyes and stretched out my arms as I yawned off the remains of my sleep.

"Sleep well?" asked Kaleeb in jest.

"Actually, I did. I feel incredibly refreshed and full of vigour."

Kaleeb silently stared at me for a good moment, and I could tell that he was trying to figure me out in his own way. You see, I'm a rather complex fellow and do not necessarily fit any one mould, unless I am of my own mould, and quite frankly, I wouldn't have it any other way.

"Then maybe all that rest has given you some idea of how we're going to get out of all of this?" I sensed his frustration and most assuredly agreed with it. I would need to reason with that inspector if we were to be free to search for our man and get on with our journey. So when he came to check on us, sometime after lunch, I tried just that.

"And how are our prisoners doing this lovely afternoon? Ready to come clean yet? You know they say God is all forgiving. Maybe you can still avoid eternal hellfire if you rinse your soul free of its sinful baggage, hmmm? What say you?"

"Inspector Groesbeck, is it too much to presume that by now you have had ample time to inspect the scene of the crime?"

"I have."

"And would you agree that Mrs. Bellmore had indeed been murdered by strangulation shortly before your arrival on the scene late last night?"

"I would."

"And in your search through Mrs. Bellmore's home, did you not find a telegram from one Nigel Palmer to Mrs. Bellmore requesting her to leave a key outside and under the window sill near the door, so that he and his friend may enter the home in the dark hours of the night to prevent waking her up, as they would be her guests for the next two days and had already paid for their stay in full?"

"I found no such document."

"Did you inspect the body?"

"What for? I know how she died and by who. You try my patience, Mr. Palmer."

"Per chance if you had inspected her body you might have found that telegram in one of her pockets, as Mrs. Bellmore was one to keep important things close to her."

"Suppose we do find such a telegram on her, who's to say you didn't put it in her pocket yourself, anticipating need of an alibi?"

"Inspector Groesbeck, imagine for one moment, if you will, that indeed Mr. Langston and myself have told you the truth. That we had let a room from Mrs. Bellmore and found her body just as you did last night. If such is the case, then I ask you three very grave questions. One, *where* is the true murderer now? Two, *what* was his motive? And three, *what if* he strikes again?"

"All right, I'll send word down to have her clothing looked at, but I'm keeping a close eye on you, Mr. Palmer. A very close eye."

"Then I pray the real killer be as closely monitored, especially as he is still at large."

Groesbeck said no more, but exhaled contemptibly through his nostrils and I swear I saw a tiny bead of sweat appear on the man's forehead. He then moistened his upper lip with his tongue, as if deep in thought, and left us to our cell.

Kaleeb and I remained quiet for the remainder of the day. Though we would have discussed our plans to China, we refrained from such conversations while under the eye of law. Prison—if you've never been there—is a lonely, dreadful place, where the mind wanders, not just to what got one into the cell in the first place, but also to life. It is a place to reflect, and for those who've not had a good life, that is, in itself, a form of purgatory.

My life has held many sorrows, and I was reminded of them during my stay there as I had been during my previous imprisonments. Yes, it should come as no shock to either of you that I have been imprisoned before. It can sometimes be expected in my line of work though upon looking at it from your perspective or as that of an outsider one may enquire exactly why the field of archaeology weaves such a perilous web.

The answer, as simply as I can explain it, lies within the extreme rarity of the items an archaeologist may seek. Usually they are of great value or involve great risk to retrieve, but the payoff, my friends, ah, the payoff is something far greater than you might imagine. For an archaeologist to unearth a prize locked away by time itself, it is as the feeling a doctor may get when having resuscitated a patient presumed lost, or of an artist putting the finishing touches on his life's masterpiece, to which I'm sure you can relate, William. These are the very moments we live for.

It was well into the evening when something caught my eye. The sky had grown dark, as night crept in, and a light flickered to life outside our barred window. A smile came to my face, though Kaleeb must have wondered why. Had he known at that moment what I knew, he too would have sparked to life, for you see, in addition to being the village chandler, Martin Abbott held a second job as the nightly lamplighter. Wasting no time, I pressed my face to the bars and called out to him just as he was climbing down the ladder he carried with him.

"Martin! Martin Abbott," I called.

He was a little taken aback upon hearing his name called in the dark and stumbled down from the last step. He is a thin man, tall, dark–haired, and rather lanky, with pale skin and a nose that protrudes twice that of the norm. His attire was common country clothing: brown tweed waistcoat, matching trousers, a raggedy topcoat, and a beige scarf and tan cap. He hadn't shaved and had dark circles beneath his eyes, which I suppose go with his trade.

"Someone there?" Martin asked aloud, as he probably doubted his sanity.

"Over here," said I. "The barred window, it is I, Nigel Palmer!"

His face perked up at the mention of the name, and he at once searched the darkness until he spotted my little window. He squinted to make certain it was indeed whom he thought, then shook his head, dumbfounded, and came right up to the window.

"Now this is all a bit dodgy then, isn't it?" he asked. "How in the name of the Queen did you end up in there?"

"I actually came back to Eyam to see you."

"Me?"

"Indeed."

"Whatever for?"

"It is a very long and complicated matter that's best not gone into at the moment."

"All right, but it still doesn't explain how you ended up in that cell."

"I'm getting to that. You see I arrived in Eyam late last night and had planned to let a room from Mrs. Bellmore."

"She's a good friend, that Mrs. Bellmore!"

"Yes, well, I'm afraid I've some bad news. When I arrived I found her dead."

"Dead? Our Mrs. Bellmore?"

"I'm afraid so."

"How?"

"She had been murdered. Strangled."

"You're putting me on now!"

"Would I? Look at our present predicament! We'd no sooner got there than her neighbour had summoned the police, and there I was checking for a pulse when they arrived. You can imagine what they must have thought. Which brings me to my present dilemma."

"They think you knocked her off?" he asked.

"Unfortunately so, but they've made a grave mistake, Martin. The real killer is still at large."

"What are you going to do?"

"I'm afraid I cannot do anything. But perhaps *you* can."

"Me, sir? What can I do?"

"I've been thinking the whole thing through in my head since my imprisonment. As Mrs. Bellmore was strangled to death with her own hair ribbon, I believe it was an unrehearsed part of the killer's plan."

"You don't think he meant to kill her?" Martin enquired.

"Precisely! I believe he was a thief, nothing more. He had gone there to steal something, only because Mrs. Bellmore was still up, awaiting my arrival, she took him by surprise, and he acted in haste. I further believe that, as nothing was out of place when we arrived, he must have only just got there himself. Therefore our arrival forced him to abandon the scene of the crime without retrieving what it was he had gone there for. If such is true, he no doubt watched from a distance to see when we'd left. Yet witnessing our arrest, and the presence of the constables, he would have fled for the night. Knowing that we had been imprisoned in his place, he will believe the house to be unguarded and will no doubt return there tonight to collect his treasure."

"Wait, you keep saying *we*?"

"Oh yes, forgive me Martin. Allow me to introduce you to Captain Kaleeb Langston," said I as I stepped aside. Martin leaned in and caught sight of Kaleeb lounging on his cot in the corner.

"Pleased to meet you," spoke Kaleeb.

Martin only subtly smiled in his bewilderment.

"So if he returns tonight, he'll get what he was after all along and you'll get the blame," added Martin.

"Unless he were to be caught in the act."

"True, but by who? I don't have to guess that the police aren't going to believe you on this one."

"That is where you come in, Martin. Will you catch the real killer and clear our names?"

"Do what? Mr. Palmer, I don't work for Scotland Yard! I'm nothing more than a chandler by day and a lamplighter by night!"

"Martin Abbott, in the short time that I've known you, you have proven to be a man of high character, with a rare intellect and keen eye. You'll pardon my pun, but if anyone can shed some light on this nasty little affair, a candle maker can. But not just any chandler—you're even more fit for the challenge because, as a lamplighter, your eyes have grown accustomed to seeing in the night. Else you'd trip over your own two feet! Mr. Abbott, if anyone is suited for this task, you and you alone can master it! Now, what do you say?"

"If anyone passes by you could say you're just making your rounds lighting the lamps," offered Kaleeb.

"You know that is a good point," reasoned Martin. "And if this bloke *is* nothing more than a common thief, he'll have his hands full taking on someone who'll give him the fight of his life."

"You'd be a hero," I put in. I had to. He was our only hope and everything depended on his cooperation.

"All right, I'll see what I can do. But then whether or not you get out of here, you must promise to tell me why it is you've come all the way back to Eyam to see me. I would have thought you'd be well into Italy by now, studying the plague route from its source in Europe all those years ago."

Kaleeb shot an inquisitive eye my way, though I was preoccupied with the current matter to humour him any.

"Then let me tell you this. It is the plague that has brought me back to Eyam," I said. It wasn't as though I were lying. It was indeed the plague research, and Mr. Abbott's obscure connection to it, that had brought me back to Eyam.

"I'd best be off, then," said he and with a tip of his cap he sunk back into the darkness.

What followed next I'd learn fully the next day. It was around eight–thirty when Martin appeared on the scene. All was quiet, and only the moonlight was cast upon the home of Mrs. Bellmore. Martin took his place among the shadows and surveyed the situation before him. The best way to ensnare the thief–turned–killer would be to catch him in the act, and the best way to catch him in the act would be from the inside.

Silently and stealthily, Martin advanced on the house. The front door was locked and so too was the back door, and all of the windows had been fastened. Had he been an ordinary man he might have been defeated. But Martin Abbott was a lamplighter, and he had with him the necessary tools to descend into the house. Martin laid his lamp–lighter's ladder upon the edge of the roof, climbed up to the top, and kicked the ladder down into the bushes below, so as to conceal it from immediate sight.

He crossed the roof and shimmied his way down into the house through—what else? The chimney. The whole incident reminds me of an American Christmas poem I once read. Ah, well, I digress. So there he was, covered in soot, hidden within the fireplace awaiting the return of Mrs. Bellmore's intruder.

The hour had grown late, though in the darkness, acute as his eyesight was, Martin did not have enough light to make out the time upon the face of his watch. He believed it was half past two or three in the morning. He could not be sure, as he had nodded off after a few hours, but blackness was all around him when he was awoken by a faint draft.

At first he attributed the draft to the chimney above, but as his mind pondered the subject, he began to realize that the draft was coming from inside the house. A window must have been opened. But he was quite certain he had not heard the breaking of glass. He also knew, from trying each and every one, that no window had been left unfastened and the doors were all locked up. He began to feel anxious and frightened. A sixth sense seemed to awaken in him, and somehow he knew he was no longer alone in the house.

The distinctive creak of a floorboard confirmed his paranoia. A man had entered the room. He was in his fifties, Martin guessed, and even in the darkness his facial features seemed vaguely familiar. He had an abnormally large forehead, a big bulbous nose, and was, Martin jested to himself, fairly fond of food, because it was clear he had a large protruding stomach, typical of someone who does clerical work. Martin knew that he had seen the man before, but he could not be sure as to where.

The man advanced into the room seemingly without a second thought about the noise he made. But then, why shouldn't he? He probably thought the police were content with us and that he would have no further interruptions in the task at hand. Martin waited and watched as the large intruder made his way over to a small globe in the far corner of the room. Martin seemed to recall it catching his eye one day during the preceding winter when I had lodged at Mrs. Bellmore's. He had been in awe of its peculiar depiction of the eastern continents and the lack of those he'd known so well. Mrs. Bellmore had told him the globe had been a gift to her from her son at the University of Oxford.

Now the globe had fallen to the mercy of Mrs. Bellmore's own killer.

Once he had it in hand, the man began to twist the northern hemisphere from the southern and when he had completed doing so, revealed that the globe was actually a hollow storage container. He removed some parchment from inside and held it up to the moonlight from the window.

Martin knew his chance had come and that if he were to seize this man, the time was upon him. From his inner coat pocket he withdrew two candles that shared a common wick at their tops, as is typical of candles made by dipping a single strand of string into two independent wax moulds (later cut to separate the wicks). Martin, I'll note, always carried some extra candles with him, just in case he thought he could persuade a passer–by to purchase one while he was out on his nightly lamp–lighting route. Now, however, the conjoined candles became his weapon and he silently spun one around until at last he flung it, like nunchaku sticks—a Japanese weapon consisting of two wooden sticks conjoined by a chain.

The candles whipped through the air with such force that they knocked the paper from the thief's hands, and gave Martin ample time to emerge from his hiding place screaming like a wild banshee. His tactic was to create as much noise as humanly possible so as to rouse the overzealous neighbour and thus the police.

The thief was taken completely off guard, and Martin then easily tossed him to the ground, where the two men struggled with each other. Martin continued to scream as they brawled. He was careful not to let the intruder see his soot–covered face. It is common knowledge that you never show you face to your opponents as they very often look there for a shred of uncertainty, a trait to be used to their advantage, if found.

It wasn't long before reinforcements arrived. The police erupted on the scene, broke down the door, and apprehended the suspect. The overall execution had been perfectly choreographed, since I had set the pieces into motion from more than one angle.

You see, shortly after midnight, Inspector Groesbeck returned to our cell to inform me that Mrs. Bellmore's clothing had been thoroughly inspected and indeed the telegram had been found in her pocket, exactly as I had said it would be. I begged him to oblige me one last time. I informed him of Martin's mission and asked that he send his men there to watch the house from a distance.

He was noticeably upset with me, but sent his men none–the–less. Once there, they found Martin's ladder where he had kicked it down. Rather than going inside, they sought cover not far away. While they did not believe someone else would show up, they plotted to jump Martin when he emerged from inside. Only what happened next took them all by surprise. Indeed, another man had descended upon the scene and used a glasscutter to remove a windowpane from the back of the house. He then slipped in, and they took the necessary positions. An officer was stationed at each of the home's four sides, so they would have the men when they came out—only it would be they who went in. Martin's cries signalled an assault from within, and the police stormed the house.

Once inside, they separated the two men, but the thief was able to knock a lantern from one of the officer's hands. It crashed to the floor, right on top of the sacred document, and within a short time the parchment was ablaze. Martin acted quickly and tried to stamp out the fire. When at last he was successful, only a small clump of dust remained.

Shortly thereafter, the true criminal was taken into custody, and Martin accompanied the officers back to our humble confinement quarters. It was Inspector Groesbeck himself who opened the doors to our cell just as the sun breached the horizon. An enthusiastic Martin Abbott stood beside him, glowing with bravado. He then recounted the tale, and I have repeated it verbatim to you. When all was said and done Kaleeb shook his head in astonishment.

"Now then," said Martin, as he escorted us to his home for some refreshments. "I believe you owe me an explanation as to your being in Eyam and what it has to do with me."

"Yes," I answered. "You've certainly earned the right to some truth."

We reached his home, which was also his workshop, and he unlocked the door and motioned for us to enter. Inside, the shop was filled with candles of all shapes, colours, and sizes lying every which way. Some rested on workbenches, others hung by their conjoined wicks from long hooks on the walls and even from a wire rack that was suspended above our heads.

"So go on then, out with it," he begged like a child in want of some sweets.

"As you wish," said I as I closed the door behind us. "My name is not Nigel Palmer."

"Come again?"

"My real name is Dr. Irel E. Vant, and I am an archaeologist, not an historian."

"Irrelevant? You expect me to believe your parents named you 'Irrelevant'?"

"What I do expect you to believe is that I am on a quest for a certain Chinese treasure, lost years ago by an ancient fleet of ships."

"You ought to think about writing a book some day. You're a marvellous storyteller."

"He speaks the truth," stated Kaleeb growing more annoyed.

"Even still, what's an ancient Chinese treasure got to do with a lonely country chandler from Eyam?"

"Ah," I exclaimed. "Therein lies our purpose here." I had made my way over to a small portrait, which had been hung on a wall on the opposite side of the small shop. "This treasure I have seen before with my own eyes, though I could not claim it, for written upon a plaque, which hangs above the chest, is an inscription that foretells of a curse onto he who opens the chest."

"A curse?" he asked.

"Yes, Martin, a curse." I had by then reached the portrait and began inspecting it as I continued. "For reasons which I will not go into at present, I believe that this curse is nothing more than a substantial dose of the dreaded Black Death or Black Plague that spread across Europe centuries ago and had originated in Asia back in the twelfth century."

"The plague that came to Eyam in 1665?" he enquired.

"The very same," I replied while removing the portrait from the wall. I presented it to him. "Who is this gentleman?"

Martin gazed at the image of an aging bearded man sketched onto a yellowed canvas.

"That's my great grandfather. It was drawn by his daughter, my great–aunt, when she was in her twenties."

"And therein lies the secret to our presence in Eyam."

"I'm afraid I still don't follow," he responded rather impatiently.

"When last I was in Eyam I checked the village records. Your lineage can be traced back well beyond the times of the plague on both sides of your family tree."

"So?"

"So in 1665, when the plague came to Eyam, the village rector, William Mompesson, convinced the village to quarantine itself in an effort to prevent the disease from spreading to other villages nearby. As a result, the majority of the village was wiped out, murdered by a disease that could not be cured. Those who contracted it grew large black boils on their skin, hence the name Black Death or Black Plague. Yet, even still, how can one account for your existence before me here today?"

"Someone in his family would've had to survive the plague!" exclaimed Kaleeb.

"Ah, but not someone, *some ones*. Two people! They would go on to bear children that we can follow down the line to Martin. Now, how is this explained?"

"Immunity," answered Martin. "You believe my ancestors were immune to the plague, and therefore did not contract it, but instead lived on well into their old age."

"An intelligent lad you are, Martin. That is precisely what I believe."

"And as a result, you think that Martin here would also be immune to it, and thereby is the only person capable of retrieving the lost Chinese treasure," Kaleeb announced, as the epiphany unfolded within him.

"Technically," I continued, "not the only one, just the only one who works out for us. You see, Martin's never been married, never fathered any children, and therefore has little of a future to gamble with. In the unlikely event that I am wrong—"

"I wouldn't be missed," said Martin plainly yet not dejectedly. Perhaps I had been too straightforward and not considered his feelings, but if that were true, he did not seem affected by my carelessness.

"I hate to be so blunt, but you've hit the nail, as it were, on the head. It is a dangerous task I ask you to undertake and can understand if you aren't willing. Yet if you succeed, one third of the treasure will be yours."

"A third?"

"Yes, and a third of an ancient treasure is worth far more than it was when it was first lost, as it is like a fine wine. It grows in value with age."

"We'd all be rich," Kaleeb whispered ,rather euphorically. It seemed to me that the idea was finally maturing in his little mind.

Martin was dazed. His thoughts must have been filled with ideas of riches, power, adventure—and confronting death head on, in an ultimate stare–down competition. A curious look of anxiousness had begun to come over him, and he trembled slightly as he fixed his gaze upon my face.

"Would … would you hand me that bottle of brandy behind you, Mr. Pal—, uh, Doctor?"

I turned around and took up the bottle. "Where do you keep your glasses?" I asked.

"Not necessary," said he, and he swiped the bottle from my hand, tore off the top, and guzzled down a mighty swig.

"You've been through a lot in the last few hours, Martin. We need not have an answer now. You take the day. Think things over. Tomorrow morning when all is—"

"I'll do it! I'll go with you."

"Please, there's no sense in rushing into this. I'd hate for you to regret your decision later."

"There's nothing for me in Eyam," he said as he gazed about the shop. "Nothing but a dying dream! Chandlery is a fading business. Gas is the way of the future. I suspect one day even the poorest of the poor will light their evenings by its clean–burning light. On top of that, I'm aging. There's no use hiding it anymore, and I've no wife to call my own. Granted, I've not yet reached forty, but my life is passing me by none–the–less. Maybe a good life–threatening adventure is just what I need to grab my fate by the horns!" With that he took another swig from the brandy bottle.

"Sea life can be hard on a man," I warned. "You should know we'll be spending the better part of a year traversing the open seas."

Martin removed the bottle from his lips and stared at me.

"Are you *trying* to talk me out of going with you?" he asked directly and seriously.

For a moment, I didn't know exactly what to say, and somewhere in that moment Kaleeb took over.

"What he's trying to do is prepare you for the unpreparable. You can't imagine what it's like, being out at sea for months at a time. Fifty–foot waves, torrential downpours, scurvy, hunger, sharks, whales, and God himself knows what else. No, sir, he's not trying to talk you out of it. He's trying to make sure that the man before him is a real man. Real men can handle the high seas. So what Dr. Vant's asking you, lad, is simple." He was now right up into Martin's face looking him eye to eye. "Are you a *real* man?"

Then it happened. As if to call Kaleeb's bluff, Martin took a step closer, so close that I was quite sure his hot brandied breath was curling Kaleeb's whiskers, though Kaleeb would never show it. "If I weren't," said Martin, "you'd be spending your second night on a prison cot right about now. So remember that the next time you question my manhood!"

The air grew quite tense, and I knew I must say something to balance the energy level in the room. "If you are to join us then there's no point in dragging out our stay. Why don't you pack your things while Kaleeb and I make arrangements for the ride to the train station. You can get some sleep on the train tonight. Depending on how things flow, we can be out to sea within a day."

And so it was to be. While Martin decided what to do with his shop, Kaleeb and I made arrangements with the village cabby to take us to the nearest train station. Later, after Martin's things were packed into the carriage and he'd gone back inside to close things up, Kaleeb joined me in the coach. He seemed consumed by thought.

"Something troubling you, Kaleeb?" I asked.

"I've just been thinking about everything that's happened to us since we arrived in Eyam. It's almost as if Mrs. Bellmore's murder was some kind of initiation test for Martin. So if he could handle sneaking into a murdered woman's house, confront her killer, and set innocent men free, he'd be ready for anything," he explained.

"Indeed," I agreed.

"As if some higher power was … was … Hang on then!" He stopped and searched my face. "You! You had it all planned out, didn't you? You were testing him!"

"Was I?"

"Only, murder? That's a bit extreme, even for you."

"Honestly, Captain Langston! At any rate, how do you know there even *was* a murder?"

"I was there. I saw it with my own eyes. I watched you take her pulse—"

I smiled faintly in my seat and glanced out the window to check on Martin's status.

"You're a mastermind, you are!" he chuckled. "But what about the man who was arrested?"

"You mean Mrs. Bellmore's son? He and I first met at the Crystal Palace at London's Great Exhibition, back in the fifties. I dare say he was no match for our Mr. Abbott. It makes me wonder what he burned that night. I'll have to remember to send him some extra funding for the university. Brilliant performance, really."

"Remind me never to get on your bad side."

"I'll keep that in mind," said I, more to myself than he.

Martin soon joined us, and we were off to the train station. That was a few short hours ago, and now I believe I can hear the distinct whistle of the train's engine signalling our arrival in Bournemouth. Therefore I bring this letter to a close. Until we meet again or by chance I should write, take care, William, and you too, Mrs. McGillian.

Yours truly,

Dr. Irel E. Vant

* * *

"For the first time, in a long time, the doctor's got me at a loss for words," stated Mrs. McGillian, as I lifted me head from the paper. We'd all been too intrigued to speak up until that point. Dr. Vant had us anxiously awaiting the outcome of such a fanciful tale, yet when it was over, and the truth revealed, we found ourselves in a state of wonder.

"But he wouldn't really have put that poor man through such an ordeal like that, would he?" Cara asked.

"He did say that he had it all planned out," I added.

"But the police surely would've known that Mrs. Bellmore wasn't really dead," Cara offered.

"He could've paid them off. Heck, that Inspector Groesbeck could have been nothing more than an elaborate ruse to keep Kaleeb in an honest state, so as to make it that much more realistic for that Abbott fellow. You know, now that I think about it, when he mentioned this Eyam man for the first time, he said the man would be practically begging them to bring him along," I recalled.

"True to his word, he was!" exclaimed Mrs. McGillian. "If there's one thing Dr. Vant is, it's patient."

And so we said no more upon the subject that day. It was as if we'd gone through some sort of life–altering event, though we hadn't even left the grounds. Mrs. McGillian and I invited Cara to stay for dinner; having read Dr. Vant's letter together kind of forged a fellowship between us, and we all had a lovely time while Victor pranced around the castle from one room to the next. Every now and then our minds would wander, and we'd find one another fixated, in a trance. Dr. Vant had proven to be a most ingenious man, with multiple layers of personality and levels of truth and—as we were reminded that day—even criminal tendencies. Nothing would come between him and his ultimate goal, though what that was we could not have foreseen.

VI
THE WOODEN WHALE

Herein you will find the log of the *Wooden Whale* and various other papers. After some cumulative consideration amongst meself and others who know the life of one Dr. Irel E. Vant so well, we have come to the conclusion that in certain instances—this being one—it's best to let history recount some of Dr. Vant's adventures. The log of the *Wooden Whale* was written in a first person narration by first mate, Morton Seadrick, and continued thereafter by Captain Kaleeb Langston himself. The dates begin chronologically on the sixteenth of April 1874, and the events were unbeknownst to anyone in England, until a year and a half later.

LOG OF THE WOODEN WHALE

16 April: I, Morton Seadrick, first mate, resume the Captain's duty of loggin' the *Whale's* daily undertakings. Today we's been at port in Bournemouth, England, whilst the Captain, his wife, and Elijah Reese took to shore with Dr. Vant and his little Irish lackey. Fog's cleared, but the view's still dismal. I's sent Thatch, Jones, and Thomas out for specific provisions under the command of John Stanton, whose leg is still recuperating after last night's adventures in Paris.

16 April, nightfall: Of the *Whale's* remaining crew of twenty–four hands—twenty–one mates, two cooks, and myself—half of them have gone into town for a night of drinking before the shove off to sea, leaving a skeleton crew of twelve. Not exactly sure when the Captain's due back, but we anticipate a day or two. In the meantime, I should probably have some fun now myself, 'cause the journey ahead promises to be a trying one. Can't leave the ship though, Captain's orders. Cold tonight. Wind's out of the south–east. A fire'd be good about now, that and some female companionship. I miss France.

17 April, morning: Fog returned in the night and is presently dissipating. Appears to be an ill wind in the air. I's a little uneasy, but all seems well. Nothing else to report.

17 April, afternoon: Terrible news. Elijah Reese returned with the Captain's wife, Isabelle Langston. She was deathly sick and lapsed into a coma sometime after their arrival. Reese claims she caught pneumonia on their way back to the *Whale*. Seems questionable to me, especially as her body's gone all rigid and stiff. Still though, Stanton agrees with Reese, and as he was a former lieutenant in the Royal Navy, I's not in a position to judge his word.

17 April, evening: Mrs. Langston's symptoms have only worsened, and the situation now looks grave. Fever's high. I should be surprised if she makes it to the morning.

18 April, early morning: It happened, as I feared. Mrs. Langston died around two in the morning. Woe to us who shall have to explain her untimely death to her devoted husband, our employer, and the Captain of this ship.

18 April, night: All hands have returned to the ship after word of Mrs. Langston's death spread. Still no sign of the Captain himself. Thatch dressed her in her favourite dress; how he knew it was her favourite is anyone's guess. Earlier this afternoon I sent Thomas to the coffin makers. He returned in the evening with a splendid piece indeed. Dark cherry in colour. Clear tonight, with a sky full of twinkling stars. The Lady of the Ship—that's what we used to call her—would have loved the sight. Suppose it's fitting.

19 April: The Captain and Dr. Vant returned to the *Whale* last night accompanied by a man from Eyam. Exhausted though he was, the Captain had been in a chipper mood. Things had gone as planned in Eyam. When he'd returned, I was summoned to give the news every man dreads giving. A glance at my face told him something was amiss, and he immediately questioned the mood of the ship. I explained as gently but as direct as I thought the situation needed. "I's afraid I have something terrible to tell you, Captain," said I. "While returning from Vant Manor the other night, the Lady of the Ship caught pneumonia, lapsed into a coma, and quietly passed away."

Darkness spread across the Captain's face draining the remaining cheer from it. He looked saddened, shocked, somewhat sick to his stomach, and even a bit angry.

"Lady of the Ship?" asked the Eyam man to Dr. Vant.

"Langston's wife," the doctor answered quietly. He crept up to the Captain and rested his hand on the Captain's shoulder, though the Captain pulled away. I swear I saw a tear fall from his eye, and then, without a word, he lurched past us and shut himself up inside his quarters where he remains.

Taking command, on his own accord, Dr. Vant ordered the ship be moved out to sea. "A ghastly ordeal this tragedy proves, and the heart of the ship has been plunged into despair. But time is man's natural enemy as it is ultimately the victor, and if we are to reach our destination at the exact necessary time and honour Mrs. Langston's memory, we must make the shove out to sea post–haste. We can hold the funeral services in the evening when the Captain has had time to come to terms with this disaster, and we can then cast her body into the ocean with a proper send–off."

19 April, nightfall: The service has only just ended, and the Lady of Ship is now the Lady of the Sea. We's set sail shortly after Vant's order and seem to be making good time. The service was short but suitable, and now the healing can begin. The Captain's meeting with Vant over business matters as I write. I think that he'd rather busy himself with work then face the truth that haunts him. Jones is taking Martin Abbott, the Eyam man, on a tour of the ship explaining emergency precautions. Stanton and Reese have been silent and stay close to one another as if to comfort each other.

Of all the men on the *Whale*, only three had been particularly close to the Lady of Ship aside from the Captain himself: John Stanton, Elijah Reese, and Stanley Thatcher. Thatch seems more depressed of late than anyone, even more than the Captain, as he cannot focus on his duties. He has been staring off into the sea all day, though his manner is not stand–offish. He has—as we all have—lost an important ally. As the only woman of this ship, Mrs. Langston had been our nurse and surrogate mother. What will we do without her?

ENTRIES OF CAPTAIN KALEEB LANGSTON

20 April, early morn: Early *mourn* is more like it. How am I to carry on with my wife resting at the bottom of the blue? Morton kept good notes in my absence and wrote in a very informative way, more than I'm sure he knows. I spent the last few hours toiling over our charts with Dr. Vant. He tried, or pretended to try, to console my present mood, but I'd speak nothing of it to him. How can I? He's a crafty lot that Vant is. Supposing I'd have a slip of tongue—what then? Then he'd be on my scent quick as a shark on blood. Truth be told, I know Vant's responsible for Isabelle's death. I just can't prove how. Not until I've thoroughly questioned Reese. In the meantime, I'll play the part of an emotionally deprived brute who drowns his sorrows in his work.

Vant is not to be trusted. Every little action, every side comment and heartfelt story is a carefully choreographed stunt to deceive or retrieve some bit of information that he's later capable of performing amazing tricks with. To think what the man would do if he knew that I'm on to his game, or that I intend to play along!

20 April, day: To protect this log I've been keeping it under lock and key in my own quarters. It's become a valuable tool that Dr. Vant could easily use against me. So it is now off limits to the rest of the crew, including Seadrick. That be said, I've just concluded a meeting with Reese and Stanton who've only just left me in my den. Shortly after noon, I heard the hearty knock of John Stanton on the door. "Come in," I says. The door opened and Reese followed Stanton into the room. As Stanton turned to shut the door, Reese stepped full into the light from the room's only window, which I might add has nothing more than the smooth edge of the ship on the other side of it. I'd constructed the *Whale* with every precaution taken, one of which was to keep my private conversations private.

"You wanted to see us?" asks Reese.

" 'S right I do. And you know about what, too. Don't ya?"

"It wasn't my fault, Captain, honest! Who would've ventured to guess that that crazy treasure tracker has his own pet snake! No, make that two! The vulture we saw was just the opening act!"

"Snakes?"

" 'S right Captain. And it was the snake what bit your wife and brought her to an untimely end!"

"I knew he was to blame! I felt it under my skin," says I. "But where the hell'd you find the things? Surely Vant's not mad enough to let 'em roam around free as that bird."

"You remember the North–East tower, what Vant was so bent on keeping William out of? Let's just say there was good reason for it!"

"So why in God's name did you go in there, then?"

"For the very reason that Vant wanted it kept a secret. If there was something he wanted hidden, we figured he'd keep it hidden from the public eye. What better way than forbidding anyone from entering the place?"

"What of the boy, William? Did he suspect anything amiss?"

"We had a run–in with him in the middle of it. That's how the situation turned on us."

"Maybe Vant's telling the truth," Stanton says butting in.

"What do you mean?" I asks.

"Maybe the only map *is* in his head!"

"Either way, he has us by the groin for now. But our chance will come. Make no mistake about that," says I. "And our friend Dr. Vant will get what's coming to him as well. Only Vant's utter destruction will avenge Isabelle's death. I'll ruin him."

Right then we heard some sort of shuffling that sounded as if it were coming from outside the window. Without a word I'd took up a hidden revolver from my desk and went over to it. I gazed out but saw nothing, nothing except the rabid waves of an oncoming storm crashing against the side of the ship.

I then turned back to Reese and Stanton. "Keep an eye on Vant, a close eye. Note everything he does, no matter how mundane, but especially the queer. Now get to it!"

"There's, uh, something else, Captain," adds Reese.

"Spit it out man!"

"While your wife and I were buying time in Leocadia, awaiting nightfall, she sent out a … um, a wire."

"A wire? To who?"

"Can't really say. It was coded. Was addressed to someone named 'S' and read something like 'Zudi by sea' and it was signed 'Niixia'. When I asked her about it, she just disregarded it."

"S?" I asks.

"'S right. Then us two split for a bit so as not to be seen together in case that O'Brien brat went out for an evening pint or what–have–you. Anyhow, I forgot all about the wire until I was carrying her back to the ship and discovered a note under her tights near the ankle. I kept it on myself and figured you'd need to read it in person to understand it," Reese says, as he removes a crumpled up piece of paper from his pocket and hands it to me.

"Niixia," I read aloud. "Countered. A, bearing. Pig reigns. S."

"What do you make of it, Captain?" asks Stanton.

"S, S. Who do we know whose name starts with S?"

They shrug.

"Eyes and ears, men. Eyes and ears!" I then motion for them to leave, they do, and I'm back where I began, more stupefied than ever.

21 April, nightfall: My patience with Dr. Vant grows thinner, and I wonder how long it will be before I snap. Since we've left England the *Whale's* made excellent time. We've been running on steam since the shove out to sea, and at two this afternoon we'd rounded Portugal and were headed en route to the Strait of Gibraltar. That's when Vant sought a word with me in private.

I was on the quarter deck going over the route with Seadrick, who was at the helm, when Dr. Vant approached.

"Splendid afternoon gentlemen," says he. "Wouldn't you say?"

"Bit refreshing after that storm last night, I'd say," says Seadrick.

"Oh I don't know," I add, "Something about a storm at sea that seems to set the mood. It's a reminder that out here you're at nature's mercy!"

"Perhaps one day nature will be at the mercy of man," says Dr. Vant. "Anyhow, I'd like to have a word alone with you, Captain, if I may."

"All right then. Run along Morton, I'll take the helm for a while."

I took the wheel as Morton Seadrick left us.

"What's on your mind?"

"I'll get straight to the point. I'm altering our course. The Mediterranean route is sure to be anticipated by our adversaries."

"Alternate route? Adversaries?"

"I speak of the vagabonds that pursued us in Paris. They no doubt followed us to England and are very likely trailing us from a distance even as we speak."

"But altering course! Where the hell would we go?"

"Around Africa."

"You're crazy! We ain't got provisions for a trip like that! And time!

Think of how long it'd take! You're barely keeping schedule now! The Suez Canal is our best bet."

"It wasn't pneumonia that killed your wife, Kaleeb."

"What? What are you talking about?"

"I saw the signs on her body. I've seen them before. She was poisoned."

"You think it was the same lot from Paris?"

"We must assume so. It's a game they're playing, a deadly game. Only I have the lead, as I am always a step ahead. That is why we round Africa. We'll keep close to the shoreline in case of emergency. If you need other provisions, I suggest you stop in Morocco."

"But—"

"Now, now, Kaleeb, no buts. I realize you are the Captain of this ship. That being said, you no doubt know the Atlantic better than most men, and will likely prove to know it better than our enemies. We'd be fools not to take that course."

"Hell, why not make it even longer then? We could take the Strait of Magellan!" I dug sarcastically.

"We don't have *that* much time."

"Then your mind is made up?"

"It is."

"And we'll still make it to China in time?"

"Trust me. Everything will work out as it should."

I didn't know what to say, or what to do. I knew there was no one following us. I knew because it was my men who had been following him in the first place in an effort to steal the map and keep the treasure for ourselves. But I'd no choice but to go along with his ridiculous request. It's either that or raise a suspicion, and I can't afford to have him on to me. Not yet.

Shortly after my meeting with Dr. Vant I broke the news to the crew. Most of them took it well. Others were angry on account that they hadn't planned at being out to sea so long. Vant was nearly doubling our time by taking us all the way around Africa instead of cutting through the Mediterranean and into the Red Sea. No telling what my men are thinking of me these days, watching Vant order me around. The whole thing makes me sick!

23 April, evening: Just left Tangier on Morocco's northern coast. The last few days have remained uneventful. The only thing that stands out in my mind is the queer way Thatch has been watching me of late. Maybe he's been watching me that way for some time and I've only just begun to notice, but something's there. His eyes seem to wince and his top lip turns upright a little. It could be mistaken for a spasm except that he only seems to get that way when he's watching me. Watching, but why? Going over the log I'm reminded of Morton's entry about Thatch picking out my wife's favourite dress for the funeral service. It struck me odd when I first read it. I even noted Morton may have put down more than he realized. There's a connection to be made here. A line needs to be cast to hook this mystery; only where should it be cast and with what bait?

EXCERPT FROM

STANLEY THATCHER'S JOURNAL

23 April 1874

My Dear Love,

How I've missed you so. It is the wicked work of Satan himself to take something from a man who's never fully tasted how sweet a thing he could have had. I'm writing to you on the advice of Dr. Irel E. Vant. Christ, I don't know how that man got to be as smart as he is, but he knew you and I were cheatin' on your husband. He told me he could see it in my eyes, in my depression, and how I looked upon the Captain with hatred. Well, why shouldn't I hate him? You had his name and he had your public devotion and praise. Even still, Dr. Vant says he knows what it is to lose the love of your life—turns out he's a widower himself.

He said the only thing that got him through his delirium was writing to his beloved in a journal similar to this. He told me it kept their connection alive and he thought we probably had a stronger connection than you did with your husband on account of how I was sulking and the Captain's plotting. If only Dr. Vant knew exactly what the Captain was plotting! It wasn't more than three or so days ago that I overheard the Captain talking with Reese and Stanton inside his den. I'd just finished mopping the quarter deck, which is directly above the Captain's den, as you'll recall, when I heard them enter.

So I lowered myself down the side of the ship and listened. I never trusted the Captain, not once, and anytime he met with Reese and/or Stanton that meant trouble of a fatal kind. 'Twas then that I learned of how you truly died, and that they planned to do Vant in just as soon as they get their bloody treasure!

Did you know that? I wonder what you would have done if you had known. Granted, I knew all about how you, Reese, and Stanton were trying to find another map to steal the treasure, but murdering a man? That's the work of the devil, and I am so close to warning Dr. Vant!

Oh, why can't things just be the way you and I dreamed them? Running away together back to where you trained in the Orient, to where the evils of Europe melt away and the inner peace of nature flourishes all around you. Where meditation is the medicine of life. There's a storm that's been brewing in my heart and I've no idea when it will strike or subside. Still, it's there, all the same. I'll write again when the urge comes, until then, good–bye my love.

Yours forever,

Stanley "Thatch" Thatcher

LOG OF THE WOODEN WHALE

CAPTAIN KALEEB LANGSTON'S ENTRIES, CONTINUED

26 April, midnight: I've spent the last two days piecing together what promises to be a web of deception. I, at this point, believe that this mysterious 'S' character Isabelle was wiring was none other than Stanley Thatcher, who was blackmailing my wife into an adulterous affair. The whole thing seems to have begun months ago, when I first starting communicating with Dr. Vant. Even in those early days we had planned to con Vant out of this hidden fortune.

A meeting had been set up one day with Isabelle, Reese, Stanton, and myself. They've been the only lot I've ever fully trusted. Stanton because he and I went back to our childhood. We grew up together and always looked out for each other. Reese because he was always like a younger brother to me—that, and he did marry my younger sister. Isabelle because she was my wife! Anyhow, this one day, after I'd got a letter from Dr. Vant finalizing the deal, we met as a group to smooth out the finer details of the scheme.

After it had all been figured out, and we had dispersed, I went back to the private room in the pub looking for some chewing tobacco I'd misplaced, only to find Thatch climbing out of an empty barrel in the corner. When I questioned him about it and about what he heard, he played drunk and claimed he didn't hear anything. Thinking back, it was after that incident that he seemed to always be eyeing my Isabelle. Every now and again he'd make an excuse to see her in private, and there was even a time when I caught him in my quarters with his pants down 'round his ankles. Of course, they both played it off, claiming he had some kind of haemorrhoids that he was having Isabelle check out, and as she was the ship's resident nurse, I let it go, without a second thought! Until now.

He had to have been blackmailing her about what he heard that day when we'd met. He's a sinister bastard, a wolf in sheep's clothing. Always just happened to be around when we'd be discussing our plans, sneaking around all weasel–like. Come to think of it, it was probably him that we heard on the twentieth, the noise outside the window. Morton did say Thatch had been mopping the quarterdeck that day. What a fool I've been! And he's no doubt been humoured by the whole of everything he's accomplished! What with Isabelle and all. But what could he have planned now? With Isabelle gone, he's got nothing to gain. Unless, Jesus, that's got to be it! He's fixin' to spill everything to Vant and swindle the rest of us out of it! I'll have to take care of him fast, but learn what he's told Vant first. There's a damp chill in the breeze tonight. If instinct serves me, there's a squall on its way. Better make the most of it.

27, April, morning: Much has taken place through the night. Best to get it all down in sequence. Shortly after midnight I'd taken to the main deck, as the wind had picked up considerably. The wind rocked the waves and sprayed a sea mist into the air with every tidal crash. The smell of the sea's salt was potent, and storm clouds rolled in, blanketing the starlit sky with gloom. The night crew was busy making the necessary preparations. Then a streak of lightning pierced the heavens in the distance, and I heard the roll of thunder just as my eyes settled on a congregation over near the forecastle.

It was Dr. Vant, Martin Abbott, and—dare I say it—Stanley Thatcher! My skin cringed as a mist of rain came blowing in. But it wasn't the rain that got to me; it was the sight before me. I then gave a few choice commands to some men, mostly to clear out any witnesses, and I approached the group.

"Storm's coming in fast; better get below decks!" I says to them.

"Now, that is sound advice," says Vant. "Come, let us do as the Captain orders." He then proceeded to escort the others past me.

"Not you, Thatch," I says, "I'm going to need a hand up here with me."

So Vant turns to Thatch and says, "We'll have to continue our conversation another time." Thatch only nodded in reply. After they'd gone down below decks, I motioned for Thatch to follow me to the back of the ship and up to the quarterdeck ,where Morton was fighting the choppy sea at the helm.

"Nasty weather, aye, Captain? Seems to have come out of nowhere," says Morton.

"That be so, and that's the worst kind!" I says. "But you've been up here since early afternoon! Why don't you go on down to the mess and fix yourself something to eat? I'll take the helm for a while."

"Are you sure, Captain?"

"Absolutely, I've been fighting the sea all my life. Besides, I've got Thatch here to keep me company in case I need help."

"Right then, have a good night. Send for me if need."

Within minutes I was finally alone with Thatch.

"So, is that all you need me for then?" he asks.

"Thatch, my friend, when's the last time you and I had a good ol' heart to heart?"

"I don't think we ever have, Captain."

"Then you're in luck, 'cause I'm feeling tonight's the night."

The rain was coming down harder now and I could sense Thatch's uneasiness. The tension between us was now thicker than the clouds and I was anxious to get underway.

"So what you want to talk about?" he asks.

"I've just been wondering why you've been acting so queer these last few days."

"Queer?"

"Giving me the evil eye every now and then and what–not."

"Have I?"

"Oh, I think you have, Thatch, I think you have. Or should I say, 'S'?"

"I'm afraid you're mistaken, Captain. I have no idea what you're talking about."

"You bloody well know full well what I'm talking about," says I, with the fury of the heavens bellowing right along with me. "I know all about you and Isabelle, so you'd best come clean while you can. I'd hate to see you die with a guilty conscience."

Fear struck hard in his pathetic face. He looked particularly weak then. His skin was pale and his eyes grew shifty.

"I don't believe you're in your right frame of mind, Captain. I think you're best left alone with your thoughts for a while," he says, whilst turning 'round. "We'll reconvene tomorrow after you've had a decent night's rest."

"Oh, no you don't, Thatch," I says, as I leave my post and snatch him by the shoulder. "I'm the Captain of this ship. You leave when I say you can leave!"

"Sir, the wheel."

"She can steer herself for a while, it'll do her some good. Come, let's walk." I then forced him to walk to the stern of the ship and pinned him into a corner. Behind him lay the ocean, roaring like mad with giant waves begging like hungry hounds for their dinner—and me in front of him, ready to feed the wild beasts.

"Now, where were we? That's right, Isabelle. I know all about your little scheme. The way you pushed yourself onto her. The way you blackmailed her about the Vant treasure scheme. And I even know what your next step is. Only," said I, as I drew my angered face closer to his so that he could feel my vile hot breath on his stark frozen face, "you're not going to get the opportunity to tell Vant anything."

"You're mad, Captain. Your wife's death ate away your sanity! I never forced myself onto her!"

"Liar!"

"I never forced myself onto her because … because she came to me, *willingly*!"

Well, that did it. I became completely enraged and belted the vermin across the face with a left hook. My knuckle clipped his lip with such a force that the friction tore a gash into it. When he regained some of his composure he spat at me, and though I tried to dodge the bloody saliva, it managed to glaze the side of my face and neck. He laughed, then says, "What makes you think Vant doesn't already know?"

"I'll skin you for such mutiny!" I lashed out again, but missed. He seized the opportunity, and counter–struck me in the stomach, then swung again, but I caught his fist in mid–air with my right hand.

"You can rest easy, you ugly ox, I never told Vant anything."

"And how do I know that?" I ask as I bent his arm back.

"Because I give you my word. And my word is just. Unlike yours! I admit that I knew your whole plot, that you now plan to kill him, and I even admit that I did have an affair with your wife. Which I continue to point out was mutual. But I haven't said a word of any of it to Vant. In fact, it was he who questioned me on my relationship with her. Seems I'm the only one who gives two shits enough to mourn for her!"

"Then allow me to thank you for that," says I. "Only don't expect me to return you the favour!" With that I bent his arm back quickly and as hard as I could until I heard his shoulder snap, then struck the poor bastard with such force that I sent him over the side of the ship to a watery grave below.

By then the ship was rocking so uncontrollably in the waves that I could barely stand. The waves and the rain made it difficult to manoeuvre, and I'd barely made it back to the wheel in time to find Morton and Dr. Vant coming up the stairs.

"Captain, you all right?" Morton asks, "The whole ship's tussling like a stomach churning with vomit!"

"I thank you for that lovely description, Seadrick, but I'm glad you came when you did. I've got some unfortunate news."

"Oh?" asks Vant.

"Whilst I was fighting for control of the ship the tussling, as you put it Morton, sent Thatch over the edge and into the sea. I tried calling man overboard, but there was no one around to hear me."

"Funny, I didn't hear anything," says Vant.

"Should we go back for him then, Captain?" asks Morton.

"No use now, we can't see anything. Anyway, I think he broke his arm on the way down; he'll have no chance out there. We've got to think of the rest of the crew now, and the mission to China. Thatch would want it that way."

"He most certainly would," Vant agrees. "And now that you've got Morton here to assist you we're surely in better hands. Indeed, Stanley Thatcher's death is a tragedy, but we must go on. I'll be in my quarters below deck should you need me."

I nodded in agreement, as Morton took the helm.

"Oh, and Kaleeb," says Vant turning around near the staircase. "You seem to have some blood on your face."

"Oh?" I ask, and wipe my cheek with my sleeve and stare at it.

Vant nodded and then left Morton and I for the remainder of the night.

30 April, evening: At four this afternoon I was fixin' myself a bowl of some sort of vegetable–beef sludge that ol' Blanford had cooked up. He's a terrible cook but Isabelle always ... Anyway, there I was at four when I felt an arm pulling me forcefully aside. It was John Stanton.

"We need to talk," he says. "Now."

So I followed him to my den, bowl in hand, anxious and confused about the urgency of his wanting to meet.

"Well?" I says.

"Not here, in your private quarters."

Now, I'm a man of iron nerve, but I admit that I was beginning to feel uneasy. When a man like John Stanton requests supreme privacy, you don't question his judgment. So I led the way into my chambers, still redolent of my late wife, and stood there beside the luxurious bed where we had many times made love.

"I'll get to the point," he whispers. "Vant's on the move, he's up to something. What, I cannot say, but I've been following his every move for days. I know his usual demeanour; I've made a mental note of every facial expression. I can practically predict his routine, but today he is jittery, aloof, and sits at the edge of the ship, staring off East, tracking the lay of the land in the distance. In the days that I've kept a watchful eye he has been calm, confident, and at the top of his game, but he is a changed man. Even now, as we speak, he confers secretly with Martin Abbott below decks.

"What do you make of it?" I asks.

"A kink in the wheel, a miscalculation—or worse."

"Worse than a miscalculation?"

"What if he's already failed?"

"I'll skin him live and feed his body to the meanest God–damned sea serpent I can find, I will!"

"I believe—"

Just then the door to my chambers burst open and there stood Dr. Vant, a sweat–soaked nervous wreck at the end of his rope.

"We have to talk," he blurts.

Behind him I could see Abbott's pale face peering up over Vant's shoulder.

"All right," I says. "Take it easy. What's all this about?"

"We need to increase our speed by five knots at the very least, now, and for the rest of the voyage."

"Five knots?" I chuckle, "We're already going as fast as the *Whale* can take us!"

"We're not going to make it in time. We'll be too late."

"And who's bright idea was it to go gallivantin' around a whole bloody continent? Huh? Yours, that's who! 'Go around Africa', you said! I told you it'd never work out! But you were so God–damned insistent on evading evil figments of your imagination that you've gone and cost us the very thing that drug us all the way out here in the first place!"

Then he said something neither Stanton nor I was prepared to hear.

"We're not going to China. We never were."

"Not going to China?" I question in disbelief.

"Do you mind telling us exactly where the hell we are going?" demands Stanton.

"The north Atlantic coast of South–West Africa, in the realm of the Namib desert. Portuguese sailors once called it 'The Gates of Hell'. The bushmen call it 'The Land God Made in Anger'."

"To hell with God," I says. "I'm the one in anger now! You lied to us! The whole damn time—from day one—you were lying to us!"

"One must be careful who he trusts with such delicate information."

"I'm the one ushering you through the sea! How do you expect me to make the necessary arrangements if *I* don't even know where I'm going?"

"*I've* known where we were going. I had it all planned accordingly. *You* lied about the speed of your vessel, Captain. *You* said she was one of the fastest ships in all of Europe, yet I've seen wild elephants run faster! We have deceived each other; we are equals once again. Only now we must find a way to achieve the impossible. We *must* reach the Gates of Hell by nightfall on the fourth of May or accept our defeat, for at the rising of the sun the secret lair wherein the treasure chest lies will be submerged below water for another nine years!"

"Nine years, huh?" I paused for a bit to think things over. "Say I can get you to this delightfully sounding place in time? If so, I keep sixty per cent, and you and the curse cracker split the remaining forty evenly.

"Twenty per cent?" whines Abbott. "For risking my life on what may or may not be true?"

"What good is it to be willing to risk your life if you never get the chance!" I add. "Be happy I'm being that generous."

"Fine," says Vant. "I accept your terms."

"Then I'll expect it in your own handwriting on my desk in five minutes. Now if you'll get out of my way—I've got a miracle to work."

Such a venture would be ludicrous. I wasn't even sure a ship could hold steady at twenty knots an hour. Had I known in the first place all those months ago, I never would have agreed to take him on this fanatical romp–around! He knew it too. He's no fool. He's played me well all this time, but now I hold all the cards. He belongs to me. Though I have to admit, as barmy as this whole thing sounds, there's a tinge of wonder in my eye. Suppose I do obtain the impossible. Go the distance never travelled in a time yet unimagined. With a treasure to boot! I'd go down in history, and Vant? Well, he'd go down, that's for sure.

The rest of the day I plotted and planned.

1 May, dawn: Didn't get much sleep last night. Too busy trying to figure out how to get to this damn desert coast in time. I've thought of every possible angle, including tossing useless provisions overboard, and no matter what I calculate, the *Whale* will not reach such a speed. That's when it hit me. It was about two in the morning when I finally thought of it. The *Whale* would never make the trip in time. There is only one shot left and, as dangerous as it is, we have no other choice. So I went out in search of Vant to pitch my idea to him.

* * *

"The *Sea Dragon*?" asks Vant, as he sat up on his cot wearing his nightshirt. He was completely alert and no doubt hadn't got any sleep either. On the cot above Vant, Martin Abbott gave a loud yawn as he woke.

"It's a watercraft that was specially designed to my needs. Think of it as a dinghy, or a self–propelled life–boat."

"Is it fast enough?" he asks.

"I've only used her three times, once on a flat surfaced lake, once on some marshland, and the other on a grassy moor. On the moor she made twenty–five miles an hour."

"You've used this *watercraft* on land?" Abbott asks.

"She's a rare breed, Abbott. She's propelled by a large fan that doesn't sit in the water, the only one of her kind. But I've never tested her on the open sea."

"Still," says Vant. "Correct me if I err, but twenty–five miles an hour is fairly close to twenty–two knots, in the sea, is it not?"

"Exactly!" I says. "And I'm not even positive that's her top speed!"

"And you have it on–board as we speak?"

“In the rear cargo hold.”

“You keep a life boat in the cargo hold?” asks Abbott.

“She’s experimental, I never really expected to use her out at sea, but where else would I store her?”

“Then,” says Vant, as he leapt from the bed, donned his dressing gown, and tied it firmly in the front. “Let’s see her.”

* * *

My lantern lit the way as we entered the cargo hold. It was the largest of the holds the *Whale* had to offer, and it was well stocked with provisions and sea essentials stacked neatly in rows. Towards the far end, directly below my private quarters, sat a huge pine–green tarp–covered mountain that I knew to be the *Sea Dragon*.

“You two get that end,” I order, pointing to a rope hanging near the left side of the tarp as I took the one on the right. “On three: one, two, three.” Together Abbott and Vant pulled on their rope and I on mine. The ropes were attached to pulleys in the ceiling, which lifted the tarp clean off the *Sea Dragon*, exposing her to the light of the lantern.

She’s an oddity, no doubt; twenty–five feet long and ten feet wide, her hull is steel, painted the same dark pine green as the tarp that covers her, and she has a raised bow. Now, on the port bow rests a guardrail, and in the rear sits the pinnacle of her power, a five–blade steel fan propeller mounted behind the seat of the driver, encased in a steel cage with rudders to steer with in the far back.

“I must say,” says Vant. “I have never seen anything quite like it.” He was staring at her in awe and began circling, inspecting every angle. “I assume it uses air to thrust it forward!”

“Right you are,” I says. “She doesn’t even really sit in the water. More like glides across the top. But like I said, she’s designed for smooth flat surfaces, I’ve no idea if she can handle the waves of an ocean.”

“How many men can it hold?”

"Probably around twelve or more, but if you want to top out her speed we'd better keep it to a minimum."

"That's fine, the fewer the better," he thought for a couple of moments. "Make the necessary arrangements. We'll depart tomorrow morning."

"Hang on then," interrupts Abbott. "How you gonna get it out of the cargo hold?"

"You leave that to me," I says, with a faint chuckle.

ENTRIES OF MORTON SEADRICK

1 May, noon: I, Morton Seadrick, first mate, once again resume the Captain's duty of loggin' the *Whale's* daily undertakings. According to the Captain, the first log has been completely filled, though I find that a little unlikely judging its size, but regardless I continue the log in a new book and begin with the Captain's departure.

Early this morning the Captain roused the crew and gave us our orders. He told us that he, Dr. Vant, Martin Abbott, John Stanton, and Elijah Reese would be journeying on ahead of us in the *Sea Dragon*. The rest of the crew will continue en route to the Gates of Hell where we will rendezvous with the *Sea Dragon* by the middle of next week.

Most of the crew had never seen the *Sea Dragon*. I was familiar with her only because it was my brother who crafted her for the Captain. He had wanted a fast–moving land and sea vessel that could be run on small amounts of steam. Took Winston—that's my brother—over three years to get the design just so before it could be constructed. The Captain had always been impressed with Winston's eye for detail; after all, it was he who designed the *Wooden Whale*!

So, at quarter past eleven, half of the men joined the Captain in the cargo hold, while the other half joined me on the poop deck high above the Captain's private quarters. You see, Winston had designed the rear of the *Whale* in such a way that a portion of it could open up like a drawbridge and rest on docks to load the cargo hold. Only now, as the chains lowered the heavy door, it came to a rest on the sea itself.

Five men then drug the *Sea Dragon* out onto the bridge, where its crew assembled.

"God speed you, Captain!" I called down from the high deck.

"You just take care of my ship, Morton," said the Captain. "I'll see you at the rendezvous point!" He then climbed up the short stepladder to the driver's seat, strapped on a pair of goggles, tied himself into the seat, and pulled a lever on his right. "Better hold on," he called out to his new crew."

Suddenly a gust of steam erupted from the dual smoke stacks at the sides of the propeller cage, and the Captain pulled another lever, this one being on his left. With that, the giant propeller came to life with such a force that it sent the men on the ramp with the *Sea Dragon* hurtling back inside the hold of the *Whale* while thrusting the *Sea Dragon* forward, off the ramp and into the waters of the Atlantic.

Though the propeller was extremely loud, I swear I could hear the Captain's hearty cackle as his crew held on for dear life while the *Sea Dragon* skipped over waves and disappeared into the distance.

After the Captain's departure, the cargo bridge was drawn and the *Whale's* crew settled down. We still have a long trek ahead of us, but not a quarter as dangerous as the Captain and the *Sea Dragon* have ahead of them.

VII
A WHISPER IN THE WOODS

Two and a half weeks had passed since Dr. Vant left on his quest. Within that time frame I had begun a new life. Cara Faulky and I had grown very close, and hardly a day would go by when I wouldn't meet up with her—either for tea, lunch, or a simple stroll around town. Leocadia was a humble village with happy–go–lucky people who spent their time socializing in church, pubs, and the local markets. They were the kind of people who lived in the moment and thought less about what tomorrow would bring. Even Mrs. McGillian, whom I'd also formed a tight–knit bond with, enjoyed playing dominoes with two lady friends she'd made while out shopping one day.

It was an easy life to get caught up in, and soon we'd all forgotten about the strange circumstances that had brought us together and the odd things that Vant Manor had produced when I'd first arrived. Victor too seemed to be a part of the family now. He had a distinct personality that we'd all grown rather fond of. He was always excellent company, and you couldn't help but feel a sense of security when he was around—as if he were our watchdog, always on guard duty.

On one particular night early in May, Victor seemed a little more on edge than usual. The four of us, Cara, Mrs. McGillian, meself, and Victor, had all assembled in the kitchen. Victor sat staring out into the hall, while the rest of us sat around the kitchen table and Mrs. McGillian began laying out the dominoes. The house had been clean for days now, and we took pleasure in having no major responsibilities hanging over our heads.

"What do you think's up with him?" I asked, referring to Victor.

Mrs. McGillian glanced over at him as she passed out the dominoes. "Maybe he's caught the scent of a rat or something," she offered.

"Do you think he misses Dr. Vant?" asked Cara.

"Doubtful," said I. "Vant told me he's been travelling this way for some time now. Victor's bound to be used to the isolation."

"Maybe he's wondering how long it'll be before *we* leave," suggested Mrs. McGillian.

"What, this bloke?" I asked as I got up and rubbed him on his head. He liked to be rubbed on the head, but tonight he seemed a little annoyed by it and sort of nudged me off. "Well, fine, rub your own head then!" He sputtered a quick snort to show me his frustration.

"He'll be all right," said Mrs. McGillian, "Now get back to this table so that I can explain the rules."

I did as she asked and when I got to the table she put two joining domino ends together that matched with five white dots on each. "Now the object of the game," she explained, "is to get rid of your dominoes, and in order to get rid of your dominoes you have to match them up to another's end of equal dots."

"Seems simple enough," said Cara.

"Aye, go on then," said I.

"Now in the version we'll play, you can all have your own lines to work off of, and we start those with a domino that has the highest double. That is, for example, a domino that has two sets of the same amount of dots on each side of the white line."

"Och, you've lost me," I exclaimed.

"Like two sixes," she clarified.

"Wait," said Cara, "I get it now. And then we build a line off a domino that has one end that matches the double domino in the middle?"

"That's it, exactly!"

"Fancy that," I commented. "I—"

'Twas then that I was interrupted by a low growling from Victor.

"What's he up to now?" I asked.

Victor was perfectly still and had his eyes fixed on the darkness in the foyer. Something had got a hold of his attention.

"Shhh," said Mrs. McGillian. "Something's not right, listen."

Dead silence spread throughout the air, and a chill crawled up the hairs on me spine. She was right; something was amiss, something that we had either neglected before or something that had simply not been there before.

"Maybe we should blow out the candles," whispered Mrs. McGillian.

"The hell we are!" I whispered back.

"Someone should go and see what it is," suggested Cara.

By someone I knew she meant me. It was me curse, being the man of the bunch. So I slowly backed me chair up and stood. Silently, I crept towards the hall entrance and stuck me head around first. As I did so, I came face to face in the darkness with a man; it scared the holy crap out of me! I hadn't any time to yell, for he was the first to speak.

"Where is Irel Vant?" he demanded.

I couldn't think, I didn't know how to act or what to say, but me only instinct was to protect the women, one of whom gave a small, startled gasp.

"I ... I ... I"

The man stared me in the eye as he came around and into the full light of the room. I'd never seen a man like him before. His skin was darkly tanned, and his hair was jet black, long and tied behind him. I thought at first that he must be from some exotic island, yet he wore a full black suit, complete with a waistcoat and a strange thin tie, the likes of which I'd never seen. He wasn't from England, that much was certain.

"Irel Vant," he repeated. "I must find Irel Vant!"

"Here now," stated Mrs. McGillian as she stood from her place at the table. "Just who do you think you are breakin' into someone's home in the middle of the night, making all kinds of demands?"

"I am Keftiuc, I come from America to find Irel Vant. Please, where can I find him?"

"America?" I asked.

"You're an American Indian, aren't you?" asked Mrs. McGillian.

"Yes, I am of Durwaihiccora. I have travelled very far to find Irel. To warn Irel."

"Warn Dr. Vant?" I repeated.

"Yes, Vant, doctor. He is in great danger. I must warn him before it is too late!"

"He isn't here," said Cara.

"Then where?" asked Keftiuc.

"He's gone on some crazy adventure," I answered. "Off to China in search of some kind of cursed treasure!"

"Then I am too late. He will not make it."

"What's all this about?" asked Mrs. McGillian. "What do you mean?"

"My people, the Durwaihiccora, sent me to warn Irel. He has been a long time friend to our people and to me."

"Well, Kef, I'm afraid he's been gone for some two and a half weeks now, and he's not due back for at least a year or so," I explained.

"I only had until tonight." He squatted down, staring at the floor in a moment of despair. "Now he will be lost forever."

"Don't you worry yourself," said I. "Ol' Dr. Vant's one crafty fellow. He always seems to get himself out of some real pickles. Isn't that right, Mrs. McGillian?"

"Right you are, William," she agreed. "Now, here, here, Mr. Keftyuck, don't go sittin' on the floor, take a seat here at the table with the rest of us."

"Aye, take mine," I offered.

"Thank you," he said as he took me seat beside Cara.

"Now, why don't you take a deep breath and explain to us why you're here and how you've come to know Dr. Vant," suggested Cara.

"Aye, 'cause you've said yourself, you're too late to get to him now," I said. The ladies shot me some ugly faces and I knew then that I shouldn't have said what I did, but the damage had already been done.

"You are right," spoke the stranger. "I am too late. But his memory can live on."

"Aye, that's it," said Mrs. McGillian. "His memory! Go on then. I'll get you a glass of lemonade whilst you tell the tale."

"And you can start by telling us how you got in here tonight," I said. "That's one tall fence out there, and I know we locked the gate."

"That was simple," he replied. "I climbed one of the trees, crawled over one of the longer branches, and dropped down on the inside of the fence. When I came up the trail from the gate I knew at once I was in the right place because I saw the totem that Abhvana—the Durwaihiccora Chieftess—had presented to Irel when he left us."

"And so the pieces of the puzzle slowly start to come together," I said.

"Like two ends in a game of dominoes," added Mrs. McGillian, as she set a glass full of lemonade down in front of the not–so–strange stranger.

"How did you ever manage to get into the castle?" asked Cara.

"The door was open."

The ladies turned their gazes on me. "The door was open?" asked Mrs. McGillian.

"Look at it this way," said I, "at least the gate was locked!"

"We'll talk later," Mrs. McGillian said to me. "But at the moment I believe Mr. Keft–yuck has the floor."

"Kef–te–uk," said he annunciating, "Keftiuc!"

"Keftiuc," we repeated.

"Correct," he said, with a satisfied smile.

"And I'm Mrs. McGillian, that's William and she's Cara."

"Now, you say your people are led by a woman?" asked Cara.

"Yes, but if you'll excuse me, when the Durwaihiccora tell stories it is customary to have a fire by which to tell them."

Mrs. McGillian got up, took one of the lit candles off a near–by countertop and set it down in the middle of the table. "Will this do?" she asked.

"It will, thank you," said Keftiuc.

"Now you were saying," I prompted.

* * *

The Durwaihiccora have lived in the north–eastern United States long before there were any states to unite. Our people had been there for nearly five hundred generations. We are a very proud and passionate people. We survive by hunting, farming, and fishing. In these skills we are unsurpassed. But it was because of these skills that we were one of the first targets of the white man. He saw us as a threat and murdered many of our people when first he came to our shores. There are less than two hundred of us now, and we are shrinking, as the elders are passing on.

Our pride had also been our stubbornness. We had refused to interact with the white man for nearly four generations. We would probably have been destroyed by now if it were not for Irel Vant. He first came to us many seasons ago during our harvest time.

Gadeiro, a great warrior and even greater hunter, was in the woods one day training, or trying to train, his younger brother, Laigasa, how to hunt deer. Laigasa was a thin, weak boy, who had always wanted to be a farmer because he did not like to see the animals suffer. This is why he was seen as weak. He could never be a farmer—not ever—because his family had always been the hunters, just as others had always been in farming or fishing. This kept the balance in the Durwaihiccora, and each of us became experts in these skills. But Gadeiro often wondered whether Laigasa would ever bring honour to their family.

So on this one day they heard a small noise. As a hunter, Gadeiro recognized the sound as the snapping of fallen branches. His instincts told him a deer was approaching, possibly two, and Laigasa would finally have the chance to redeem himself. He told Laigasa to crouch low in the leaves and aim his bow. Laigasa did as he was told. He was good at paying attention. Then Gadeiro stooped down next to Laigasa, and they waited. Laigasa could not see anything, and he shared this with Gadeiro. His elder told him that he would need to listen, and to smell the air. He told him that seeing was not as important as knowing, and you know when you focus on your surroundings.

So Laigasa began to focus. He could hear the wind blowing the leaves free from the limbs of trees, the crickets singing to each other in the autumn air, the trickle of a brook in the distance, and then at last he heard what his brother had been talking about. There was the sound of a footstep—a *whisper in the woods*, as the hunters call it. Laigasa raised his bow, as did Gadeiro. Laigasa thought that if they both released their arrows at the same time, then he would not know whose arrow had hit the poor creature and could then sleep in comfort that night. They heard the footstep again, and Gadeiro nodded to Laigasa. They pulled back on their bows together, and at the sound of the next footstep an arrow went slicing through the air, and they heard their prey fall to the ground.

Laigasa, relieved that it was now over, looked to his brother, who had not released his arrow. Gadeiro smiled. He knew what Laigasa had been thinking, and he also knew that part of hunting was coming to terms with the cycle of life. Laigasa had been the one to slay the deer and so too redeemed himself as a member of their family.

Still, Laigasa's task had not been completed. He needed to ease the deer's pain during death and then bring it back to their village. So Gadeiro motioned for Laigasa to follow him and when they came upon the creature they had downed they fell back in horror. There, with an arrow lodged in his chest, lay the body of a white man.

* * *

"Dr. Vant?" I interrupted.

"It was," confirmed Keftiuc.

* * *

And they saw that he was still breathing. Unsure of what to do they argued until Laigasa won. They would bring the man back to their village and let the Cheiftess decide the white man's fate.

When they returned to the village, Abhvana, the Chieftess, was very angry. She did not like to be put in such situations. She, as did the rest of the Durwaihiccora, hated the white man. The white man had killed many of our people, and part of her felt they should have left him to die where he was. Yet another part of her saw something good coming from this. Maybe if the other white men saw that the Durwaihiccora was a peaceful tribe they could find a way to co–exist. So she arranged to have Sekhettepi, the village shaman, restore the man's health.

Abhvana was a very beautiful woman; she had the Durwaihiccora black hair but cut short; she was very fit, and had powerful, thought–provoking eyes that could easily bring down a snake in a contest of stares. Still, for all her good looks and curved features, she was not considered one of the most desirable women of our people. She was too strong–willed for most of the men. Most of the men wanted their mates to clean and gut their prey, or tan the hides and keep general household order. But the order that Abhvana kept was over all the people. She was the supreme power of the Durwaihiccora, which was why many other tribes would have nothing to do with us. You see, though there are tribes in which the chief is chosen by women, such as the Iroquois, and those that trace their ancestry through their mothers, very few are led by women. But it was tradition that a female had always led the Durwaihiccora, and that fact could never be challenged.

Likewise was the fact that the village shaman was always a male, and Sekhettepi was considered as great as all those who had come before him.

* * *

"Sek–ah–tepy?" I interrupted again. "If you don't mind me askin', where do your people come up with your names?"

"Sekhettepi is a very old name in our history. It best translates into 'Son of the Wild Cat'. No! Not a wild cat exactly. A … a lynx! Yes, 'Son of the Lynx'. That is as much as I can say. How do you explain your name, William?"

"Oh, that's easy, it's um, er … well, I know it means something."

"May I continue?" asked Keftiuc.

"Go on," said Mrs. McGillian, giving me the evil eye. "Pay no more attention to Master William."

* * *

When Irel's body was brought into the small longhouse of Sekhettepi, it was lain upon a very special patch–work quilt. The quilt carried the Durwaihiccora sacred symbol: a tree with its branches connecting to its roots so as to symbolize the cycles of life.

* * *

"The tree of life?" I interrupted once again. "Like the one Vant's got in stained glass high over the front door?"

"I did not observe," said Keftiuc, turning his head.

"You can observe later," said Mrs. McGillian. "For now, continue with your story. And you, William, if you've got something to say, keep it 'til he's finished!"

"Fine. Me lips are sealed."

* * *

By this time Irel's body had stopped breathing, and Sekhettepi knew that he must work fast. Many of us, myself included, gathered around to watch. Some of us had never seen a white man before, and it was always astonishing to see a shaman at work. He tore the clothing off Irel's torso, removed the arrow from Irel's chest, and in a wooden bowl he lit some crushed qas'ily—a type of sage—and took in the fumes. He then smudged some of the smouldering qas'ily onto Irel's forehead and laid a solution–soaked cloth onto Irel's wound. He took up his wooden staff, which had been carved from the branch of a very special tree. He then began to chant as the smoke from the qas'ily filled the air. A small fire in the central pit was the only light in the small longhouse, its smoke seeping out several small ventilation holes in the roof. Only now, it slowly began to die down to its embers, leaving but a soft glow.

Sekhettepi went to the fire and took up some of the ash. He blew the ash onto Irel's chest and then said a prayer to heal Irel's wounds. He pled with our deceased ancestors to help him in his task, for Irel was chosen as the man to bring peace between the Durwaihiccora and the white man. After he spoke we were all silent. Lastly, he took up a bucket of water, said some final words, which I did not understand, and flung the water onto Irel's body.

Irel sprang up to a sitting position in shock, as one who has been sleeping might when a bucket of water wakes him. He coughed, and his chest heaved for air. When he shifted himself again, the solution soaked–cloth fell from his naked chest. The cloth was now crusted with dried blood, and Irel's wound had been completely healed, except for the scarring of the skin during the healing process. At this sight we all gasped, for we were in awe at Sekhettepi's great powers.

Irel looked around at Sekhettepi and the rest of us. He did not try to speak. Sekhettepi stared Irel in the eye, but he too did not speak. Irel looked down at his wound then back up at Sekhettepi and he knew what our people had done for him. By now Abhvana had entered the longhouse and said something to Sekhettepi privately into his ear. He lay out his palm to present Irel to Abhvana. She gazed into Irel's face, saw that it was trustworthy, and patted her chest.

"Abhvana," she said.

Irel understood immediately, patted his chest gently, and said, "Irel Vant." He looked around at all of us again and asked, "Durwaihiccora?"

"Yipchie," acknowledged Abhvana. "Durwaihiccora."

Everyone was now quietly chatting to each other. How did this man know who we were? The Durwaihiccora were not sociable outside the tribe. Most white men did not even know we existed. Even other Indians thought we belonged to one tribe or another. But here was a man who knew exactly who we were. This only confirmed to us that he must, in fact, have been sent by our ancestors and thus would be the one to bring peace to our worlds.

Abhvana stooped down to Irel, brought her hand to her mouth, grasping an imaginary apple. She took a large bite from the air and offered a bite to Irel. He looked at the space in between her fingers and said, "Yipchie."

Abhvana smiled and forced her arms around Irel's chest and lifted him up from beneath his underarms. When he was at last standing, Abhvana motioned for him to follow her out of the longhouse. We all stood aside so as to let them exit easily. But before Irel followed her he stopped. She turned back from the entrance as Irel stood before Sekhettepi. He then bowed to Sekhettepi to show his thanks. We were all taken aback by his act of gratitude, and Sekhettepi nodded, his mouth forming a small smile.

That night Irel joined us for dinner around a large fire. Dinner was salmon with slices of apple, carrots, and potatoes all tossed together in wooden bowls. We ate from the bowls with our hands and Irel seemed to be observing everything very closely.

Abhvana then addressed us. She confirmed that she believed Irel would be able to unite our worlds and expressed her concern with the language barrier. Someone had to learn Irel's language and teach him ours. She asked the elders for recommendations.

Someone suggested Laigasa, since he wasn't any good at anything. But Gadeiro pointed out Laigasa's potential and how it was Laigasa who caught the white man. So it would not be Laigasa. But if not Laigasa, who? The hunters were too busy hunting all the time, the farmers and fisherman with their trades. The women were too busy. Yet there had to be someone.

You see, in the Durwaihiccora, your trade follows that of your mother's people. If your mother's family were hunters, you would be a hunter if you were male or the cleaner of the kill if you were female. There was only one lineage that was slightly different. This was the chieftess' family. The daughter of the chieftess would be the next chieftess, but if the chieftess had a son he would become the shaman. This means, of course, that Sekhettepi was Abhvana's uncle. But on rare occasions, when the chieftess had more than one son or daughter, that child would become the chieftess' advisor.

This particular generation was unique in that Abhvana had two brothers and one sister. So the eldest brother became the apprentice to Sekhettepi, who is not allowed to sire children, and Abhvana's sister became her advisor, also fated to never bear children. This left the youngest of her siblings, who had taken on the honorary position of head storyteller. It was he, they decided, who would learn the ways of English and teach Irel their ways, because who better than one who was not needed but who specialized in communication? I am that man.

* * *

"You do tell a wickedly good story," I said happily.

"Thank you, William."

"You can call me Billy, if you prefer."

"Thank you, I prefer not," he said, with a sense of seriousness and then continued his tale.

* * *

That night, Irel was given a bed of branches covered in furs in the longhouse of a travelling fisherman who was away at the time. Sometimes our fishermen must travel great distances to follow the migrating fish. In the morning, when the first light appeared over the horizon, my sister Abhvana took me to see Irel. We were surprised to see that he was not only awake but already finishing the remains of his breakfast, while he jotted down some notes in a small book with a pencil. He had been eating a biscuit of some kind that had been kept in one of his pockets along with the book.

He smiled warmly to us as we entered and offered us some of the biscuit, though we both declined. Abhvana introduced me by pointing to my chest and saying, "Keftiuc." She then wasted little time and, as the American white men say, got down to business. She pointed to Irel, shaped her hand to look like a mouth, placed her hand near her mouth and then opened and closed her mouth while doing the same with her hand. After that she pointed to me. Irel understood right away; he is very intelligent.

"You," he said pointing to Abhvana.

"Abhvana," she said.

"You, Abhvana, want me, Irel," he pointed to himself, "To teach Keftiuc," he pointed to me, English?" He then mimicked her hand gesture, as if it were a mouth speaking.

"Yipchie," she confirmed.

"And Keftiuc teach Irel Durwaihiccora?" he asked.

Abhvana thought for a moment then said, "Yipchie," again. She then patted me on the back and left the two of us alone in the longhouse.

Irel began right away and started picking up objects. The first was the fur blanket. He walked over to it and picked it up off the ground. "Fur," he said, as he brushed the fur with his hand. He then wrapped it around himself and said, "Blanket."

"Fur," I repeated as I brushed the fur while he handed it to me. "Blanket", I said as I wrapped it around my shoulders. He then pointed to my mouth and said, "Durwaihiccora?"

It was then understood that for every word he taught me in English, I would teach him the same word in our language. We continued this way for many days. I showed him around the village and he mastered our terminology very well. I took him to the woods and the fields and even the lakes. The more time I spent with him, the more he became my mentor. I wanted to learn everything there was to learn about the white man. He had become a better friend to me than anyone else had ever been. Most people would just come to me to hear stories, but Irel listened to my opinions and my dreams.

One day, after we each had a fair understanding of each other's language, I sat down with Irel and Abhvana. I was to be her translator. Although Irel had learned our language fairly decently, he wanted to be sure that nothing was lost in translation. We had met at the top of a great mountain overlooking the valley where the signs of winter melted away in the spring sun.

She immediately began to speak, and I rushed to translate as best as I could.

"You with us long time," I translated, "Long enough to know why we let you stay."

"I *have* wondered about that," answered Irel and I rephrased it for Abhvana.

"White man not friendly; you are friendly. Many generations fought with white man. Fighting must stop. We want you to bring peace. Peace between Durwaihiccora and white man."

Irel raised an eyebrow; I knew this to mean that he was thinking deeply. After a few moments of silence he spoke.

"Peace does not come easy. The white man may not listen to me. I am from far away and am not well liked by white men here."

"But we need peace," I said, speaking her words. "Only you can help us."

"The American white man is stubborn. He believes he is entitled to this land and that you are like wild buffalo in his way. He is not friendly because he fears you, and he fears you because he does not understand you. To make the American white man understand you, you cannot work through me. The fight must be your own. But do not be upset. I will give you the necessary tools to help you. I will teach Keftiuc more than my language. I will teach him everything I know about the white man. Communication is the first and most difficult barrier to break. You need one of your own to speak on your behalf and teach the white man your ways and what concerns you. You must then pass this gift of knowledge on to the rest of your people. If you are to truly gain peace you must accept that the white man will not learn your ways easily. So you must learn his and work for a compromise."

"She agree," I said. "She believe you very wise, but does not understand why American white man not like your tribe."

Irel then surprised Abhvana by speaking directly to her in Durwaihiccora.

"It is a very long story that I will tell you and the rest of your people one day. History is very important."

"What do you want from us in return for such a gift?" she asked him, intuitively.

"As I was saying, history is very important. I am very interested in your people, particularly your shaman ways. I believe those teachings were handed down to you from a very old, very intelligent people who were lost long ago. I ask only to learn these ways. As you can see, I am a fast learner and have already grasped most of your language. Let Sekhettepi be my teacher as I am to teach Keftiuc."

She suddenly became very uneasy. The shaman ways were very sacred, and only a shaman could know of them. She was hesitant but then spoke, "I will meet with the elders and all will discuss. A decision this important must not be made fast."

"I understand and will await the word of your council," said Irel.

So that night, as the half moon rose in the sky, the Durwaihiccora council of the elders met around a large fire in the great community longhouse, where most of us call home. I was asked to attend, but Irel had to wait in his quarters. There was talk among the elders over what was to be discussed. They knew it had to do with the white man but did not know to what extent. There were perhaps forty of us in the great longhouse: Abhvana, Wyvonx—our sister and thus her advisor—

Sekhettepi, Sekhettepi's apprentice Asuras, myself, fifteen elders and twenty or so prospective elders. Abhvana was listening to Wyvonx as she whispered into her ear. Abhvana nodded then turned to address us.

"Irel, the white man," she began, "has agreed to help us in our quest for peace—" Cheering cut off her words, though she pressed on louder. "But in return he asks that Sekhettepi teach him the ways of the shaman." The cheering ceased immediately. All was instantly quiet.

"The ways of the shaman are sacred," declared Asuras. "I do not trust this white man."

"Did he say why he wished to learn these ways?" asked one of the elders.

"He believes we are descended from an ancient people who were lost long ago. It is my belief that he wishes these people be remembered. Learning our shaman ways may help him to do that."

"He is evil," interrupted Asuras. "These are all lies. The Durwaihiccora have always been Durwaihiccora. None other came before us."

"The peace fight," asked another, "He said he would fight for us?"

"He said he would give us the tools to fight for ourselves."

"Ha," said Asuras, "He is making a fool out of us. He is tricking us. Maybe he is really Aingidha, the trickster wolf–god, come in the form of a white man to test us!"

"Asuras, calm yourself," said Sekhettepi in a very quiet yet commanding tone. "What kind of tools will he give to us?"

"He has offered to teach Keftiuc the ways of the white man in full: how they function, what their rules are, and how to sway their thinking."

"Lies I tell you," shouted Asuras, "All lies!"

"If it is the will of the elders, and you, my chieftess, I will teach this man my ways," said Sekhettepi.

"You cannot!" declared Asuras.

"We must think of the greater good, Asuras. That remains to be something you have not yet mastered."

"But I have trained in your ways since childhood. To teach this white man those ways would take far too long."

"He is a fast learner," I said. "And I believe he is sincere."

"This is true," said Abhvana, "He has already learned our language just as Keftiuc has learned his."

"We should take a vote," offered Wyvonx.

"Yes," said Abhvana. "Raise your hand if you agree to Irel's terms."

After some hesitation the vote swayed in Irel's favour twelve to eight; prospects do not vote. After the meeting I hurried along to tell Irel of the verdict. He seemed very happy. I was happy too. I would do anything for my people and now I would have the chance to save them all.

And so the seasons came and went. During the day I learned from Irel and during the night Irel learned from Sekhettepi. They quickly formed a bond, which was much to Asuras' dismay. With each passing day, Asuras grew more and more jealous of Irel. Feats that had taken Asuras many moons to comprehend were mastered by Irel in under a week. Sekhettepi tried to console his apprentice by telling him that since he had learned much of this as a child, he had been trying to grow as well, and that forces of nature had been fighting for his attention at the time. But Asuras' anger was not eased. And so he began to think of ways to make the white man leave.

There was one thing, above all else, that Asuras knew Irel would ask to see once he learned of its existence. Only the shamans knew of it, and Asuras aimed to keep it that way. On the far edge of our territory raged the waters of a powerful series of waterfalls. Hidden beneath the falls, in the foaming basin far below, lay a secret underwater cavern. To get there you needed to swim far down into the water and then into the cavern, where a pocket of air was the only source of oxygen. Inside the cavern rested great texts with gold bindings and a large chest painted purple with gold trimming. There was a scripture written upon the chest that could not be read. In fact, none of the volumes of text could be read because as they lay unseen they became forgotten and with them the knowledge of their meaning.

So it was that on one cloudy night Asuras set out on his quest to keep this knowledge hidden carrying only a satchel of shaman tools. He climbed down the steep edge of the falls, and dove down deep into the basin. As he swam, he kept course by feeling the edge of the rocky walls. He could no longer hold his breath by the time he reached the cavern, so he took a few moments to draw in the fresh oxygen. He was exhausted, but he felt compelled to go on.

Working in the darkness, he produced a flint quartz from his satchel. He felt around near one wall and found a clay bowl filled with powder and a steel knife beside it. Not far from the knife he also found a small bundle of dried leaves and sticks resting in the centre of a stone circle. Carefully he used the knife to sprinkle a little powder unto the leaves. Next he bent down low and struck the flint quartz against the steel knife, which produced a spark. The spark feel down upon the leaves and light burst forth as the powder created a small explosion, just enough to kindle the leaves and sticks into a small fire.

With the cavern now illuminated, he walked past the sacred books and came to the purple–and gold–trimmed chest. Although it was locked, he used a small tomahawk from his satchel to brake the latch. He then remembered the words of his master. He was never to open the chest, as its power was far too great for any man to possess. Recalling that, Asuras made a decision. He would destroy the contents of the chest and therefore never have to worry about it falling into any wrong hands, especially those of the white man.

Asuras opened the chest and was momentarily blinded by a radiating purple light from within it. Once his eyes adjusted, he found that the chest contained a crystal submerged in water. He reached in and removed the crystal. Its power seemed to course through his veins like liquid lightening, but he was not tempted by it. Instead, he sensed the potential for evil and, with all of his might, smashed the crystal against the side of the cavern wall. An explosion of energy and light erupted from the crystal as it fragmented, thrusting him back through the cavern's entrance and knocking him unconscious. Rock and debris rained down, sealing off the cavern for all time.

The texts were now lost, and Asuras' body floated up to the surface of the basin where it was discovered by a man from another Indian tribe, the Onguiaahra. Asuras' body was recognized at once as being Durwaihiccora and, since the Onguiaahra held great respect for the dead, was taken back to the Durwaihiccora village.

Chaos broke out in the village immediately. Sekhettepi and Abhvana were summoned at once and were taken to Asuras' body. Sekhettepi placed a hand on Asuras' chest. "There is no time to lose," he said, "He has not yet crossed over."

Together they brought his body into Sekhettepi's longhouse, where Irel was reciting some prayers.

"What happened?" asked Irel.

"Asuras was found drowned, but his soul remains in his body," explained Sekhettepi. "We must hurry to revive him before it is too late. I have taught you these ways, Irel Vant. This must be your ritual to perform."

"Mine? Me? But I cannot. I mean, I don't know *if* I can."

"Now is the time to find out. Our ancestors have presented you with a test. You must accept the challenge."

Irel thought silently for a moment. I understand. Please, place him before me."

Abhvana and Sekhettepi lay Asuras' body flat on his back atop the sacred symbolic quilt before Irel as I entered the longhouse. Irel knelt beside the body and pumped on Asuras' stomach, expelling much of the water from his chest. He then lit a bowl of crushed qas'ily and inhaled its fumes. After this he smudged some of the qas'ily onto Asruas' head using his right thumb and then placed a solution–soaked cloth onto his chest. By this time the body had already been turning blue, and it seemed as though Irel would be too late. But Irel was not intimidated.

He took up a staff, which had been carved specially for him in the shape of a deer—due to his run in with Laigasa—and he began to chant. The smoke from the qas'ily burned on as he scooped up a handful of cinders from a low kindling fire. He prayed in our tongue to our ancestors and begged them to return Asuras to us as he was next in line for the shamanhood and Sekhettepi was too old to go on forever. He then blew the ashes onto Asuras' chest. Sekhettepi handed Irel a bucket of water, and Irel said a final prayer. He then flung the water onto Asuras, who immediately sat upright.

He coughed and spat up more water. His body convulsed and heaved as he gulped in the air around him, and slowly the colour returned to his skin. By smelling the qas'ily he knew what had transpired though he was stunned to see who had revived him. He then saw the potential for a great many things within Irel. He knew that he had made a terrible mistake and had been wrong to judge this white man. At once, he confessed his deeds to us and begged for forgiveness.

Sekhettepi was very saddened. He knew that the hidden chamber held a great purpose. That was why the shamans were destined to be its guardians. Although he was sad and angry and disappointed, Sekhettepi openly forgave Asuras. His main concerns were that the crystal would now never fall into the wrong hands and that Asuras had learned a valuable lesson from his ordeal. Our people had never learned the true significance of the crystal or the sacred texts and, while they never would, Irel was very interested in learning as much about them as he could.

Soon it was autumn again, and Irel explained that I had now acquired all the skills he could teach me about the American white man. Yet my learning was not finished. Irel enrolled me into an American university, where I continued my education. I spent six years there taking classes year–round on every subject you can think of, and Irel Vant funded it all.

On Irel's last day in our village, Abhvana presented him with the totem pole, and it warms my soul to see that it proudly stands on his grounds today.

* * *

"And whatever became of your people?" I asked Keftiuc.

"After I obtained my last degree in political studies, I sought an audience with the government, first the local, then the state, and finally of the United States. A treaty was later forged, and my people won the plot of land on which our village rests. So you see, Irel really did keep his word."

"That must have been a very long time ago," said Cara. "Why look for him now?"

"It is, as I've said, I … I beg your pardon, I did not say, did I?"

"All you said was that you had only until today," reminded Mrs. McGillian.

"You're absolutely right. The reason I'm here is because of a dream Asuras dreamt about Irel. Ever since his rebirth, Asuras has been able to see many things in his dreams. One of those things was a dream in which Irel was drowning with his arms and legs bound by ropes or shackles. Asuras was confident the dream was a premonition that would manifest on the fourth night of May this year."

"Maybe this Asuras bloke is just having nightmares about his own experience," I suggested.

"But Dr. Vant is out at sea," stated Mrs. McGillian.

"And you are certain there is no way to warn him?" Keftiuc asked again.

"Not if tonight's the night," replied Mrs. McGillian.

"Then we must pray to my ancestors," ordered Keftiuc.

"But I'm Catholic," I informed.

"Then pray to whomever you pray to. The important thing is that our prayers reach him before it is too late."

So there we sat, meself and the two ladies with our heads bowed and hands folded, and Keftiuc seated on the floor with his legs crossed and arms extended. In retrospect, I suppose the whole situation seems kind of odd—the three of us praying with an American Indian we'd met just a little over an hour ago after he broke in to our home. But when it came to matters of Dr. Irel E. Vant, odd was the norm.

VIII
THE TREASURE

With the approval—or rather the persuasion—of one Mr. William O'Brien, I, Martin Abbott, would like to recount what would otherwise be considered a missing link in the epic story of the man I first knew as Nigel Palmer, namely Dr. Irel E. Vant. So much had happened so fast. It was like I was living in a fantasy world. The day I closed up my candling shop and joined Dr. Vant and his seedy shipmate, Kaleeb Langston, my entire life changed. I think I knew it too. Dr. Vant, as I'm sure you've learned by now, has a way of altering the lives of almost everyone he encounters.

Things were queer right from the start. The first night when we'd arrived at the ship there was Langston's wife dead. The very same night we set out to sea. Then there was a bizarre, yet oddly fitting, funeral for the woman as her body was cast into the ocean. As we pressed on I stayed close to Dr. Vant. I personally saw very little of the blond–bearded beastly Captain, but I'm not complaining. From the first day I saw him, sitting there with Dr. Vant in that Eyam prison cell, there was something about him I didn't trust. It was written in his face, and I never forgot it.

Anyhow, life at sea was no picnic, as you can imagine. The ups, the downs, the crashing waves, the smell of the salty air, the ups, the downs, the greenish frigid waters sloshing to and fro as the ship rocked and thrust itself farther and farther out into the realm of no–man's land.

Frankly, it made me very nauseous, but I tried not to show it. I wanted to come off as strong and self–contained, but in my head I just kept thinking about the ups and the downs. We stayed on course that way for a little over two weeks.

During that time, we faced scattered storms and lost a shipmate or two and, just when I thought things couldn't get any worse— any crazier, any more off the beaten path— Dr. Vant pulls me aside and takes me into his confidence while sharing his frustration with me. Apparently he never planned on going to China; he was really taking us to some desert coast called the 'The Land God made in Anger' on the shores of South–West Africa. Now the icing was that nobody else even knew about it. I mean here was old Captain Manly–pants sailing or boating, I don't know what you call it when you're running on steam, off to someplace he didn't even know about. That's when I told Dr. Vant that the only thing he could do was explain the situation to Langston and hope he'd have some kind of secret lever he could pull to make the ship go faster. That was the first time I put my foot in my mouth and didn't know it.

So he agreed and went to see Langston. After a fit of rage, the Captain calmed down and devised a plan to get us to this desert coast before nightfall on the fourth of May. We'd be taking his experimental *Sea Dragon* out to practically skip over the waves like a skipping stone you fling when you're little. Well, let me tell you, that's what it felt like. It was the first of May when we'd left the *Wooden Whale*—the five of us, including me, Vant, Langston and two of his men, Reese and Stanton— with two empty barrels and a few sacks of supplies. Now, if you thought I was sickly on the *Whale*, you flat out know I was aboard the *Sea Dragon*!

It wasn't ten minutes after we'd left the cargo hold of the *Whale* when I first tossed my breakfast over the side of the propeller–powered mini–ship. Stanton and Reese laughed it up at my expense, but Langston was too busy steering and Dr. Vant was too busy holding on to pay me much attention. We were moving fast, damn fast, and when you don't have a whole ship to walk around on, you feel just how fast you're going. Hell, we were going faster than the ship! That was the point, afterall. Soon I couldn't even see the *Whale* anymore. The whole thing was suicide. That's the only way to truly explain it. We were going so fast that when we hit a wave, we hit a wave, literally. We'd be crashing head on into them and I've no idea how in God's name we survived, but we did, and kept on going too! Over three days straight we lasted that way. I don't expect you to believe me, but that's how it was.

It was the morning of the fourth when Dr. Vant ordered Langston to slow us down. There was a substantial fog hugging the shore that must have been five or six miles thick.

"This is it," said Dr. Vant. "This, gentlemen, is the Land God Made in Anger."

"We're stopping there?" I asked nervously.

"Yes," he said to me. "Bring us in slow Kaleeb, the waters are shallow and there's no telling what might be protruding up out of them."

"Ain't seen a fog this thick in a while," replied Langston, as he yanked a lever that brought the fan to a low rumble.

"The coast has a very ill reputation," explained Dr. Vant. "Many ships have gone down here since ancient times."

"Doesn't sound too good for us, then," I commented.

"Quite the opposite, Mr. Abbott," said Dr. Vant. "It is that very unlucky aspect that finds us incredibly fortunate. You see, the shallow water and the thick fog cause the majority of the shipwrecks. One such shipwreck was that of Admiral Yang He back in 1421. After leaving China in May of that year, under the orders of Emperor Zhu Di, the ship had rounded the Cape of Good Hope, staying close to the African shoreline so as to map it. In August or September He's monumental junk, as that type of ship is known, sailed into the fog and never sailed out from it. The rest of the ships steered clear of the fog–infested coast, but did send a scout out to search the area. The scout returned to the others saying Yang He's ship had vanished. So the remaining ships pressed on."

"What about this Yang He guy?" asked Reese.

"His vessel had, indeed, been shipwrecked. Most of the survivors made it to land safely enough. Those who did brought with them some of the riches they had carried in the hull of their ship. One such item was a treasure chest, a treasure chest with a very long and important history. They took the chest ashore and hid it within a cavern that remains under water for years at a time. It is that treasure we are after."

The *Sea Dragon* was creeping along slowly, now easing us deeper into the fog. Soon you couldn't see a foot in front of you, but it didn't seem to break Dr. Vant's concentration.

"The rest of the treasures were kept with the refugees and were used to barter with local tribes," he continued.

"Then what made them hide the chest in the cavern?" asked Stanton who was now just as curious as the rest of us.

"The chest had belonged to a band of Arab tomb raiders, who had stolen it from an Egyptian pyramid. No one knows who put the treasure inside the treasure chest, but as the Chinese found out after trading the Arabs for it, the treasure was cursed with the bubonic plague. After being opened it was immediately resealed but the plague spread across the land. Years passed and Zhu Di came into power and ordered that one of his ships take the chest with them on their journey to chart the world and cast the chest deep into the bowels of the earth's oceans. When the ship was wrecked, Yang He ordered his men to conceal the chest the only way they could, by hiding it within the secret cavern. It remains there today but will be ours before tomorrow."

"Land ho!" called Kaleeb, as he brought the *Sea Dragon* ashore steadily.

"How'd you learn all of this?" asked Reese in a voice of sarcastic doubt.

"I'm sorry," said Dr. Vant. "I'll not be answering any additional questions directly related to the treasure again at this time."

"Come again?" asked Reese.

"Are you really sure you *want* to get at this treasure?" asked Stanton, cutting in on Reese.

"I can say this. I'm not leaving without that chest, " said Dr. Vant, and I swear I caught an ever–so–slight smirk on his face, as the fog was thinner on the shore. "We mustn't dawdle. Bring the packs and the two barrels, time is against us." With that the doctor strapped a pack to his back and leapt ashore with his walking stick while the rest of us scrambled to follow suit.

It was still dark as we walked, following the shoreline. The waves were crashing along at our feet, and there was an eerie quietness that gave me the chills. As we walked on, we could see pieces of debris strewn about. There were large splintered planks of wood jutting out of the shallow water like jagged spears. There were even some old metal pots and pans, dented and rusted by the ages. Still we pressed on, and Dr. Vant led us this way for more than a mile. At last he brought us to a stop at the edge of a small cliff.

"Just a brief jaunt down, and we'll be there, " he said, plainly enough.

Some rustling sounds in the fog caught Reese's attention. "Did you hear that? " he asked.

"I definitely heard something, " I agreed. "Should we check it out? "

"Gentleman, we mustn't dawdle!" said Dr. Vant. "Now is not the time to investigate every random sound. We mustn't lose focus, not as we are this close! "

"Too right, " agreed Langston. "Now let's get a move on! "

And so we followed Dr. Vant down the side of the cliff, though Reese couldn't help but keep glancing back behind us. When we had reached the bottom we helped Dr. Vant shift the position of a decent–size boulder, which revealed a hole about eight feet wide.

"And here we are," he stated. "This whole area is usually under water and the cliff is usually the edge of the shore."

"You want us to go down there?" asked Reese.

"That *is* where the chest lies," said Dr. Vant.

"Guess it wouldn't be a good time to mention I'm claustrophobic," I remarked.

"Come now, you shimmied down a soot–filled chimney all by yourself back in Eyam," reminded the doctor.

"Yeah, but I knew I was headed into a house."

"The pit is merely a short drop. We'll go down by rope after we tie one end to the boulder," he explained.

"Let's get on with it," ordered Langston.

With that Stanton broke out his pack and removed a long rope that he fastened to the rock as Dr. Vant had advised. He then tossed the length of it down into the hole.

"Who's first?" Stanton asked.

"I'll go down and survey the structure," suggested Dr. Vant, as he dropped his cane down into the abyss. "When I reach bottom I'll light my lantern and the rest of you can slither down one at a time."

"Shouldn't one of us stay up here and watch the rope?" asked Reese.

"What do you expect it will do Mr. Reese?" asked Dr. Vant. "Jump in after us?"

"Suppose there are natives lurking about?"

"Will you trust me if I tell you there are not?" questioned Vant.

"I guess so, but what if a bird or something should happen by and—"

But Dr. Vant had already disappeared down into the pit. Shortly thereafter a light flickered to life about ten feet down.

"Everything seems sturdy enough," he called from below. "We're starting to get the better of the moment, let's keep it that way."

"Right," said Langston. "In we go. You first Abbott, then me, then you two can fight out who goes last."

"Lovely," I grumbled sarcastically, as I took hold of the rope and slowly lowered myself down.

Once inside the damp darkness, we followed a narrow path, descending deeper until we came into an enormous underground cavern. It must have been fifty or sixty feet high and more than an acre in width. Each of us carried a lantern, and we spread out from each other to get a better feel for the size of the cave. Our footsteps echoed through the emptiness, and you couldn't help but feel you were being watched.

"Think there are any bats?" asked Reese.

"The hole was sealed up when we came down, so I doubt it," replied Stanton.

"Look," stated Langston, "A tunnel." He shone his lantern forward, which was off to our right, and sure enough there was a tunnel.

"Over here," said Stanton, off to the left. "There's another tunnel."

"There are eight tunnels in various directions," said Dr. Vant.

"And how do we know which to take?" I asked.

"This one," exclaimed Dr. Vant, as he stepped up to a tunnel and shone his lamp on it. When he did so, you could plainly see that the opening had been outlined in silver, which lit up brilliantly in the light of Vant's lamp.

"Look at that," Langston whispered, with a hint of euphoria.

"I painted it nine years ago," explained Dr. Vant. "I learned the technique from historic paintings. It's called illumination. You mix powdered silver into the base of clear pigment and paint like you would with any ordinary shellac. The result is a sparkling feast to the eyes when light is cast upon it."

"You really are a genius," I stated.

"I'm a careful planner," corrected Dr. Vant. "Now then, come along."

"Hey, wait just a minute," said Reese. "There's a tunnel over here outlined with gold paint."

"Yes that would be the tunnel that leads to an untimely death," replied Dr. Vant.

"Pit of snakes?" asked Reese, to which Stanton gave him an elbow in his side.

"Ceiling with lowering spikes that seal off your exit," stated Dr. Vant. "Very effective," he paused. "I disguised it that way so that if anyone, save myself, made it into the cavern seeking the prize, they would naturally associate gold with treasure. Thus they would foolishly follow that path and wind up empty–handed," he paused again. "Either that or a human pincushion. Ah, well, I digress. Victory awaits us down this path."

And so we followed our anxious leader into the tunnel and into the unknown. As we pressed on, there was a subtle yet obvious decline in the ground. It was as if we were on a very gradual ramp leading us deeper into the earth. The path began to curve, first to the right, then at times to the left. Eventually we were able to see a faint glow in the distance that got extraordinarily brighter the closer we got to it. Just ahead of us was a silver pond, which shone magnificently in the lantern light.

"Am, am I seeing things?" I asked astonished.

"Indeed, as we all are," confirmed Dr. Vant. "That illustrious illuminant was deposited here by our Chinese friends in order to keep anyone from getting to the treasure."

"What is it?" asked Reese.

"Looks like mercury," I replied.

"Indeed," said Vant. "But it isn't. If it were, we'd already be dead from the odourless vapours."

"Then what?" questioned Stanton.

"According to Sir William Crookes, an acquaintance of mine, it is yet to be officially classified by science. I took a sample to him after stumbling upon it the first time. He named it *metallum vivum*, living metal. Now do not be deceived. Though there are no vapours, the liquid itself is quiet poisonous."

"It's a booby trap," said Langston.

"Not quite," said Vant. "It's just what it looks like, a hurdle."

"But the path continues up ahead, and the ceiling's too low to get a decent jump across it," Stanton observed. "Must be a good fifteen feet wide."

"Excellent observation," added Dr. Vant.

"So tell us," Langston spoke directly to Dr. Vant. "Exactly how *do* we get across?"

"Like this," he said, and with that he took off his pack, rummaged through it, and produced a small cross–bow.

"What do you plan on doing with that?" asked Reese.

Saying nothing, Dr. Vant then removed an arrow with a rotating metal spinner on the end of it, fastened one end of a rope around the spinner, and aimed the arrow at the wall across the metal pond. He pulled the trigger, which thrust the arrow carrying the rope, through the air and into the wall a ways off. The other end of the rope was wound round his right arm. He then let out a little slack and shot another arrow into the wall behind us. That arrow also had a metal spinner on the end of it. He tied one end of the rope to the other, making it taut, and then we realized he had made a pulley system.

"Here now," said I. "Just what else do you have in your pack that we don't have in ours?"

Ignoring my comment, he returned to his bag and produced a rag. "You will all note that each of you has a rag in your pack. This is to hold onto the rope so that you might not blister your hands. The object is for us to cross one at a time by holding onto the bottom rope; the top rope will then be pulled by the remaining members on either side of the liquid mercury so that we may cross. Now, are there any questions?"

"Is it safe?" I asked.

"Of course it's not safe, but it's the only solution I have," said Vant as he raised his walking stick, aimed it at the path ahead and darted it through the air like a spear. It made it safely to the other side, crash–landing on the rocky ground.

"And the barrels?" asked Stanton.

"I took the liberty of adding make–shift hooks to them during our voyage aboard the *Wooden Whale*. You'll find that they are quite sturdy and can handle a tremendous weight." Dr. Vant then fastened his pack to his back and grabbed hold of the bottom rope with the rag. "Now then, give me a hand, will you?"

Kaleeb and Stanton grasped onto the top rope, which wasn't too high off the ground, and began to pull on it, sending Vant forward. On his journey, he had to keep his legs bent and up a little, so his feet wouldn't accidentally splash the metallum vivum. When he made it safely to the other side he gave us the signal to send over the next man. Again this man was me. If I had to compare climbing down a ten foot rope into the unknown or cramming myself down into a chimney where a notorious murderer was still at large to being pulleyed, if that's a word, across a pond of toxic liquid metal, I'd have to say that although the others had their share of anxiety and danger, the most stressful for me was hanging on to that makeshift pulley system with my legs dangling over my doom, all the while being eased across by a band of pirate–like barbarians and an archaeological doctor whom, up until a little over two weeks prior, I had known as an historian by a completely different name!

Before the others came over, they fastened the barrels to the rope and we collected them on the other side. Once everyone and every *thing* was intact, we continued our way down the path leading to God knew where. Well, God *and* Dr. Vant. Eventually we came to what looked like the end of our journey.

"It's a dead end!" said Mr. Langston referring to a pile of rocks that completely blocked our path.

"It is a trick," said Dr. Vant. "Press on it, go ahead."

Langston went up to the wall of rock and stared at it. "It's just rock!"

"Mr. Abbott, *you* press on it."

I remember thinking that it wouldn't make a difference, but I'd humour him anyhow. So I went up to this wall of rubble and I pushed it. To my surprise, well, to all of our surprise—except Dr. Vant's—the wall moved. "I'll be," said I.

"You are looking at a carefully constructed ruse," explained Dr. Vant. "Those rocks were fastened tightly together on a very strong piece of reinforced cloth, which was hung from the ceiling."

When I pulled the cloth aside—I'd like to point out that it was a heavy cloth—the light from our lanterns lit up the room beyond, and within that room, a circular sort of cave, sat a treasure chest painted violet with gold trim. It was a miraculous sight. The chest was about seven feet in length, and even from where I stood, which at best guess was about thirty feet, I could see something inscribed on its lid, as well as a plaque hung on the wall directly over it.

“Ain’t she a beaut,” said Mr. Langston.

“What are we waiting for?” asked Reese as he came forth with his lantern lighting his way. Dr. Vant twirled his cane very swiftly bringing it chest level to Reese thus preventing him from going forward.

“The lantern must stay here,” said Dr. Vant.

“And why is that?” asked Reese.

“Because the room is protected by a semi–circular trench of oil from whale blubber. The slightest spark could seal off our only exit. So the lanterns—all of them—will remain here.”

“But how will we see what we’re doing?” questioned Stanton.

Saying nothing, as seemed to have become his second nature, Dr. Vant took his walking stick and jammed it in such a position that it held back the heavy rock–covered cloth. “We should have just enough light for our purpose.”

And so we followed Dr. Vant, leaving our lanterns behind and stepping widely over the three–foot–wide trench.

“It almost seems too easy,” I pointed out.

“You call all of what we’ve been through easy?” asked Reese.

“I mean, that’s just it,” I continued. “We climbed down a cliff that’s under water for nine years at a time, discovered a boulder–covered hole, which we shimmied down, took one particular path of eight possibilities, crossed a pond of ‘living metal’, moved a dodgy wall of rock, and stepped over a trench of whale oil! I’d think there’d still be one or two more obstacles in our way.”

“And you would be correct,” said Dr. Vant as he made his way over to the chest. He tried to lift it, but it must have been too heavy, so he motioned for each of us to take a side, and we all pulled with every ounce of muscle that we could muster but to no avail. The chest wasn’t moving. “Still as stuck as ever, and as you hypothesized, Mr. Abbott, indeed it isn’t as easy as all that. This chest has been fastened to the floor.”

“So,” said Reese. “We’ve got the barrels, let’s just empty it into ’em. After all, that is why we brought ’em ain’t it? Just in case?”

"Quite right, Mr. Reese, only what do you remember about this specific chest?"

"It's ancient?" he asked, like an idiot.

"No, you fool," said Langston, "The damned thing's cursed with bubonic plague!"

"Oh, yeah," recalled Reese.

"Look in your packs," ordered Dr. Vant. "Each of you will find a special bundle of clothing tied by twine. These garments are made out of India rubber and come complete with a pair of gloves and boots as well as a facemask, goggles, and a hood. These items will protect us from the plague's presence but not from directly touching that which is contaminated with it. Especially not with such a high concentration as this."

"Then how do we get it out?" asked Stanton.

"Our friend Mr. Martin Abbott will assist us," stated Dr. Vant with a smile. "Only he can get close enough to touch it."

"Right then," said I as I, untied my bundle only to discover it contained just about everything but clothing.

"Where's mine?"

"For you, who are immune, such cumbersome attire would only slow you down," explained Dr. Vant.

When fully clothed, the others resembled something out of a nightmare. Their coats were very long and reached their knees, which were donned in a pair of India rubber trousers. Together they were all kind of shiny in the golden lantern light, and I could smell the stink of fresh rubber.

Dr. Vant reached into his pack once again and removed a set of keys, which he took over to the chest. He bent down next to it and placed one of the keys into its lock. He gave it one good hard turn and the latch opened.

"Now where do you get a key for an ancient Chinese treasure chest?" Reese asked.

"Well," said Dr. Vant. "When last I was here I filled the keyhole with melted wax, thus making a cast, and then had a metal key fashioned when I'd returned to England." His answer kind of shut Reese up, on the account that it seemed like a perfectly logical way to get a key made. "And by the way," said Dr. Vant, as he stood up to open the chest. "This isn't a Chinese chest."

As soon as he'd begun to raise the chest's lid, a bit of smoky gas hissed out from it which forced me to cough and a blinding glow filled the room as the lanterns from afar shone and danced on the golden coins, brilliant gems, and numerous other sparkling treasures. Soon we'd forgotten all about Reese's stupid question and stood staring, mesmerized, at the sight before us.

The feeling was indescribable; here, we'd come all this way, and now there it lay, ripe for the picking, and only I had the power to take the prize.

"Go ahead, Martin," said Dr. Vant. "It is up to you now. Reese, Stanton, open those barrels."

"Are you sure it's all going to fit?" asked Langston, not wanting to leave any behind.

"Quite sure! Absolutely," he said proudly. "At least, I think so."

So I got down on my knees, brought a barrel up beside me, and then hovered over the treasure with one foot in heaven and the other in hell. I mean there I was about to become rich beyond anything I could ever have guessed, and yet there was still the possibility that Dr. Vant's theory about my immunity to the plague had been wrong. I stayed there for a moment on my knees rolling things over in my mind.

"Come on then, are you going to do it or ain't you?" demanded Reese in a childish whine.

"If you'd like to take a crack at it, you go right ahead," said I, as I'd had enough of his yammering. "The way I see it, I'm the only one who can help you right now, so unless you want to leave this place empty–handed you'll shut your yap and keep it closed, because quite frankly,"—and I turned to face his rubber–masked mug—"I'm tired of your God–damned bitchin'!"

"Well put, Mr. Abbott," said Dr. Vant. "Now, pray, continue at your leisure."

"Thank you," said I and then I faced the treasure again. This time I slowly dipped my hands deep into the pile of gold, scooping up two handfuls and emptied them into the barrel at my right. I continued this way for what seemed like hours, until at last there remained only two golden coins and an emerald.

The coins bore some symbols that I could not make out, but I could plainly see that they did not match those of the inscription on the chest's lid nor the Chinese writing on the plaque. When I'd finished, Reese and Stanton sealed up the barrels, and I took to my feet.

"Never was there a more splendid occasion for a celebration," said Dr. Vant. "When we return to the *Whale* we'll drink a toast to our victory. I have there, in my quarters, a very rare bottle of Chinese wine that will—"

"There's just one thing," interrupted Mr. Langston.

"What?" asked Dr. Vant.

"This," he said, and in a blur of speed I'd never have given him credit for, Langston slammed his fist as hard as he could—which is pretty damn hard—right into the forehead of Dr. Vant's mask. As Dr. Vant flew backwards I felt my arms being seized by the Captain's goons. Vant's body was on the ground now, motionless.

"Have you lost your bloody mind?" I screamed.

"You should be happy," chuckled Langston. "Now there's one less person to share the treasure with!"

"You'd have to be nuttier than a drunken squirrel to think that I'll help you get this treasure out of here without Dr. Vant!"

"Yeah," sneered Reese. "You sure we need this one?"

"He's the only one that can transport the treasure into the sanitation bins aboard the *Whale*," said Langston.

"Right," said Stanton. "But what about him?" He pointed to Vant's body.

"Vant?" asked Langston, as he returned to his pack and searched its contents, "We'll give him what he wanted all along."

"What's that?" questioned Stanton.

Langston had removed some rope from the sack and stepped over to Vant. He produced a knife and sliced the rope in half. He then tied one end of each rope to Vant's wrists and the other ends to the handles on each side of the treasure chest.

"Why, his treasure of course," said Langston with a titter.

"I don't get it," said Reese.

"Didn't he say he wasn't leaving without that treasure chest?" laughed Langston. "Guess he was right after all!"

Reese joined in the laugh and I felt as though I were going to be sick. I began to struggle until I was elbowed hard in the stomach. Langston passed us by and the others picked me up clear off the ground and carried me, kicking wildly, out the doorway.

"I'll not leave Dr. Vant," I shouted, "Do you hear me? I won't!"

"You don't have much choice," said Langston, and with that he threw Dr. Vant's lantern, which crashed down into the trench of whale oil. In half a second fire erupted in an explosion of the likes I'd never seen. Soon a wall of flames high as the ceiling itself surrounded Dr. Vant, sealing him off from us.

"This can't be happening," I whimpered.

"What makes you think Vant's so different from us?" asked Langston, as the others dropped me to the ground.

"What do you mean?" I asked.

"He's a confidence man, the truest definition of the word if there is one."

"He's no con man," I said, doing my best to stick up for him.

"No? So exactly how long have you known Dr. Vant, or should I say Nigel Palmer? You know what he was doing in Eyam all those months ago? He was finding the perfect fool to do his bidding. That, and he set up the most elaborate show I've ever seen. He staged that murder of Mrs. Bellmore to test your allegiance! And like a good dog, you obeyed his every command. He's played us all and would no doubt squander us out of the treasure just as we have him. Deception's in his veins. *He's* the reason my wife was killed! If there's one thing I've come to know about that man, it's that he makes no mistakes, even when he appears to be making a mistake. The bastard's got it all planned out, some freakish grand scheme to screw the world, no doubt. So I think I just did the world a favour, don't you?"

"I don't believe a word of it," said I. "Not a word."

"His name is *Irrelevant*, for God's sake! You think that's normal?"

"I don't care what he calls himself, I'd still trust him over you any day."

"Then you leave me no other choice," said Langston. "Tie him up, we'll hoist him over the silver pool and get out of here before it's too late."

"Christ," said Stanton as he got out some rope. "I forgot about the incoming water! How long have we been down here?"

Langston felt his rubbery side, "No good, can't get at my watch. We'll just have to assume the worst."

"Then let's get the hell out of here," cried Reese in full agreement, as he assisted Stanton with my bindings.

I glanced back at the blazing barricade one last time as I was carried past the wall of rock, which was sealed back up as Langston had taken down Vant's cane. That was the last time I ever saw Dr. Vant, or Nigel Palmer, or whoever he really was. But my journey was just beginning, and when once we reached the sparkling pond, the Captain was the first one over, followed by me, and then came one of the treasure barrels. Its weight pressed heavily down on the rope, and I could see some of the strands starting to unravel themselves just as Langston intercepted it at our end.

Now it was time for the next barrel. Stanton raised the barrel high into the air, and Reese hooked it on the bottom rope. They eased the barrel across, going slowly because it was so damn heavy. I was watching the rope carefully as more and more of it unravelled itself, but then something that none of us had taken into consideration surprised us. One of the arrows with the pulley—the one on our end—detached from the wall and, thanks to the weight of the barrel, flew backwards through the air, dropping the second barrel of treasure into the pond of metal where it sank almost immediately.

"Not my treasure!" hollered Langston. "Curse you, Vant, curse your damn antics!"

"What about us?" shouted Reese.

"What do I care?" asked Langston. "I've still got half an ancient treasure!"

"But we'll both be drowned when the water floods in!" declared Stanton.

"Your efforts will be duly noted," said Langston. "But if you'll excuse me, I've got to save my own hide. Come on, Abbott," he said, and he grabbed some of the rope binding me and hoisted me up onto his back.

"You'd leave your own brother–in–law?" demanded Reese.

"Lad, I'd leave my mother herself!"

He then leant the barrel over onto its side and started to roll it up the inclined path while Reese and Stanton were left to their demise.

"What kind of captain leaves his men behind?" I asked, trying anything to irritate him.

"A wise one," said he, and he continued to advance forward, though all I saw was what lay behind us.

"I wonder what the rest of your crew will think when I tell them about how you got rid of Vant and left the others to die."

"If they want a cut of the treasure they'll thank me. And if you know what's good for you, you'll shut your yap." As we returned to the main cavern, he threatened, "First thing I'm going to do when we get back to the *Sea Dragon* is muzzle that mouth of yours!"

"*If* you get back," I taunted. He only snorted. "Think I'm exaggerating? Listen closely. As a man of the sea I think you'd be able to hear the sound of crashing waves."

He stopped then, as we reached the smaller tunnel on the other side of the main cavern. His feet made a splashing sound in some small puddles of muddy water, and then he began to hurry.

"We'll never make it! That water's going to come down on us like a ton of bricks on a camel's back. Or is it straw?"

"Blarney!" he blurted. "There's plenty of time."

When at last we reached the point of our first descent, he set me on the ground and grabbed hold of the rope that hung down from the top of the pit. Water rushed in every few seconds, but he wasn't deterred. He tied the bit of rope to those that bound me.

"You'll never be able to get me, the treasure, and yourself out of here all in one piece!"

"That does it," said Langston, and he stuffed some kind of cloth into my mouth and wrapped yet another piece of rope around my head to keep the gag in place. "If there's one thing I should give Vant credit for, it's that he was right about needing all this rope!" With that he leapt up onto the rope that was dangling from the ceiling and began the short climb up to the seafloor. I watched as some water sprayed down onto him, but it didn't slow his momentum and within a very short time indeed he had reached the top of the pit. Once he'd made it out I felt a tugging on the ropes at my back. Having tied me to the main rope, Langston could easily haul me up and out, just by pulling on his end.

Once I was out of the pit I took in the scene before me. Granted, I was happy to be out in the open again, but the water level had got within ten feet of the pit and every now and then a wave would reach the pit's edge, spraying water down into it. The full moon rested directly overhead, and all I could do was wait while Langston sent the rope down into the cave below, looped it around the hook on the barrel, and yanked it up as he had me. In the meantime, a nasty sort of taste had filled my mouth from the cloth he'd gagged me with. I tried not to think about it, but it was no use. I couldn't exactly place the taste; it was something along the lines of a salty sweat and bitter fungus mixed with dried mud and a bit of sourness.

"No time to rest now," Langston told himself aloud as he wheezed. "Tide's coming in, and if I want to get out of here a rich man I've got to hurry." He then made his way over to the giant boulder that had once covered the pit and tried to shove it back into place. "No good," said he. "It'll take too much out of me. Besides, a good shower will do the others some good," he chuckled to himself.

I wanted to tell him that the first thing to go was the mind, but being unable to speak I only shook my head.

"What are you looking at?" he asked me. "This is no time to be sitting around; we've got a boat to catch!"

Then, rather than being dragged back to the *Sea Dragon*, I followed behind Langston like a dog on a leash, and he carried the barrel along in his arms. We'd stop every now and then to take a short rest. The day had taken its toll on the bawdy, burly Captain, and he had begun to show it. By dawn we had reached the *Sea Dragon*, which rested just off–shore. We crashed there, exhausted, and I dreamt of Eyam and my simple life. I was a chandler again, and it was as if I had never left. But darkness flooded across the dreamscape sky, and everything I had known suddenly disappeared, and I found myself drowning in a pool of darkness. As I gasped for air I suddenly woke up to find that Langston had removed the gag from my mouth and that I really was gasping for air.

"Think you can be quiet now?" he asked, and behind him I could see that it was late in the day. I nodded. "Good, now eat this." He had tossed a roasted fish my way, and I was surprised that I was able to catch it in mid–air. He had untied me completely, stripped me of my clothing, dressed me in a sleeping gown, and had himself changed out of the rubber apparel. I said nothing but eagerly devoured the food.

"I've untied you because I need your cooperation," he explained. "I know that, and I know you know that. A portion of the treasure's still yours if you want it. I know that you don't want to agree to anything, especially anything I offer. But if you help me, I'll see that you make it safely back to Europe. Defy me, and you'll be giving my regards to Dr. Vant in hell. Are we clear on that?"

Again I nodded. I had no choice. I didn't know the first thing about Africa and the *Wooden Whale* was my only ticket back home. I felt for

Dr. Vant, possibly even a little for Reese and Stanton, but they were gone now, and I had myself to look after. At that moment I made a pact with myself. If I ever saw England again I was going to find myself a good woman, marry her, and start a family. I'd been given a new lease on life and I wasn't going to gamble with it.

Two days later, the *Whale* drifted in and we went out to meet it on the *Sea Dragon*. When we'd got aboard, Langston made up a story about how Reese and Stanton knocked off Dr. Vant and tried to take the treasure for their own, but Langston and I were able to get the upper hand and come away with half the treasure intact. I didn't say anything. I couldn't. But one day I would.

That night—I think it was the sixth of May—there was a large celebration aboard the *Whale*, as we had returned to sea, and Captain Langston helped himself to Dr. Vant's private stash of Chinese wine to top it all off. In the morning, I would be cleansing the treasure in the sanitation bins in the cargo hold where the treasure rested. For the moment, though, I was enjoying a greatly needed night off. I went to bed early that night with my stomach stuffed to its maximum, but an empty feeling stayed with me all the same.

Sometime during the middle of the night I heard a scream that woke me and curdled my blood. At first I thought I was hearing things, but then I heard it again. As the screaming continued I crept slowly out of my chambers and up to the main deck where the noise originated. There I found Morton Seadrick, the first mate of the ship, trying to console a crew member of whom I had not made the acquaintance. As Morton stepped aside I caught sight of the poor shirtless fellow and large black boils formed beneath his armpits. He stood there shivering in the wind and screaming in hysteria.

Soon the screaming caught the attention of the Captain, and he came to see what all the fuss was about. When he came upon the scene he froze in his tracks.

"He just started to break out," explained Seadrick to Langston, while he tried to calm the man down.

"But that's impossible," said Langston under his breath. "We took every precaution. It's not possible."

"Beg your pardon, Captain?" asked Seadrick.

"Captain, Captain!" I heard someone call from behind. "Someone's been at the treasure! I went down on my watch and found Thomas unconscious and the seal broken off the top of the treasure barrel!"

"Abbott!" Langston accused.

"That would be a negative," said I, as I came forth from the shadows.

"Then, who?" demanded the Captain.

"Who, indeed," came a grave voice from a shadowed figure high up on the quarterdeck.

"You!" hollered Langston. "But you were dead!"

"Maybe I am," said the voice, and soon the figure descended to the main deck and into the light. It was Langston's old mate Thatch, and with his pale skin and malnourished body he certainly did resemble the dead.

"I thought you fell over the side of the ship in that big storm," said I.

"I was thrown over, by the Captain, but not before he ripped my arm out of socket to ensure that I'd not be able to swim."

"Is that all I did?" asked Langston. "I thought sure I'd broken it."

"So did I, at first. But when I'd gone overboard I managed to grab hold of the rudder. There I forced my shoulder back into its socket and there I remained for days, eating anything that came along my way." Thatch stopped and looked around. "Where's Dr. Vant?"

"He didn't make it," said Langston.

"Now, there's a surprise," sneered Thatch.

"Very glad to see you're all right, Thatch," said Seadrick. "But now we've got to get Ab here some help. He's got boils of the likes I've never seen!"

"That's all thanks to our good friend Thatch," explained Langston.

"Blaming me for more of your misfortune, Captain?"

"You popped open the lid on the barrel of treasure, did you not?"

"I was only taking what's rightfully mine!"

"And in doing so, you released a curse onto all of us. That treasure's tainted with bubonic plague—hell maybe even pneumonic plague for all I know!"

"You're out of your mind," accused Thatch.

"I'm afraid he's not," I stated. "Granted, he's a lying, stealing, murderous malicious vagabond out to keep the treasure for himself, but he's right about the plague. It's the reason they needed me on this expedition. I was the only person capable of touching the treasure, since I'm immune to it. Or so said Dr. Vant before his demise."

The truth set into Thatch's eyes, and he began to sulk. "What have I done?"

"You've damned us all," cursed Langston. "The whole ship's going to die a slow, agonizing death because you had to have your revenge! Think of all the innocent lives you've doomed. Maybe I am a killer, but the handful of people I did in is nothing compared to your stunt! You've probably got poor Isabelle turning over in her watery grave as we speak!"

That was all the fuel Thatch's fire needed. He suddenly came to life with a burst of astonishing energy and attacked Langston head on. The two began to brawl, and by looking at Thatch's size next to Langston's one might have guessed the outcome, but still the mate fought, and the two became entangled in a mess of flying fists.

"If we're going to die anyway," said Thatch. "Then I'm taking you out first!"

"Best of luck to you!" snapped the Captain, and before anyone knew what happened, they both fell overboard, fists still flying all the way down.

"What should we do?" asked Seadrick, as he went to edge of the deck.

"Nothing you can do," I said. "Their lives are lost no matter what. The only thing we can do now is comfort those still alive."

"Are… are we all really going to die, Mr. Abbott?"

"I'm afraid it does look that way," said I.

He stayed silent for a few moments, and then spoke: "Then you must take the treasure."

"No, I—"

"If you don't, what good will it do us?" he asked, as he took off his coat and draped it over the man named Ab. "Dr. Vant would have wanted it that way. You can believe that. You can take the *Sea Dragon* and get out of here before you lose your mind."

"Nonsense, I'll stay and take care of you all. I'm probably the only person who can. Then I can take the ship back to England and have you all properly buried. In the meantime you can teach me how to steer the *Whale*."

"One man can't control this ship by himself, sir. Besides, if this ship should reach land there'd be an even bigger epidemic. No sir, you'll do us all a favour if you let us die out at sea with our dignity. Knowing that it wasn't all for nothing, that's enough to let me die with a smile on my face. Take the *Sea Dragon* back to Morocco and burn her once you've reached land. Burn her *and* your belongings. You can use the sanitized treasure to buy yourself a new life."

"But, but when would I go?"

"Go now, Mr. Abbott, before the men find out the truth. Before they go mad and have a chance to stop you. I'll steer a course out into the Atlantic and set the *Whale* ablaze myself. There's no time to argue, sir."

So I didn't. Instead, I followed him down into the cargo hold, submersed the treasure in a sanitation bin, which was a large metal tub that reeked of alcohol or something, sealed it closed and loaded it aboard the *Sea Dragon*. Seadrick then lowered the rear ramp, and together we pushed the *Sea Dragon* up onto it.

"Well," I said. "I guess this is it then."

"Follow the directions on this paper," he said, as he stuffed something into my front pocket. "That'll get you to Morocco."

"Right then, thank you, Morton, Captain Seadrick." He smiled.

"Do me a favour, Mr. Abbott," he said. "When you get back home, send a wire to my brother Winston; he lives in Norquecaster these days.

Tell him I'll miss him and send him and his family my love."

"I'll do more than that, Captain. I'll take him your share of the treasure!"

A single tear descended from behind the old man's spectacles and down into his moustache. "God bless ye, Mr. Martin Abbott."

I smiled, gave the man a hearty handshake, and stepped up to the *Sea Dragon*. I then climbed up the short stepladder, strapped myself in, put on a pair of goggles, and pulled the lever on my right. A plume of smoke erupted from the smokestacks and I waved good–bye to Morton Seadrick. I then yanked the lever on my left and the fan–like propeller sparked to life sending me down the ramp and out into the open sea.

I never looked back at the *Wooden Whale*, but I suspect that if I had, I would have shed a tear of my own. Instead, I pressed on with thoughts of living and made it to Morocco some days later. I burned the ship and my clothing as instructed and used the remaining solution in the metal bin to rinse the container itself as a final precaution. I then carried the lot, stark naked, into port.

Eventually I was able to get back on my feet, very well off I might add, and followed through with my promise to Morton. I told his family of the honourable way in which he sacrificed himself and then, having found—after years of research—that Dr. Vant had had no family of his own, I discovered that one William O'Brien, the closest thing Vant had to family, still resided in Vant's home town of Leocadia. Upon my journey there, I met and fell in love with a wonderful woman named Iris; we're to be married soon, and I give credit for that to Dr. Vant. That brings me back here, where, under Mr. O'Brien's persuasion, I have filled in a gap in Dr. Vant's life.

IX
THE SHROUDED

A fortnight had passed since that irregular evening at Vant Manor, when Keftiuc came to warn Dr. Vant that his life was in danger. An irregular evening, I suppose, for those whose lives had not been christened into the world of one Dr. Irel E. Vant. It had been a month since I had come to Leocadia; a month since I had met the love of me life, Cara Faulky. A month is an interesting period of time, when you come to think about it. In one way, you feel as though time is passing quickly; yet in reality, it's only been a month. What can a month tell you about a person or a place?

Well, a month told me that Dr. Vant was quite possibly the most mystifying individual I'd ever met; that Mrs. McGillian was the sweetest old lass I'd come across since me Great Aunt Lill; that Victor was as strangely comforting as he was, well, strange; that Vant Manor was full of more secrets than a leprechaun's treasure trove; that Leocadia was a village of friendly faces and humble strangers; and that it was about time I met Cara's family. Actually, it was Cara herself who told me that it was about time I should meet her family.

"They'll love you," she cooed, "You're a determined man who fights for his dreams and believes in himself. You're kind, sensitive, caring, a hard worker, and a dear, sweet friend."

"Och, friend is it?" I teased. We were sitting on the edge of Vant's stone pond in the front yard with two dried–up dragon heads beside us, while their bodies towered overhead forming a massive ten foot tall water fountain.

"You seem disappointed," she jested lovingly.

"I just thought that maybe we'd moved beyond that now, that maybe we could advance to something of a—dare I say—courtship?"

"That's why I want you to meet my family. I could never date someone they haven't met," she said as she ran her fingers through me hair and gazed into me eyes. "What's there to be scared of?"

"Scared? Huh, me?"

"Then what's there to stop you?"

"'T ain't nothing woman," said I.

"Good, then you'll join us for dinner this evening. I'll set the whole thing up with my parents. It'll be a lovely time, you'll see!"

"I'll be on pins and needles until then," I promised, with a hint of sarcasm.

"Now listen, because this is important: My father's name is Henry, and he'll try to get you to call him so, but don't do that, because he hates it."

"Then why would he ask me to call him that?"

"It's one of his tests."

"Tests? God blind me, should I be taking notes?"

"Don't mock! He'll ask you to call him Henry, but he is very traditional and believes that as a form of respect, people—especially those who intend to court his daughter—should refer to him as either Mr. Faulky, or sir."

"Mr. Faulky or sir," I confirmed.

"It's his way of telling whether or not you respect your elders."

"I see. And what about the Missus? What's your Mum like?"

"She's very soft–spoken and very nurturing, very much the opposite of my father."

"Sounds like we'll be having a real dandy time, just the four of us."

"Well there's also my younger brother, Adam."

"Och, the list goes on and on!"

"No, that's where it stops. Just my mother, my father, myself, and Adam."

"Can I call your brother Adam or do I have to call him Mr. Faulky as well?"

"Billy!"

"Wait now, think about it. If they both go by Mr. Faulky how will they know whom I'm talking to? Maybe I should call one of them sir and the other Mr. Faulky. But what if I get confused and mix up the two? It's useless; I can see no good coming from it."

"Oh, will you stop," she giggled. "Call him Adam."

"So what time should I pop by then?"

"We usually have a late dinner, nine o'clock, after I get in from the shop and father returns with the stock shipment from London."

"What do your mother and Adam do all day if you and your father are always busy working?"

"Oh we all have jobs. My mother tends to the shop from dawn until my shift then tends to the household chores at night. As for Adam, it really depends on what day of the week it is. Twice a week, on Mondays and Fridays, he goes with my father to the city. But the rest of the week he takes on odd jobs, such as sweeping the streets, delivering groceries, delivering telegrams, and on occasion he'll help out with the ironing at my uncle's tailor shop."

"I'm beginnin' to think you and your family run this town."

She giggled again. "We just do whatever we can to get by. Not everyone's as rich as Dr. Vant."

"Aye, you can say that twice."

She smiled cheerfully, and then caught sight of the sun's height in the sky.

"Oh it's getting late. I better get going. Mother will be expecting her relief."

"So then I'll see you at nine," I said, as I walked her to the front gate.

"And don't be late," she minded. "My father hates that."

"I'll bet he does," said I, and waved her off as she went.

I don't remember exactly what I thought, but it was something along the lines of: *Her father must be crazy!* or *What did you get yourself into now?* Either way you get a sense of the moment.

After I closed the gate, I went back inside to find Mrs. McGillian seated at Vant's piano in the parlour, the room with the boarded–up door to the North–East tower. Victor was beside her with his head resting on her lap.

"Why don't you play something?" I asked as I entered.

"Because I never learned how," said she. "I always wanted to learn though."

"I'm sure you'd master it too, what with how you cook and clean and all."

"That reminds me," she said as she rose from her seat. "I should get started on dinner."

"None for me, thank you, I'll be eating out tonight."

"Oh?" she asked, as she plopped back down at the bench.

"Aye, Cara invited me over to her place. She thinks it's time I met the family."

"Getting as serious as all that, then, is it?" she asked.

"I'm a man in love, and I cannot deny it."

Victor snorted.

"Victor's right," said Mrs. McGillian. "Tread lightly, young Master William, tread lightly. After all, remember what Dr. Vant said. He didn't even want you to see this girl one more time, let alone start a relationship."

"Well, if the bugger's going to be mad about anything, it'll be about that North–East tower," I said, pointing to the boarded–up door. "He told me that if I went in there I'd forfeit this whole arrangement, and here I did so on the very first night!"

"You were trying to protect it though, so that's different."

"I just hope he sees it that way."

"When is this dinner of yours?"

"Nine o'clock," I replied. "In the meantime, I figured I'd do a little painting, maybe take a bath, then stop off for a bouquet of flowers along the way. Something for her mother, I was thinking. You know, some kind of friendly, gentlemanly gesture."

"You're a sweet lad, William. You'll make a fine husband one day. Now, if you'll excuse me, one of us is eating here tonight, and I'd better get started on something." She turned to Victor. "Maybe Victor here would like your share. What do you say Victor?"

He sniffed the air a bit.

"I haven't started making it yet!"

"Perhaps I *could* have a small snack," I reasoned. "You know, just a little something to tide me over. After all, I'm not used to eating so late."

"All right, just be sure to pace yourself. We wouldn't want to insult Mrs. Faulky's cooking, would we?"

"Too true, that," I added, as I followed her out of the room.

At eight thirty that evening I departed from Vant Manor. There was a cool spring breeze in the air, and I began to whistle as I went on me way. The gas–lit street lamps illuminated the darkness with a warm golden glow, as Vant Manor's narrow private drive became Westbrook Avenue. I was en route to a local market I'd once passed down Heather Street, which was just off Barkly near Town's Square. Usually, I made it a point to visit only Faulky's, on account of Cara and because they really were a very well–run place, but on this occasion I was out to get some flowers for the Missus and thus could not stop there. So the place I sought out was called *Botanical Bliss*, and it was mostly in the business of produce, houseplants, and flowers.

I had picked out a dandy bouquet of daisies and daffodils, which were held together by twine netting and tied with a bright yellow ribbon, and next thing I knew, it was five minutes to nine and I was bringing me hand up to the door of Twenty–five Ravenwood Road. It was a strong door, I observed, stained dark brown and decorated with a wreath of dried flowers. I stood there with me fist in mid–air, finding the courage somewhere inside meself to knock.

"Oh, for the land's sake! Damn thing's made of wood," I heard a voice from behind me say. "Ain't gonna bite ya, if that's what you're worried about!"

I lowered me hand a little and swivelled me head to catch sight of a stocky man with a grizzled beard, dirty shoulder–length hair, and the general appearance of a wild mastodon. His clothing was dishevelled, and he seemed to sort of hunch forward in his normal stance.

"Are you Mr. Faulky?" I asked, as I turned around completely, flowers and all.

"That I am, but please, call me Henry. Look at that, you brought me flowers and everything. I'm touched, truly," he said, mockingly taking them from me hand and sniffing them. "Not very fragrant, but still, they'll do. Now then," said he, as he moved past me and stuck a key into the door. "Come inside so I can get a better look at you. Don't mind the door now, it won't get ya."

I wasn't sure exactly what to do, but I knew I had to follow him in, so I did. The Faulky home was a rustic townhouse with wood panelling, a few paintings, and plenty of candles. There was a small tea table, which rested in front of a beige sofa with a brown throw blanket tossed over its back, a fireplace, two sitting chairs, and a dining room table with a lovely floral centrepiece near the back. It was all located in one enormous room along with a rocking chair, china cabinet, and an old wooden chest.

"I'm home, Annabelle," he called. "I'm home and I'm hungry." He then glanced back at me whilst he removed his coat and hung it on a hook on the wall. "Oh, yeah, and I brought home a stray."

"A stray?" asked Annabelle Faulky as she came out from the kitchen with a large metal pot in her mitten–clad hands. Her plain brown hair was pinned up, and she wore a simple brown dress with a white apron. "Oh," she seemed a bit surprised when she saw me. "You must be William O'Brien, I'm Annabelle, Cara's mother."

"Oh, here, ma'am," I said and I went to help her carry in the pot. "Let me take that for you."

"At last," she sighed. "Someone with manners and a good upbringing." She gave her husband a quick glance and handed me the pot. "Careful now, it's hot."

And hot it was, damn hot, and I didn't have any mittens to hold onto it with. So I made a noise, something along the lines of *Owowow!*, and brought it to the table as fast as I bloody well could.

"Manners he's got," said Mr. Faulky. "But brains—"

"Hen–ry!" scolded his wife.

"Ah, it's no sweat, Mrs. Faulky," said I. "I know he's just jokin'."

"Am I?" he asked with a strange sort of gleam in his eye.

"So, uh, where is Cara?" I asked.

"She's getting washed up," replied Mrs. Faulky.

"Here," said her husband, as he handed her the bouquet. "These are for you."

"Flowers, Henry? What's the occasion?" she questioned. "Our anniversary isn't until August," and she took them from him.

"They're from me," I said. "Something of a thank– you for having me tonight."

"Oh, isn't that sweet," she said. "Such a nice young man. Wait, speaking of young men, where's Adam?"

"He'll be along," Mr. Faulky replied. "He went over to Danny's to see if he wanted to join us for dinner."

"But we already have company," she whispered under her breath.

"What's a father to do?" he asked. "I can't tell one of my children she can invite someone over for dinner and tell the other that he can't. That'd be favouritism!"

'Twas then that the night was made right, for there in the doorway between the rooms appeared Cara.

"Hello, Billy," she said with a smile as she came to greet me.

"Hello to you," said I, as I reached for her hand and gave it a wee peck.

"Aw," cooed her mother.

"Quick, get me a bucket, I'm gonna be sick," jested her father.

"Here," said Mrs. Faulky as she swatted her husband with the flowers. "Put these in a vase, would you?"

"Be happy to," he said through his teeth and disappeared into the kitchen.

"Please, excuse me," said Mrs. Faulky. "I have a few more dishes to get on the table before dinner," and with that she followed her husband.

"I'm so glad you came," said Cara, as she gave me a proper hug. "My family means a lot to me, and I just want everything to work out."

At that moment, the outside door opened and in came two fourteen–year–old boys. One had a dirty mop of brown hair atop his head and was dressed in some shabby trousers and a dusty shirt, and the other had a short shock of orange hair and wore somewhat cleaner clothing.

"This is my brother Adam," said Cara as she introduced me to the dirtier of the two.

"Hi," said he.

"And I'm Danny, Danny McArthur, you must be William, Cara's suitor come callin'. Adam's told me all about you." Adam elbowed him in the side. "What?" asked Danny.

"Call me Billy," said I.

"Billy's a boy's name," commented Mr. Faulky, senior, as he entered the room carrying some bowls with his wife trailing behind him. "Are you a boy, O'Brien?"

"Em, no sir," said I.

"Then why don't people call me Daniel?" asked Danny.

"Cause last time I checked," began Mr. Faulky as he set down some bowls, "you weren't a man!"

"Come on, now," said the Missus. "Dinner's on the table."

With that, Adam and Danny headed on over. "Not you, Adam," said his mother. "Not until you wash up!"

"Yes, ma'am," he sighed as he left the room.

'Twas then I realized that Mr. Faulky himself had cleaned up a bit. I'd noticed so as he took his seat at the head of the table, while his wife made for the seat directly across from him and Danny took a seat on one side.

"Smell's lovely," I stated, as I took a seat beside Cara, next to her father.

"Yeah, what are we having?" asked Danny.

"A slow–roasted cider brisket, with boiled potatoes, steamed carrots with broccoli, biscuits, and one of my home–made apple pies," explained Mrs. Faulky.

"Sounds delicious," I added.

"It'd sound a lot better if it were coming from my stomach," remarked Mr. Faulky. "Now where is that boy? Adam!" he called. "You coming to the table, or am I going to eat your share?"

"Coming, Pop," he said, as he hurried into the room and took his seat beside Danny, near his mother.

"Now, Henry, why don't you say grace?" asked his wife in a tone that implied she wasn't asking so much as telling.

"Right," said he, as we all folded our hands and bowed our heads. "Dear Lord, we thank you for the food that we are about to receive—"

"And for being able to share our meal with our friends, Danny and William," added his wife.

"Christ, woman, are you saying grace or am I?"

"Henry, watch your tongue when you speak to the Lord!"

"Sorry, Lord, we do appreciate all you've given to us and we ask that you please bless this meal. Amen."

"Amen," we all repeated.

"So, William," said Mrs. Faulky, as she reached for her carving utensils and began transporting some of the brisket onto her plate, "Cara tells us you just moved here, not too long ago."

"Aye, ma'am, I'm originally from Ireland."

"Hey, I'm Irish too," said Danny whilst he scooped up some of the boiled potatoes onto his dish. "Not that I've ever been there, but my grandparents were born in Dubloon."

"That's Dublin! Oh, you'd love it! 'Tis a beautiful country, Ireland," said I.

"If you love it so much," asked Cara's father after buttering his biscuit, "Why'd you leave?"

"He's a painter," said Cara.

"A painter, eh?" said he. "Ireland's a decent–sized country; don't they have need for painters over there?"

"Truth be told," said I, "I could probably paint anywhere, but I thought I needed a proper education in the field. That's why I left home last autumn."

"And you came to England for it?" questioned Cara's father. "Well, you shouldn't have any problems here. Take Leocadia, for instance, average village, something along the lines of three or four hundred families, five at best," said he, filling his plate with a bit of everything as he spoke. "Say you commission to paint a room for half of them. That's around two hundred and fifty rooms. If you charge them an honest price, I bet you could make a pretty good living."

"Oh, I'm not that kind of painter," I tried to explain.

"Mostly exteriors, then?"

"No, actually, I—"

"Well," he began to chuckle, "What other kind of painters are there?"

"Billy paints portraits and still life," said Cara. "Artwork. Creative painting."

"Oh," said Mrs. Faulky. "That's very different."

"You're not serious," stated Mr. Faulky. "A man can't make a living painting a bowl of fruit!"

"Not at first, sir," I agreed. "But after I learn the proper techniques and get enough practise—"

"Thought I asked you to call me Henry," he said, and the table instantaneously became silent.

"He's only being polite," stated Cara.

"I didn't mean any disrespect, Mr. Faulky."

"I said, Henry!" he demanded, with a firm thump of his fist on the table.

I swallowed hard and glanced at Cara. She remained motionless.

"Henry it is, then," I squeaked, and then stared at the food I had been sampling on me own plate.

"I'm not familiar with too many schools of the arts," said Mrs. Faulky, as she tried to salvage the conversation. "Is there one near here?"

"Do you know, come to think of it, I don't really know," I realized.

Mr. Faulky coughed a little while stuffing some more of the brisket into his mouth.

"I left Ireland for Paris and sought out a very distinguished arts school, but they were only interested in French–speaking students."

"Now, I'm no geography teacher, but Paris *is* in France," stated Cara's father as sarcastically as possible.

"Aye, Henry, that it is," I replied.

"I'm a bit confused, then," said Mrs. Faulky. "How did you end up in Leocadia if you were staying in Paris?"

All eyes were on me now though Mr. Faulky continued to stuff his face.

"While I was over there I met Dr. Irel E. Vant, and—" Mr. Faulky began to cough and sputter as I continued, "and he offered to commission me paintings if I watched over things at his castle down the way."

Mr. Faulky was choking now, and the situation began to look serious.

"Are you okay, Pop?" asked Adam, as he patted his father on the back.

Soon he regained his composure, took in a deep breath, and his expression changed from one of hysterics to one of pure evil.

"Get out of my house!" he ordered spitting food chunks from his mouth.

"Pardon?" I asked.

"I won't say it twice," he said rising to his feet.

"Did I say something wrong?" I asked.

"OUT!" he raged.

"Father," said Cara.

"Henry!"cried her mother.

"If there's one thing I won't tolerate it's the mention of that man's name in my home! Let alone someone in cahoots with him!"

"You mean Dr. Vant?" I asked.

"You try my patience, boy!" he stormed and he grabbed me shirt by its collar and pulled me out of me seat.

"Put him down!" screamed Cara and she started pounding her fists on his arms. The force must have been like a flea on a dog; he knew she was there, but he was in control. With not another word he carried me to the door, opened it, and cast me out into the night.

"Heed my warning," he declared. "You stay away from my daughter! And if I ever catch you or him who ain't worthy of mentioning anywhere near my home, hell won't look so bad afterall!" Then he slammed the door.

I struggled to me feet and tried to catch me breath. I could hear the rampage continue from behind closed doors.

"How could you do that? How could you throw him out like that?" I heard Cara cry.

"You listen to me, girl. If I ever catch you so much as even looking at him again I'll ship you off to live with your Aunt Celia in Norquecaster!"

"I'll never forgive you for this father, I won't," she cried, her voice fading away.

"For God's, sake Henry," came the voice of his wife. "Have you lost your mind?"

"You know how I feel about that man! Anyone who has anything to do with him is no good for anyone else!"

"But William's just moved here."

"Don't get me started on that boy! He's a useless freeloader without a future and I'll be damned if he's going to steal mine! For God's sake, did you hear him, Annabelle? He called me Henry! You can't get any more disrespectful than that!"

"You made him call you that!"

"A real man would have stood his ground. Now, I've said all I'm going to say on the subject. We're going to sit down and finish our dinner!"

Some tears trickled down me face and I wiped them away with the sleeve of me shirt. I walked on, crushed and alone. I didn't know exactly what made him hate Dr. Vant so or what had made Dr. Vant so leery of their family, but Mr. Faulky's words cut into me soul like a hot knife into butter. Not all men made their livings killing themselves with physical labour, and I certainly wasn't going to. Still, it's hard when the world's against you. Certain professions aren't readily accepted, and Cara's father shared that view with me own brothers back in Ireland. I wanted to succeed at that moment more than ever. I'd show that monster of a man that I could support meself off me craft. I became determined and me dejection turned to a restless anger.

I made me way back to Vant Manor as quickly as I could, a rogue tear or two still streaming down me face as I tore open the front door, hastened from room to room, passing Mrs. McGillian in the hallway as I made me way into the library.

"Here now," I heard Mrs. McGillian call. "What's all this about?"

She trailed after me and found me in the library with a single lantern lighting the room from the table where I'd put it and watched as I tore at book after book, searching the shelves.

"What are you doing? Why aren't you at Cara's?" Then she must have caught sight of the drying tears. "What's wrong?"

"I *was* there," I explained as I searched. "We were all eating, when her father started belittling me dreams and making me feel like dirt. Then," said I, facing Mrs. McGillian with a book in me hand, "when he found out I live here, at Dr. Vant's, he had himself some kind of tantrum and threw me out of the house telling me never to see Cara again." I was in a convulsing bit of hysterics now meself. "And I heard him saying in so many words that I'll never amount to anything. But I'll show him! I am going to make it as an artist. I just need to learn the business side of it, and that's what I'm doing now." I returned to the bookshelf. "I'm going to find and read every godforsaken business book in Vant's library until I've come up with a foolproof plan to make me art into a living."

"Here, now," said Mrs. McGillian in a very calming tone. "Calm down, you can't let him get to you. He's just hot–headed, that's all." She forced me hands to drop the books and held me like me mother used to when I'd get upset. "It's all right, William. I believe in you, so does Cara, and so does Dr. Vant, else he never would have put up that kind of proposition."

"Vant, what is it about him and this place?" I asked as I left her arms. "Why doesn't he trust the locals, and why does Cara's father hate him so?"

"We can sort it all out in the morning. You need to relax, maybe get some sleep."

"Och, I can't sleep! Not now. I'll not sleep until I've found at least one book worth reading in this mess."

The library took up the North–West tower; its bookshelves lined the walls like wallpaper clear to the ceiling, and one long winding staircase led to each level.

"Then I'll make you a nice cup of tea," she said. "You'll need it if you're going to stay up all night. Just promise me you won't do anything foolish."

"Foolish? I'm upset Mrs. McGillian, not suicidal!"

"I'll go and get you that cup of tea, then."

The hours passed, Mrs. McGillian's tea came and went, and sometime in the night—after finding a stack of books to read—I fell asleep on a chair near the table with the lantern on it.

I woke the next morning to find Mrs. McGillian casting open the drapes allowing the morning light to shine in on me face.

"Good morning," she said.

"Mornin'," I replied wiping me eyes. "Mrs. McGillian, I want to apologize for me behaviour last night. I don't know what came over me."

"Don't give it another thought," she said. "Did you get any sleep?"

"Aye, that I did. I must've fallen asleep about an hour or so after drinking your tea."

"Chamomile has that affect on some people. Especially when you mix in a bit of lemongrass, spearmint, and a dash or two of peppermint."

"You bewitched me then, is that it?" I jested.

"Sometimes we all need help getting to sleep and calming our nerves."

"Too true, I thank you for that."

"Find the book you were looking for?" she asked, glancing over at a globe on a pedestal near me table.

"Some seem promising. Titbits really. There doesn't seem to be any on how to start or manage your own business."

She was now inspecting the globe rather curiously.

"Funny little globe, isn't it?" I asked. "Like the map on the doors to the West End, it's upside down. Oh, and get this," I added, as I leaned over and touched it. "Unlike most globes, this one doesn't spin. It doesn't move at all!"

She caressed it with her hands. "Perhaps it's hollow like the one Dr. Vant mentioned Mrs. Bellmore had in Eyam. Here, this is a bit strange, then," she said as her right hand came to a rest over Africa. "This continent's raised somewhat."

"What do you mean raised?" I asked.

"Raised, as in higher up; it sticks up just above the rest of the globe," and with that she gave it a little push. The globe made a *ca–chunk* sort of sound, and soon clockwork–like noises filled the air, and shortly thereafter, a six–foot section of one of the bookcases popped open like a door.

"Look at that," said Mrs. McGillian in awe.

"Aye, I'm lookin'. Only I'm not so sure I want to know where this one leads!"

She headed over to the entrance, and I hurried to catch up. As we opened the bookcase wider we saw a descending stone staircase.

"Is there any oil left in that lantern of yours?" she asked.

"No such luck, I'm afraid. But I could go fetch one of Vant's candelabras!"

"Hop to it then, Master William. Maybe we'll get some answers yet!"

When I returned with the candelabrum, we lit it and then crept down the stone staircase, heading deeper underground into the dark abyss. It grew much colder as we descended further down the winding stairs with stone walls enclosing them on all sides. At the bottom we followed a hallway and eventually came to a wooden door, which was unlocked. When we opened it we found ourselves in an extremely large, circular room that had a ceiling near twenty feet high.

Around the perimeter of the room, a three–foot–wide worktop followed the wall's curves most excellently. Beneath it were a series of cupboards, and in the centre of the room rested a raised stone platform that came up about four–feet high or so. More peculiar, though, were the objects that rested on the worktop and hung upon the great stone walls.

There were charts, scrolls, notebooks, inkwells, hundreds of broken pen nibs, and blots of ink stained on the counter. Strange masks hung from the walls, ugly faces they were—scary too. There were wind chimes and astrological charts, shelves full of oddities such as dark dolls made of cloth and racks of spices and herbs, but what took up most of the wall space was a large map of the upside–down world. It had numerous notes on it, as if Vant had stood on the worktop and jotted down ideas as they came to him. Certain specific locations had more notes than others, and all of it had us captivated.

"This must be his private study," reasoned Mrs. McGillian. "This must be where he figures out all of his great plans."

I strolled over to a spot on the counter and opened up a pamphlet of documents.

"Curious," said I, as I flipped through some other pamphlets beneath it. "These folders are full of official documents like certificates of birth, bank accounts, property deeds, and God himself knows what else. What do you make of it?"

I handed one of the pamphlets to Mrs. McGillian and she glanced through it. "I'll bet each one pertains to a different person. I don't think it'd be too much to suppose that each one of these is one of Dr. Vant's aliases."

"You mean like Nigel Palmer?" I asked.

"Exactly," she said. "He could be anyone at any time in any place."

"Aye, but why?"

"To blend in, to observe the world in its natural state or even to protect himself."

"But why all the secrecy?" I asked, as I left the pamphlets and browsed the room.

"Again, a question with multiple possibilities, perhaps each one a part of a bigger whole, like layers of an onion."

"That's a bit too deep for me, so early in the morning," said I.

"Do you think maybe we should leave?" asked Mrs. McGillian. "I mean he went to so much trouble to keep people out."

"That he did, but he told me I could go anywhere in Vant Manor that I wanted, just so long as I stayed out of the North–East tower. He said nothing about keeping out of private studies hidden behind secret entrances in his library bookcases."

"Yes, but it wouldn't be secret if he had told you about it."

"Why are you gettin' all righteous on me now?" I enquired. "You were just as eager to dig up some adventure as I was. Maybe even more so."

"Aye, William, I was," she agreed as her eyes shifted among various artefacts, including some of the frightening masks. "I just have this sudden overwhelming feeling of discomfort."

"You mean you're scared?"

"I mean I'm uneasy." She began to move back towards the entrance.

"All right," I stated. "But I want to take something up with us. Something to whet me curious appetite." I began to search the worktop.

"Make it snappy, please," she said, with a hint of desperation in her voice.

"Here," I announced, taking up a book of Vant's notes with the words *THE KRIDE* written upon the leather–bound cover in black ink. "This looks promising."

"What is it?" she asked, as I met her at the door.

"I'm not sure; the title says something, but I don't know exactly how to pronounce it."

"Then we'll take a look at it in the light of the day," she proposed and led the way up the staircase as I closed the door to Vant's study behind me.

Once we had reached the library again, I positioned the bookcase back into place, and Mrs. McGillian let out a great sigh of relief.

"It really was gettin' to you, wasn't it?" I asked.

"It was just the most unworldly feeling, but it's gone now. Let's go into the kitchen, and I'll fix us up some breakfast. I'll feel better after we eat. You can read to me about this," she glanced at the cover. "*Kride*." She paused, then concluded, "Yes, like 'bride' but with a 'K'."

And so I followed her into the kitchen, having forgotten all about the events of the prior evening, that had led me to Vant's hidden lair in the first place. There was just something enthralling about Dr. Vant, and whenever there arose an opportunity to learn more about him, we took it.

X
THE KRIDE

"Dearest Ristila," I read aloud to Mrs. McGillian from the pages of the leather–bound book titled *THE KRIDE*, which we'd only just retrieved. "That's his wife," I said.

"I might have guessed," she replied. "Anyhow I think I knew that. But go on, I'll boil some eggs while you read. I need to get my mind off the aura of that study."

"Right then." I cleared me throat and continued. "Dearest Ristila, I write to you this day, the twenty–first of October, 1865."

"Sixty–five?" asked Mrs. McGillian as she placed a pot of water onto the stove. "That's a year after he and I first met. After all that ruckus with the Morrigan."

"Aye, so 'tis," I acknowledged, and then went on with the text:

* * *

I write to you because you are my sanity, my inspiration, my bliss. Writing to you allows me to sort out my thoughts. You had always listened so patiently to my ravings when you were alive, even if you hadn't the least bit of interest. In death you are my sole confidant. Oh, how I long for you now! I can think of little else. My only digression is my work, and it is of this that I write to you tonight.

At present, I am in a railway station in Buda, just across the Danube River from Pest, awaiting a ride back to the civilization I've grown accustomed to. I am returning from a most interesting trip, perhaps *the* most intriguing of any I've endeavoured on before. It began when I arrived in Rumania one week ago. My destination was the Transylvanian sector of the Carpathian Mountains, and it was within a very small village called Craiontina, near Sibiu, that I sought out my interpreter and guide. Although Rumanian is a Romance language, I never had the opportunity to sit down to learn it myself.

When my coach pulled into Craiontina, it was pouring rain. The sky was bleak and overcast, and the Transylvanian Alps overlooked the land. This sight would undoubtedly cause most to feel a sense of sadness, despair, or one type of depression or another. To me, however, the dismal backdrop carried a certain bit of comfort, for as you know, I have always enjoyed a good storm. I find the rain to be invigorating if not soothing. Add to that the jagged peaks of the picturesque mountains, and indeed I had found a sense of tranquillity. The village, however, was a poor one, where all the shack–like homes were made completely of wood, as they had been for centuries.

I stood there—in the rain—with my umbrella in one hand hovering above my head, and a carpet bag in the other, which I then used to remove a sheet of stationery from my inner coat pocket where I had written down the address of the man who was to be my companion on that day. I followed the street, gazing up at the addresses, and eventually found the one I was looking for, though it appeared at first as if there were no one at home. I rapped upon the rotting door and waited. Nothing. I knocked louder this time. I did so love the rain and usually the cold, but the chill was beginning to get the better of me. I must have knocked for a quarter of an hour before the door finally opened. The man in front of me was rather short, with a bushy grey moustache, matching eyebrows and a cap upon his head, and he was dressed in the usual peasant attire.

"Owen Hubert?" he asked in rough English, betraying nothing in his demeanour.

"Of Halperstein, Whitberry, and Associates," I lied. You see, my darling, I had used an alias to acquire information about the region and was acting on behalf of a made–up brokerage firm that I had claimed was foreclosing on some property within the mountains.

* * *

"There he goes again," interrupted Mrs. McGillian. "Another assumed name," and with that she lowered some eggs into the boiling water.

I nodded, then continued with Vant's words:

* * *

The man looked at me doubtfully. Then he stepped aside to bid me entry. His home was constructed of two rooms, and there was but a solitary candle to light them both from a table near his pot–bellied stove.

"I've been knocking for quite some time, Mr. Von Orten. I cannot imagine that you could not hear me from within one of these two rooms," I asserted.

"I was finishing my dinner," said he, pointing to an empty plate on the table near the candle.

"So I see. Well, sir, I shall be most monetarily obliged to you if we could take to our trek as soon as possible."

"That is what is wrong with you foreigners, you businessmen, always in a hurry."

"Quite right, Mr. Von Orten, you certainly are an intelligent man." I knew I was acting pompous, but it was all part of the act. I had a role to play if I was to be believed.

"Be better to wait until the storm clears," he added, as if that statement were going to shut me down.

"How long would you suppose the storm will last?" I asked.

"Two, three days," said he, devoid of any emotion.

"Mr. Von Orten, I am on a tight schedule. I have other duties to attend to. Might your mind be swayed by a doubling of our negotiated fee?"

"Not even triple," he reasoned in his own way.

"Then I do believe we are wasting each others' time. If you'll excuse me," said I as I reopened the door through which I'd come. "I have another guide to find."

"There is no one else who will take you where you seek to go. Best to wait, I think."

"And why might that be, Mr. Von Orten?"

"The people are afraid," he answered, while entering the other room. "I was the only one in town to agree to your firm's request, because I need the money. But I will not go in the rain," he added. He sat on his tattered bed and began removing his shoes. "Dark things happen during storms, Mr. Hubert—unnatural things—and I will not bear witness to them."

"Bah, nothing more than local folklore, superstition at its best," I stated firmly.

"Could be, but then, I am not willing to risk it. If you want to go, we wait until the rain stops. Unless you want to find it on your own?"

"Then I have no choice, Mr. Von Orten. We shall wait. But if it's so, our initial offer stands," and I closed the door once more.

That evening I stayed at Mr. Von Orten's and pressed him for any information he could give me on our destination, Castle DeCarlo, formerly Castle Grigoryev. Although he claimed to know very little, he explained that ten months prior news had spread that Oleg Grigoryev had passed on and that an Italian man named Giovanni DeCarlo had purchased the estate. He proceeded to say that no one had seen DeCarlo move in and that, in truth, no one had ever seen DeCarlo *or* Grigoryev for that matter. To this I laid down a web of fabrication, saying that my brokerage had issued Mr. DeCarlo a mortgage, which he had failed to uphold, and that we were now going to foreclose on the estate if he could not produce the back payments.

As luck would have it, the rain had stopped sometime during the night, and the morning sun rose to dry up the watery remains. Towards this Mr. Von Orten seemed rather impartial but nevertheless he gathered his gear: a heavy coat, some hiking boots, a rifle, and a hiking stick. The journey to Castle DeCarlo would be made on foot, as no one in town owned a carriage and those that owned horses, he assured me, would not be willing to lend them out for such an occasion.

We departed shortly after eleven. As I did not have a hiking stick I was forced to use my umbrella for the job and it proved very useful as the path Von Orten took me on was quite steep. The ascension took nearly four hours, and as we climbed higher, the air grew much colder, and I noted that the ground at this altitude was covered with snow. At last, I laid my gaze upon Castle DeCarlo. There she stood, an ashen–grey nightmare nestled atop a cliff as if she had been carved from the mountain itself. The signature architecture was quite unidentifiable, though it was clear that it was an extraordinarily large castle, much larger than Vant Manor, made purely of stone that had the look of centuries' worth of weathering and decay.

"I will wait for you here," stated Von Orten.

"I beg your pardon," said I. "You mean that you'll not be accompanying me inside?"

"That is correct."

"But are you not my interpreter?"

"I do not speak Italian."

Rather than argue with him I agreed that he should wait outside. I wasn't exactly sure of what would transpire inside anyway, and it was better that he have no part in it. It would allow me to keep up appearances in the future. Thus, I trudged up some two hundred feet to the main doors; there were two, both nearly eighteen feet high. Mr. Von Orten was no longer in view. I looked about for bell or a knocker and when I had found the bell cord an odd feeling came over me. I would suggest that it was the old feeling that I wasn't alone, but it was more than that. I could not place it. It wasn't as if I were being watched, but rather felt, on some esoteric level. I contemplated my situation. I knew that if I pulled the bell cord there would be no answer. To knock would be equally fruitless. You see, darling, I already knew *what* lived there.

I decided it would be best to seek out the nearest window and, as luck would have it, I found one approximately twenty feet above me. I then opened my carpet–bag, which contained a pamphlet of notes, a rope with a grappling iron, a packet of matches, a small case with three pint–sized glass bottles wrapped in padded cloth, and a few other objects that I will explain later. I naturally removed the rope with the grappling iron, closed up the bag, and swung the rope in a circular motion around my head until at last releasing it—in a perfect trajectory, I might add. The grappling iron shot directly through the glass window, which in turn was shattered. I was not worried, however, because I knew that the owner was already aware of my presence. This would be the only way in.

So I then tucked my umbrella beneath my arm and placed the other end of the rope through the handle of the bag, pushing it before me with each advance as I climbed to the window. Upon reaching my destination, I used my elbow to break open a suitable entry hole and struggled to get myself and the carpet bag inside. The whole ordeal seemed as if were taking forever, and I nearly dropped the bag twice. Still, though, I had prevailed. I was inside the castle. And what a castle it was! Darkness enveloped the hallway I had entered, and though I could make out little, the furnishings appeared to be rather lavish. The castle seemed to me a contradiction. As dull as it had seemed from the outside, the inside gave the impression of being quite remarkable, even though I couldn't really see it.

In fact, the only light within the hallway came from the very window I ascended through; it was a dim periwinkle, hardly a glow, but my eyes soon grew accustomed. I searched the corridor and found a single unlit candle resting within its holder upon an obsidian side table that sat beneath a painting of a tropical paradise. I produced a match from my bag, lit the candle, and continued on my hunt.

It was there, somewhere, and I would find it. I searched from room to room, each wrapped in the stateliest decor, until I descended a staircase to the main floor. I felt an instant surge of energy—it seemed to coalesce before me—and there, at the bottom of the staircase stood a tall, solemn figure shrouded in black robes. Its cranium was quite large, nearly twice the length of my own, and its skin was a stark white, that slightly reflected an array of blue hues from a distant window somewhere unseen. Its eyes were of the exotic sort, and its facial features were more Nubian than European, but one thing was most obvious: It was not Italian.

"Mr. DeCarlo?" I asked.

There was no answer.

"Mr. Grigoryev? No? Hmmm, indeed. Well, my name is Owen Hubert and—"

"You are intruding in my home." It spoke in a firm whisper.

"Do be honest," I said, as I continued down the staircase until I stood beside it, nearly two and a half feet shorter than it, with my candle illuminating the pale, placid face. "If I had rung the bell, would you have let me in?"

"No," it said.

"So then you see I had no other choice," I then paused and took a good look at it. "My, my, you certainly are a most intriguing creature."

"You realize," it said. "Now that you have entered, I cannot allow you to leave this castle."

"I had thought you might say something to that effect, yes," I answered.

"And still you came?"

"I am rather stubborn."

"Foolish," it corrected.

"To each his own," I said with a smile.

We then stood silent for a few moments, and I could nearly feel its energy probing my thoughts to no avail. It wore a black robe and had long, string–like thinning hair.

"As I see it," said I, "we have two courses of action to choose from. One would be your typical game of cat and mouse from which I narrowly escape with my life and live to tell the tale of the evil vampire in the mountains who tried to thirst upon my blood. Or two, we could handle this like civilized people and discuss my reason for coming here over a nice cup of tea. You will, of course, be the one who makes this decision, as this is your home and I am in no position to force my will upon you. Now then, which option do you fancy?"

Within a mere fraction of a second its hand came hurtling through the air in an attempt to slap me, giving me barely enough time to smack it away with my umbrella, the force of which bent it in half. Then suddenly it came at me like a whirlwind of flying slashes, chops, and side–swipes, all of which I narrowly avoided. My best bet, as I saw it, was to get behind the creature and gain some distance, and then try to rationalize with it. I moved to one side to confuse it, then darted to the other side, and actually pulled off my little stunt . I was now behind it and gaining some ground.

"This isn't exactly what I had in mind, still I must admit that I am not surprised," I informed my attacker.

When I looked back, it leapt up on top of me; somehow it had gained the distance I had tried to widen. My carpet bag and deformed umbrella went flying into the air in opposite directions, and I found myself pinned to the floor by the creature, which leaned forward to stare me in the face.

"Tell me why I should not drink from your veins here and now," it demanded in the same firm whisper, but this time with a bit of phlegm spraying my forehead and its nose a trifling two inches from my own.

"Because Atlanteans don't drink blood," I stated directly.

Almost immediately its rage shifted, and it struggled to find its most intimidating face.

* * *

"Hang on—Atlanteans?" I questioned aloud, rereading Dr. Vant's handwriting.

"Atlanteans you question, but vampires you don't?" asked Mrs. McGillian.

I gave her a sour face. "Better read on for an explanation," I decided, and picked up where I had left off.

* * *

"You know not of what you speak ," it insisted.

"I know quite a good deal more than you can imagine," I replied. "How else would I know how to protect my thoughts from you?"

"You don't think that I will kill you?"

"Kill, perhaps. Drink my blood? Doubtful. Most likely, as I have previously mentioned, you would choose to scare the wits out of me so that I can spread your demonic legacy that allows you to live out your immortal days in virtual peace."

The creature's eyes expanded, and I knew I had got to it.

"Now then," said I. "Do get off me, this floor is hurting my sciatica!" To my surprise it did just as I asked, and even helped me stand up. "How do I know you're not trying to trick me into trusting you so that you can take the final blow?" I asked as I gathered my strewn belongings.

"You don't," it replied, but this time in its full and natural voice, which was, on the whole, rather deep yet androgynous.

"Fair is fair," I reasoned.

"You must tell me how you came to know of such things."

"In time," I agreed. "But I will have that cup of tea I spoke of earlier. It's rather cold in this dungeon of yours."

"I've grown accustom to the cold over the years…" it said, trailing off. It paused then and turned abruptly to look at me. "I go by many names, but my title is 'Kride'."

"Yes, I know all about your aliases: Oleg Grigoryev, Giovanni DeCarlo, countless others. How else can you live forever in a world of mortals? I too know something about multiple personas. My real name is Dr. Irel E. Vant. I'm from England."

"It would seem that we have much to discuss," said the Kride. "Come, I will brew some tea."

I retrieved my bag and the deformed umbrella, which the Kride bent back into shape for me without effort, then followed the Kride as it led me through a series of halls until we reached a large sitting room. The room overlooked the valley, and I could see that it was snowing outside. I was not surprised to discover that Von Orten had apparently deserted me. I had a clear view of where I had left him.

There was a small fire burning in its place, and there were some cushiony parlour chairs, a sofa, and other antique furniture. The floor was covered by an enormous bright violet area rug with tessellated patterns produced by zigzagging lines of golden thread. Its impeccable craftsmanship left me without much to say. My host bent down to the tea table in the centre of the room, where a kettle contraption sat. It was silver, bulbous, and stood on four legs just above a small metal cylinder with a tiny hole in its side.

The Kride removed a winding key from its pocket, much like I've seen used on old watches, and inserted the key into the hole of the small cylinder. The Kride twisted the key, and I heard a faint snapping sound, of which produced a blue flame from the centre of the cylinder to heat the kettle.

"Please, take a seat." It motioned to the sofa behind me.

"Thank you," said I as I took my seat.

"I want to know what you know and," it thought for a moment as it took a seat in the chair across from me, "how you've come to know it."

"I am an archaeologist; I study old things left behind by ancient civilizations. I dig them up, consult global experts, and pose a conjecture."

"A conjecture?"

"An educated guess as to what the object might have been used for. For example, a few years ago I received a letter from an old classmate who was down in the Caribbean excavating a Mayan temple. The Maya, a people native to Meso–America, were conquered by the Spanish in the sixteenth century. Their language, and therefore their culture, was practically outlawed. My friend had been at the University of San Carlos searching for a text to aid him in the translation of the hieroglyphics he had found at the temple. It was at the library that he and his colleague stumbled upon a copy of an ancient scripture called the *Popol Vuh*, a communal book that explained the creation beliefs of a Mayan tribe and told of a time of terribly cold weather.

After receiving his letter, I boarded the next ship to Guatemala. When I reviewed the materials, I realized they added fuel to a theory I had: that the continent of Atlantis was actually North and South America combined and that the capital city—the heart of Atlantis—had been destroyed by an age of ice brought on quite accidentally by their power source, which was a grid of energy transmitted by great radiating gemstones fuelled by either the sun or the moon. This grid of energy, which your people learned to utilize, brought on their downfall, as it increased the earth's gravitational pull and derailed the cyclical passing of an otherwise harmless comet, forcing it to collide with the earth. The results of the impact caused a heating up the atmosphere followed ultimately by a blocking out of the sun. The polar icecaps melted at a rate still unsurpassed due to the extreme heat, and the sea level rose to submerge the capital of Atlantis. Shortly thereafter, the rest of the area froze over in the age of ice brought on by the blocking of the sun."

"And what of this comet?"

"I believe it struck the main source of the energy grid, which was located within the capital itself, and helped the rising sea to bury what was left of the city into the depths of what is now the Caribbean. Even the name Maya comes from the name of the first daughter of the Greek Titan, Atlas, who held up the celestial spheres of the universe, though it is often written with an 'I' instead of a 'Y', Maia. Even the first king of Atlantis was named Atlas. Could that not have been because in some sense it was true and that the ancient Greeks had learned of this tale, thereby creating this Titan in the image of a king whose people brought down the heavens?"

The Kride sat across from me, rather perplexed. I couldn't decipher whether it was because I'd left something out and therefore got things wrong, or if it was because I'd got it exactly right. Something told me it was the latter.

"You see," I tried to explain. "My knowledge is an accumulation of years of research from multiple sources. To identify each thread would take endless amounts of time. Now I, unlike yourself, am not immortal and thus cannot afford to waste the time I have."

"You seem to know everything," it stated. "Why do you come to me?"

"I know bits and pieces. From an archaeological standpoint I am the leading theorist on Atlantis, but on an anthropological level I am left uneasy. I know about the objects but I want to learn more about the people, your culture, things that left no clue as to how your community thrived. The little I've scraped up about your culture I've taken from the offspring of your satellite states: the Chinese, the Egyptians, the Maya, the Africans, the Arabs—in short, the whole of the world. But I have no direct correlation to the primary source. And as you are the sole remaining survivor of that empire, I can only get the answers I seek from you."

The kettle began to whistle and the Kride twisted the winding key in the opposite direction, forcing the flame to die out. It then poured the hot water over two cups of dried leaves on set saucers and returned the contraption to its base. I couldn't help but notice a peculiar lavender tint to the water.

The Kride then focused its exotic eyes on me in a straight yet sombre way.

"Come," it said. "I wish to show you something." It stood up, cup in hand and shepherded me along. "Bring your cup, the tea is no good cold," it added. We walked down a long corridor and up a flight of stairs; when we'd reached another hall we came to a stop at a doorway. The Kride opened it and led me out onto an enormous stone balcony overlooking the backdrop to the castle's rear. There—to my bewilderment—lay a sea of headstones nestled within the mountains, completely surrounded and secret. By this time the snow had begun to accumulate on top of the headstones. The scene overwhelmed me, and for the first time, in a long while, I was left without words. I stood there for a moment trying to contemplate the gravity of the situation.

"These graves," I began to say.

"These memorials," it corrected. "Our people did not believe in burying their dead. Cremation was the chosen way. Some, those who governed, were entombed within temples, but the majority had their bodies burned. Those stones you see before you have no bodies buried beneath them."

"But we've never found any such stones in Meso–America," I stated.

"This is because Atlanteans did not leave any markers."

"But these—"

"This was my decision. After the fall of our great city, Pontus, there remained a large number of survivors. The survivors were power figures, called the Posse, who had drunk from the elixir of immortality—an impressive name for nothing more than a specialized tea derived from steeping our energy–radiating crystals in hot water. This tea, *aeternus*, prevented those who drank it from the toil of age and the death of natural causes." The Kride was now gazing out over the balcony railing as he held his own tea cup.

"After the fall of Pontus most of us went out into the world, going our separate ways to start anew. The Posse were a hermaphroditic breed of Atlanteans, highly regarded for their knowledge of how each sex experienced the world. They were honoured as power figures and given the gift of everlasting life to teach their knowledge to the future generations of Atlantis," it then turned back to face me. "I should like to differentiate the term 'power figure' from how you might interpret it. The Posse were not rulers but rather teachers, guardians of *Awen*. *Awen*—essence—is our term for the all integrated concept of being, which is present in every *thing*. The Kride was at the centre of the Posse, even the title translates into 'the all–knowing'.

"Truly intriguing," I uttered whilst finishing the contents of my cup. "But that doesn't explain the graveless tombstones."

"Throughout the centuries the Posse saw a shift in mankind. Gone was the thirst for knowledge, replaced by the quest for land and power by force. These new men even robbed the Posse of their title, turning the word 'possession' into one of greed and control over another. Eventually the Posse went into hiding and ultimately all found their way to my home, here in these mountains. We devised a myth to seclude ourselves from mortal mankind and became vampires. For nearly a millennium this seemed to work, but then a new plague overcame the Posse: depression. The meaning of life had been vanquished amongst them; they had lost their will to live and as such came to me for the only therapy available to them: death. As the Kride, only I knew the ways to terminate an otherwise immortal life. There were two: One, sever the head; or two, silence the heart. As I performed these brutal procedures, after being heavily persuaded by the very individual, I burned the remains and erected a stone to the memory of each here, in what I named the Valley of the Posse."

"Nearly unfathomable," I uttered.

"The story of my people is nothing more than tragedy. But I sense that there is something else you are searching for. Is there not another reason you have sought me out?"

I was amazed at the Kride's uncanny intuition. It was pointless for me to go on concealing my main purpose for coming. So I told it. I explained everything in great detail and when I had finished the Kride seemed somewhat moved.

"Now *there* is something hindering on the unfathomable," it remarked. "Even I would not attempt such a feat. You are certain that these three pints of my blood will prove useful in this endeavour?"

"You are the all–knowing; surely you can see its importance," I suggested.

"All knowing as I am, the centuries still feed on my memory as they would on any human. I am not privy to a single instance of your plan ever being attempted by an Atlantean or even our descendants. Still, I understand enough of the ancient tales to believe that what you strive for may—however unlikely—actually be possible. Therefore, Irel, I shall provide you with what you seek, but on one very *finite* condition."

"Anything that I may give," I offered.

"After you take what you need, you will end my depression and set me free."

"You mean … kill you?"

"I mean restore my mortality."

"Understood. You have my word."

"Then follow me," said the Kride. "We must act in haste so that neither of us may change our minds."

* * *

"He wouldn't really kill the poor creature would he?" I asked Mrs. McGillian as she finished off her eggs.

"I don't know. Part of me doesn't trust it. Suppose it's just stringing Dr. Vant along until it can take him out when his guard is down."

"I disagree," I argued. "We've no idea what it's like to live for centuries. I had a grandfather, who lived to be ninety–eight. He used to sit up in bed, smoke his pipe, stare out the window, and complain about how death had abandoned him and he wished they could settle their differences, because he was flat out tired of living in a filthy broken bed with useless children and his loud–mouthed grandchildren."

"What a lovely outlook on life," she said, and then paused. "But listen to us go on as if this whole tale of his were true! Still, might as well find out what happens, I suppose. Read on," commanded Mrs. McGillian.

* * *

Before I had time to stop it, the Kride had disappeared back into the castle from whence we had come. I gathered my thoughts together and followed post–haste. Once back in the upper hallway I glanced around in the darkness until I heard the Kride's voice.

"This way," it called. "To the main floor."

"Forgive my lack of enthusiasm," I announced as I descended the staircase. "But I have so much more to learn from you. Perhaps we could postpone the actual finale a week or so until—" Suddenly the Kride was in front of me on the staircase staring into my eyes.

"Out of the question," it stated. "Your coming here today was an answer to my prayers. You are here as an ambassador of *Awen*, you are here to restore balance to the essence. There are unseen forces working to counteract your destiny here today. We must not delay." With that the Kride pressed onward, and I soon found myself in a large room in the back of the castle with large window panes that let in the pale blue light that reflected off the snow–covered tombstones, if I may even call them that at this point.

The room was fairly devoid of furniture, save for a large stone platform that the Kride knelt before. It smoothed its hands out along the surface of the ten–foot long stone and then turned to look up at me.

"When I am at rest, this castle will belong to you, this castle and all of its secrets." The Kride took to its feet once more and pulled open a stone drawer from under the top of the platform. It removed a long wooden spike with various hieroglyphics carved into it and a stone hammer that reminded me of Mjölnir, the hammer wielded by the Norse god, Thor. "You must forgive the brutality of this act. My guillotine was broken during the last ritual."

"I hate to bring this up," I hesitated. "But I believe I should extract the pints of blood while you're still alive."

The Kride only tittered quietly. "It would seem to me that you are more the vampire than I." It then removed a very large white mask from the stone drawer and closed it again.

The Kride held up the mask. It was striking, a sight to behold. It was elongated, and pure white; except for two large, coal–black almond–shaped eye slits fixed at symmetrical angles. Its presence forced the hairs on my neck to stand erect. The shape of the mask reminded me of something along the lines of a jackal or the skull of a buffalo. At its top were two large pointed ear or horn–like structures, beneath them an expressionless face, and lower still an extra line forming either an oblong jaw or a snout. Perhaps the most intriguing aspect of the mask was that it was one solid material, as though it might have been carved from a solid slab of ivory. Simple as it was, it was also very striking—strikingly good or bad, you could not decipher which, yet striking nonetheless.

"This is the ceremonial mask of the Kride," spoke the Kride. In the days of Atlantis it was worn in educational service, in ritual, and in addressing the people. Since then I have worn this mask during every silencing, and I now pass it along to you to wear in during mine."

"You want me to wear that?" I asked. "But I couldn't. Surely I am not worthy."

"*You* will be the all–knowing one now. The knowledge you possess is your validation, and setting my soul free shall be your initiation." The Kride set the mask upon the stone surface beside the stake and hammer. "Now, how shall you extract this blood?"

Taking the Kride's cue, I set my carpet bag atop the stone slab and opened it. I removed the glass bottles from their case, unwrapped them from the padding and set them aside. Thankfully, they were all intact. Next I removed a pouch, opened it, and withdrew some tubing, a small hand pump, and a syringe. The Kride remained silent as I prepped the materials. I attached one end of the tube to the top of the syringe and the other to the small hand pump that fit over one of the glass bottles.

"Please," I coaxed. "Take a seat and roll up your sleeve."

The Kride sat down on the stone slab and pulled back its left sleeve. I then took some of the remaining rope from the grappling iron and tied it around the Kride's left arm tightly, in a tourniquet style so as to aid with the removal of blood. I took the Kride's arm and inserted the syringe. Once it was inserted, I pressed down on the pump, and the blood began to flow through the tubing and into the pint–sized glass bottle. I continued in this manner until each of the three bottles was filled. I then returned the pump and the rubber stoppered bottles to the case. I covered the syringe with a tattered cloth and placed it in my coat pocket until I could discard it.

"Humankind has indeed come a long way," stated the Kride.

"Agreed, but we are not yet at the level of your people, and in that we are not even what we once were."

"You are very philosophical, my friend," it said.

"Thank you," said I. "Well, now that I am finished I believe it is my turn to keep up my end of the bargain. And the sooner I get it over with, the better off we'll both be."

"Now you're thinking like a Kride," it stated.

"So how do we do this?"

The Kride stood up and removed its top robe, revealing its large bosom and a pendant with a golden Yggdrasil, the world tree. Around its waist the Kride remained dressed in a *schenti*, a skirt–like loincloth. I had not expected the Kride to disrobe, and now found the idea of planting a wooden stake in its breast all the more difficult. Although I knew the Kride to be between genders its breasts were so feminine that I stood there fascinated by nature's irony. Driving the wedge into its cleavage would be like doing so to you my love, as my eye has only ever seen your bare bosom before.

The Kride took up the mask and came towards me. I leant my head down so that the Kride could place the decoration on my head, and when I opened my eyes the world became a deep green colour. I realized then that emerald coverings protected the eye slots, though they had seemed black from a distance. Saying nothing, the Kride untied its schenti and discarded it upon the floor. I suppose that wearing the ceremonial mask somehow made me worthy of witnessing the Kride's last great secret. It returned to the stone slab and lay down upon it, exposing its unique combination of genitalia. I then took up the stake and the hammer and made my way to the end of the slab where the Kride's head rested.

"There is a stone button just below the lip of the slab," it explained. "Depress it for me, please." I did as the Kride asked, and—like clockwork—stone slots in the slab opened and iron shackles emerged and clasped around the Kride's wrists and ankles.

"But why confine yourself in this manner?" I asked. My voice muffled by the mask, sounded otherworldly.

"It is the body's natural response to prevent death. No matter how strong my will may be, the body is a separate entity, a vessel that exists only to live."

"I never thought of it that way," I replied, as I prepared to aim the stake.

"Wait," it ordered. "If you really are to become the next Kride it is fitting that you know something else."

"Such as?"

"Within the Americas exists a tribe of people directly related to the Atlanteans who have never had external breeding. They live in a world unto themselves, pure, but without knowledge of their true history. They are the Durwaihiccora and they practise the ancient ways on which Pontus was founded upon. They were my people's last hope at a second chance, a chance to start over. Seek them out and from them you can learn more than I can explain about the culture of Atlantis. Perhaps you may even unlock the keys to *Awen* itself."

"That was very selfless of you, and I thank you for all you have given to me."

"It was my honour, *Kride*," it spoke, addressing me by its title for the first time.

I then aimed the stake vertically, with the point resting in its cleavage just below the Yggdrasil pendant. "One question," I mentioned as I prepared the hammer. "What name shall I engrave upon your memorial?"

"My true name is…" The Kride's face seemed to lose colour.

"Yes?"

"There is no time, you must drive the stake now."

"But—"

"Now!" it yelled.

I raised the hammer and struck once. A blood–curdling scream filled the air. To my surprise, it did not come from the Kride but rather from a distance, at the entrance to the room. There, in the doorway, stood a tall thin man with elven–like features and long white hair. Beside him stood a shorter man, perhaps five feet tall, with long black hair, who was poking his beak–like nose into the room to see what the other was shrieking about, and in doing so resembled a scrawny little troll.

"Don't stop!" ordered the Kride in a gurgle, as blood filled its lungs. "Hurry!"

Abiding by the Kride's wishes, I continued to hammer with all of my power, driving the stake further into the heart of the world's last true Atlantean, as its body went into spasms and blood erupted from within. The Kride's body fought back against the shackles, but soon it could not hold out any longer. The white–haired man sprinted towards me howling madly. When the man reached me, it was evident that the deed had been done. I stood before the body of the Kride wearing the blood–stained white mask, while the man felt for a pulse.

"You fool!" he stormed. "You do not know what you have done!" he turned on me as his companion crept closer. "This being was the last of a noble race of people! A race that is now lost forever on account of your actions! I was going to learn the secret to immortality! Do you have any idea how long I've sought out the key to immortality? I'm an alchemist, it is what I do! It is what I live for! And you have robbed me of it! You have no idea what I've had to endure to try to pry that secret from this creature. Do you know what it is like having sexual relations with a hermaphrodite? I was this creature's servant of affection and I despised the whole affair. Now all of my agony was for nothing. Nothing!"

"I didn't know the Kride had a mate," I said.

"Mate? Mate! Do not insult me! Had the Kride not sent me into town on a fool's errand I would have been a god. A *god*!"

"Then," I said, removing the mask as I backed away, "I did the right thing. Clearly you were not worthy. The Kride must have known that."

"What?" he demanded as he laying his eyes upon my face. As he did so, his companion's eyes grew large with a sudden realization.

"Spencer," squealed the smaller man. "Have we not seen this man before?"

"What is this you speak of, Malachi?"

"Think London, think the Morrigan," stated Malachi.

"The Morrigan?" asked Spencer. "Of course!" He pointed at me. "You were the highest bidder at that auction, Dr. Irelanous or something. They kicked you out and awarded the Morrigan to the Earl of Norquecaster!"

"And it was later stolen," added Malachi.

"You stole it, didn't you?" asked Spencer. "That crystal, mistaken as a fancy diamond, is the philosopher's stone: the main ingredient in obtaining immortal stature. That must be why you sought out the Kride, to learn how to activate the Morrigan. You *will* take me to it!"

* * *

"White hair you said?" asked Mrs. McGillian.

"Aye, that's what Vant's written. I think you may have mentioned them."

"Yes, I do have memory of two men who fit that description. I remember them only because they bid against Dr. Vant for the Morrigan."

"You mean to tell me this whole fairy tale Vant's written to his late wife is true?" I asked.

"I wasn't there when he wrote it, but it certainly seems to at least be grounded in true events, though I suppose most legends and myths are."

"Best to continue and find out," I proposed, and continued the text.

* * *

"I believe you are mistaken," said I. "My name is Owen Hubert and I am—"

"Going to die, unless you take me to the Morrigan!" stormed Spencer, his nostrils flaring.

Contemplating the gravity of the situation, I said nothing but instead hurdled the blood–stained hammer through the air at them, grabbed my carpet bag, and ran out another doorway.

"After him you fool," I heard Spencer shout as I ascended the nearest staircase. I ran faster than seemed humanly possible, made it upstairs, and came to a dead end at the balcony overlooking the Valley of the Posse. Within seconds Malachi was upon the scene, no doubt tracking the blood dripping from my hands. Darkness had overtaken the mountains and the moon barely shed any light from behind growing grey clouds as the falling snow quickened its pace. That's when I caught sight of Malachi's sharpened fingernails.

"One last chance," proclaimed Malachi. "Tell us where the Morrigan is!"

"Just what are you?" I sneered, "some kind of apprentice? A troll? Or just Spencer's flunky?"

He growled angrily. "I am Malachi Lachgustav, maleficium maestro."

"Honestly," I taunted. "Do you hear yourself? Why not just say sorcerer of the silly?"

Ignoring me, he reached into his pocket and produced a handful of powder.

He then chanted some gibberish under his breath and then flung the powder at me. I only just evaded the powder, which struck the stone railing with a small explosion that left a hole where it had stood.

"You still question my power?" he asked.

"Gunpowder and a match, for all I know or care," I said, and I struck him with my right fist. We then locked in battle of brawn, fists flying every which way. "All right, then," I stated after the scuffle. "I suppose

I can humour you."

"What nonsense do you speak?" he asked, striking me in the side.

We had turned now, and I was facing him with my back to the doorway.

"How did that rubbish of yours go again?" I did my best to repeat his gibberish and then struck Malachi's pocket with my fist where I knew the powder rested. In the instantaneous explosion Malachi was thrown backwards through the air, passed through the hole in the railing, and fell down to the valley below, where he struck his head on a memorial stone.

"Perhaps it was magic after all," I muttered aloud.

"Perhaps you shall share his fate," came the voice of Spencer, and I felt a sudden rush of force slam into me from behind. I fell over the balcony, but managed to grab the edge on my way down, smearing the Kride's remaining blood from my hands onto the stone.

"Now; the Morrigan or your life," demanded Spencer, as he lifted his foot over my hand.

"Very well, you have me. The Morrigan resides in my English home, but only I can take you there."

He bent down and grasped my arm with his. "If you try to betray me, you *will* die."

"I understand," I said as he pulled me up. "There's just one thing," I added as I took to my feet.

"What?" he asked.

"I'm not a very trustworthy fellow," and with that I pelted the man across the face with a backhanded slap and leapt up unto the railing, from which I pulled myself up to the vaulted snow–covered roof of the castle—in retrospect, probably not the best choice. Still, though, as I climbed and slipped, climbed and slipped, behind me I could hear my attacker cursing his way after me.

The wind whipped, the snow stung like ice pellets, and I found myself at the castle's highest point. All around me the white of the whirling snow mingled with the dark of night nearly blinding me in their insensible dance. Somewhere I heard a crunch in the snow, and I turned to face back the way I came.

"Do you really think you can keep me from my destiny?" Spencer's voice asked, as it cut through nature's deafening silence. Slowly his pale face came into view in what muted light was left, and he stopped directly before me. "I am destined to live forever, I am destined to become a god!"

The time had come, the end was nearing, and it was at that moment that I began to think about joining you in eternity, my love. I was reminded of our life together, what my life had come to and how it would all end with this crazed villain. But I had come so close in my quest. Too close to let this pitiful man claim dominion over me. Desperately I fumbled my pockets, and then suddenly it came to me. It was my only chance and I took it. With the swiftness of a vampire, nay a Kride, I removed the discarded syringe from my coat pocket and drove it into Spencer's left eye. He fell backwards, clutching his wound, and slipped off the snowy summit, plummeting downward somewhere far into the wintery abyss. I then collapsed in the snow, exhausted and stupefied.

Later, when I'd returned to the castle below, I retrieved the bodies of the Kride and of Malachi. I burned them separately. The Kride's pyre perked up the gloom of the Valley of the Posse as I imagined the Kride had enlightened them all in life. The icy breeze curled the smoke high into the air, where I am certain it diffused into that natural essence the Kride had spoken of.

There was much weighing on my mind then. There still is.

* * *

"Go on," urged Mrs. McGillian. "How's it end?"

"That *is* how it ends," I declared. "That's all he's written."

"Are you serious?" she questioned and stood up to have a look for herself. "Well, I'll be."

"It doesn't make any sense, though. None of it! The whole thing's too bizarre to be true. There's no such thing as an Atlantean! And even if there was, what would Dr. Vant need with bottles of its blood?"

"True," agreed Mrs. McGillian. "But then why would he go to such lengths to hide this manuscript?"

"Do you think he's daft?"

"I'm not sure. But I would like to know what all this life's quest claptrap means."

"Aye. You know, on some level I can't help but find the whole story a bit inspiring."

"How do you mean?" she asked.

"I just seem to have this incredible urge to paint, perhaps a snow scene or some mountains." I sat still for a moment and let the idea fully form in me head. "Yes, I think that's a grand idea," said I as I rose from me seat.

"What about your eggs? They've probably gone cold now."

"'Tis all right, Mrs. McGillian. I'm not very hungry anyway. I'll do some painting to work up me appetite. But I'll warn you, now," said I with a grin. "You best have a feast with all the trimmin's when I'm finished. 'Cause nothing works me up more than gettin' out me thoughts on a blank canvas!" And with that I took up the pamphlet, gave the old gal a peck on the cheek, and headed off for me makeshift studio.

XI
KINDRED
PART ONE: SHEDDING INNOCENCE

For the next few chapters I will be joined by a guest author, who will explain how he came to know our unusual friend, Dr. Vant, and will transcribe a series of events that—while unrelated to the tale I too will tell herein—merit being presented to you now, in unison. I ask you to draw your own comparisons. The guest author is named Kamahni, and I think you'll agree that his unique view is a welcome addition to the literary portrait we have been painting. To alleviate confusion, me own text will be written plainly, as you see before you here, while Kamahni's will be italicized.

* * *

There is an old saying my people have. "Speak with your heart, listen with your soul, act with pride, and honour your father." I am Kamahni, from South-West Africa, and I am of an Iboruba tribe. I was but a boy when Dr. Irel came to our land for the first time. It was April 1865. My father found him and his guide roaming the desert on camel back, half starved. So my father invited them into our village, where we helped nurse them back to health. At first our people were angry with father for this. White men were not often trustworthy. We had known of many tribes that had been taken away to live as slaves throughout the ages. There were even tales of our people being eaten by the white man. But they acknowledged that ***these*** *white men needed our help and hoped that one day they would take word of our kindness back to their people. Dr. Irel, through his guide, explained to us that he was exploring Africa and that he would love to stay with us for a while and learn about our culture.*

I can only wonder what he must have thought. We are a people of simple things: thin lightweight cotton clothing, straw huts, and fires for cooking. He was a man of elaborate dress, who wore what I now know to be a tan tweed suit coat. Apparently this was typical fashion of Englishmen in Africa.

There was a gathering that first evening, and it was decided that the two strangers could stay, but only if they could pull their own weight. As mentioned, we lived in straw huts and each of my father's three wives had their own. Each week, for two days, my father would sleep in each hut with each wife. It was very important that he treat them equally in every way. Well, almost every way. His first wife, my mother, died during child–birth, and so father decided not to have any more children, for fear of losing a wife every time. Wives were greatly valued for the chores they did when the men went off to do their jobs. So my father built a fourth hut surrounded by the huts of his wives. This was to be my home, and on the seventh day of the week he would take a much–needed rest from his wives and spend the night teaching me important manly things. Those women drove him crazy, each in her own way. The rest of the week I stayed alone with my dog, Azi. So the village came to the conclusion that Dr. Irel and his guide could stay with me in my hut, as I would have the space, and father would have to work something out with his wives.

Dr. Irel and I became fast friends. He had a thirst for learning that I have not seen in anyone else. As a boy of twelve this was very inspiring to me. He wanted to know everything there was to know about our people. Many were the days I spent explaining things to him and his guide. There was always something going on in the village. Sometimes there would be a robbery; sometimes there was a curse to be lifted; sometimes there was even a fight with a deadly snake; but always there were chores to do. There was always meat to be cleaned, clothing to be washed, vegetables to be harvested, meals to be prepared, and illnesses to be cured. It was this monotony that Dr. Irel enjoyed the most.

One day I was teaching Dr. Irel how to play sneak attack with Azi and Dr. Irel's walking stick when we heard the village warning drums. The beat spelled out danger. People were soon running in all directions. They were fleeing to their huts and Dr. Irel seemed to be lost in the confusion. I tried to explain to his guide that we needed to run and hide but our time had run out.

A poisoned dart sliced through the air and lodged itself into the throat of Dr. Irel's guide. We were shocked at being caught off guard and as we searched to see where the dart had come from, we were confronted with the sight of a great evil. The Maasahanti tribe was attacking. The Maasahanti were known as great warriors who had rarely been defeated in battle, and certainly not by any Iboruba. The Maasahanti carried few weapons. They wore armbands with darts and necklaces with a hollowed stick to blow them through. The poison itself was kept in sachets tied to their waists, and they wore war paint to symbolize their intent. Only their leader carried a sword and wore the traditional mask of their war spirit.

We began to run and all around us came war cries and poisoned darts. I knew we would not be safe in the huts so I led Dr. Irel far from the village and took him to where father worked in the fields. When we got there, I explained to father what had happened, and he gathered the other men and hurried home. Time passed very slowly. I was scared, and Dr. Irel tried to comfort me. He kept saying things that I could not understand, but his voice was calming, and I knew he meant well. The next day we cautiously returned to the village only to find it in ruins. Many had died, and many more were now left homeless. I returned to where my home had been and found my father, who now lay dead beside his wives. They had been beaten to death. Dr. Irel found me and clutched me to his side as I stood there, tears glossing my eyes.

That day we worked with the remaining Iboruba to burn the dead. Most of the men had been killed, and most of the survivors were women, children, and a few of the elders. The elders presided over the funeral service, and that night everyone left gathered to deliberate. In the end no one could explain why the Maasahanti had attacked us. We had always had a truce with their people. The choice was made that we would move the tribe farther to the south where we could seek help from the Yobandi in case of another attack. It would be a great undertaking, but it was our only choice.

Dr. Irel was not convinced. He did his best to explain that he would travel to a nearby town of white men and seek out information from the people there. The elders were sceptical.

* * *

I hadn't seen Cara Faulky for a month, not since the incident with her father. Luckily, though, I had formulated a grand plan that kept me in touch with me love. Old Mrs. McGillian became our personal telegram service and delivered letters between us twice a week. Most of our letters detailed how we missed each other or told of what we'd been up to in the absence of one another. I had turned to painting and immersed meself its grasp. Vant's *Kride* tale rekindled that imaginative flame and I hadn't stopped painting since. I called me first painting *Perception*. I had crafted it so that it looked as though a blurred face were gazing straight out at the viewer. In some ways it reminded me of how someone might look if they were looking out a window in the rain. In other ways it was as if the viewer were looking into a fogged mirror, and since the face was blurred, it was hard to argue whether it was in fact your own reflection.

I was well into me second painting entitled *Leocadia Sunrise*, one morning, when I was interrupted by Mrs. McGillian.

"Morning, Master William. Up early again I see," she observed.

"That's the trick," I said gazing out the window. "In order to paint a sunrise you have to start it at the same time every day. But then it never stays for very long. Anyway, how are you this morning?"

"Fit as an aging widow can be," she stated plainly. "I came up here to give you this," she said, and held up a letter.

"Wednesday already?" I asked turning to face her.

"Nay, 'tis only Monday. I was taking a morning stroll when I happened by the letter box. That letter's from Ireland; it must have been in there since Saturday."

"Ireland?" I said, as I snatched the letter from her. I got a good look at it, and sure enough, it was from Ireland: from me brother Glenn. I wasted no time tearing it open and reading the letter aloud to Mrs. McGillian. "Dear Billy, for God's sake where have you been? The family's been trying to reach you since April, but it looks like you've traded in countries again. I'll get to the point. Mum's deathly ill." Me voice began to quiver.

"Easy now," Mrs. McGillian said soothingly as she held me arm.

"Dr. O'Grady says she's got pneumonia and is fading fast. Seems to have come out of nowhere, but the winter was hard on all of us, and without your added income Mum was forced to beg old Rooney Malone for a job down at the docks, and that man had no shame at all. He had poor Mum guttin' fish for a quarter of what he'd pay a man. But Mum was too proud and never told either Arlen or meself. Seems only Erin knew, and as far as I'm concerned that puts her as much to blame about this as you." I turned to Mrs. McGillian. "He's blaming me?"

"Don't let him get to you. There's anger and intense emotion written all over that letter and he's probably just upset about your mother."

I continued: "We'd begun to give up on you until we got your letter saying how you're now in England somewhere. If you know what's good for you, you'll grab the next boat to Kinsale and give up all this painting crap. Don't disappoint Mum. Signed, Glenn."

"It is rather harsh," added Mrs. McGillian.

"Disappoint Mum? The only way I'd disappoint Mum is by giving up on me dream. I'll never give up painting. Not now."

"What are you going to do?"

"I'm going to Ireland. Just to nurse Mum back to health. Then I'll return."

* * *

After some persuasion, I convinced my people to let me accompany Dr. Irel to this strange town he had mentioned. They had quibbled for a short time, but as my family and home lay in ruins and I had no one to watch over me, they granted my request. We spent two days on camel back until we came to the Afrikaner town. I do not remember the name. Back then I did not know much of the Afrikaners. What I would soon find out though, was that they were not friends of the British. I can recall some stone buildings and a few dirt roads. When we arrived Dr. Irel took me into the most official–looking building. When we entered we came into a tiny vestibule, passed a room with a few empty desks, and came to a small hallway where we could faintly hear voices. There were three doors in the hallway, two on the left and one on the right. The voices were coming from the first door on the left; we listened, but I could not understand, and it was obvious to me that Dr. Irel did not understand either.

Slowly he turned the knob of the door and opened it a crack. This, to me, was odd. Even in my village it was customary to knock before entering one's home. Yet here was a white man spying on other white men. The idea made me nervous. Why the secrecy? Since I was smaller than Dr. Irel, I peered through the crack at my height and looked into the room. There I saw two white Afrikaners and an African man who I knew to be of the Maasahanti. You could always tell a Maasahanti apart from other tribes because when they are young children their faces are scarred with a sharp razor and a specific pattern, like a tattoo, is carved into their skin. Over time the wounds heal but the marks are a permanent statement of who they are.

As the men in the room talked, one of the Afrikaners—the heavier one—began to laugh as he picked up a fountain pen off his desk and turned to a large map of the surrounding area on the wall behind him, just left of the room's only window. There he used the pen to put a large "X" over a word on the map. As he stepped aside I could see that there were many X's on the chart, though I could not make out what words they covered as I had not been taught to read. This map made Dr. Irel shudder, and I could feel his uneasiness as he quietly began to close the door. The door was closed, though his hand was still on the knob and he looked at me with a keen look in his eye, and rather than turn the knob softly back to its place, he released it all at once, so it made a clicking noise.

The voices inside the room stopped, and when the door opened, there was no one to be seen. Dr. Irel was concealed, crouching beneath one of the desks and I was hiding beneath a desk next to him. I could hear the men rush towards the main entrance, open the door, and step out. The next thing I remember is Dr. Irel removing the chair in front of me and pulling me into the room the three men had just left. I stayed close to the closed door and listened, while Dr. Irel set down his walking stick and rummaged through some papers on their desks.

I listened quietly as my heart pounded in my chest and then I heard a faint sound coming from the outside room. As I turned to give a warning to Dr. Irel, I gasped to see the Maasahanti man's arm rush through the open window and pull Dr. Irel backwards, catching him by surprise and slamming his body into the wall. The struggle brought the Afrikaners in through the door, and I stood by watching helplessly. When they saw the scene before them, one of them grabbed me and held me, covering my mouth. The other Afrikaner spoke in his language to Dr. Irel, but when he received no response he tried another. To this Dr. Irel gave a reply. By now the Maasahanti man had crawled in through the window, never once letting Dr. Irel go and never taking his eyes off me.

"Are you scared, little Iboruba?" he said to me in a general tongue. "You should be. The time for Maasahanti rule is upon us. With these men's help our people will dominate the land as far as the sun shines."

I was hesitant to speak, but my father did not raise a coward. So I bit the hand of the thinner Afrikaner, forcing him to release me as he grasped his wounded hand inside his other.

"Why would they help you do that?" I asked in a cold tone.

The thin Afrikaner wanted to hit me, but the heavier one kept him back with his hand, as the Maasahanti spoke to me.

"Because they know power when they see it."

"Or because once you have destroyed all the native peoples these men will turn on you, and because you think they are your friend you will not be ready for them. Then they will murder or enslave the Maasahanti and rule the land you cleansed for them."

"You speak without fear little one, but you will learn fear soon enough."

"Oh, but I am afraid. It is only after finding your fear that you can overcome it." My father had always told me that, and I thought it fit the moment. Perhaps I was too cynical for my own good. The Maasahanti rushed me and was nearly upon me, but was suddenly called to a stop by that heavy Afrikaner.

"So you are a slave after all," I said to him.

He then slapped me with the back of his hand and I flew into a wall. My head swooned on the edge of unconsciousness, and both Afrikaners stopped him from coming after me. The heavy one explained something to him in their language and this made the Maasahanti man very angry and he spit at the ground by my feet. He then left us, and I felt the darkness close in around me.

* * *

It was nearing the end of June when I laid me eyes on me homeland again. I stood aboard the deck of a meagre fishing boat and took it all in. There it was, those famous shades of green, like arms stretched out to embrace me and welcome me to the place where it all started. When I came into the harbour I felt all the memories pouring back into me soul. Then I spotted Malone's fishery and—instead of it reminding me of the happy times I came to watch me father work, the friends I'd made when I worked there meself, or the pictures I painted sitting on the benches during lunch—a dark image came to mind: me ailing mother. Worry washed over me now, and I hurried ashore when the boat docked.

It was a short walking distance to the village of Summerstone Cove where I'd grown up. I made it there just as dusk approached, and I soon came to me old home, where I saw me sister Erin sitting grimly on father's chair on the tiny porch his father had built. The closer I came, the more I must have stuck out and eventually caught her eye. When she realized it was me she squealed with excitement, sprang from her seat on the porch, and rushed up onto me with a good strong hug and a face full of happiness.

"It's great to see you too," said I. "Here, let me have a look at you."

She stayed in me arms for an awkward moment, and when she finally showed herself, I could see that the happiness had faded away into the shadows of despair. Tears haunted her face now, and as much as I wanted them to be, I knew they were not tears of joy.

"What's all the shrieking about?" asked Glenn as he came out from within.

"Is everything all right?" asked Arlen, as he followed up behind Glenn.

It seemed strange to see them again. Glenn with his broad shoulders, ochre–brown hair, and square jaw, towered high above Arlen in the doorway. He had always been an intimidating fellow, especially when paired against someone like Arlen, who, you see, was far less daunting and got all the family's good looks. I was jealous of him as a teenager.

He was fifteen years older than me, and in his thirties he was in his prime. Women used to flock to him, swooning over his dark eyes and smooth skin. That's usually when I'd make fun of him, on the account that women were supposed to have the smooth skin in a relationship. Still, it was a long while before he found the right lass; he spent most of his time working long hours, trying to impress his employers. He was a bookkeeper for a bank and always had his eye on the prize: the next step on the ladder. But that day, even his lady–killin' features had grown pale.

"Look who finally showed up," sneered bitter Glenn.

"Billy!" declared Arlen. "Thank goodness you're here."

"Goodness indeed," Glenn muttered under his breath.

"Where's Mum?" I asked. "How is she?"

"She's in the house, dead," said Glenn coldly. "Not more than an hour ago."

"Dead?!" I cried. I felt an instant weakening in me knees and would have collapsed had it not been for Erin, who now held *me* up.

"Oh, Glenn," scolded Erin. "For God's sake, don't you think you could have broke it to him a little more gently?"

"I'd like to break his nose, if you want the truth."

"Here, stop it," said Arlen. "Erin's right. This is no time for those kinds of thoughts. If anything, this should be a time of togetherness. We're all we have left now."

"I cannot believe it," I babbled, tears soaking me stubbled face. "Not Mum, Jaysus, not Mum."

* * *

When I awoke, I found that I had been imprisoned with Dr. Irel. We were confined behind steel bars in a cell with a dirt floor. The only light came from a small window far across the way. Next to us were a few other cells, but only one held a prisoner, and there was an empty one in between us. Dr. Irel had been pacing, and when he saw that I was awake he came to me showing concern. I smiled faintly to let him know that I was fine. He nodded and sat down beside me on the ground. He was fed up. And then something unexpected happened: The other prisoner—surprisingly he was an Afrikaner—spoke to Dr. Irel.

Dr. Irel seemed indifferent to the man's words. He was a dirty–looking old man with ragged clothing and a balding head that sprouted sprigs of grey. He had not shaved for a long time. He then looked to me and asked me, in Iborubi, how I felt. I was taken a little off guard, but Dr. Irel seemed ecstatic that this man could speak to me. Dr. Irel spoke to the man, and the man introduced himself to me as Charl. He said that Dr. Irel wanted to know if he would translate between us. I asked him what he thought. He said it would be better than sleeping and so agreed. I asked him what he had done to get imprisoned. He gave me a warm smile, showing his rotted teeth, and said that there were some things a boy my age should not know.

I told him that in a few weeks I would soon be thirteen, take part in the circumcision ceremony, and thus be a man. He laughed long and hard at this and when he finally found himself he explained to Dr. Irel what had set him off. Dr. Irel did not laugh, but instead gave me a pat on the back. The older man shook his head. And that was the beginning of our three–way conversation. Throughout the evening, we discussed many things: prison, the Afrikaners, the Maasahanti attack, and life in England, but it was not until deep in the night that the conversation became engrossing.

We had been discussing the history of Africa when Dr. Irel mentioned that he was an authority on cultures of the past and made his living digging up their remains. He reached into his coat pocket and removed a corked vial of gold liquid and then one of silver. He called these his markers. When we asked why, he explained that whenever he finds something that he cannot remove, he marks it so that he may return to it at a later date. It was a technique of his trade. We reasoned with him that it must be very difficult to piece together ideas about how a society lived merely by studying what the people left behind. He acknowledged this and said that he most enjoyed studying the ways of the people that still exist. His only problem was that museums would only pay for artefacts, not information, and so he could not sustain his living studying living people.

Charl was intrigued by our conversation and said that there was only one people he had ever tried to study—a mysterious people from long ago that had come from the sea. He said that they were white but not white like those of today. These men had narrow eyes, straight black hair, wore thick armour, and possessed fighting skills that were unsurpassed anywhere in Africa. He had heard of these people from legends carried down from various tribes. They were said to have been shipwrecked centuries ago and had brought with them a multitude of treasures. But there was one treasure that they sought to conceal. Why? He could not say. Yet the legends claimed that these strange men hid this treasure in a cave that rests on the ocean floor. Every nine years, he explained, the sea pulls back for one day to allow access to this treasure and that day was almost upon us.

Charl had first told this story to Dr. Irel, who seemed completely enchanted by it. When Charl told me, I told him that I remembered hearing stories of such a people, and Dr. Irel seemed even more excited. He told Charl and me that in his studies of the world, he had come across documents that led him to believe that centuries ago a people called the Chinese set out to traverse the world and barter with foreign rulers. He went on to say that some of their ships were lost at sea, and one of them was rumoured to have gone down off the shore of South-West Africa, 'The Land God Made in Anger'. He believed this ship was carrying a chest with powerful qualities. The chest had been passed down through time from one civilization to the next, and it was last seen in China days before the ships were to set sail. He said the chest was invented in a place called Atlantis and that it had been primarily used to transport powerful violet crystals that these people had mastered. He said that once something was placed inside, it could never get out unless it was opened from the outside. The chest the Chinese had encountered had been used by the Egyptians to hold the treasure of a fallen pharaoh and held a curse for whatever man opened the chest. The curse, Dr. Irel explained, was a powerful disease that the Egyptian high priests had manufactured from ancient texts that predated them and had once belonged to their ancestors, the Atlanteans.

When Charl asked him what happened to the Atlanteans, Dr. Irel said that power had been too much for them, and the violet crystals caused their destruction. I thought about all of this for some time before I made a suggestion. I proposed that if Dr. Irel could find this chest it might make him rich enough for him to study living people. He smiled and looked at me proudly for a few moments.

Charl said that the coast was not too far, three or four days away, and that he had once tried to find the cave, but had failed. Dr. Irel said that if we got out of prison in time we would take Charl with us and find that treasure chest. Charl laughed and said that once these particular Afrikaners imprisoned you, you did not go free. But I was not so sure.

* * *

At the wake, Father Murphy led us all in prayer. He was very old and very frail, and I couldn't help but think that it was cruel of the Lord to take me mother, who was just in her mid–sixties, while this man teetered before us well over eighty. The service was held in mother's family room, which was packed with people who had known and loved her. I sat quietly beside Erin, who sat beside Arlen and his wife, and off to the side was Glenn's family. He had five children, all boys.

When the service had ended, Arlen saw that the guests were fed whilst I went over to see Mum. She lay in her best dress surrounded by ice and rested there very peacefully, looking very much like herself, though she had grown somewhat thin from the pneumonia.

"Hi Mum," I whispered to her body. "'Tis Billy, your young artist. So much has happened in the last ten months … I should have written more. I should have … Och, I don't know what I should have done. I should have never have left you. I should have been there to take care of you. I'm sorry Mum, I'm so, so sorry. Please forgive me," I begged, with tears staining me face.

"She wouldn't want you to blame yourself," came Erin's voice from behind me, and she put a hand on me shoulder. "She believed in you. You're out there living your dream and her's too. Can't you see that, Billy?"

"But if I'd been—"

"What?" she'd cut me off. "If you'd been what? Here? Wasting your life away at the docks like poor Daddy did. Killing yourself from sunrise until sunset so you can spend two hours with your family, reek of fish guts, and collapse of a heart attack? You're better than that, Billy. Mum knew it too. It would've broken her heart had you given up on your dream for her, and then she might as well be dead anyway."

"You know," said I, wiping me tears with a hankie. "You were always me favourite. Mum's too."

"Mum had no favourites," explained Erin, though I disagreed with her in me mind. "She loved us all equally," she paused, "which is odd really. I mean, what's there to love about Glenn anyway?" she chuckled.

"You know, he's like a … a tree, sort of, strong, stable … stubborn."

"How is a tree stubborn?" she asked.

"Think about it," I stated. "A tree's too stubborn to get out of the way of a storm, or carriage, or a man with an axe. It just stands there like no one else even exists. Kind of selfish really when you consider it."

Erin chuckled some more. "Glad to see you haven't lost your dry sense of humour."

"Aye, there were times it seemed all that I had left. But what about you, Erin, how have you been getting on?"

"Do you remember the bench over at the pond on the outside of town where we used to go with Mum?"

"You mean *Fara's Frolic*?" I asked.

"That's right," she giggled. "I forgot that's what we called it."

"What about it?"

"Would you like to take a walk over there? See how it's changed? We can play catch up on the way."

I knew then that she wanted to talk with me openly and didn't feel she could do so in the house. *Fara's Frolic* was our special place with Mum. She and Mum had found it long before I was born, and when I finally did come into the picture, she agreed to let Mum bring me there, and it had since been our special place. A place where we would often go to talk things out, appreciate the natural things in life, and just be. None of the others even knew where we'd go, but that just made it all the more special.

They had named it *Fara's Frolic* based on a fairy tale mother and Erin made up together about a fairy named Fara who danced in the breeze and frolicked along the surface of the water. Fara was said to be very graceful and had charmed the heart of a dragon so much that this dragon, Aidan as I recall, fell in love with her and prayed to the sky, the moon, and the storms to allow them to be together forever. Well, as their story goes, the *sidhe*—fairy–like spirits, I guess you could call them—granted Aidan's wish but in a tricksterу way, as gods often do. They turned both Aidan and Fara into the stone legs of the bench that rests there and formed the seat from their love so that they would always be connected to each other. I knew that if we were going to *Fara's Frolic*, something heavy was on Erin's mind, so I agreed to accompany her.

Darkness had taken over the land as we trudged off into the night with a lantern lighting our way. The walk to the pond was about twenty minutes, but we filled in the time with conversation, which was really the point of going there in the first place.

"I can't take it anymore, Billy," Erin said flatly when we'd got far enough away from the house. "These people, this place, it's not me. Maybe it was once, but there's nothing here for me now."

It was true, in a way. You see, Erin had been married when she was twenty–five. She never wanted to get married, but it was expected. It took until she was twenty–five before she gave in to the idea. She was married for about two years when her husband ran off with a younger woman and I honestly think she was happier for it. It meant she would be free, at least for a while. That was three years earlier. Since then she'd moved back in with Mum and I, and we took care of each other.

"Mum was the only thing keeping me here," she added. "Now that she's gone I feel like a new chapter has turned in my life. Part of me could feel it coming; somehow I just knew."

"So what exactly are you planning on doing about it?" I asked.

"I've been thinking about that all night. When I was about fifteen, I used to imagine heading out into the world, seeing it first–hand. Back then Daddy used to get the paper every morning and read it over breakfast. One day when I was cleaning up the table I caught an article on London. I read a little of it and was so enticed I sat right down at the table with dripping wet hands from the dishes and read the entire thing. From then on I would fantasize about going to London and gazing out into the Thames while Big Ben tolled to signal the hour. But then I never did. I was swept up into a life of conformity, and my dreams were stifled. But now I have a second chance—a chance to take back my dreams and live my life the way I see fit. Like you."

"Och, you don't want to be out in the real world, Erin. It's hard. Damn hard. I've never experienced anything like it in me life. But I'm one lucky fellow running into Dr. Vant when I did. His presence changed me life in a single evening."

"Yeah, you mentioned this Vant character in your letter," she said, as we ascended a hill and continued to walk. "Tell me about him."

"He's different, that's for sure, but I think it's what he strives for. Almost like he fears being part of ordinary life. Everything he does seems to be done for the sole purpose of being strange."

"What's he done that's so strange?"

"See, that's just it. I can't place a finger on any one thing he's done. It's more like the world around him. Like he attracts the odd."

"Try not to confuse difference with the need to be different," she said. "Just because you're not used to things being done the way he does them or the way things happen around him, doesn't mean he's out to prove himself the most unique man in the world. Maybe he's just being himself, and because you're not used to that, you see him as being something else."

"You're gonna give me brain an awful headache talking like that," I stated.

"What I mean is that you've lived the majority of your life in one spot with one state of mind based on the stimuli of your surroundings. Once you break free from that, you realize what you've been missing: a whole world of different stimuli. A world in which what's considered the norm in one place may be a taboo in the next."

"I guess that makes sense."

"And see that's it. That's what I want for myself. A chance to experience everything I never did while I still can. That's why I want you to take me back to England with you."

"Take you where?" I questioned, quite surprised, though I knew full well what she'd just said.

"I've always dreamed of going to England, Billy. Take me back with you. Take me to London."

* * *

Two days had passed since Dr. Irel and I had been imprisoned. In prison there is not much one can do. Sometimes we talked with our new friend, Charl, and sometimes we sat silent. However, during those silent moments I took turns watching a scorpion eye a mouse about eight metres away, and watching Dr. Irel as he thought deeply about his plans for escaping, though he never once mentioned that was what he was doing. Soon after he began to pace.

Eventually the scorpion forced the rodent into a corner, and when it knew that its prey had no way out, it finally seized it with a claw to hold it in place and stung the mouse with its tail. Dr. Irel had stopped pacing to see what I was staring at, and when I looked back to him he raised his fingers in a claw–like fashion and pinched the air. What neither of us knew was that the silence was about to be abruptly interrupted. A powerful yet soft blowing sound cut through the air like a diving bird. It was not loud exactly, but in silence everything is amplified. Afterwards, we heard a gargled choking sound and as Charl and I stood up, the Maasahanti man who had helped to imprison us entered the main room that held our cells.

"There is no time to lose," he said to me as he held up a key and unlocked us. "You were right about these Afrikaners. I saw some of their hidden plans. They plan to take control of Maasahanti territory before the start of the next season."

"Why free us?" I asked.

"They will be powerful enemies. The Maasahanti cannot defeat them alone. We will need the help of your surviving people."

Charl translated for Dr. Irel, who seemed very cautious but stepped out of the cell just the same. When the two of us were free, the Maasahanti warrior told us to follow him.

"What about him?" I asked, pointing to Charl.

"I do not know what he is imprisoned for. It would be unwise to release a man like him."

"You'll release him," I demanded, "or we will not go."

"He is Afrikaner," reminded the Maasahanti. "He is not to be trusted."

"Have you not heard," asked Charl, "that the enemy of your enemy is your friend?"

The Maasahanti then said something back to Charl in what could only have been the Afrikaner language, because even Dr. Irel did not know what was being said. Charl said nothing further, and the sound of someone opening the outside door forced us to leave him behind. When we entered the other room, we found the heavier Afrikaner kneeling beside his companion holding the poisoned dart he had just removed from the man's throat. Before he had time to react, the Maasahanti man cracked his hand down on the back of the Afrikaner's neck and over he fell. The Maasahanti man shouted for us to follow him, but Dr. Irel returned to the room we had entered days before and retrieved his walking stick. He kissed it on the handle, and together we ran outside where the Maasahanti man had some of his people waiting, hiding, just in case. There were three of them.

"Quickly," said our acquaintance, "Before word spreads."

They led us to the back of a small building where four horses stood waiting. Our acquaintance took me onto his horse with him, while Dr. Irel joined one of the other men.

"We will head to the Iboruba and bring them the message that my people will be waiting to join them at the edge of a nearby river. Then we will come together as the true people of Africa and drive out these Afrikaner men."

I was hesitant and looked to Dr. Irel for some sort of sign, though I did not know what I expected him to do. To my surprise he lifted up his hand and pinched the air. I knew then what he was thinking, and I knew that he was right.

We rode on for a day and a half until we stopped to figure out the direction to head in next. "We must now travel west," I announced to them.

"West?" questioned our acquaintance.

"Our people—what was left of the tribe—were forced to migrate further to the western shore, where they hope the fog and inhospitable soil will keep others away. But we must be cautious when we come upon them, as they will not be very trusting of the men who killed their families."

Our acquaintance grumbled at the idea, but drove us westward anyway. Of course, my people had actually gone south, near the Yobandi, but I had to keep them safe. There was, indeed, another reason I wanted to go west. The shore was where Charl and the legends placed the sea cave with the hidden treasure chest. So we continued west for a few days more until, at last, the smell of the sea air took a strong hold. It was evening when we came upon the fog–infested shore and descended from our horses to take a rest.

"How much farther?" asked our acquaintance.

"Half a day's journey north," I stated. I began at this point to wonder what Dr. Irel was thinking. He did not understand our language, but he knew we had not gone south and, what is more, we had come to the shoreline. Surely he would make the next move. Or so I hoped. My plan had been a good one, but it would not free us of these men. Sooner or later something would have to be done; I just wished I knew what and when.

That night we settled down in the sand to sleep, blanketed by the fog. We were exhausted from the trip so far, even though it were the horses that most deserved the rest. I slept beside Dr. Irel, and the others were scattered beside us. The Maasahanti did not feel a night guard would be worth the trouble, as we were miles from other people and were all equally tired. So we all drifted off to sleep.

Sometime in the night I felt a small pinch at my side and batted at it to go away, but I felt it again. I remember thinking it might be something like a scorpion getting agitated with me; that made me think of Dr. Irel and his pinching motion after the scorpion in the prison had conquered the mouse. I woke up, surrounded in fog, which had gotten thicker during the night. A cloud of dark, smoky grey prevented me from seeing very far in front of me and then Dr. Irel's face came into view. He put a finger to his lips to signal silence. I stood up quietly and took his hand. The crashing waves of the shoreline helped to muffle the noise our footsteps made, and we cautiously began to retreat.

Yet we must not have been quiet enough, because we startled one of the horses into a giving a loud whinny that woke the Maasahanti suddenly. That was our cue to run. We ran so fast, I cannot even tell you. We ran and ran and had good reason to run, because we were now being chased. The Maasahanti knew that we realized they were plotting against us, and they were angry. But the fog was too much for them. They could not see us. The waves crashed loudly, and they could not hear our feet. They must have felt bewildered because try as they did, they could not find us. We had escaped.

Dr. Irel and I continued running until we came to a small cavern on the coastline. We did not know what to make of it at first, but there was an opening big enough for us to hide in. As we crawled inside, I thought how clever we had been. The Maasahanti would surely expect that we would head inland away from the openness of the shore. What is more, as I discovered the following morning, the water had receded even more, so that now, in the misty morning light, there lay even more uncovered caverns! We had found the Land God Made in Anger.

* * *

I was never any good at turning anyone down for anything. Particularly not when it came to family, and especially not when it came to Erin. Somehow or another she'd managed to talk me into bringing her back to England. The truth of the matter is that I didn't mind Erin coming along with me. Part of me was even a bit keen on the idea, but when it came to telling the brothers the news, I'd much rather have been a continent away. I think the only reason I actually got through the moment was because, in the back of me mind, I kept thinking that I'd soon be far away from them and not have to deal with their tempers.

Erin had decided that it would be best to wait until after the funeral was over and all the legal affairs were tied up before we mentioned the news to Glenn and Arlen. That day ended up coming faster than I'd hoped. The funeral had been very lovely indeed, and we buried Mum right next to Dad under the old red maple tree in Saint Sylvester's cemetery. We then had a grand meal and spent the rest of that week dealing with financial matters and divvying up our parents' property.

I took only a white onyx candleholder for meself. It might not seem like much to the average person, but I considered it to be a family heirloom. It had been handed down through me family for some time and had been used to hold the unity candle at me parents' wedding. So you see, it reminded me of them both. Almost everything else went to Glenn or Arlen; Erin didn't have much use for anything. We then came to the agreement that Arlen would sell the house and divide the profit amongst us, and since he would be doing most of the work, he'd take a bigger piece of the profit. That suited me just fine, because I had no interest in making a profit at me parents' expense.

Eventually Erin and I knew the time had come to tell Glenn and Arlen about her leaving. We chose to tell them after dinner one night, so that no one would lose their appetite but before any serious drinking could begin. Arlen was at the kitchen table, sipping his tea and mulling over some papers regarding things he felt the need to triple check. Glenn was standing in a corner with a pint in his hand, staring off into space and gnawing on his nails. I was calmly rocking back and forth in Dad's old rocking chair, when Erin stood up from her seat on the sofa and cleared her throat to speak.

"Um, Glenn, Arlen, we need to discuss something," she said.

"Discuss what?" asked Arlen, though he never bothered to look up from his papers. "Everything's settled. This time next week we can start to put this all behind us."

"That's not what I'm talking about," she rebutted.

"Hold on," said Glenn, as his mind joined us again. "Why just me and Arlen? What about Billy? Don't you want to tell him something too?"

"He already knows," she added. "It's something we'd both like to discuss with the two of you."

At this Arlen must have felt the gravity of the situation because he set down his papers and turned towards us in the other room.

"Go on then," said Glenn, as he spat out a nail. "Spill it."

Erin looked uneasy, but she kept her stance and drew in a deep breath for strength. Then she said it. "When Billy goes back to England tomorrow, he'll be taking me with him."

Up until that moment I don't think I'd ever experienced a deafening silence that could make the hairs on me arms stand at attention—and boy, did it seem to linger! I'd expected cursing, yelling, spit flying, and possibly a fist or two—but not this kind of torture. It was almost unheard of. It was as if the brothers were thinking the whole thing through though neither showed the slightest hint of emotion. Perhaps it was the strain of the last few days, or maybe they'd seen it coming, or otherwise they didn't care, but after a long moment one of them finally spoke.

"It's getting late," said Arlen, "I should be going."

"Didn't you hear what I said?" asked Erin.

"Oh, we heard you," muttered Glenn under his breath. "We just have better things to do with our time then waste it on the likes of you two."

"Oh hey, hang on then," said I. "What's that supposed to mean?"

"Take it how you want," said Glenn as he opened the door for Arlen who stepped out before him. "But you know how I meant it." With that he closed the door behind him.

XII
KINDRED
PART TWO: MATURATION

Morning had soon become afternoon and Dr. Irel and I had searched caves of every size and depth, yet try as we did, we could not find any cave that seemed to contain long lost treasures. I could sense Dr. Irel's frustration. The sea had pulled back several hundred metres in a single morning; there was no telling when it would return to cover the shoreline again.

I sat with my thoughts as I rested my back against the entrance of a cave. Something Charl had said came to me and would not leave my mind. He said that the cave rested on the ocean floor. I looked around. All the caves we had explored were from a very steep exposed shoreline that descended as a cliff would. But they were not on the ocean floor itself.

Without saying anything I began to walk towards the ocean. I passed Dr. Irel where he stood drumming his fingers on a rock. If he took notice of me, I did not pay attention. I was seeking out the bottom of the steep cliff where the land became flat once more. Upon the ground stood a single boulder three times my size. I inspected it and gave it a slight push. It did not budge. Soon Dr. Irel was beside me. He smiled down on me as he had done at various times since I met him, and the two of us pushed the boulder together until, finally, it gave way. It must have been the muddy sand around it that made it move so easily, because I do not think the two of us would have been able to move an object of that size on dry land. Together we looked down.

There, where the boulder had been, was a very wide hole in the ground, on the ocean floor. Charl had been right.

* * *

A light mist had settled in on the docks, as I watched Erin set foot on the English shoreline for the first time in her life. She seemed excited, but somewhere inside she was uneasy about the way things had gone with the brothers. We had tried to talk to them again before we left Ireland, but they would not see us. That was behind us now.

I had talked Erin into staying with me in Leocadia, where she could get a job and earn enough money to make the official move to London. Truth be told, I wasn't very fond of the idea of her moving to London alone. London was a hard city, and although she was older than me she was still just one girl. As we drove up in the carriage to Vant Manor later that evening, Mrs. McGillian came out to greet us. She had spotted the carriage coming up Wigington Circle from her usual spot on the roof.

"Seriously," Erin commented as she stepped out of the cab and gazed up at the entrance to Vant Manor. The place had regained its regal stature since Mrs. McGillian and meself had put in a lot of hard work to get her back in tip–top shape. "This is where you live?" she asked turning back around to me. I smiled. "St. Brigid's finally answering your prayers!"

Mrs. McGillian opened the black iron front gate and smiled at me sister. "You must be Miss O'Brien."

"Mrs. Calhoone, actually," she corrected. "Though my husband left me."

"Oh," replied Mrs. McGillian. "My apologies."

"Don't be sorry. Lord knows I'm not. Call me Erin. You must be Mrs. McGillian. Billy's told me a great deal about you."

I retrieved our bags from within the cab and it was soon on its way leaving us all together at the front gate.

"Erin's going to stay with us for a few months."

"Just long enough until I earn a little money to move to London," she added.

"I see," said Mrs. McGillian. "Then, welcome to Vant Manor Ms. Erin! Allow me to show you in."

On the way up the front walk, Erin marvelled at the estate. It was all rather astonishing to her. As we walked, she pointed to various objects, and I explained what I knew about them. Once inside, Erin enquired about a wash–down closet.

"They're calling them water–closets now, I hear," I replied. "But as wealthy as Dr. Vant seems, he hasn't installed one in Vant Manor. Least not that I've found. There's a privy though, just under the stair case there, so at least you don't have to go outside."

"They're called garderobes in castles, Master William, added Mrs. McGillian.

"Well, whatever you want to call it, I need to pay it a visit," said Erin. "Please excuse me."

"We'll be over here in the parlour," I added as she entered the privy.

On our way into the parlour, Mrs. McGillian turned to me. "Master William," she said quietly to me. "Are you sure about this arrangement?"

"Absolutely," I said. "She's me sister. I couldn't let her just run off to London."

"What about Dr. Vant?"

"Crikey, Mrs. McGillian, this is me home, it's not a prison. I can entertain company if I choose, especially me own flesh and blood!"

"Perhaps it won't matter much. By the time the doctor returns home she'll have been gone for a spell anyway."

"There, that's the ticket," I stated.

Suddenly there came a shriek from the foyer and we heard a snort and the flapping of wings.

"Guess she's met Victor," I chuckled.

* * *

Dr. Irel tossed a rock down into the hole and listened for the sound of it as it struck bottom. He smiled when he heard the thud. I reasoned that it must as deep as my father with me on his shoulders or perhaps twice his size. This made me sad as I thought of my father again. But my sadness turned to thoughts of anger, and I kicked a rock into the pit at the thought of what had happened to my people.

Dr. Irel tugged my shoulder. I did not want to look up at him. Instead, I stared down at the ground with a pouting face. He leaned down to my height and looked up at me. He then lost his balance and fell onto the mucky ground. I laughed and he winked at me. After that, we hugged and I felt the anger pass. We then decided to focus on how to get down into the hole.

Rope would have been nice, but we did not have any. Our clothing would not do. We needed something strong and plenty of it. We began to search our surroundings, but there were no branches or vines—only the mud, the water, and the seaweed. The seaweed! We must have come to that conclusion at the same time because the moment we saw an abundance of it we ran out toward it.

Hastily, we gathered as much seaweed as we could and began tying the ends of the pieces together. We each started a strand and finished by combining the two into one long piece, long enough to take us down to the bottom of that hole! Nowadays I understand that most children my age would have been terrified of the idea of dropping down into the ground like that, but not an Iboruba boy. To me, it seemed a great adventure.

Together we made a second seaweed vine. We then anchored one seaweed rope to the boulder; the other Dr. Irel spun around his arm. We then climbed our way down into the mouth of darkness. When we reached the bottom, I could not see anything. All I could do was listen. It is amazing how much your other senses improve when you temporarily lose one of them. I am sure you are aware of this, as I think everyone closes their eyes at some point in their lives just to listen. This is what I did, except that my eyes were wide open. I heard Dr. Irel tear something and then there was rustling in what I guessed was his pockets, and finally the spark of fire emerged in the cloaking darkness. Dr. Irel had struck a match.

I saw that he had torn the sleeves from his coat and wrapped them around the end of his walking stick. He now lit the bundle with the match, and with our makeshift torch we set out to explore the cave.

* * *

After Erin had thoroughly explored the castle, we sat down for a bit of dinner. Mrs. McGillian had prepared a fine meal while I had been showing me sister the grounds. During the feast we took turns embarrassing each other in front of the old gal, reciting early memories from a life long ago, or so it seemed. That meal must have lasted for hours while we jabbered away. Yet somehow it wasn't until our evening stroll on the estate that the conversation took an interesting turn.

"So Ms. Erin," began Mrs. McGillian. "What do you intend to do once you actually get to London?"

"I'm not sure, really. I just always assumed I'd find my niche."

"You can take it from someone with London experience. Life in that city is not for the weak of mind, heart, or character. If there's one thing I learned from Dr. Vant it's that you've got to *make* your niche. Make a name for yourself. Find something you're good at. Make it your craft. Own it. Then you can begin a life. All you need to do is tap in to your inner compass and follow it to your destiny. That's what Dr. Vant told me the first time we met. Nothing's ever seemed more fit."

"What was it you were good at?" Erin asked.

"Isn't it obvious? Taking care of others! It all started when I was a housemaid. But when I was let go I ended up on the streets until I met the good doctor. An adventure or two later, and I found myself tending to one Master Hugo, whom I had met on account of Dr. Vant. Ten years later, and here I am again, repaying my debt the best way I can: by taking care of others."

"Well, I don't think *I* could be anyone's servant. It's not who I am. I'm independent, strong–willed, and—"

"Stubborn, headstrong, and naive," I added.

"Billy!" she gasped.

"Awe, come on, Erin. You know Mrs. McGillian is right. We just need to figure out what it is you're good at."

"Maybe you can perfect a talent?" asked Mrs. McGillian. "Do you know how to sew?"

"What woman in this day and age doesn't know how to sew?" asked Erin. "Of course I can!"

"There you go," I stated. "Hey, you know, now that you mention it, Cara's got some uncle or something who runs a tailor shop in town. I bet she could get you a job there for a while."

"And at least you'd be getting a start on your savings," added Mrs. McGillian.

"I guess I could try it out. I don't see the harm in that."

"Great!" I cheered, as we shuffled through the dew–covered moor. "Only … only don't tell anyone we're related."

"What?" she giggled.

"Seriously," I stopped. "There's been a misunderstanding with Cara's folks, and I wouldn't want them to prejudge you. Best not to even tell them you're staying here at all. The town doesn't take lightly to the mention of Dr. Vant."

"Any particular reason?" she asked.

"If I knew that I'm quite sure I'd be able to figure out Dr. Vant once and for all."

* * *

The caverns beneath the ocean seemed, to me, to be endless. In truth, there were around eight tunnels spreading out from a larger central cavern, like the legs of a spider stretched out before you.

There was the tunnel that led from the main entrance and, as I recall, two of the tunnels curved together to form one, both leading you back into the central cavern. Another tunnel was nothing more than a dead end. The fourth led somewhere I cannot remember, but the three remaining were all linked to each other.

One of these special three led to a pool of liquid metal. I can recall being very taken with it. Dr. Irel was too. He sniffed the air and slowly crept closer to it. The light from his torch danced magically over the pool and I knew this would be a fantastic place filled with wonder. To a child my age, it was as if the heavens themselves were contained in that pool. In a way that is true, for you see, my friend, the heavens exist within everything and everyone. It just so happens we can't always see them until a little light is shone.

After thoroughly inspecting every angle of the pool, Dr. Irel reluctantly gave up and signalled me to move on. The second of these three tunnels came to an abrupt end, where we came upon a hole in the ground. This pit was so vast that when Dr. Irel stopped to drop a rock down into it, we never heard it reach bottom. But there was something else in that tunnel that sat shyly awaiting our attention. It was a thin stone bank on the far side of that pit—a puny ledge, perhaps a foot wide. Now this bank—this rail of wall—began at our left in darkness and continued deep past our right, returning to darkness. This sight brought a smile to my companion's face, but I must admit that at the time I was a bit confused. To me it was just another dead end but with a pit.

Hurriedly, Dr. Irel flew back down the tunnel from which we had just come, and I struggled to keep up. When we returned to the large cavern, he stopped me suddenly and spun me around. I was facing the cave we had just left. He pointed to our right, and there was the tunnel with the metal pool; he then pointed to our left and took me by the hand to follow him. I began to wonder whether he was slowly losing his marbles, but I followed him anyway. Soon our path began to shrink and before I knew it the path was no longer wide enough for our feet. So he put his back against the wall and shimmied his way onward on a space just wide enough for his heels to rest on!

When I saw this I knew exactly what he was doing. Soon enough, we passed by that same endless pit and the tunnel through which we had passed before. Only now the pit seemed more frightening as it was right before us and even the slightest wrong move would surely mean the end of us. Yet he pressed on, and I followed.

* * *

The following day Mrs. McGillian took Erin into town to introduce her to Cara. They were gone for a long time, but I tried not to think about it. Instead I focused on me next painting, *Fara's Frolic*. It would be an ode to our mother. Of course, a painting this important needed to be drafted first. So I used pen and paper to plot out the key components of the composition. Victor kept me company in the art studio. He stared out the open window, sitting peacefully, and I tried to imagine what sorts of things he might be thinking. When I finished me first draft of the composition I heard a rustling from Victor as he stood upright and stretched out his wings. I took to his side and gazed down to the walkway outside, up which Erin and Mrs. McGillian were strolling. It was evening now.

Within a moment I was at the front door holding it open for them. They were snickering about something.

"Well," I asked. "How did it go?"

Erin turned to Mrs. McGillian and they busted out laughing.

"Here, now, what's so funny?" I begged.

"Nothing at all. Don't work yourself up," said Erin.

"That's right," added Mrs. McGillian. "We'd hate for you to have an accident."

That set them both off again, this time to the point of a tear or two welling up in Erin's eyes. It was then I knew what was the topic of their private joke.

"Not the school–play story, Erin! Tell me you didn't!"

They laughed harder now.

"You see," said Erin to Mrs. McGillian, "I told you he'd remember!" And they tittered some more.

"Here, here, that was a long time ago. I couldn't have been no more than eight. A roomful of people's a nerve–racking experience when all eyes are on you."

"That and … what was her name again?" asked Erin. "Oh, that's it. Little Stacey McCourt!"

"Hang on now, you didn't tell that story to Cara now did you?"

That set them off again.

"Jaysus, what *am* I going to do with you Erin? Come on; let's get you two inside so you can tell me everything."

* * *

The walkway we had been on began to widen again and then came to a sudden end where the room opened up. We were standing at the edge of the ground, and below us, down perhaps ten or so feet, was a cavern and, at the end of said cavern, lay a curious gold and violet chest. I knew then that we had found it: the treasure Charl had talked about. But was it what Dr. Irel was hoping it would be?

He sniffed the stale air. I copied him. Surely there was an unidentifiable odour in that room that I could not place. But he could. He dug a small hole into the ground and fastened his stick–torch into it. Next he took the remaining seaweed vine from around his shoulder and fastened it to a rock that stuck out of the wall like a tongue. Slowly we descended into the room below.

When we were on solid ground again, Dr. Irel went right for the chest. Upon the wall above it rested a painting with black symbols on it. To this day I do not know what those symbols meant. But I do not think Dr. Irel did either. He did, however, begin to laugh. This led me to believe that these markings must have been placed there by the Chinese people he had spoken of when we were imprisoned with Charl. That meant Dr. Irel had been right and that this was his missing treasure.

But if he was right about the treasure, might he also be right about the curse? We would not be able to open it there. So he motioned for me to assist him in lifting the chest. Together we bent down, each grasping an end, and heaved, but it would not budge. This angered him, and he kicked the chest. When he did, a bit of rock gave way at the bottom edge. We inspected it and discovered that the chest had been sealed to the ground with some kind of rock adhesive. Concrete, I believe, is what it is called.

Dr. Irel paced the length of the room for some time. The entire room was surrounded by rock. But something seemed interesting to me. Why was this chest at the far end of the cave near the wall? Why not in the centre of the room, with the painting in the ground before it? I searched the ground for a clue and found that surrounding a portion of the room was a trench of stinky liquid. It gave off the same odour we had discovered from above! It was strongest here.

But what was its purpose? I followed it around until I was at the opposite end of the room from the chest. All at once I felt a draft blowing from somewhere. But where? Beneath the rock in front of me! I pressed on the wall, and to my surprise it gave way. This portion of the wall was false. It concealed an entrance to another tunnel.

When Dr. Irel witnessed what I had discovered, he immediately came over to the wall. He stepped across the trench, pushed aside the wall, which moved as if it were cloth, and entered the hidden tunnel. He stood there for a moment. It was too dark for him to go any further without the torch. I wondered where it went, and he must have read this thought by the expression on my face, for he stepped back into the room and reached into his coat pocket. From there he removed the corked vial with the silver liquid inside. I knew then that he was telling me this tunnel would take us to the other side of the metal pool. I also knew that we would not be able to take the chest. We would have to come back.

* * *

"So," said I, as I poured some coffee for meself and Erin, "Now that the two of you have settled down a bit, why don't you tell me what happened today? How did things go with Cara?" I asked, addressing Mrs. McGillian as I poured her some tea. "Did you get the job?" I asked Erin.

"I took Ms. Erin straight over to Faulky's and introduced them to each other," stated Mrs. McGillian.

"Oh, she's a lovely girl, William, really she is," said Erin.

"William?" I asked. "What happened to Billy?"

"We—Mrs. McGillian and I—talked it over and agreed William was a far better name to call you than Billy. Mother would have wanted it that way anyhow. You know that's all she called you."

"Forget it, just get to the good stuff."

"I'll tell you, I don't understand what a girl like her sees in you but any fool could sense she's downright smitten. Her face seemed to light up at the mere mention of you. She's so well mannered too."

"I'm glad you like her, but will she be able to help you out?"

"I'm getting to that," she said, as she sipped some of her coffee.

"After the introductions were made," said Mrs. McGillian, sensing me eagerness, "Miss Cara gave us a note to bring to her uncle's tailor shop."

"Her uncle is a very nice man," added Erin. "Thin, with a thin moustache and spectacles and a nose the size of which you would not believe!"

"Ms. Erin!" interrupted Mrs. McGillian. "It's not polite to poke fun at another's expense."

"Aye," said I, "and you ought to remember that the next time you giggle at mine!"

The old girl got a little red in the face and said, “Point taken.”

“Yes, well we gave him Cara’s note and introduced ourselves. He knows me only as Mrs. Erin Calhoone and that Mrs. McGillian is my old friend.”

“He told us he could use the help in his shop and told Miss Erin to come by on Monday to begin.”

“Crikey,” said I. “That’s great news! I knew if anyone could help it would be Cara. If I could see her now I swear I’d give her the biggest kiss.”

“Easy there, Aiden—dragon of love,” jested Erin. “One thing at a time. Cara explained more of your situation to me and I think we’ll be able to figure something out. But it’ll take time.”

* * *

Before we left the cave, Dr. Irel had withdrawn a bar of wax from his inner coat pocket. He softened an end of it by holding it near the torch and then hastily descended back down into the room and inserted the wax into the chest’s keyhole. We waited for it to cool, and when he removed it from the lock it had taken on a whole new shape—that of a key.

Once we returned to the central cavern, Dr. Irel once again removed the silver and gold liquid vials from his coat pocket. Only this time, he also removed a small brush. He then painted a thin layer of gold paint around the entrance to the path we’d just left and a silver layer around the tunnel to the metal pool. When he’d finished, he held his torch up to the light, and the entrances seemed to sparkle to life like stars in a desert sky. Satisfied, he returned one of the empty vials to his pocket and we took the other one back to the metal pond where he gingerly extracted some of the liquid metal. Once done, he gave an approving nod, placed the vial in his pocket and beckoned me to follow him out.

That night, after we recapped the boulder, we made camp on the shoreline and watched as the water slowly crept back in to conceal the hidden world for another nine years. Within a week's time we had returned to my people. A day later it was time for the initiation ceremony. I was about to become a man.

In our culture, tradition is sacred. To be Iboruba means to uphold the laws of our forefathers. The ceremony to become a man is a hardship unto itself. Not just anyone can become a man. Manhood must be earned. First, the village celebrates with a large feast. But the feast is not for those who are to become men. They must learn what it means to take the life from another, so as to learn about the balance of life, what it means to kill and what it means to lose a loved one. For this we must slay a member of our own kindred—our faithful companions, our dogs. I had dreaded this moment for a long time. I loved Azi. But the law is the law, and I swung the club that delivered the fatal blow to poor Azi's head. His flesh tasted terrible. I wanted to vomit, but knew I could not. This was how I would honour his life. It was this that seemed particularly difficult for Dr. Irel to behold. He could only watch the rite of passage unfold.

With this—our final meal before we boys turning men leave the village—comes a song and prayer. The elders gather around the boys and ask the gods to honour the boys' families and bring us back as men; this was imperative now that the Iboruba were now short on males. Then, after goodbyes have been made, we are sent off into the forest to live on our own for seven days. At the end of this time our fathers are to come to us, perform the ritualistic circumcision, and bring us back as men.

As my father had been murdered, I did not know what fate was to bring me, and it was not discussed. But I did not question anything. I took to the forest willingly and survived on my own for the seven days. When the eighth day came, I had begun to lose hope. I would not be allowed to return. Tears began to stream down my cheeks not those of a man, but of a boy. Boyhood was my fate. And then I heard a sound from outside my make–shift hut. I gazed up, and there was Dr. Irel.

He pointed to my eyes, and I dried my own tears. He was playing the part of my father, my Baba. What I did not know was that he had undergone a ritual of his own in order to adopt me, even if for only a few days. This was after he learned what my fate would be. The adoption rituals are rarely performed, so I cannot say what he went through, but I was grateful. Shortly after his arrival, he executed the circumcision, and we returned to my village as men—Baba and me. The final ceremony involved the new men chewing the bark of the iboga plant and donning the masks of our ancestors. We then sang to the beat of the elders' drum–playing and danced around the communal fire in the moonlight. As the ceremony comes to its close, each man stands full in the light of the moon and is overtaken by the spirit of his ancestor. I stood there, in front of everyone, wearing the yellow–and black–painted mask of my ancestors. Although this seems to be a hard concept for people of the western culture to understand, for a moment I became my father. In that moment I could feel his peace. I could feel his pride. And then he was gone. I was myself once more.

Later that night, after the ceremonies had ended and my people were settling in for sleep, Baba came to bid me farewell. He brought one of the Yobandi women with him. This woman spoke English and resumed the lost role of the translator between us.

She explained that Baba wanted me to learn his native tongue, now that I was his son. This Yobandi would be my teacher. She was around my age and seemed knowledgeable enough, so I agreed. She said that Baba would write to me whenever he got the chance, and that one day—in nine years—he would return to these lands seeking my help. He was to leave until then, as he had much to take care of in his own village. Before he was to leave, I returned to my tiny hut, retrieved my ancestry mask, and presented it to Baba as a parting gift.

"No," he said through the translator. "This belonged to your father and is rightfully yours now."

I said, "But Baba, you are my father now, and you must keep this until you die. Then I will take it back. If ever you need guidance or spiritual help, seek out my ancestors by the light of the full moon as they are now your own."

He nodded, with a single tear in his eye. He gave me a whole–hearted, fatherly hug, though I tried to squirm away, as I was a man now. Then he departed on a horse that he had been given from the Yobandi.

The years passed, and every so often I would receive a letter from Baba telling me of all the lands he had visited. Then one day, nine years later, I received a very different letter and with it a package.

* * *

Erin had been working at Faulky's Tailor Shop for just over a week when she found a way to bring Cara to me. The two of them became fast friends, and one evening Erin asked Cara to stay with her for the night, as she pretended to live alone. Cara's folks agreed, and what a pleasant surprise it was to me! Back then people really didn't ask where you lived which was all to the good, given me situation. That night we all talked for hours, and at last the idea of sleep came up.

"Yes," Mrs. McGillian repeated to Cara, "sleep. It's what we do when we're not awake. Where would you like me to fix your bed?"

"With Erin taking the sixth bedroom," I said, "that doesn't leave a vacancy. No way she can stay in either of Vant's two personal rooms and I don't think she'd want to sleep in me art studio."

"Well, it's not like she's going to share a room with you!" declared Mrs. McGillian.

"Oh," stated Cara bashfully. "We would never!"

"That's right," added Mrs. McGillian who turned to Erin. "These two aren't married. It wouldn't be proper."

Erin chuckled. "Sometimes I wish I'd slept with my husband before I married him. It might have saved us both a lot of aggravation! You know, some women do sleep with men before marriage."

"Yes, *whores*."

"Mrs. McGillian!" I interjected.

"Don't Mrs. McGillian me," she said. "I maybe old and from a different time, but in those times people had respect. Marriage was holy and sacred."

"For goodness sake," said Cara. "I'm not going to sleep with William!"

"You're not?" I asked in jest.

"No," she affirmed. "I'm not that kind of girl. Oh, I may be a bit flirtatious, but—"

"Requesting young Master William to paint you nude seems a bit beyond flirtatious to me," said Mrs. McGillian.

"I never said *nude*!" Cara insisted.

"Maybe not," conceded Mrs. McGillian, "but it seemed to be headed down that path."

"Even so," said I, "seeing one nude and touching one nude are two very different things. Why Leonardo Da Vinci—"

"I won't have it. Not while I'm on watch."

"On watch?" I asked.

"You know," said Erin. Billy and Cara are both twenty years old. Romeo and Juliet were merely in their teens when they—"

Mrs. McGillian cut Erin off. "Yes, and I'm not about to let them end up like those two. I do believe they are meant for each other, and that means they're both worth waiting for."

"I don't believe we're having this conversation," said Cara.

"Believe it, Miss Cara, because you will be sleeping with Ms. Erin tonight."

"I will?" said Cara.

"Either that or you can sleep with me."

"Erin it is."

That night I lay in bed staring up at the ceiling, unable to sleep. Knowing me love was just down the hall invigorated me. When your soul mate is near, and the love is strong, you feel like you can do anything. So I got up, left me bed, and made for me studio room. I was inspired; a higher force was guiding me. I grabbed a fresh canvas and some oils and began to paint. I didn't know what I was painting; it really didn't matter. The object—no, the *point*—was to create, to get me feelings, the energy, out of me system. When I'd finished, I studied the image before me. It was a tree. Its limbs were naked, as in the winter, but it was silhouetted against a midnight sky. It reminded me of the tree of life entombed in stained glass high above the front entrance to Vant Manor. But why had I painted it? What did it mean? That's what I was asking meself when I turned and noticed Cara in the room. I jumped a smidge.

"You startled me," I said.

"Sorry, I couldn't sleep and I noticed the candlelight from the hall. Would you rather I leave?" she turned to go.

"No, no, no. Stay. It was you who inspired me to paint tonight."

"Well, I'm glad to be a part of it. It's a tree, isn't it?"

"Aye, but I've no idea why I painted it."

"What does a tree mean to you?"

"Oh, I don't know. Nature, wood, things that are sturdy … family."

"A family tree," she suggested. "But this tree's lost all its leaves."

"But still it stands," I added, "Distressed, dormant perhaps, but not dead."

"Don't you think it's interesting that you painted something that represents your current situation with your family?"

"You might have a point there. Even more interesting that you inspired me to paint it." I added as I approached her and wrapped me arms around her from behind as she gazed at me painting.

"Now that's the real odd part of it," she stated as she leaned back and looked up at me. "Maybe you think of family when you're with me?"

"Maybe. But we don't get to choose our family. We're stuck with them. Friends and lovers mean more to me than family."

"I believe that life is about both choosing what you want and getting what you need."

"And what do you need?" I asked.

"I need you," said she as she turned her body in towards mine.

"You've got me."

We looked at each other for a long moment and then kissed. It was tender—not forceful, not carnal, just soft. Her kiss was almost like a feather blowing across me lips. It began slowly like that, off and on, a small peck here, a stronger, longer–lasting embrace there. It was magic. It was love.

"Draw me," she cooed. "Draw me on the canvas bag I gave you when we first met."

"The bag?"

"As a symbol that I control my life now … and my body."

I was nervous, I can admit that, but I needed an outlet for the creative energy wellin' up inside me. So I did as she asked. I tore through me stacks of paper and paints until—at last—I found the canvas bag she had given to me when first we'd met.

Clothed in her night attire, she took a seat atop an old desk and did her best to make herself comfortable. When she was settled, me eyes explored her body, genially, as I struggled to force me quivering fingers to grasp the quill and sketch her as the flickering candlelight illuminated her feminine curves.

The quill danced across that old canvas bag while her eyes fixed on me. Over and over I was forced to dip the quill back into the inkwell to keep it moist. I think it's safe to say that it was the most fun I'd ever had with ink. After a while—as she struggled to maintain her pose—I put the finishing touches on me masterpiece, flung it aside, and embraced her lips in a fit of fervour. Like a whistling tea kettle, we were finally able to release the pent up passion within us. We kissed off and on until we fell asleep.

We woke the next morning in each other's arms, our relationship consecrated by the rays of the sun . In that moment, when she went creeping back down the hall to Erin's room, I knew that she was the girl I wanted to spend the rest of me life with. She was the girl I was going to ask to be me wife.

XIII
KINDRED
PART THREE: PARADIGM SHIFTS

Today I keep Baba's letters with me. Here is the letter I received nine years after our parting.

* * *

Dear Kamahni,

How are you, my son? I am well. Tonight I write to you from my hotel room in Paris, France. Today has been quite an eventful day. I toured a fantastic boat this afternoon, one that I will return to Africa on. Yes, Kamahni, the time has finally come for us to achieve our goal so long in the making. However, the situation, you must understand, is not ideal. My eagerness to return in time for the chance at the treasure chest has found me in the company of an untrustworthy party. I am quite certain they will try to deceive me, if not attempt to kill me, and escape with the treasure. For these reasons you must follow the proceeding instructions exactly as I have written them.

Our adventure begins on the fourth of May. Sometime on this day I shall come ashore with a party of questionable men—no doubt the most questionable of the bunch. You will recall that the shoreline is usually steeped in fog. You must use this to your advantage and remain hidden. You are to come alone. I cannot trust another, and an army of warriors is not as effective as an agent of the shadows. I will enter the caverns below the sea with these men. I do not believe I will be returning to the surface with them. It would be ideal for them to somehow leave me for dead where I would not be found. Therefore, you must wait for them to return topside and seal the pit with the boulder. Once they have left the area, you will need to act in dire haste.

It is extremely likely that you will find me beside the treasure chest. They will not be able to remove the chest, as it will still be fastened to the ground. But make no mistake the treasure from within will be gone. They will have removed it in barrels. But do not fret, my son. They do not know the real treasure they will be leaving behind. You see, I have never had the least bit of interest in the treasure itself. It is the chest that holds all the potential for me. Now, you will enter through the gold lined tunnel when you come for me. I will have taken them through the silver tunnel and over the silvery pool of mercury. Even if a man is left behind, which we can almost count on with men of such low calibre, he will not be of any trouble to you, for he will not even know you are there. As mentioned, you will find me there, and we will then remove the chest itself. Included within this package you will find dynamite, which we will use to separate the chest from the ground. Do not worry about the chest. It will survive the blast. If I am right about it, it is virtually indestructible. Enclosed you will also find a strange bit of clothing with which you must adorn yourself. I have provided a diagram to instruct you on how to dress.

When I left you, you had become a man, when we meet again you will become a legend. Farewell for now, my son.

Yours,

Dr. Irel E. Vant, Baba

* * *

And so, a few months later there I was, an agent of the shadows concealed within one of the cliff side caves, watching, listening, waiting in the fog. Much time had passed before I finally heard voices. One of the voices was all–too familiar. Only now, for the first time, I could understand it. I had been successful in my English studies and could not wait for Baba to hear me speak his language. But in the moment I was silent—that is, until I stumbled upon some rocks in the fog, alerting them to my presence. Thankfully, the fog that blinded me also blinded them, and I heard Baba convince them to press on. I was far away in distance from the ocean floor where they were headed, but when I heard the boulder move for the first time, I began to dress as I had practised countless times before in the strange clothing he had sent to me.

The material was black as night and shiny. It covered all of my skin, and I wondered if it was for protection. But protection against what? Time passed. I began to worry, as I knew the tide would be coming back in soon. It was a few hours later when I heard some more noise. They were voices, and I waited until they'd passed before I crept down to the sea floor, only to see that the hole remained uncovered. I then fastened a rope that had been in the package to the boulder and lowered myself down into the pit. It was very dark, especially with my mask on. I then lit a match and touched it to an oil lamp, also provided in the package, and entered the main cavern. It was exactly as I had remembered it, and I continued, past the gold–lined tunnel and across the narrowing edge of the pit. It seemed far narrower then I remembered. This must have been because my feet had grown to full size by this time. When I had last taken this path I was but a boy.

So I slowly entered the treasure chamber from high above, and there I saw him. His body and the chest were blocked from the other entrance by a wall of fire. Although he was dressed in clothing like mine, I knew in an instant it must be him. He lay upon the ground, unconscious. I then heard muffled voices through the wall. He had been right about that too. The men he had been with had left some of their own behind. I would need to be quiet. Slowly I began to unshackle him.

* * *

The months passed. Summer had faded. Erin had become quite the seamstress. You might also say that she made it her business to be up on all the town gossip. She made friends with practically everyone she met. But try as she would, she couldn't find a way to patch things over between me and Mr. Faulky and one night she found out why.

"It was sort of queer," Erin began, as I, Mrs. McGillian, and Cara sat 'round her in the foyer. "How the conversation started," she added. "We were in the back, Cara's uncle and I, behind the storefront, where we keep the clothing to be mended. I was taking a break from my sewing and had taken up a pad of paper and begun drawing some of my own clothing ideas when Cara's uncle —his name is Jacob—turned away, face to the window, and started to cry."

"Cry?" I asked.

"For no reason?" asked Cara.

"Well, that's what *I* thought," Erin explained. "So I asked him if everything was all right."

'Pay no attention to me,' he said. 'It isn't right for a man to cry anyway,' then he paused, as if trying to keep his voice from breaking. 'Ah, what's the use? I need someone to talk to, and here you are and all.'

'You can tell me anything,' I offered. 'Come and sit, I can fetch you some tea, if you'd like.'

'No, no, I'll be fine by the window here. Tea isn't necessary,' he said gazing, out into the darkness. 'What I'd like to tell you is this: Twenty–one years ago on this very night a terrible tragedy occurred. I was younger then, not quite your age, but I remember it all very plainly just the same.' He removed his spectacles and took out a handkerchief to dry his eyes. 'Back then my grandfather owned this shop. I was his errand boy then. Anyway, during that time he had employed a young woman. Ristila was her name. Ristila Vant.'"

"Dr. Vant's wife, Ristila?" I asked Erin, shocked. I pointed to her portrait hanging above the foyer's fireplace.

"Aye," said Erin. "The very same."

"Finally, now we're getting somewhere," I stated. "Go on, please continue."

Erin cleared her throat and began again, "So I asked, 'What was this tragedy?'

'She died,' he said flatly.

'I'm so sorry,' I said. 'Did you know her well?'

'Well enough. She was a dear, sweet friend—a friend to the entire family. She had only been with us for scarcely under a year, but she had this presence about her. One talk with her and you felt as if you were speaking with an old friend.'

'And you said it was tragic?'

'Terribly so. The idea of it makes me sick to even consider it.' He stared out again, not bothering to stop the tears this time. 'But how can I not think of it, today of all days?'

'Do you mind if I ask how?'

Then he turned to me and looked me dead in the eye. 'She was murdered.'"

"Murdered?" we all gasped.

"By whom?" I asked Erin.

"'By her husband,' he said."

* * *

"Baba," I whispered, putting my mouth where I guessed may be his ear; (the mask was very concealing). I was bent down near him, trying to be quiet. "Baba ... Dr. Irel!"

I nudged his shoulder; he did not move. Then I was reminded of that scorpion from being in that jail with Charl long ago and so I pinched his side and said, "Baba, get up!"

He came to in an instant.

"Hello?" he asked, still in a daze. "Who's there?" He looked up at me.

"Baba," I repeated. "It's me, your son, Kamahni."

"Kamahni?"

"Yes, Baba, but we must be quiet. There are men on the opposite side of the fire wall."

"Men?" He was still confused. "Of course, Reese and Stanton. Kaleeb must have abandoned them. Quick, my boy, did you bring the dynamite?"

I removed the sticks from my coat pockets. "I would not disappoint you, Baba."

"My boy," he said, as I helped him to stand. He was slightly shorter than I. "You've certainly become a fine man."

"Thank you, Baba."

"Now," he said, as he closed the treasure chest. "Let's set the explosives and get out of here before the tide washes us away with it."

"But won't the noise bring the men upon us?"

"The flames will hold those two back. Now quickly," he said, and he took the dynamite from me, lit the two sticks in the fire from the flaming wall, and wedged them beneath the chest. We ran to the other side of the flame–circled room and waited. Then it happened. ***KABOOM!***

"What the bloody hell was that?" I heard a man say from beyond the flames.

"It's gotta be Vant," said another. "The scheming slime's not done yet!"

When the dust cleared the chest was toppled on its side, but it was no longer attached to the ground. We had been successful.

"Excellent," said Baba. "Now, we'll use the straps I sent you to fastened it to my back so that we can get it across the narrow passage."

"The chest is too long, Baba. It would be better to strap it to my back as I am taller than you."

"Vant?" called a voice. "Vant! It's Stanton. Langston's left us here to die."

"So now you understand my position," Baba called back.

"Look," said the other voice, which I took to be the man named Reese. "Can't we put our differences aside? That tide's gonna come in and drown us all!"

"Correction," said Baba, as he helped me fasten the chest to my back. "The tide will come in and drown you."

"Baba, no," I said. "Whatever these men have done, you can't let them die, not here like this."

"Who's that?" the Stanton voice asked the Reese.

"He's got company," said Reese. "He double–crossed the double–cross!"

"You knew how this would turn out, didn't you, Vant?" asked Stanton.

"That must've been the noise we heard on the shoreline, " added Reese.

"You knew we were out for ourselves the whole time," stated Stanton, ignoring Reese.

"Perhaps the idea had crossed my mind," said Baba.

"Then I don't get it," said Reese. "You've lost the treasure—what else is there? What do you get out of all of this?"

"The chest!" said Stanton. "My God, that has to be it."

"What are you talking about?" Reese asked.

"Langston said Vant got what he wanted, remember? He said he wasn't leaving here without that chest!"

"Bloody hell!"

"It's worth more than the treasure, isn't it Vant?" asked Stanton.

"More than you will ever know," stated Baba. "Come," he said to me, "These men do not deserve to be saved."

"Look," said Stanton. "We double–crossed you, Langston's double–crossed us, that puts us all in the same boat. If you help us get out of here alive we'll help you get back at Langston."

"I've no interest in Langston anymore," Baba said.

"And Abbott? You'd leave him to die with Langston, after you brought him into this mess?"

"I'm quite certain Mr. Abbott will be fine. Langston wouldn't kill him; he needs him to cash in the treasure."

"Fine, then. But look," Stanton continued. "I know you're a crafty one, but I know you'll be wanting to get back to England. Unless you've got another boat handy, that's a long trek to make. No, it's a dangerous one. You get us out of here, and we'll be your indentured servants until we reach England. Then we all go our separate ways and never speak of any of this. What do you say?"

"I say," said Baba, "That I have enough to worry about without wondering whether I'm going to be killed in my sleep or not."

"Baba, some mercy."

"These men are merciless. Now let's get going. We've wasted enough time."

"I will not move unless you do something to free them."

"You'd jeopardize both our lives?" he asked.

"It is the right thing to do, Baba. You know this, I believe that you do."

"You're wrong, these men are—"

"Still men, Baba. But are you?"

"Even if I agreed, how would you propose we save them? That wall of flames would easily eat through us."

"The chest," I said.

"What about it?"

"You said in your letter that it was indestructible. We could lay it on the flames and give them enough room to pass into the chamber."

"Sounds like a plan to us," said Reese.

"If we must," said Baba. "But let us make dire haste."

Although Baba could not see it, I was smiling. You see, being a man is not easy. It means doing the right thing even when you do not want to. And so we followed my plan and we placed the chest on top of the flames. The flames parted, the two men came through, we fastened the chest to my back—it was not hot, to my surprise—and together we made the climb up the overpass.

* * *

"I don't believe it," I said to Erin. "I don't believe it's in Dr. Vant to kill someone. Let alone his own wife!"

"Whether he did or not is irrelevant," said Erin. She paused for a second to take in what she'd just said. "The point is, that's what people think."

"Did he say anything else?" asked Mrs. McGillian.

"Said he didn't want to talk any more about it, just that it'd been years since he'd even spoken her name."

"The Vant name isn't spoken in my family," said Cara. "No one ever mentioned why. I never asked. It never really seemed important before."

"What secrets lie in the heart of man?" asked Mrs. McGillian. "Only God knows."

"He … he's not the type," I stated, trying to reassure meself. "Is he, Mrs. McGillian?"

"Lord, I hope not … I hope not."

We didn't speak much about anything after that. A silence needing no explanation blanketed the lot of us. That night, when we'd all gone to bed, I lay there thinking about Dr. Vant. About how much I really knew about his life, about who he was. And then I felt a compulsion to get up, go downstairs, and enter the West End. There I found Cara staring up at the moonlit statue of the late Ristila Vant. She glanced back as I entered the room. She'd mentioned to her parents that she'd be staying over at Erin's. These sleep overs were becoming a regular thing.

"Do you think he killed her?" I asked.

"Does a man build a shrine to a murder?"

"The truly deranged, perhaps," I stated.

"Do you think he did?" she asked.

"No, no, I don't think he did. You never heard him speak of her. His whole demeanour changed. I think there has to be some kind of misunderstanding somewhere."

"It was twenty–one years ago tonight. On their anniversary no less."

"I wonder where he is right now," I said. "You know, what he's thinking."

"And where are you right now?" she asked.

"Come, I want to show you something." I led Cara out of the West End and into the North–West tower, the library.

"What's in here?" she asked.

I lit a candle and made me way to the globe in the middle of the room.

"This," I said, as I pressed the raised continent on the upside–down world. It gave a familiar *cha–chunk* sound, and the six–foot section of the bookcase opened up. Her eyes widened.

"Follow me," I said as I took her by the hand.

"I don't know if I like this," she said. "Couldn't this wait until morning?"

"I discovered it with Mrs. McGillian. She wouldn't want me to show you. You know how she is. It's just a ways down."

She held me hand firmly, and I led the way down the stone staircase and into pure darkness with but a candle to light the way. We passed through the wooden door and entered the private chamber.

"This is Dr. Vant's private study," I said. "It's where he houses all his secrets."

"It's freezing down here," she commented as she looked around. "What is all this?"

"His collection."

"Collection of what? *For* what?"

"Now, that I can't answer. But when we stumbled upon this place, Mrs. McGillian and I, we found one of a series of pamphlets that read as a diary he was keeping."

"That's not so unusual," she said.

"He writes to his dead wife, and in the tale we read he spoke of the lost city of Atlantis and vampires and this creature called the Kride."

"Maybe he's writing a novel," she suggested.

"Maybe we'll find out more about his wife if we go through some of his notes," I suggested.

"All right, if it means finding an answer to all this. I'll start on this counter."

"There's me girl. I'll take these over here."

"Strange," said Cara. "Look at these masks. Where do you suppose this one came from?" she asked holding up a yellow–and black–painted wooden mask.

* * *

"Son," said Baba, grasping my shoulder to prevent me from falling backwards. The weight of the chest was great, and I was now wearing it across my torso and moving along with my heels against the wall and my feet hanging over the ledge where the pit waited to swallow me up.

"Just a bit further," he encouraged.

"Did you say 'son'?" asked Reese, who was on the other side of me.

"It's a long, drawn–out story," began Baba, "and I—"

"Quiet!" ordered Stanton. "What's that sound?"

We were silent as we crept onward. Baba made it onto the narrow but pit–less path ahead of me.

"It's faint," stated Baba, "but it's—"

"It's the tide!" declared Reese.

"Everyone," ordered Baba, "on the double!"

Suddenly, and without warning, water came flooding into the cavern and down into the pit, just as Stanton and Reese joined us in the other part. We ran as quickly as we could and soon found ourselves in the main chamber up to our waists in rushing water.

"Son of a—," began Reese.

"How do we get out with the water coming in on top of us?" asked Stanton.

"We'll never make it," said Reese. "We'll all drown!"

"Wait a minute," said Baba. "How do we know we'll drown? It is true that if we attempt to go up now we'll be facing enormous pressure as the entire ocean rushes in around us. But if we wait—"

"Then we can swim out," I said. "Oh, Baba, you are truly the wisest man I know."

"That's all well and fine," said Stanton. "But how long do you think it'd take to fill up that pit? And what do we do when the water mixes with the toxic liquid metal?"

"Yeah, and how are we supposed to swim in these get–ups?" added Reese, referring to the protection we were wearing.

"All valid points, gentlemen," Baba agreed. "Kamahni, is the dynamite dry?"

I felt my pocket, "Yes Baba, it is dry."

"How much do you have left?"

I searched my pockets, "Four, Baba."

"That should do. You three: Each of you take a stick of dynamite and wedge it into the rock above each of those three tunnels leading to the pit. With any luck we'll knock down enough rubble to seal them off and flood the central cavern faster."

"Faster?!" asked Reese.

"Don't worry," added Stanton. "I think I know what he's planning."

I handed a stick to each man while I took a third one to the gold–lined cave. When the dynamite was in place, I lit the fuses and waded my way back towards the main entrance with the others. And then ...

KABOOM! *The rocks erupted in a great explosion and, just as Baba predicted, they sealed off the tunnels.*

"Success is ours gentlemen," said Baba.

"Great," said Reese with a sigh of relief. "Now let's get out of these outfits." He reached to unfasten his coat.

"Not yet," Baba interrupted. "There could still be some contamination. We need to be cautious. We've no choice but to try to swim our way out as is. Once ashore we can burn the clothing."

"Just how bad is this stuff?" asked Reese.

"Life–threatening, Mr. Reese."

By now the water had risen to our necks and we were forced to begin paddling to stay afloat. Within fifteen minutes we were floating with our heads inches from the ceiling.

"It's now or never, gentlemen," ordered Baba. "We must leave now if we are to maintain enough strength for the swim to shore. On the count of three, we all take a mighty breath. Make it a good one, it may be your last."

Everyone felt the anxiety.

"On my count: one, two ... three!" A great sound filled the air as we all took a great breath in. Baba led the way, and we followed him in the darkness, while he pushed the floating chest before him. I did not think to ask him how he would guide us without the light of the lamp, but somehow we were able to exit the hole in the ocean floor. Still, darkness surrounded us, and my lungs began to ache. I pressed on. When at last my hands found the open air, I sprang my head up, removed my mask, and gulped in the sweetest air imaginable. It was the breath of life.

It was night now, and the sea had returned to claim the cliff–side. Baba was beside me. He helped me bring the chest ashore where, Stanton was already standing, naked. He helped us out of the water.

"You'll pardon me," said Baba. "If I don't have any extra clothing. You see, I didn't plan on rescuing anyone. Kamahni," he said to me as we stepped ashore. "Where did you hide the rest of the package I sent you?"

"Oh, Baba! Oh, I am such the fool."

"What do you mean?"

Then Reese's head popped up out of the water. He too removed his mask and gasped for air.

"You'll never believe what I found floating in the water," said Reese. Then he held up the remains of Baba's package.

"I hid it inside my cliff–side cave," I explained. "The water must have swept it away when it rose!"

"Perhaps it would have been too easy," said Baba. "Very well, we'll have to make clothing out of—" he looked around. There was only sand, fog, and water. "What's left in that pack?" he asked Reese, as the man came ashore.

Reese handed the pack to Baba. He inspected it and removed a wet pair of trousers. "Looks like this will have to do until we can get to Kamahni's village."

"How are four men going to dress themselves in one pair of trousers?" asked Reese.

"Are you a fan of the loin cloth?" asked Baba.

* * *

Cara and I must have been rummaging through Dr. Vant's things for nearly fifteen minutes. The study was dark, damp, and dismal. But curiosity kept us going. Then it happened. I pulled open the bottom drawer of one of the cupboards and removed a wooden box. I opened it up and there, before me eyes, rested the biggest, brightest, clearest jewel I'd ever laid eyes on. I was holding the Morrigan.

"Cara," I called. "Cara, come here! I want you to see this."

She came over. I balanced meself on one knee, having just been at the bottom drawer, and I held up the box for her to see. She gasped.

"Billy! It's … oh, it's beyond beautiful!"

"Aye—"

"Of course I'll marry you!"

"Of course you'll—*What?*"

"I'll marry you, Billy."

"Oh, hey, whoa—"

"Father will have to learn to like you, that's all," she said as she helped me stand. She then reached inside the box and removed the Morrigan. She placed it on her ring finger.

"It's a bit large, but Uncle Jacob knows a jeweller in town who can set it right."

"Now, Cara, hang on."

She kissed me passionately on the lips.

"Oh, Billy, this is the happiest day of my life. Imagine, fooling me with that ridiculous vampire tale just to get me down here! I can't wait to tell the others," she said, as she ran up the staircase.

"Cara," I called after her. "Cara, no!" I said.

"What's wrong, Billy?" she asked as we returned to the library.

"It's … it's the middle of the night, you know. At least wait until morning."

"Of course, what was I thinking? I'm just so excited. Just think of it. Mrs. Cara O'Brien!"

"Does have a bit of a nice ring to it," I said with a smile. Then I thought about the ring again. Mrs. McGillian was never going to go along with this. I would have to get to her before Cara did. That night I didn't get an ounce of sleep. I stayed up in bed praying for an easy way out of the mess. That's when I came up with the best idea I could think of.

"That's your plan?" asked an exasperated Mrs. McGillian after I'd explained it to her. I had caught her over her breakfast. The great thing about Mrs. McGillian is that she's always been an early riser. "Letting her keep the Morrigan until you've found a way to replace it with an amethyst?"

"Have you got a better idea?"

"Yes. Tell her the truth!"

"I can't do that. You didn't see her face when she thought I'd proposed."

"Good heavens, listen to yourself. Do you even want to marry the girl?"

"Yes, of course I do. I'd planned on proposing one day, just not yesterday, er, last night … this morning … whatever! Look, just do this one thing for me, and I'll do anything that you like. You've but only to ask! I'll owe you me life."

Just then we heard Erin and Cara coming down the stairs.

"Oh, Mrs. McGillian," said Cara as she entered the kitchen. "I'm glad you're up."

"You little devil, you," chuckled Erin as she rubbed me head with her knuckles.

"Master William's already told me all about it," said Mrs. McGillian.

"Here's the ring," said Cara, as she held it out for Mrs. McGillian to see.

The old gal gasped at its beauty.

"There it is, right in front of me," she said, almost in a trance. "In all its glory!"

"Mrs. McGillian?" I asked.

"All right, Master William, you win," she said, and she glanced up at me with a wink. "Pancakes with lemon and sugar it is!"

* * *

After days of travelling we had finally reached my people. There was a celebration to commemorate Baba's return and our successful journey. I introduced him to my first wife but he already knew her. She was the Yobandi woman who had translated for us when last we parted nine years earlier. She was pregnant with our first child. Although Baba has never yet met him, I named the boy after him. His name is E.

And so, I have little left to tell. Baba stayed a few days more and then departed with the two salvaged sailors. We gave them a wagon and two horses and plenty of food to last them for a good long while. I have not seen Baba since, but a Baba to me he will always be.

XIV
THE SPANISH AFFAIR

The following is a letter from Dr. Vant addressed to meself and Mrs. McGillian. I offer it here now to maintain chronological order and so as not to interrupt the pace of the chapter in which it arrives:

My Dear William, Mrs. McGillian,

I trust that all is well. Indeed it has been several months since I've last written. Over half a year has passed and in that time so much more than I can comprehend or put to words. Never–the–less, I have been lucky enough to have made it thus far. You might have guessed that Kaleeb was not a noble man. As I predicted months before my initial voyage aboard the *Wooden Whale*, he attempted to deceive me and made off with the treasure within the chest I had been so long seeking. Of course, I let him take it. The prize was not what was in the box but rather the box itself. I do not know what became of Martin Abbott. I last saw him back in May. I speculate that he was taken captive by Kaleeb and his crew. I've no idea if he was able to escape. However, I have a feeling he's doing well somewhere.

And so, after having evaded death on more than one occasion with the help of my adopted African son, Kamahni, and Kaleeb's own Stanton and Reese, who turned over a new leaf, so to speak, I found myself entering Morocco in the middle of December. Oh pardon, as I now think of it, I believe I've quite forgotten to mention that I have an adopted son. My past is a strange series of tales, the majority of which are irrelevant to this tale in particular. Still, after such a time I feel I do owe you some explanation as to where I have been and what I have been doing. So I shall continue.

Morocco, December 1874. If there's one thing that can be said about Morocco, it would be that it has mountains, mountains of mountains. Beautiful, my word, yes, and vast. Part of the Sahara lies within Morocco, which was how we came to enter it from the south. Every evening we were slowly advancing towards England. The journey had taken longer than I'd liked but my destiny never seemed closer. I learned throughout my trek that Reese and Stanton, for all the initial trouble, turned out to be decent companions. I had made the same journey nine years prior, and I must say that travelling with others has its advantages. We took turns cooking, sleeping, keeping watch, and so on. We had come by horse–drawn wagon. Our goal, once we'd reached Morocco, was to seek out Casablanca and catch a ship home, or at least to Europe. We arrived there by the end of the month, which is really where this story begins.

Casablanca, Morocco, December 1874. We entered the city during the late hours of night and so waited until sunrise before seeking a potential escort home. We decided we could cover the most ground if we split up. I believe Stanton chose to check the piers, while Reese went to enquire on the streets and in the market square. My tactic was to scour the restaurant scene. At this time of morning I'd be likely to find the captains shovelling a last meal into their gullets before shoving out to sea.

I entered a fine–looking establishment and asked the host for some information on the diners. He was a chubby but clean gentleman with the air of French descent and he beckoned me to follow him. We came to rest at the table of a man seated with his back to us and his legs propped up on a stool. He was reading a book and smoking a coca–laced cigar.

“Good morning,” I said. The host nodded and left us. “You speak English, yes?” The man made no attempt to reply. “I was told you may be able to assist me in my quest to reach London.”

The air grew stale. The man sat for a long time and then finally spoke.

“Indeed, I am en route to England,” he said, in a quiet calm voice that possessed traits of a foreign ethnicity.

“Excellent,” I stated. “Then are you in a position to allow me and two of my companions to accompany you on this voyage? For a very generous fee, of course.”

“A very generous fee, I’d expect. There’s just one thing.” He took a long draw from his cigar. “I have some business that I must attend to in Spain on my way. You don’t mind, do you, … Dr. Vant?”

He turned to face me and I recognized him in an instant. His name is Shih–Chieh (pronounced *shŭ–je*) Ling. He’s a sixty–five–year–old Chinese man of refined culture. He always appears to be in the best shape of his life. He is fit, he is distinguished, and he has a thin pepper–and–salt moustache that curls up into a half circle on each side of his perfectly symmetrical face. Upon his head he usually wears a black bowler, though at the time it was on the table beside him. He was dressed in a black morning suit complete with grey gloves. His face is most certainly his trademark feature. He can look wise, show sympathy or respect, and appear humble, while underlying the surface is the keen, sharp, and very cunning intellect that comes subtly through in his mannerisms and subconsciously gets his general point across.

Shih–Chieh’s background has always been somewhat mysterious. He was schooled in dozens of higher–level universities and holds four degrees. As I recall, they are archaeology, psychology, trigonometry, and physics. He speaks five languages fluently and held tenure at my alma mater, where I was first introduced to him by the university’s provost, Professor Stone Greyson. Since his departure from teaching, Shih–Chieh has become a somewhat famous archaeologist, dabbling mostly within the realms of Atlantis and the Library of Alexandria.

"Professor Shih–Chieh Ling," I exclaimed merrily. "Good heavens, what are you doing here in Morocco?"

"Business, naturally," he said, plainly and with little emotion.

"But of course. And just how did you know it was I who had come to your table?"

"You'll find there is very little that escapes me, Dr. Vant. I would think that you, having taken several of my classes, would know this."

"It *has* been a while, hasn't it?"

"The lapsing of time is an improper excuse for a student of your calibre."

"Doctor, now," I corrected him.

"The best doctors of philosophy are always students first."

"Touché," I chuckled. "Still the same old Professor Ling, aye Shih–Chieh?"

He said nothing, and in that nothingness I found my answer.

"So then." I pulled out a seat. "May I?"

"Please."

I sat down and continued: "What of my offer?"

"Your money is of little value to me, Irel. What I choose to seek is something of a different end to a means."

"You mean, means to an end. "

"Do I? "

"If not, what other end?"

He smiled. "That, my pupil, shall remain to be seen. What I need from you now is your expertise."

"Is that all? Then you shall have it."

"That is what I've come to enjoy about you, Irel. You are always willing to give as long as you're getting in return."

"May I ask how my expertise may possibly assist your ever–expansive intellect?"

"You will learn in time. Gather your companions and meet me on pier seventeen. We'll discuss the details en route to Spain."

"Pier seventeen," I repeated as I committed it to my short–term memory.

"The *Atlas* departs at seven sharp."

The *Atlas*, I thought, a fitting name for the vessel of one Shih–Chieh Ling. The very name conjures up images of the character from Greek mythology. One Atlas was Poseidon's son and ruled over Atlantis another held the weight of the world upon his shoulders. There's even a mountain range named after the Titan in Morocco. So you see, it is only fitting that the ship bear such a name.

Shortly thereafter, I caught up with Reese and Stanton in the market. Reese had had a lead, but we all decided it would be better to take Shih–Chieh's offer. We returned to our belongings, sold our horses and wagon, and carried the chest to pier seventeen.

Pier Seventeen, Casablanca, December 1874. The *Atlas* was nothing short of miraculous. It was an enormous sailing yacht as smooth and as white as ivory, with a solid gold–bow splicing the air before it in a razor–sharp point. Never had I seen such a clean vessel. It was in immaculate condition. We were met at the dock by one of Shih–Chieh's crew. He was a huge man, rather obese, I must say. Although the ship was clean this man could've used a shave, as his face was rather stubbly. I imagine I looked no better, perhaps a bit worse, even. Months in the desert can do that to you. There was something about the man that I could not place. I felt almost as if we had met before, a lifetime ago. He introduced himself as Hector Arnold. He appeared to me to be in his fifties.

"Professor Ling will see you now," he said. "Follow me please. Watch your step."

We followed Hector up the ramp and on board the gleaming vessel. We were taken into an interior cabin, where Shih–Chieh was seated with that same book. He stood up when we entered, shook our hands, and, after introductions were made, sat back down on a luxurious white sofa that curved around the entire cabin. I think it worthwhile to mention that during the lapse of time while I was catching up with Reese and Stanton, Shih–Chieh had changed clothing. He now matched the rest of the ship in a suit of white. The hat he wore was a thin–brimmed straw fedora with a pheasant's feather extending from its black ribbon.

"Gentlemen, please be seated," he said. We took him up on the offer and sat down on the sofa. "You are, of course, curious as to why I agreed to allow you passage on my ship. I suppose if there is one thing I am, it is to the point. Dr. Vant has undoubtedly explained to you that I am one of the foremost Atlantean scholars on the whole of the planet, though I receive little recognition. Which is partly by design, but I digress. The question is why? Why Atlantis? What secrets could it reveal that could be beneficial to me in today's thriving world? Not fame, not fortune: such things I have and yet have not need for. I am on a very different quest, a journey that has taken me my entire life and thousands of others' lives before me to achieve: power—absolute, raw power—pure, crisp, clean."

I felt the yacht stir and I could see from the cabin window that we'd left port.

"How does one obtain power from a long–lost continent?" continued Shih–Chieh. "The secrets they left behind hold all the keys. Crystals, diamonds, gemstones, whatever name you ascribe to these delightful objects, they are violet in colour and are capable of harnessing the very power of the sun and moon. Here." He extended his hand and removed a white glove. "This is what they look like." Upon his finger was a gem, a fraction of a crystal that I am in possession of, called the Morrigan, as you'll recall, Mrs. McGillian. But it was his pride and joy. "Magnificent, I know. I hypothesize that this tiny rock holds more power than a factory of coal. Imagine the possibilities. Now imagine a crystal the size of this cabin. What could *it* do?"

"Bring about the end of a civilization, I would suppose," I stated.

"Ah, Irel, forever caught up in your own doom's–day theory."

"There is evidence beyond belief that will one day be put together in such a fashion so as to prove my theory, Shih–Chieh."

"Perhaps, but not in my lifetime."

"So," said Reese. "What you're telling us is that you're after some big purple diamond?"

"I did not mean to lay down such an impression, Mr. Reese. No, I am already in possession of such a crystal."

"Preposterous!" I declared. "Crystals of that size were either damaged, lost, or destroyed ages ago."

"I do not ask for your belief. I merely seek your assistance. Your guidance."

"Guidance on what?" I asked.

"How to unleash this power."

"I haven't the least idea of such things."

"Nor do I, but somewhere in Spain there exists a people who do. They have passed its secret down for generations. It is the very reason they have been wanderers, nomads, never staying in any one place too long. They are a self–reliant band of brethren living among the Spanish. They are the—"

"The Gitanos," I replied. "The gypsies."

"You see, Irel, that is why you continue to be my favourite pupil."

"I'm sorry, but I fail to make the connection between gypsies and Atlantis," said Stanton.

"You're not alone," I said. "Few people know the truth behind the peoples of the lost continent."

"You both keep referring to it as a lost continent," he continued. "Wasn't Atlantis just the myth of a city?"

"Atlantis a city?" laughed Shih–Chieh. "How ignorant the world has become!"

"Plato," I began, "described Atlantis as an island beyond the Straits of Gibraltar. He explained that Atlanteans went to battle with the Athenians and conquered the whole of the Mediterranean world from their home in the Atlantic. They are described as greedy, power–hungry people who perished by earthquakes and erupting volcanoes. Their island was said to have sunk.

"Note that I am world–renowned for my own Atlantean theories and believe that their greed brought about their demise. It is my strong belief that those colossal crystals were affixed to various superstructures, such as obelisks, and the capstone on the great pyramid of Giza, all of which were used to transmit energy across the world and power their cities—much like the electricity becoming ever–so–popular today. Yet they did it without wires!

"But this power was cleaner than electricity, without a single by–product. There was just one catch. Comets, falling stars, however you wish to think of them, come close to our planet only once or twice each millennium. One such object I have dubbed the 'Natural Regulator'. This Natural Regulator was on its usual orbit during the time of the Atlantean rule. Normally it would continue on its trek around the cosmos but it felt a strong tugging. This traction, this force, caused by the enormous crystals, enhanced the earth's gravitational pull as they transmitted their energy from one superstructure to another. And so, what happened?

It is not unwise to suggest that this Natural Regulator was drawn in by the energy and came hurtling down upon the largest of these crystals, the place where the energy culminated, the great temple in the heart of the continent's capital city that some say bore its name, Atlantis, but others know as Pontus. The collision was catastrophic, to say the least. It demolished the city, melted the polar icecaps, which caused flooding of what was left of the city, and at the same time plunged a great portion of the western hemisphere into an age of ice, as the debris blackened the sky for years. And so the city was lost forever, but not the continent, not really. The continent, my friends, was none other than the Americas, North, South, and Central. Atlantis, the city, resided between the United States' coastline, Bermuda, and Puerto Rico, in a sort of triangular pattern. When we refer to the lost continent we are speaking of this lost knowledge of its true existence."

"You've been out in the sun too long," sneered Reese.

"I admit," said Shih–Chieh, "there are many parts of Dr. Vant's theory that I disagree with." He turned to me. "However, some spark my curiosity. The name Pontus is new to me."

I said nothing.

"But what does all of this have to do with gypsies in Spain?" asked Stanton.

"However one imagines the fate of Atlantis—Pontus," began Shih–Chieh with a smile, "the truly dedicated scholars came to the conclusion that some of the Atlantean descendants had survived."

"Yes," I continued. "Various tribes still populate areas of the world. Most of them chose to forget their past so as to escape a similar downfall."

"The least noted ancestors are the Durwaihiccora and the Yishnalta," explained Shih–Chieh. "But various others still exist. One such people are the Roma, the gypsies. As Dr. Vant mentioned, most of these groups covered up their pasts, but some continued to pass down the secrets of their forefathers. The Roma are such a group, though most of them do not even know it."

"And what makes you so certain?" I asked.

"Let us just say that I have my resources," he replied with a faint grin.

"True, if you knew of the Durwaihiccora, perhaps the Roma could be as you suggest."

"But if it destroyed a city and caused an ice age, why would you want to unleash that power again?" Stanton asked.

"*If* is the question," added Shih–Chieh. "Perhaps it was that the world grew jealous of their advanced intellect and smited *them*. Regardless of their disappearance, we are in a different age today. As civilization has flourished, so too has our capacity to reason. We are ready for the responsibility of that power."

"The power of gods should not belong to humans," I argued.

"My friend, are you not a preacher of atheism?" Shih–Chieh asked. "I've read your theories. According to you, the power of the universe is within all of us humans alike.

"That does not make me an atheist. And that energy—that essence—belongs to every *thing* in this universe, Shih–Chieh, not just you and me.

"In your presupposition we are *all* gods. I am merely suggesting we find a way to tap into that energy for the benefit of mankind."

"I will not support the return of such madness," I firmly stated.

"All I ask of you is to accompany me to Spain and help me to find the one who can answer my questions. Maybe there is no secret. But there is someone who will know and that is who I must speak to. If you wish passage to England you will assist me in this search. Otherwise, I believe you know the way back to shore."

I sat silent for some time. Now you both know that I am known for my deceptive powers, but putting something over on Shih–Chieh would be like telling a man standing in a thunderstorm that it is not raining. I agreed to his terms, but schemed under my breath.

Atlantic Ocean, The Atlas, December 1874. The voyage aboard the *Atlas* was, at first, a pleasant one. Shih–Chieh is crafty, and so he used his many talents to try to put us at ease with the arrangements we'd made. That night we drank a fine bottle of merlot, played a few hands of cards, and slept well. I awoke to the sounds of the gulls flying overhead. Shih–Chieh had provided us each with a clean set of clothing. I wore a white suit myself. When I'd finished dressing, I left my room—we all had our own—and found Shih–Chieh sipping a drink while over–looking the Spanish coastline, with the Strait of Gibraltar to our left.

"Beautiful, isn't it?" he asked, without turning around to greet me.

"Very," I replied. "You know, my wife was part Spanish."

"Is that right?" he asked. "What was her name again?"

"Ristila."

"Yes, that's it," he said. "And speaking of your dead wife," he added in a suddenly cold tone, "Why do you carry an Atlantean chest with nothing in it?"

"I've no idea what you're referring to," I answered.

"Have you forgotten that Professor Greyson was the one who introduced you to Winston Seadrick?"

"Perhaps you do know more than I'd like you to," I stated.

"We all have our secrets, Irel. Secrets are dangerous. They make us … vulnerable."

"Just what are you hinting at, old boy?"

"Irel, you misjudge me. I do not hint. Negotiate, yes. Threaten? There *are* times. Just something to consider if you should decide to walk out on our agreement."

"I see," I said, as I glanced down at his drink, which he held in a silver goblet. It was very dark but held remnants of a red colour. "Rather early for merlot, don't you think?"

"Oh, it isn't wine," he said with that grin. "I suppose in some countries they may mix it with a rice wine, but not I. No, Irel, this is a very old concoction: fresh snake blood with a hint of its bile. The essences of these creatures are very beneficial to my health and my spirit."

"I believe I read that somewhere."

"I have a glass every morning. In the back there is a room where I keep the snakes caged up. You see, " he paused for effect, "you must taunt the snake first to truly get the blood flowing. Once it's ready to deliver a fatal attack on you, you deliver the final blow to it." He began to chuckle. "Did you know that their bodies continue to quiver long after you've drained them of their blood and skinned them? The deadlier the snake, the more fulfilling the drink. You have a snake or two, don't you, Irel?"

"Well, it isn't that I've enjoyed this conversation," I said. "Because I haven't. But if you'll excuse me, I must check on my companions."

"Not at all," he replied, turning back to the view before him. "Not … at … all."

I suppose you're wondering what all that was about. I'm sure everything will come to light soon enough, so fear not. But where was I? Ah, yes, so I explained to Reese and Stanton that Shih–Chieh was not to be trusted, and they acknowledged that they too found him somewhat queer. It was around noon when we finally docked in Málaga.

Málaga, Spain, December 1874. Upon the shore waited a very stunning Chinese woman. Her hair was long but worn up and anchored in place with chopsticks. She wore a form–fitting red dress with gold and black sequences swirling into unrecognizable symbols and patterns. Her lips were painted red and she stood perfectly straight, as if made of porcelain. She, like Shih–Chieh, had perfectly tanned skin.

"Gentlemen," said Shih–Chieh, as we followed him down the ramp and unto shore. "My wife, Kien."

"That's your wife?" asked Reese. "You sure she's not your granddaughter?"

"Kien is a very young forty–five–year old," he said. "Age means little to us."

When we gathered closer, Kien was the next to speak.

"We sighted you some hours ago," she said to her husband.

"I trust everything is in order?" he asked.

"Come," she said to us all. "We've much to discuss, and the time is right."

"Excellent," Shih–Chieh muttered to himself. "Excellent."

From the port we took carriages to a private club just up the shoreline. The club was called *La Adivinanza del Mono* or in English, *The Monkey's Riddle*. It was a Chinese themed club owned by Shih–Chieh. We followed him into a private room where there were no windows. The room was dark, lit only dimly by a low red light. We were seven in total: There was Reese, Stanton, Shih–Chieh, Kien, Hector Arnold, a Chinese man that I took to be either Shih–Chieh's or Kien's bodyguard, and, of course, myself. The bodyguard stayed behind the happy couple, and we were soon joined by two waiters who served us baijiu, a warm Chinese spirit, and put out a plate of dim sum, which is a type of steamed bun appetizer.

Shih–Chieh glanced up at the waiters and, as if he'd said 'leave us,' they were soon gone. Shih–Chieh leaned back in his chair and lit a fat cigar. He took a long drag.

"Reports have come in," began Kien. "That indicate a calming trend among the Roma."

Shih–Chieh exhaled, which covered his face in smoke.

"What exactly does a *calming trend* represent?" I asked.

"In this case," said Shih–Chieh. "It represents very much."

"When the Roma are at ease," Kien explained, "it becomes easier to gain their trust—to infiltrate their encampments—and they become more trusting of useful information."

"This is where you will become a superior asset to us, Irel," stated Shih–Chieh. "You possess a rare talent to finesse people with an enchanting charm surpassed only by myself."

"Then why have you not *finessed* the Roma yourself?"

"There have been complications, and the Roma no longer have faith in me."

"I see."

"Each year, a particular sect of the Spanish Roma, the Ubatta Lahros, hold a secret festival within a public festival to reflect on their culture," informed Kien. "It is during this festival that the ancient secrets of Atlantis are discussed in a coded language."

"That festival is nearly upon us, is it not, my dear?" asked Shih–Chieh.

"The festival of Nemontemia begins on the first of January and ends on the fifth," she advised.

"And the first is tomorrow," Shih–Chieh reminded.

"The New Year already?" asked Reese. "That means we've missed Christmas."

"But think of the joyful time you'll have during Nemontemia," offered Shih–Chieh.

"Nemontemia, Nemontemia," I repeated. "Why does that sound familiar?"

"Nemontemia is a festival that comes from the idea of Nemontemi, which was a period of five days in the Aztec calendar representing the empty days that transitioned one year to the next," Kien stated.

"Yes, yes, that's right. I'd forgotten."

"Aztecs?" asked Reese.

"An ancient Mesoamerican people in Central America and Mexico," I answered. "Remember that Pontus was relatively close in proximity to

Central America. The Aztecs' ancestors were or were heavily influenced by the Atlanteans."

"How will we be *tracking* these special gypsies?" asked Stanton.

"Straight to the point," stated Shih–Chieh. "A man after my own heart."

"Identifying the Ubatta Lahros is rather easy," said Kien. "During public festivals they must distinguish themselves from other gypsies so their travelling brethren can easily recognize them. In general, the women wear a deep purple headscarf sequenced in gold patterns. The men wear these same coloured kerchiefs around their necks."

"Of course there is no written recipe, if you will, for extracting the information we need from these people," said Shih–Chieh. "We have to play it by ear, work fluidly with the pace of our conversations, and emerge victorious. Irel, you should be flawless at this."

I smiled faintly, perhaps scowling at him.

That night we feasted gluttonously and were taken to Shih–Chieh's private villa, which also overlooked the Mediterranean. There was a glorious display of fireworks to ring in the New Year. Afterwards, we retired for the night. There too we each had our own room furnished with clothing and, while I cannot speak for the others, mine came equipped with a bottle of wine and assorted fruits and cheeses. The following morning was fairly uneventful. Shih–Chieh kept us busy with a tour of his estate while Kien must have been attending to business elsewhere. Eventually, evening set in and that was our cue to set out onto the streets.

We began our trek in the Candelaria district along Tello Street, where the gypsies had set up stands. There we separated, each going a different direction. The moon was out, and the stars were spotting the dusky sky, setting the mood for a night of festivities.

"Come," beckoned an elderly gypsy woman in a robe of pinks and lavenders. She spoke Spanish, naturally, and I understood but pretended not to. "Come, Señor. I know just what you need. An elixir!" I glanced her way. "Ha, that's it!" She was smiling now, and I could see her yellowed teeth. “You need an elixir to set your heart on its true course.” I kept walking. “Wait, don’t go! Here, here,” she called, as she struggled to follow me. “Drink this,” she requested, as she handed me a small cup of some greenish tea concoction.

“If I drink this for you,” I began, “will you go about your business and leave me to mine?”

“Of course, Señor. I am not a pest!”

I smiled. I brought the cup to my nose and inhaled. The smell seemed strange, but I was eager to be rid of her, so I downed the odd brew in a single gulp. I then handed the cup back to her.

“There, now,” I said. “Please keep your end of the bargain.”

“Certainly, Señor. That will be three reales.”

“Thre—”

“Oh, now, Irel,” I heard Shih–Chieh whisper from the shadows, though she apparently did not. “You didn’t think you could get something for nothing did you?”

I said nothing and paid the woman. Shih–Chieh had been kind enough to exchange some of our money into the local currency. The woman walked away chuckling to herself.

“Irel,” Shih–Chieh called me over to a shaded area. “You seem to be doing the opposite of what you need to do,” stated Shih–Chieh. “We’re here to get information not avoid these people. Maybe the old hag was right. Perhaps you do need to get your heart back on course.”

“Shih–Chieh, you know me. My heart is always in the right place.”

“Perhaps I’d forgotten,” he remarked calmly. “ Now then, go, mingle. I’ll be around.”

I had many encounters that night. Not all the gypsies were old and unkempt. On the contrary, there were numerous young folk about. They were playing their instruments, reading fortunes, performing various stunts, and selling delicious foods. None of which were healthy mind you. But one does not go to a festival to be healthy. I engaged myself in a lot of idle conversation, and, although it was highly interesting, nothing was of particular value. It wasn’t until just before midnight that I caught the possibility of a lead.

I was now walking back up Tello Street when I spotted a fortune teller's stand that I had passed earlier. Only this time I took notice of a highly attractive woman in her early forties. Her hair was long and emerged out from under her violet and gold headscarf. Gold earrings dangled on each side of her almond–coloured oval–shaped face.

"Pardon me for staring," I said in Spanish. "But do you have any idea how radiant you are?"

"Tell me something," she requested. "Is that what you usually say when you first meet a woman?"

"Do you know, I don't believe I've ever said that before," I said with a chuckle.

"Then it pleases me to be the first to hear it."

"I was by here earlier. I didn't see you. I would've noticed."

"My sister left for dinner. You might say it's my shift."

"I'm Irel," I said, and I offered my hand.

"My name is Renata," she replied, as she reached to shake my hand. In an eloquent move I manoeuvred her hand just so and bent down to give it a kiss. "Ah, an old–fashioned gentleman. It must be your refined British upbringing."

"If you knew anything about my upbringing, you'd change your mind."

"Point taken. Though, I may not know much about your past, if you'd like I can tell you your future."

"Is that so?"

"Oh, yes," she said. She smiled in such a profoundly charming, confident, and innocently coy way that I could not resist.

"How can I refuse?" I asked, as I took a seat on a chair across a small table from her. She reached for my hand and focused her deep, large eyes on it. "Anything of interest?" I asked.

"Hmmm, well, here's something. It says that you are often overconfident, self–reliant, and that you have a way with the ladies."

"Very nice, very nice indeed. I'd like to come back to that last one, but pray, continue."

"You travel often and make friends wherever you go."

"This I know, but what about my future?"

"Patience, Irel, the future comes about from the energies around us. I need to pick up on those subtleties." She then spit into my hand and rubbed the saliva into my palm.

"And what does that do for me?"

"Nothing, I just wanted to make sure I had your trust," she said with a wink.

"But I barely know you."

"It says here," she claimed pointing to a line in my hand. "That we were destined to meet."

"*Now,* you're talking."

"But you are trapped," she added, and her voice changed to a more serious tone. "There's a wall, a prison or something around you. Inside is a great sadness, and it is very dark. If you do not learn to deal with this sadness … it will destroy you."

"Interesting. Is that all?"

She looked up at me and gazed into my eyes, almost as if in some sort of trance. "You will soon find yourself at a crossroads in your life. Be careful. There is a great deal of power surrounding the wrong decision."

"Which would be?"

"I do not know. But you will, when the time comes."

"Well, I—"

She gasped at the sight of something behind me.

"What?" I asked as I turned around. "What is it?"

I saw Shih–Chieh in the distance. He had just emerged from a small shop.

"It is nothing."

"Do you know that gentleman?" I asked.

"No, but I've seen him before. There are evil rumours that stir up like dust in the breeze when he is near."

"Because he's Chinese?"

"Don't be foolish. It is because of *who* he is."

"And *who* is he?"

"Never mind," she said. "I've said too much already. It is late. I must go for the night."

"Wait, wait," I begged. "When might I see you again?"

"I've already read you your fortune. What more do you seek?"

"Dinner! Breakfast? Lunch? A walk? I'd like to see you again. That is, if you would do me the honour. Think of it as my way of repaying you for reading my palm."

She smiled, obviously taken aback by my directness.

"OK," she confirmed. "Meet me at the Chapel of Jeremiah at first light."

"Where is that?"

She pointed behind me. I turned and saw it. I hadn't noticed it at first, but there it was, its enormous steeple piercing the night sky. When I turned back to her she was gone. Suddenly there was Shih–Chieh.

"Ah, Irel, there you are," he said. "The night is over. I think it's time to retire."

"I quite agree," I said as I stood up from the table.

"Any leads?" he asked.

"No, none yet I'm afraid."

"Well, it *is* just the first night," he said as we began our walk back.

* * *

The next morning, as I'm sure you can imagine, I departed from Shih–Chieh's villa while it was still dark. I hadn't slept much or deeply so it wasn't difficult for me to stir. When I left, I thought I was going to be followed, but as I walked I didn't notice anyone trailing behind. Not that that meant anything, mind you. Before too long I could see the towering steeple of the Chapel of Jeremiah peering up over the Spanish rooftops. The sun was coming up now and I hastened my step. Shortly, I arrived at the entrance.

It was a remarkable church, made of stone, and there was a large, stained–glass image high above the entrance. It reminded me of Vant Manor, and I took it as a sign that the universe was working with me. I crept up the few steps to the door, opened it, and went inside. It was much taller than wide or long, which must have been for the acoustic effect, but it was very beautiful. The light shone in through the stained glass, lighting up the wooden pews and the stone altar where the priest or minister would preside over his congregation. I turned to gaze up at the stained glass. It was a curious image. There was a seated man with his chin resting in his hand and the arm propped upon his knee. This man was in contemplation. It could not have been Jesus, as I had never seen him depicted in that way before.

"That is Jeremiah," said a soft voice from in front of me. I brought my eyes back down and took in Renata's beauty. She no longer wore the violet and gold headscarf but had let her long, wavy, black hair flow freely. "You're not the first to question his portrait."

"Perhaps it is fitting, as it is a chapel in *his* honour, but shouldn't Jesus be depicted instead?" I asked. "At least above the altar?"

"A hundred years or so ago this chapel was built by a gypsy artisan who was intrigued by the prophet Jeremiah. He arranged to have that glass image made as a copy from Michelangelo's ceiling in the Sistine Chapel. Jacinto, the gypsy, was a devout Christian, who wanted to remind the world of Jeremiah's presence. At the same time, he wanted to construct a meetinghouse for gypsies. Jeremiah, if you don't know, prophesized warnings, which were rarely listened to. This was Jacinto's way of reminding everyone of a greater power."

"I hadn't realized you were so religious," I said.

"I'm not," she said. "But I do believe in a greater power."

"You refer to your kind as gypsies. Are you not also known as the Roma?"

"So there is more to you than you let on," she replied.

"I am most certainly very fond of the Roma culture, and of late seem to find myself rather smitten with a particularly lovely Romani woman."

"You are very direct," she observed. "Not to mention a bit mysterious."

"No more mysterious than yourself, I should think."

"That's what puzzles me."

"Perhaps that's what draws you closer?" I said, taking note that she had come within a pace of me.

"Who are you, exactly?" she asked.

"I am student of the world: an explorer, a researcher, a philosopher, an illusionist, and if I am lucky, a thief."

"A thief?"

"Yes, of your heart."

"Come, I'd like to take you somewhere," she said.

I said nothing more but merely followed. She took me up a winding staircase through the heart of the steeple and up to the bells. There, awaiting us, was a black iron kettle resting over a toasty fire. Beside it was a box of curious–looking items.

"Tell me," she asked. "Have you ever tried xocolatl?"

"No, but it sounds as if the root word is chocolate."

"It is an ancient elixir made of cacao."

"So I was right. Doesn't sound like something of the Roma culture."

"It's more Roma than the name Roma. Only nobody knows it."

She took a ladle and spooned some of the dark potion from the kettle into a golden chalice for each of us. She then removed a long wooden stick, perhaps a foot in length, which had various exotic designs carved into it and had several wooden rings surrounding the slightly larger bulbous bottom.

"This is a *molinillo* stick," she informed me as she placed it into my chalice and rubbed it quickly between her hands, rather erotically, in such a fashion so as to force the brew to froth up. "It's also called a frothing stick." She handed the cup to me and began frothing her own drink.

I inhaled the brew gingerly, its aroma stimulated my salivary glands. When she had finished preparing her own, we each took a sip.

My senses were in ecstasy to say the least. There was a sweetness, a spiciness, a thick creamy taste, and hints of chillies.

"This is quite the cup of hot chocolate."

"My grandmother used to make it for me. Every morning in the winter she would make a fresh batch. Just before she died, she passed the secret family recipe on only to me. She said I was to do the same some day."

"I never knew my grandparents," I stated. "I actually know very little about my own mother and father. On occasion they would take me to visit my grandparents estate in a small English village but otherwise I saw very little of them growing up. I was always in a boys' school or at the university." I sipped some more of the cocoa. "Just before I graduated they were killed in a freak train derailment," I could see the morning sunrise and felt a sudden alienation. "They never got the chance to meet my fiancé, Ristila."

"Are you married, then?"

"Widowed, actually, but enough about me," I said as I turned back to her. "Surely your past is much more compelling."

"Why do you say that?"

"You're a gypsy. Entertainment runs throughout your history. Aside from that, as I mentioned, I find your culture fascinating."

"The life of a gypsy is a hard one. Being scowled at on the streets, cursed, threatened for being who we are, for not *belonging*. Then having to *entertain* those same people who change their views when they see something or some *one* they want. No, the life of a gypsy is *not* entertaining. Not for us. That much is myth."

"Surely it cannot be as bad as all that?"

"The trick is to find happiness in whatever you do. And to keep home with you wherever you go."

"That's very poetic," I remarked, as I crept closer to her. "Are *you* married?"

"No, but I've been with my share of men. The Spaniards call me 'slut' in the day and 'sweetheart' at night. I don't know what I am but I know I'll never belong to anyone other than myself."

I leaned forward and brushed a lock of her hair out of her face. "When I look at you I see a strong, beautiful, and independent woman full of creativity, curiosity, and life."

"You're kind," she replied. "But you don't have to compliment me to win a kiss."

She came right up towards me and would have kissed me had I not pulled back.

"Is something *wrong*?" she asked.

"It's just that ... I haven't been the slightest bit intimate with a woman since my wife passed."

"Oh, I am sorry," she said, taking a few steps back. "How long ago did she die?"

"Twenty–one years ago."

"Ah. I, uh, I understand your nervousness," she said, with a hint of humour.

"I should go," I said as I set down my chalice.

"I hope I did not offend you," she said.

"No, no offence taken. I just need to be alone for a while."

"When can I see you again?"

"I'll find you," I promised. "Until then," I bent down and kissed her hand. "Thank you for this lovely morning, but I must be off."

And then I left. Truth be told, I didn't know what to make of my behaviour. At first I had been 'finessing' her for secrets I knew she possessed. Then something happened. Something real. I began to care for her, nearly long for her. Or was I longing for companionship? Was it the cocoa? Was I longing for Ristila? I had to be alone. I had to catch my breath, gather my thoughts. I would not have the chance.

As soon as I emerged from the chapel there was Shih–Chieh waiting for me.

"Do you have a lead *now*?" he asked.

"It's too soon to be sure," I said hastily without thinking. "But the prospects are definitely promising. It'll just be a matter of time, that's all."

Shih–Chieh seemed satisfied with that, and I still don't know why I told him what I had. Perhaps it was a way to safeguard my own heart from hers. Had I known the damage that statement would cause, I certainly would not have uttered it.

"Take all the time you need," said Shih–Chieh. "I have always been a patient man."

The afternoon came and went in an otherwise uneventful way. However, when evening came Shih–Chieh, his guard, Reese, Stanton, and I were back on the prowl.

"What would you say your chances are of seeing this woman again tonight?" asked Shih–Chieh as we neared the gypsy haunts.

"It may be premature to say, but I believe there is a strong chance."

"Excellent, excellent. Then we should disperse beforehand. I would hate to think that our *presence* would in some way jeopardize what you've accomplished so far."

"A wise decision," I stated.

We then nodded to one another and split up as we came to Tello Street once again. That night the street seemed to have changed either that, or something within me had changed. I was suddenly more aware of my surroundings. Everything I saw was vivid with colour—with life. I noticed rats scurrying on the streets, the smell of black iron stoves, screaming children, their screaming parents, and the poor who slept on the roadside. For the first time in a long time, I was living in the moment.

As I strolled, I paid full attention to my senses and had I not I would have missed the soft–spoken Renata whispering to a large man in the shadows of a bakery shop's canopy.

"Is that all?" I heard the brute ask. "In that case, how much for the whole night?"

Realizing what was happening, I acted prematurely and marched right up to the man.

"Is something the matter?" I asked.

"No, but if you don't know what's good for you there may be," he said to me.

"Irel, what are you doing?" asked Renata.

"There must be some confusion, my good man," I proclaimed in my most proper Spanish. "This lovely lady is not for sale."

"Is that so?"

"Oh, it is. Did you not know? This woman is promised to me," I said, as I gave her a wink.

"Promised?" he asked.

"Yes," she broke in. "My apologies, sir, I was only using you to test my fiancé's loyalty, and as you can see, he is most trustworthy."

"You're serious?" he cursed loudly. "Take her then, but don't let her out of your sights again, or I might not be so cooperative next time. Oh, and make sure to put a ring on her, hmmm?"

"Very good," I added. "Come darling, we must *away*."

"You're lucky I'd rather be with you," she said when we were far enough away from everyone. "I could've made a lot of money off him tonight."

"Money? Good gracious! Money *is* the root of evil. How much money would keep you off the streets for a lifetime?"

"A lifetime," she laughed. "Do you know how much money I can make in a week?"

"Yes, for now, but a woman your age has likely only a decade of this kind of work left for her before she must depend on the income of the next generation."

"Then what do you propose I do?"

"Is there a place we can talk in private?"

"I have a regular room at the inn down the street."

"No, no, I couldn't stand to be in a place where—"

"Then I'll take you to my sister's house, where I live."

I nodded and she led the way through the back alleys where we allowed ourselves to be swallowed by the darkness of night. The home was a dilapidated townhouse in the seedier outskirts of the city. As we approached, I noticed that all the windows were dark.

"They're all in town for the festival. We should have the place to ourselves for a while."

I said nothing but merely followed, and she took me inside.

"Can I get you anything? Something to drink?"

"No," I replied. "I should be fine, thank you."

"Then come with me, my room is at the top of the stairs."

When we reached her room, she closed the door behind me and began lighting incense and a few candles.

"Oh, no, you have the wrong idea," I said.

"Shhh," she cooed and she pressed her finger to my lips.

I eased her hand away. "I didn't interrupt your meeting with that man so as to fill in for him. Nor did I mean for you to satisfy my sexual urges when I asked to speak to you in private."

"Then you admit that you do have *urges* for me?"

"A—a certain appeal, cannot be denied."

"Then give in to that and let's enjoy each other, fully," she coaxed.

"It isn't that you're not a beautiful woman. Goodness knows you're gorgeous. And I can't say that I haven't thought, briefly, what it would be like to be with you, but that is not my intention here with you tonight. I gave my heart to someone long ago. Although she may be dead, it remains hers."

"I don't need your heart," she said. "I just need someone."

"*You?* You who are so independent, so strong?"

"It's a defence, a front to hide my loneliness. Do you never feel that emptiness?"

"Every day of my life for the last twenty–one years I have felt that void. But I don't mean to fill it with every woman I meet! That wouldn't bring my wife back."

"All right, we won't be intimate," she said. "But you are tense. At least allow me to give you a massage?"

"But I still haven't told you what I have to—"

"I fear that whatever you're going to tell me will end the night very abruptly. I don't want you to go, not yet. So please let me enjoy your company for now. Tell me later before you leave."

I sat quietly and she removed my topcoat. Slowly she worked her magic and had removed my waistcoat and shirt. She then set me down on the floor in front of her bed where she took her position. She wrapped her legs around my torso from behind, straddling my back and I was suddenly aware that she wore no undergarment beneath her dress. She then began to massage my shoulders very deeply.

"When I was a little girl and could not sleep, my grandmother would sing me a lullaby to help me relax. As the song is in English, it took me some time before I came to understand the words. Sometimes I still sing it to myself when I'm feeling uneasy. Would you care to hear it?"

"Please," I whimpered quietly, allowing myself to enjoy both the massage and her presence.

"Over seas and far away
Live the lands of yesterday
There were no kings
There were no tsars
All were equal beneath their laws
Education reigned on high
Until the day that greed came by
From that day on things weren't the same
Power and slavery became their ways
They conquered nearly all the earth
Until the hand of God set forth
And put an end to their control
Spreading winter ever more
And so their kingdom had been destroyed
But new ones would one day fill their void
The hope was that they would not forget
The greater power that overall sits."

She had hit a particularly high note on that last line, so high that I wondered if the glass in the window would shatter. That's when it came to me. Her song was the key to releasing the energy from the crystals! Much as that last note in the right pitch would break glass, so too would it stir, on some level I'm sure, the energy built up inside the crystals. Here she carried the key with her all along, and so perfectly wrapped up in a story about the dangers of power. I was dumbstruck to say the least.

"See," she said. "I knew it would ease your stress."

"Funny, you wouldn't think a song about greed and destruction would do that. And then there's that high note. Rather loud for a lullaby, don't you think?"

"I was always fast asleep before my grandmother ever got to the ending. But the song is about learning from our mistakes. That it's never too late to change. "

"Optimism in a world of despair."

"It's what gives me strength when I'm ready to give up on myself. My grandmother told me to keep it with me always, and that during Nemontemia I am to wear her headscarf and sing that song to my travelling ancestors to put them at ease in much the same way."

"That is a very beautiful concept," I stated. "But I wonder if you've ever really learned anything from it."

"These are my ways, Irel. The ways of my people."

"You said yourself that it's never too late to change."

"It's just a song to help ease the pain."

"There's more truth in that song then I've heard in years," I said, as I turned over to face her, accidentally catching a glimpse of her femininity as she rose slightly, allowing me to shift. "Renata, listen. I am wealthy beyond your comprehension. I have enough money to take care of your needs, if it means you'd be off the streets."

She bent down and looked me closely in the eye. "What good would money bring if I cannot share your life?" she asked, as she tenderly kissed my lips. "You stir places inside me that I've never known," she added in a whisper. I could feel her bosom pressing tightly against my chest. The air was cool and dry, but she provided warmth, and we were now both perspiring. I felt her pulse race.

"I, I don't know what to say," I stated.

"*You?*" boomed an–all–too–familiar voice from behind me. "Imagine what your wife would say ." We were both taken by surprise, and when I turned to look, there was Shih–Chieh, his guard, Reese, and Stanton. I could not believe we hadn't heard them enter.

"I—I'll be sure to ask her one day."

"Then you *do* have a death wish?" asked Renata.

"No," I stated, as I shifted her aside and struggled to stand. "Not at all.

"Pity," said Shih–Chieh. "Still, you know why we're here." He tossed me my shirt.

"You *know* him?" Renata asked me.

"Oh, my dear," said Shih–Chieh. "Irel has always been my most prized pupil."

"She didn't tell me anything," I lied, putting on the shirt. "I don't think she even knows the answer you seek."

"I see," he said, as he came closer towards us. "Then the question I am asking myself is: How can a man so devoted to his late wife that he's practically taken a vow of celibacy suddenly be found at the bedside of a gypsy whore? Answer? You tell me."

"It's complicated."

"Is it? Irel, there's something I never told you about me. For thousands of years my people have been hunting down the secrets to our ancient heritage. In each generation one man is chosen as the leader of that clan and—make no mistake about it—our clan is vast. That man, Irel, is me. So do you think that after searching for so long that we are going to let any lead go unfollowed? Especially when we know we are so close?"

"You're a Yishnalta?!"

"Do you think it was a coincidence that I was in Morocco when you came through? That the waiter just *happened* to bring you to me? True, I expected you under the reign of the pig—"

"The pig?" I asked.

"Yes, the pig is the Chinese zodiac sign for November to early December, which is when I expected you."

My mind began to race at that moment, and suddenly I was back aboard the *Wooden Whale* speaking to Stanley Thatcher in confidence about a conversation he'd overheard Langston, Reese, and Stanton having that dealt with a wire Isabelle had received from a man named 'S'. The pieces were coming together now. I shot a nervous glance towards Stanton, whom seemed to understand.

"For a long time I've known that you would be my most valued asset in returning the Atlantean descendants to our true place in this world: in command of it," Shih–Chieh continued. "Irel, I know what it is *you* seek. And I know that that power can only come from the Atlantean crystals. Help the oldest race on the planet reclaim its power before it's too late, and I will help you—"

"Too late?" I questioned.

"You see, Irel, there is much you have yet to learn."

"You want the key to unlocking the crystal's power? Fine. The answer lies in a song that Renata just sang to me. Even she doesn't know the truth behind it."

"A song?"

"The incantation is wrapped up inside a lullaby, which is why your people have never been able to track it down."

"No," Renata cried. "Please! This man killed my grandmother!"

"What?" I asked.

"She was old," Shih–Chieh said with an eerie calm. "It was her time. I admit, I'm not above threats. Shing!" he ordered. Suddenly, his bodyguard unsheathed a sword and in one swift motion plunged it into Reese's chest and removed it just as easily. Reese fell, coughing up blood. Renata shrieked.

"But my threats are not empty," added Shih–Chieh. "The song, what is it?"

"In order to get a true demonstration, the crystal needs to be either in the full light of the sun or the moon while the incantation is spoken," I said, on a whim.

"Very well," said Shih–Chieh, and he took his ring to the window.

I gave a nodding signal to Stanton, and all at once he grabbed Shing and I ran up to Shih–Chieh and shoved him through the glass of the window. Shing tossed Stanton aside like a rag doll, and while he headed for the window, Renata, Stanton and I hurried out of the room.

"The chest," I said to Stanton as we ran. "Is it safe?"

"Reese and I took it to the train station this morning. You'll pick it up in Mérida at the lost and found, just as you planned."

"Excellent," I stated, as we hastened our pace. We had left the home and taken various alleys.

"You didn't tell him," said Renata.

"Of course not," I said. "But I did underestimate him. I never dreamed he could be in the Yishnalta, let alone be at its helm."

"What did he mean by 'Atlantean'?" she asked.

"Your ancestors, and his, once belonged to the same people. Their greed destroyed them as in your song, and he wants to restore that greed," I explained. "Now, which is the quickest way to the train station?"

Before Renata could speak, a carriage crossed in front of our path and Kien flipped out of the doorway through the air and came down in front of us.

"Going somewhere?" asked Hector Arnold as he stepped out of the coach.

"Enough's enough," shouted Stanton, and he drew two pistols from his inner coat and began firing at Kien. She skilfully dodged each bullet through various martial arts moves and was eventually able to knock both weapons out of Stanton's hands with her feet.

"I haven't seen moves like that since—"

"Isabelle Langston?" Kien asked. "It was imperative that we infiltrate Langston's crew with one of our own. Niixia was a great asset to us. Winston Seadrick masterminded that little twist. Afterall, he did also design the *Whale* to be the strongest, fastest ship in the world. How else were we to lure Vant to us?"

"Isabelle and Winston Seadrick part of the Yishnalta! It's just one stab in the back after another!" declared Stanton, as he and I began to realize the full force of the Yishnalta.

"It explains her ridiculous accent which was clearly overlooked by all, except me. She must have been romancing Thatcher to help her overtake Kaleeb. She never loved either of them," I said aloud as pieces of my thoughts now fit together.

"She loved her people," stated Kien. "She believed in our destiny."

Stanton searched the ground with his eyes until they rested on one of his pistols. Each had been flung to a different side of the alley. He then looked to me and nodded. Together we split, each of us heading for a different gun. Kien could act on only one of us, as Hector was still too far, so she chose Stanton. I reached my weapon and fired over and over again.

Kien was holding Stanton with his arms pinned back and the other pistol at his feet. She turned to me. "You missed."

"Did I?" I asked, and I pointed up the alley to Hector, whom I had shot in each of his four limbs. In that moment he fell to his knees in pain. I then fired at Kien, but she leapt backwards, all the while kicking Stanton square in the jaw. He too fell back, and she disappeared into the shadows.

Renata and I ran to Stanton's side.

"Are you all right?" I asked.

He tried to speak but found that he could not. He then reached up to his dislocated jaw and forced it back into place.

"Go," he said weakly. "Get out of here. I'll cover you."

"But—"

"Go, now!" He took to his feet, picked up his weapon and ran forward. We followed after him and entered the carriage. As I urged the horses onward, Stanton stayed back with his weapon. We heard a shot and then silence. It occurred to me, in that moment, that what Renata had said was true. It is never too late to change. Stanton proved that to me. One day he was working for one of my enemies, the next he was saving my life.

Soon it was morning, and Renata and I found ourselves in Granada, where I extracted large sums of money from a bank account I have there.

"Come with me," I said, as we brought the carriage to a stop at the train station. "Let me take you away from this life—from such a profession. You would want for nothing!"

She smiled a sad smile, and in that moment I knew she would not be joining me.

"A life with you, but without your love is not worth living."

"Then here," I said, handing her a wad of bills. "Use this to keep yourself off the streets." I then removed my wedding band and placed it into her palm while closing it tightly. "And take this to the island of Sicily. There, in a small village called Ragoto, seek out a man named Gordon Winthrop and present it to him. Tell him I sent you."

"I don't know—"

"You must go into hiding. Now that Shih–Chieh knows you possess what he seeks, you will never be safe."

"But my sister, my family—"

"If you believe in what your grandmother's life has stood for, you will honour your ancestors and keep their secrets."

"What am I supposed to do?"

"Change your name, change your appearance, use my money to set up a new life for yourself and find a way to fight back from the shadows."

"I'm just one person—no—a gypsy whore!"

"You are a Roma, a descendant of the most prominent people to ever walk this earth, the Atlanteans. Your only limits lie within yourself," I stated and I kissed her firmly. Saying nothing more, I departed. It was the right thing to do. At least I tell myself so. From the window of the train, I caught a glimpse of her in the carriage brushing tears from her eyes. I knew then that my presence, for better or worse, had altered the life of yet another person.

I never saw Stanton again and fear the worst. The days I spent commuting wreaked havoc on my thoughts; I felt alone again. I felt that I had betrayed Ristila. In the night I call out her name from my nightmares, forcing myself awake to face the sad reality that my life has become. It is time I righted some wrongs. I am returning home as you read this. It should just be a matter of days.

Yours truly,

Dr. Irel E. Vant

XV
PRELUDES

As the autumn slipped by, so too did various secret outings between Cara and meself. She kept the Morrigan hidden inside a tiny wooden box that she kept beneath her dresser where she hid such private things. So when we weren't talking about the wedding, her father, or Dr. Vant, I found time to continue me craft. By the end of the autumn I'd painted dozens of works. I was quick, as you may recall from when I first met Dr. Vant. Ideas came in and out of me head easily, and it was a though I were channelling the energy of creation itself. Glorious times I had that season. Many times I painted until sunrise, with only Victor to keep me company. He'd become more than a companion. He was a right critic, and a good judge of all things nature–related.

Well, as I said, autumn had passed. I had since explained to Erin me dilemma with Cara and the Morrigan, and, of course, she thought it was an act of God, Mum, or some other greater power that was forcing me to start the next phase of me life. Erin had been working her fingers to the bone to save enough for her move to London. The year seemed to have picked up pace, and soon the Christmas holidays were upon us. She and I sent a card to the brothers, but we never heard anything in reply. You don't really realize how much your life has changed until the holidays come 'round. That Christmas Erin and I mourned the loss of our mother but honoured her with some carols she used to sing every year. We sat by the fireplace, just the two of us and Victor, reminiscing about good times.

Mrs. McGillian had been gone visiting her family during that week. But when she returned it was as if she had been rejuvenated. Family has a way of reminding you what's important in this life. After all, life is about experiences; you can't take nothing else with you. 'Twas the beginning of January when she returned, and she returned with a plan.

I could hear Mrs. McGillian humming a merry tune before she even had the door open. She continued to hum it as she opened the front door and stepped into the foyer. The snow blew in with her, and I met her at the door to help her with her things.

"Someone's in a cheerful mood," I said to her.

"And why not, Master William? What's not there to be cheerful about? Life is grand. I'm not getting any younger, and I don't intend to spend the rest of my days in a sour gloom."

"What's all the ruckus?" asked Erin, calling over the railing from above.

"Mrs. McGillian's returned home," I announced happily.

"And better than that, Master William," she added. "I've returned with a plan."

"A plan?" I asked.

"What kind of plan?" Erin asked as she descended the stairs and greeted Mrs. McGillian with a hug.

"One so glorious that I've had to pinch myself every morning since I thought of it, just to make sure I wasn't imagining things."

"Go on then," I said. "Out with it."

"Uh–uh–uh! Not so fast. Not until I've settled in and had a nice cup of tea."

"I see you haven't changed *too* much," I chuckled.

"Mustn't mess with perfection, dearie."

"Dearie?"

She then pinched me cheek and was off up the stairs with her bags, humming again to herself.

After she had settled in and made a pot of tea, we all sat down around the dining room table to hear what grand things the old girl was up to.

"I believe," she began, "That I've come up with a way for you, Ms. Erin, to get set up in London; for you, Master William, to begin selling your art; and for the Morrigan to be replaced comfortably back into its home well before the return of Dr. Vant."

I had, of course, already confessed to Erin the truth about the so–called proposal.

"'Twill take a miracle to do all that," I replied.

"What's your idea?" asked Erin.

"While in Edinburgh I had just sat down to write out my Christmas cards, when it came to me. You see, every year I write to my friends Hugo and Desiree to catch up and to ask them how they're doing. Now, Hugo and Desiree live in London. I first met the day Dr. Vant after all. So I wrote to them this year explaining Ms. Erin's little dilemma. Well, a day or so before I was to come back to Leocadia, I received a letter from them. They've offered to give Ms. Erin room and board for a few months until she gets her feet on the ground."

"That … that's wonderful," I bellowed.

"And extremely generous," offered Erin.

"And that's only the half of it," added Mrs. McGillian. "Desiree's father, Mr. Jervis Cronley, is the curator of a museum. He's worked out a deal with some colleagues of his to set up an art show for Master William's work."

"That's … that's beyond words, Mrs. McGillian," I practically blubbered.

"And with the money you make off the show, you can afford to buy your lady fair a proper engagement ring and replace the Morrigan."

"I think I'm the one who needs a good pinch now!" I yelled.

"When are they expecting us?" asked Erin.

"They said to wire a telegram to them whenever you're ready."

"It'll take me at least a day or two to get things straight with the paintings," I pointed out.

"And I guess I should give Mr. Faulky a couple of days notice," Erin added.

"So ride out the week and leave on Friday," suggested Mrs. McGillian. "That way you have the weekend to get used to things and set up Master William's art. Why, if all goes well," she began as she turned to face me, "you can open up shop a week from today."

"So you'll not be coming with us, then?" I asked.

"I'm an ambitious old crone, but my bones have had enough travelling for a long while. You can give them my best. I'll set the whole thing up tomorrow."

"Then," I said, as I raised me cup of tea. "Here's to the magic of Mrs. McGillian and may the best be yet to come!"

"Here, here," chanted Erin as she raised her cup to clink against mine.

"Cheers," said Mrs. McGillian, as she too clinked her cup with ours.

So from Monday to Friday we all kept busy with preparations. Mrs. McGillian had wired her friends, Erin had given her notice, and Faulky was sad to see her go but wished her well all the same. As for me, I boxed up me best work and packed me finest clothes. This would be a trip to remember.

Friday finally came upon us, and Cara joined Mrs. McGillian to give us a send–off. She kissed me, wished me well, and told me not to worry about me art. Erin and I then drove out in a local hansom to Avebury, where we boarded the next train to London. The day before I'd sent me paintings out ahead of us via an in–town shipping company, Simon, Granaham, and Portwater, or something like that. It's hard to remember after all this time.

Anyhow, Erin and I were ecstatic the entire way to London. We were each feeding off the idea that our dreams were about to come true. I'll tell you, nothing compares with that feeling. It's like living on the top of the world, it is. Things were finally shaping up for us. At least that's how we felt.

When we arrived in Waterloo Station, neither of us could scarcely believe it. To this day, I still get that same feeling whenever I smell burning coal. The station was a modern world wonder to be sure. There were locomotives and people everywhere. I began to wonder if we'd end up missing the Deerings in all that commotion, but when we found the ticket counter, as Mrs. McGillian instructed us to, there they were. Though I'd never seen them before in me life, they were the spittin' image of how she'd described them to me. Picture a king–sized Quasimodo without the hump but with a timid, skittish nature, and that's Hugo Deering all right. His wife, Desiree, was very endearing, indeed. She was plain but elegant. Her auburn hair lay behind her, which accentuated the almond shape of her smooth, feminine face. She seemed to be around Erin's age, and both she and Hugo had a humbling presence about them.

"You must be Mr. and Mrs. Deering," I said, as we met them where they stood off to the side of the counter.

"And you must surely be William O'Brien," replied Desiree. I took up her hand and gave it a small peck.

"Oh, this is me sister—"

"Erin Calhoone," stated Erin.

"And, and I'm Hugo Deering. Th–that's me!"

I could see why Mrs. McGillian had first described the man as having a childlike innocence. He certainly reminded me of a boy, only friendlier.

"Welcome to London," Desiree stated proudly.

"I–i–it's not f–for everyone, it's not. But we do fine. Yeah, we like it."

"Oh, it's great," said Erin. "I just can't believe I'm finally here. I've been dreaming about this moment my entire life, and now here it is. It's just … just …"

"Don't worry," said Hugo. "I have trouble w–with words too."

We all chuckled.

"Come, we'd best be off," said Desiree. "There is much to do yet, and my father is awaiting our arrival at our home, not far from here."

"Have me paintings come in yet?" I asked, as we followed them to a four–horse coach. The cabby eagerly assisted Erin and me with what few travelling bags we had, while Hugo began his climb in.

"Paintings?" asked Desiree. "No, not that I've heard. When are you expecting them?"

"They were to be delivered this morning to the address your father wired to Mrs. McGillian the other day, the one where me show is to be," I explained. I followed her into the carriage and the cabby closed the door behind me.

"He's not mentioned it, but you can ask him when we arrive at the house. He's been at the site off and on in preparation for your arrival. Father exudes a feverish energy when he sets his mind to something. He's hoping you'll be the next Da Vinci or something and that he'll be the one to discover you."

"I hope I live up to the expectation."

The ride to the Deerings' house was a short one, and Erin stayed glued to the window the entire way. I don't think I'd ever seen her so mesmerized. Or that quiet. When we arrived, Hugo reached to pay the cabby, but I held out me hand in protest.

"You've given us so much already. Please allow me," I insisted, and I reached into me back pocket for me wallet. I felt for the bulge but couldn't find it. So I checked me other pocket, thinking I'd probably switched pockets in all the hustle and bustle. But no, it wasn't there either. I checked me inner coat pocket then me outer pockets—nothing.

"Something wrong?" asked Erin.

"Me wallet. Me wallet's gone."

"Gone?" she asked. "What do you mean gone? Did you misplace it?"

"No, I … I could have sworn I had it on me when we went into the carriage. I always feel for it out of paranoia. Now I know why."

"It was probably stolen," suggested Desiree.

"S–s–stolen?"

"It happens often in the city," said Desiree, while she nodded to her husband, who dished out the doll for the cabby. That bugger took down our bags from up top, tipped his hat to us, and smiled with a wink before he crept up to his riding post and drove off.

"Wouldn't surprise me if that cabby took it!"

"You're probably right," Desiree agreed. "Don't trust anyone you don't know in London, and if I were you, I'd be a little leery of those you learn to know."

"Take me, f–f–for instance," said Hugo. "I–I–I've been robbed th–th–three times in the last six years."

"Well Erin," I said, turning to me sister, "Welcome to London."

She gave me half a smile to acknowledge me sarcasm, and we turned our attention to the front door of the quaint townhouse as it was unlatched from the inside and opened with a creak. An older gentleman emerged. His hair was white and combed back to one side, and his wrinkles were deep, but his face was warm. He wore a complete suit of ash grey, and you might guess that he never wore anything less than that.

"Greetings, friends," he offered.

"This is my father, Jervis Cronley," stated Desiree.

"Pleasure to make your acquaintance, Mr. Cronley," said I as I extended me hand. He shook it and wrapped his other hand around it as well in one of those political sort of handshakes to help you feel at ease. He succeeded.

"Mr. O'Brien, I presume. And Mrs. Calhoone?"

She nodded, and he pecked her hand. "Welcome to our fine city. Tell me, how do you like it so far?"

"It does seem a bit busy, and I did get me wallet stolen—"

"*My* wallet," he corrected. "Good grammar is paramount if we are to weave you into high society."

"We love London," Erin butted in.

"Excellent," said he to her. "My apologies on your wallet though, William. I'll have a man of mine file a report with the precinct for you. Pray, do come in."

We followed him inside, and I remember feeling a sense of serenity as I entered. It was the same sort of feeling I felt whenever I was near Mrs. McGillian. Part of me wondered whether she'd left her mark on them or they'd left theirs on her.

"Oh, father, William was enquiring about a shipment of paintings that were to be delivered to the Maples–Riverondon House. Has there been any word?"

"Not that I'm privy to, I'm afraid. But don't be disheartened, my lad. Sometimes it takes shipping companies a while to find their way. I assume you used one native to Leocadia?"

I nodded.

"There you have it, then. I should be surprised if it arrives today at all. London is a very large city. If you don't know where you're going, getting around can be somewhat of a nightmare."

"Would anyone care for a cup of tea?" Desiree asked.

"I've already taken the liberty of preparing the kettle," stated Mr. Cronley. "Do take off your coats and sit for a spot."

After the first round of tea, the conversation shifted to Erin and what sort of work she might be interested in.

"Since coming to England I've been working as a seamstress for a Leocadian tailor shop, but I don't think there's anything I wouldn't be willing to try."

"Quite right," added Mr. Cronley. "You should know that work is hard to come by in London, especially for women. You have to have the right attitude and a great deal of determination to make it here. Take Hugo, for instance, he's had a hard life since birth but makes no excuses for what most deem a disadvantage. He works hard as an accountant."

"You're an accountant?" I asked, surprised.

"He's a very good and thorough one at that. Checks every figure three times, at least. It's his obsessive compulsion, but he's put it to work for him. He's mastered something that would overwhelm the average man. And in doing so he has gained the respect of a great many employers and businessmen alike."

"It's a h–hard life," added Hugo.

"I appreciate your frankness, as I'm sure I can only benefit from it," said Erin. "First thing in the morning I'll set out to find work. I'm not one for procrastination, by any means."

"That's the spirit," said Mr. Cronley. "You can begin with the paper," he added as he tossed the newspaper across the way to where Erin sat. "I picked up a copy for you this morning. It's never too soon to take the lead."

Erin seemed a bit uncomfortable and taken aback, but acknowledged his deed and let it slip by without a word. Later, sometime after dinner, Mr. Cronley departed, and when he was out of sight Desiree addressed us.

"Don't let my father worry you," she said, as she'd no doubt sensed our uneasiness. "He's a great and lovable man, but he worries about his family and just wants to ensure that we're not taken advantage of."

"Oh," I began. "We would never dream of—"

"It's just his way," she stated. "Come, I'll show you to your rooms."

That night I slept soundly, but felt odd upon waking. It must have been a dreamless sleep, because although I felt refreshed in the morning, I also felt somewhat unfulfilled. Perhaps it was just a feeling in the air. After breakfast, Erin and I took separate paths in this new world.

She went off to hunt down some prospects she'd circled in the paper during breakfast, and I joined Mr. Cronley at the Maples–Riverondon House. It was a terribly tiny establishment—really just a brick hole in the wall—down one of the busier thoroughfares, but Mr. Cronley assured me not to judge it by my first impression.

The shop was one large, grey–brick room; cold and damp, it had been gutted in some previous life and was in need of remodelling.

"As the Maples it was a fine clothing store offering only the very best in ballroom gowns. As the Riverondon it seated a mere thirty diners but all of them from the topmost layer of the upper crust," explained Mr. Cronley. "Everything it has been has been a success."

"Then may I ask how she came to her present state?"

"The Riverondon needed to expand to keep up with its clientele, so it moved across town. When the owners did the relocation, they took every bit of the ambience with them and used it to energize a new atmosphere with old origins. That being said, renting an establishment such as this is no small undertaking. However, I take pride and joy in helping the aspiration of today's youth. You will owe nothing for the rent I pay on this space, but I do require a nominal fee of fifteen per cent of your net earnings. Do we have a deal?"

"Aye, sir. 'Tis a small price to pay for such an opportunity."

"Quite right, my lad," he said as he patted me on the shoulder. "Oh, and I have some supplies being dropped off at ten this morning for you to renovate with. You can design this storefront any way you see fit. Just remember that you'll be the one doing the work, as I can't possibly afford carpenters alongside everything else."

"Thank you, sir," I said.

"You are welcome. Just make us proud!" He turned to leave.

"Oh, Mr. Cronley, could you show me where I might send a wire back to the Leocadian shipping company? I just want to make sure there hasn't been any official delay with me paintings."

He smiled, sort of, then said. "*My* paintings."

"My paintings," I repeated.

"Follow me."

As I was sending and receiving wires, Erin was, as she'd later tell me over dinner, having a very trying day indeed.

"As you might recall," she began, "I left the house after breakfast and started my search about three blocks from here. There was an ad I'd circled in the paper for a cleaning position at a local hotel. Much to my disappointment, they said they'd already filled the position, and I'm sure they hadn't, because the manager looked at me in disgust on account of me being Irish and all. That's one, I thought, and headed down the street to another inn. In all I must have tried five inns, a turn at a textile factory, a position waiting tables, one as a nanny, two as a teacher's assistant, one in a bakery, and there was a moment I even applied for a wound–washing position in a hospital emergency ward. Everywhere I turned seemed to be a dead end. Either the position was filled, or it was because I was a woman, or Irish, or a lower–class citizen. Sometimes because of all the above! I swear, I never thought it'd be *this* hard to find work in London, especially when I'm literally willing to do anything short of sell my own body."

"Aye," I agreed, as I melted some butter into me baked potato. 'Tis a different calibre of life out here. It's like you're nobody in a pool of nobodies that the somebodies pass over."

"You mustn't be discouraged so easily," Desiree advised. "For most newcomers it takes weeks—sometimes months—before they find work, then years before they can even begin to dream of owning a home—if ever! Today was your introduction to the idea of city life. Nowadays we are one of thousands. You must find a way to single yourself out."

"That's right," added Hugo across the table from his wife. Erin and I sat across from each other, as dinner was just the four of us. "Sometimes you have to … have to make a need and be the only one who can uh … uh … fill it!"

There was more truth in that statement then I'd heard in all me life up to that point. Hugo's advice was so simple, and yet that was surely the secret to many a man's fortune. Find or create a need and fill it. Then, as Desiree suggested, single yourself out. Set yourself apart from the rest of the lot just like yourself. I took some mental notes on the subject and went to bed that night with a head full of ideas.

* * *

The next morning, Erin and I departed together and parted a third of the way to me shop. When I arrived, much to me amazement, there was the wagon from Simon, Granaham, and Portwater. I marched up to the door where the driver sat smoking a cigarette. He was a hefty man, rotund in appearance, in his mid–fifties, and he had a stubbly beard and pale complexion. He was not the driver who had picked up me paintings in Leocadia two days prior.

"You're late," I said. "And where's the other driver?"

"Came down with somethin' at the last minute," said the driver. "Name's Hector, and I take it you're O'Brien?"

"Aye, William O'Brien."

"Sign here," he said, as he handed me a crumpled–up form from his pocket and a pen that he'd already dipped in ink; fountain pens were still somewhat of a luxury back then. I signed the slip and opened the shop door.

Hector opened up the gate on the back of the wagon while his horses rested. "Where you want these things?" he asked. I came 'round to help him.

"Anywhere inside's fine. I'll be settin' them up later meself, so anywhere will be good."

"You're a … you're in from Vant Manor, ain't ya?" he enquired, while handing me some of me paintings, which I'd wrapped in cloths.

"Yes, sir, been keeping the place occupied while the good doctor's away on business."

"That a fact?" he asked, as he picked up a few boxes with some obvious difficulty—he seemed somewhat weak in his limbs, but managed to bring them inside just the same. "Where's he go? Seems like he's never at home."

"Who, Dr. Vant? Aw, he's a world traveller. Always hunting for one thing or another."

"You know when he's coming back?"

"Not exactly," I said, as we continued to unload. "I guess he'll be in around April or May. Said his latest endeavour would take him about a year. Why, there something you need to talk to him about?"

"You might say I've something to deliver to him."

"Anything you have for him you could leave with either me or Mrs. McGillian."

"McGillian?" he asked.

"Aye, she's the old gal who's been keeping house for me while we keep watch over the estate."

"I see. But, I'm afraid I'm under orders to give it to Dr. Vant myself. You understand?"

"Of course. Dr. Vant's a very secretive man. No offence taken."

He struggled with the remainder of me paintings and then he closed his wagon gate.

"Are you all right?" I asked.

"Some old battle wounds. I'm fine."

"Been in Her Majesty's service, then?"

"Something like that. So, what about you? You're a painter, I take it?"

"Trying to be anyway," I said. "I've been given the opportunity of a lifetime to have me work—pardon, *my* work—showcased right here in the heart of London."

"Why'd you do that?"

"Do what?"

"Correct yourself."

"Just trying to fit in, you know."

"To hell with that. Be true to your roots."

"I just want to sell some paintings."

"They're your paintings, ain't they? They're as much you as your brogue."

"You have a point. You know, I should have everything set up tonight. If you're interested in popping by to see how it all comes together, me benefactor's putting on a party tomorrow night to unveil the goods. You're welcome to come ..."

"I might just do that."

"Well, listen, nice meeting you," I said as I handed him a tip. "See you around."

"You will," he said with a smile, as I closed the door behind me.

Our conversation at dinner later that night picked up where it had left off the night before, only this time there was a bit of good news to go around.

"So after me paintings arrived," I continued. "I spent the remainder of the day working on the set–up, and I tell you—you've never seen a display like the one you'll see tomorrow during the unveiling."

"That's terrific, Billy," cheered Erin. She too was in a good mood, and I'd soon learn why. "I've a bit of good news myself. Today, after five hours of searching, I happened upon a laundry service with a help–wanted sign. I guess the owner couldn't afford to advertise in the paper but was looking for a laundress just the same. When I went inside, I saw a weaselly man standing behind a small wooden counter. The shop was small, moist, and hot. The owner has a broad moustache and wears thick spectacles, but he can't be more than forty–five. He wore a wrinkly but blindingly bright white shirt."

* * *

"Here to pick something up?" he asked.

"No, I, uh, saw your sign in the window and was wonder—"

"Do you have any experience with washing clothing?"

"I've always done my own laundry, if that counts."

"Can you handle severe hot water, brutal hours, menial pay, and all around poor working conditions?"

"Well, I'll give you this," said I. "You're an honest man."

He stood there and stared at me.

"Look, sir, the bottom line is that I'll do whatever you're willing to pay me to do. I'm a hard–worker, I keep my mouth shut and—"

"You've no experience, your hands look as if they've never seen a hard day's work in their life, you've got an attitude that needs to be broken, an accent from across the seas, and you probably think that on some level you're above me."

"Uh—"

"You're hired," he said plainly and devoid of emotion. "I'm Andrew Massey, and this is my shop," he continued, as he lifted the side of the counter and came around to fully address me. "You'll work Monday through Saturday from six to eight, take a half–hour's break, and wear this," he said as he handed me a grey uniform. "The price of the uniform will come out of your pay. The cost is ten shillings. You'll earn two shillings a day, which means you'll work for five days to pay off the cost of your uniform. If you work hard and keep to yourself you'll see tuppence added to your pay after the first six months. Do we have an understanding, Mrs.—"

"Erin Calhoone, and yes, I agree to your terms," I told him while looking him dead in the eye. "See you in the morning, Mr. Massey."

* * *

"Well," I said to Erin after she'd finished relaying the tale, "looks like we've both got something to celebrate. Our luck's finally making a change for the better. Maybe soon we'll even get a lead on me wallet!"

That night, after I'd laid down for bed in me guest room, I thanked God for everything he'd given me and I vowed to pray more in the future. As strange as me life had become, given everything I'd gone through in that last year, it was somehow turning out right. I thanked God for that too, and somewhere between me prayers, fell fast asleep.

Morning arrived before long and I went back to the shop, where I finished putting the finishing touches on me display. Soon it was the eve of me unveiling party, and I'd bought a second–hand suit in town to fit the scene. Imagine, me in a suit! There I was, all monkeyed up in a brown tweed suit with a matching waistcoat. I'd always liked waistcoats. 'Course, I've no idea whether I pulled the look off. I'd never worn a waistcoat in me life. I was clean–shaven, with hair combed, and hands free of paint for the first time in a while. That night I was *William* O'Brien.

I stood beside Mr. Cronley on the front steps of the shop entrance as a small crowd gathered 'round, obviously people he knew from the museum, but they were there for me art and that was enough for me.

"Ladies, Gentlemen," began Mr. Cronley. "Today you shall bear witness to what I hope and suspect, will be history in the making. This young man here,"—he placed his hands upon me shoulders—"is a fine artist, an artist who sports a modern trend in the world of painting. I've been told he's trained under the French and even lived for a time in Paris. Please, join me in celebrating the collected works of William O'Brien, in what will surely be the first of many shows to come!"

There was a small, humble applause, and I took a brief moment to address them as well.

"Thank you all for coming this evening," I said, as I looked out into the crowd of faces. It wasn't long before I'd recognized one of them as Hector from the shipping company. "Me hope is"—I could see Mr. Cronley's face contort into disapproval— "that me work leaves you with a sort of lingering feeling. In a good way, of course, but—well, I hope you get something out of it, is all. 'Tis all that any artist can hope for, to entertain his audience, but to go a step beyond that, to teach or inspire or somehow enrich his or her audience is what makes it all worthwhile. Now," I said, as I opened the door, "follow me."

I led them into a part of me mind then, for I had been in charge of everything beyond those doors. Everything within was something I had thought up or crafted. It was an expression of feelings, a reflection of meself. Upon first entering, the guests were welcomed by a painting of dozens of hands forming one large hand that seemed to almost extend out of its framed universe. It was supported on an easel with the label *Power in Unity*. Beyond that, the room really opened up and, in all honesty, looked very similar to how I'd found it a few days before. Only I'd given it a few choice touches here and there.

"William," whispered a somewhat alarmed Mr. Cronley. "I thought you had decorated, cleaned the place up, or for heaven's sake, at least put a fresh coat of paint on those old brick walls."

"Magnificent," declared a fine, upstanding older gentleman from behind Mr. Cronley.

"I, uh, beg your pardon?" said Mr. Cronley.

"The decor, of course. I find it quite ingenious the way young William has deliberately depicted the entire storefront as though it were an artist's studio. Bravo, William, you're off to a good start!"

Mr. Cronley gazed out at the room before him as if suddenly seeing it for the first time. There were paintings hung on the walls and strewn about on tables, in what was meant to look like a random fashion but were actually arranged so as to add to each of the surrounding paintings' charms. Paintbrushes and palettes lay here and there, and I'd draped the floor in white sheets with paint spots on them, as though to cover the floor beneath. I'd spent the last few days trying to come up with something but that idea hadn't come to me until I'd talked with Hector the day before. After that, it was just a matter of getting it all worked out in me head, and some of the paintings were even suspended from the ceiling at all sorts of angles. I even had me ink drawing of Cara hung off in one corner on an easel. She had encouraged me to sell it, even though it was on her own father's canvas bag. She lay there in her nightdress, in a moment of absolute serenity.

I couldn't wait for Erin to see everything. She was still at work, and as it was her first day, I knew better than to ask her if she could leave early to make the opening. So I just sort of stood there, in the middle of me spectators. I enjoyed watching people's reactions to me work. Some were impressed, some were confused, some looked humbled, and others maintained a quiet damnation. Me art, you see, was very closely related to what is known today as Impressionism, as I think I've mentioned before. This was no doubt due to the many lessons I learned from Monsieur Pierre de Croismencer, who himself was an avid fan of the coming new movement even before it was considered a movement. I believe he even spent some time with Degas, Monet, and possibly Morisot, though I could be wrong. But that was before anyone knew who they were. I, meself, was not limited to painting any one thing in any one way. I believed, and still do, that to be free in your expression is to experience who you are.

"Where do you get your ideas from?" asked Hector, as he stood near me inspecting a piece I call *Living Exile*. In the painting stands a man at the far edge of a village glancing back as others turn their backs on him. The canvas colours were mostly browns, greys, green, and blue, yet all were pale.

"Sometimes ideas just come to me," I replied. "Other times I stare out into nature, or nothingness, and let me mind wander over thoughts. On occasion I see or think of people and wonder what their life is like. Do you like this one, Hector?"

"Just reminds me of someone is all."

"I believe they're meant to invoke what each individual person feels. There's no wrong answer."

"Do you ever get tired of that sentimental Romanticism crap?"

"How else can you explain thoughts and feelings?"

"Who says you have to explain anything?" asked Desiree, as she happened upon us.

"Oh, Desiree, this is a new pal of mine, Hector. He's the one who brought in me goods from Leocadia."

"How do you do?" she asked him.

"Not bad, thank you."

"Desiree, her husband, and her father are the ones who made this evening possible for me. She's even opened her home to me and me sister."

"That's an awful generous gesture. Wouldn't let that one slip by unnoticed, aye?"

"Too right," I agreed. "If there's ever anything I can do for you, Desiree, you just name it!"

"Oh, William," she said. "Life isn't about balancing debts. You help those you can without ever expecting payback. That's the true inner nature we all need more of."

"More Romanticism," huffed Hector. "Just when I thought it was runnin' dry!"

I could tell Desiree wasn't too keen on me new friend, so I stole her away, and we discussed some of me other works. The night was going better than I'd planned. Apparently people had begun approaching Mr. Cronley about purchasing me art, and he soon found himself busy with potential buyers. A little while later, the door to the shop opened, and some newcomers had entered. As I was in the back I couldn't rightly see who they were. Then I heard it.

"That's why you brought me here, ain't it?" bellowed the familiar voice.

As I made me way through the guests I came face to face with Mr. Henry Faulky, his son Adam, and the love of me life herself, Cara!

"Bless me eyes," said I. "I don't believe what I am seeing."

"You nor I," agreed Mr. Faulky, which—had he thought about it more, I'm sure he wouldn't have agreed to. "This is why you wanted to come with Adam and me, ain't it?" he asked Cara, point–blank.

"There something wrong?" asked Mr. Cronley, as he came round from the back.

"Don't mind us. We were just leaving," said Mr. Faulky, as he tried to shuffle his children out the door.

"Oh, why must you act like a child? You're *my* parent. Not the other way around."

"Excuse me?" he snapped. You could feel the tension thickening.

"You've had it in for poor Billy before you ever got a chance to know him. You said being an artist isn't a way for a man to make a living. But if you would only look around you'd see that's exactly what he's doing."

"Look, Cara," I said. "I don't want to force him to like me."

"This isn't open for discussion," he said. "Anyone who fraternizes with that … that murderous Dr. Vant has no place in your life, Cara."

I suddenly noticed Hector, as he stepped up behind me to where Mr. Cronley, Desiree, and Hugo now stood.

"You've something against Dr. Irel E. Vant?" asked Mr. Cronley.

"As I do any man who's murdered his own wife," Faulky sneered back.

"Murder?!" declared Desiree.

"What the devil are you talking about?" demanded Mr. Cronley.

"Look," Faulky said, as he tried to gain composure. "I don't mean to start a ruckus. I'm sorry you all were brought into this mess. This is a family feud between me and my daughter. Leave it at that, and we'll be gone." He opened the door. "Cara, out."

"I'm nearly twenty–one years of age, father. I can make my own decisions. That being said, I choose to stay here."

"Adam, out." Adam did as he was told. "You listen to me, and you listen good," he said to Cara. "If you don't walk out of this door now, you'll never walk through the door of my house again. You'll be dead to me. Do you understand? Dead!"

Cara seemed shaken up, because she knew he meant it. The room was silent as she made her next move. She went up to where her father stood by the door, and for a brief moment he smiled, as if to say he'd won. Yet Cara took up the door and said, "Good–bye, Father. Give my regards to Mother."

The man's eyes turned stark raving mad, but he said nothing else as he departed. And on his way out, Cara vocalized the unthinkable:

"And don't think for one second that I'll be inviting you to our wedding." With that she slammed the shop door.

"Wedding?" Desiree asked me in a whisper.

"'Tis a long story," I whispered back.

"Well—," Mr. Cronley began.

"I apologize for this interruption," I announced to the gathering. "I only hope you can look past this and continue to review me art, which is the reason we've all gathered here in the first place. Thank you."

Slowly and quietly, the guests resumed their previous positions, and a few minutes later some mild chatting spread out amongst them.

"I feel terrible about everything," Cara said to me. "Honest, Billy. I … I mean, I guess I knew he'd be angry, but I didn't think he'd cause such a scene. I just wanted him to see that he was wrong about you."

"I understand, darlin'. You had the best intentions, but I didn't want the man to disown you. That's not the way to settle this."

I then heard a faint knock at the back door. Hugo took it upon himself to check it out.

"I love you, Cara. But that man is your father. You know he'll make it impossible for you to see your family after all this."

"I just wish I knew what to do. Life doesn't come with instructions."

"Wa–Wa–William!" called Hugo nervously and loudly from the back of the shop.

"God, what now?" I asked, as I raced to the back. Cara followed me, and, as we emerged outside, I saw before me the unthinkable. There lay Erin, with her new uniform torn and muddy. A man held her up, and I'd find out later he was her boss, Andy. He eased her down as I took to her side.

"Erin? Erin, Jaysus, what happened?"

She was disoriented and filthy, with a far–off look in her eye.

"A man attacked her with an intent to rape after she'd left work this evening," explained Andy. "I heard her scream from afar and was able to beat the miscreant off her. I don't believe she was breached, but the shock of it all seemed to be too much for her."

I held her as the tears streamed down her face. She couldn't speak. I couldn't think. I just held her. London had proved to be a force greater than either of us could have reckoned. When the highs came they were indeed glorious, but the lows—the lows could kill you. Sometimes they did.

"I'll fetch a coach," offered Mr. Cronley, as he too had witnessed the scene.

Hugo and Cara helped me to get Erin to her feet, and we guided her through the alley to the street where—to me surprise—we saw Cara's father and her brother waiting outside the storefront, as though the man was duelling the demons in his head that continued to prevent him from going back inside. He then caught sight of us. He and Adam rushed right over.

"Not now," said Cara.

Mr. Cronley opened the carriage door, and I stepped up inside while

Hugo slowly handed Erin to me.

"Isn't that Jacob's shop girl?" Mr. Faulky quietly asked Cara.

"Yes, that's Erin Calhoone. Billy's sister."

"His sister?!" he asked in surprise. "What happ—"

"She was assaulted," said Cara, as she joined us inside the carriage. Soon we were off, Hugo, Erin, Cara, and meself. Mr. Cronley and Desiree would take care of things back at the shop. As for Mr. Faulky and Adam, who could guess? But I wasn't thinking about that then. I could only hold me sister and blame meself.

XVI
THE RETURN

Sometimes you can have something planned out perfectly in your head. You think, maybe it won't work out exactly as I plan, and deep down you think of your plan as a sort of rough guide to get you to where you want to be. But you never think of the hardships that await. Not really. But how can you? Who could have foreseen Erin's assault or the battle between Cara and her father? I couldn't.

Erin didn't speak until supper time the following day. Mostly she had just cried. It was a bitter pill for me to swallow. Here was a woman who had defined the idea of women for me. She was as strong as stone, independent, free willed and able to tangle with any man. But it took only one man to rob her of that spirit. Andy, her boss, had beaten the man so badly that he had been caught a few blocks away after he'd stumbled to the ground for loss of too much blood.

Andy was good to us. He gave Erin a few days off to regroup and he replaced her uniform free of charge. Erin's never been the same. Oh, she eventually recovered enough to return to work and tried to get by as she always had. Still, something was different. She'd lost that spark—that old flame she once had. It's that demystifying moment in one's life when the carpet seems to have been pulled out from under you. Call it growing up. Call it learning the ways of the world. Call it whatever you like, but when it comes, it takes its toll and you're never the same.

As for Mr. Faulky, Desiree explained to Cara and I that after we'd left with Erin, he'd gone into the shop with Adam and quietly glanced around. He remained in the shop the rest of the night, and purchased the ink drawing I'd done of his daughter on his own canvas bag. When he left he told Desiree to tell his daughter and her fiancé that they were always welcome in his house. Little did we know then how fortunate that would turn out to be in the very near future.

I had stayed on an extra week in London to see to it that Erin got on all right. The day before we left, Cara and Desiree took lunch to Erin while Mr. Cronley, Hugo and I went to secretly shop for an engagement ring. I'd explained the situation to Mr. Cronley and the Deerings in private whilst Cara was busy looking in on Erin.

"I still find it rather taxing to understand how you inadvertently proposed to young Miss Faulky with the Morrigan," said Mr. Cronley as he opened the door to the third jeweller we'd see that day.

"Yeah," added Hugo. "A–a–and, do you really think an ama–, uh, ama—"

"Amethyst," said Mr. Cronley.

"—will take the place of the M–M–Morrigan?"

"It'll have to," I said. "Cara's not likely to have the diamond appraised, so she probably thinks it's an amethyst anyway. I just hope we can find one big enough to replace it."

The money I'd taken in gave us a foundation for the ring, though I wasn't sure if it would cover the entire cost. Still, Mr. Cronley agreed to loan me the difference until me future shows could pay off the rest.

"What do you have in the way of amethysts?" I asked the jeweller, a thin, black–coated gentleman who stood behind a glass case.

"Hmmm," he muttered. "Not much I'm afraid. There's a bracelet and a pendant, but I'm sure you'd find a simple solitaire diamond with a gold band much more to your liking. Searching for an engagement ring, yes?"

"Can we see the amethysts?" I asked.

"As you wish," said the man, and he disappeared around back and returned with a small iron chest. He removed a set of keys from his pocket, unlocked the latch, and pulled out a small drawer, where the amethysts lay side by side in a black–velvet–lined tray. Needless to say me eyes nearly burst out of their sockets when I set me sights on the pendant's gem: It was every bit the same size as the Morrigan.

"That one," I said, as I pointed to the pendant. "How much to have it set into a ring with a silver base?"

"The pendant itself is a hundred pounds. To have it set into a ring would be at least another two for the service and ten for the band."

"Whatever the cost, can it be done by tomorrow morning?" I asked.

"Tomorrow morn—. Listen, sir, I need at least three days to find the time. Running a shop with minimal staff is hard enough while trying to turn a profit these days."

"We'll give you an extra hundred pounds to close your shop for the day and work on the ring through the evening," stated Mr. Cronley.

"An extra hundred?"

"Come, now," said Mr. Cronley. "We both know how hard business is for a man in your profession *these days*. You'd be very lucky to find a better offer on a gem as this."

"You may have a point," said the jeweller. "Would you like it gift wrapped, too?" he asked, with extra sarcasm.

"Not necessary," I replied. "I'll be by first thing in the morning to pick it up."

The next day I did just that. The amethyst's resemblance to the Morrigan was uncanny. All that remained to be done was to make the switch once we'd returned home. Hector was generous enough to give Cara and meself a ride back into Leocadia, as I'd had only one train ticket between us. I left the ticket for Erin so that she might save some money on her next visit.

When our baggage was loaded into Hector's wagon, I held onto Erin for a time. Neither of us wanted to part, but we both knew it was for our own good. We had separate lives to lead but we would always be brother and sister. And so Cara and I thanked the Deerings and Mr. Cronley for their kindness and departed for home.

* * *

When we arrived in Leocadia, it was the middle of the night. I gave Cara a gentle kiss when Hector and I dropped her off at her parent's home. I decided not to go in this time. I knew I would have me chance to make amends with her father eventually. I just wanted to get back home and crawl into bed.

Back at Vant Manor, Hector dropped me at the gate, and I thanked him again for his generosity. He and his wagon trotted off while I opened the gate to the estate. When I entered the castle, I found Mrs. McGillian hurrying down the staircase to meet me.

"Master William, thank God you've returned. I got your wire about Ms. Erin. How is she?"

"Better, but she's a changed woman, you can be sure of that."

"How dreadful the scorn of man?" she seemed to ask the air. "We can go over those details later. Here," she said, as she handed me a thick envelope. "Read it, it's from Dr. Vant."

"Can you give me a second to get in? I've kind of had a rough week."

"You don't understand. Vant's on his way back."

"What?"

"He said he was just a few days away in the letter. It came on Wednesday; today's Saturday. You have to read it."

"All right, OK. I'm reading it," I said, as I dropped me bags and opened the envelope.

"The Morrigan—did you get the Morrigan back?"

"Not yet. I bought the replacement, though, just haven't had the time to make the switch."

I then proceeded to read the letter that I enclosed a couple chapters back, in 'The Spanish Affair'. I had no sooner finished than we heard a sound in the distance.

"Hooves!" declared Mrs. McGillian. "Quick—the amethyst. Give it to me!"

I took out the box with the amethyst in it and tossed it to the old gal.

"You keep him busy while I stash it where he kept the Morrigan."

"Then how will we ever make the switch?" I asked.

"We'll figure that out later," she called, as she hurried out of the foyer towards the library in the North–West tower. "Just keep him occupied!"

I heard the clank of the gate in the distance. A short while later the front door opened and there, in a dishevelled glory, stood Dr. Irel E. Vant. He had returned.

"I see that I am not the only one returning from afar," he proclaimed, as he made a mental note of me luggage.

"Dr. Vant, welcome home!"

"Indeed, William. I take it Mrs. McGillian is at rest?"

"Em, yeah, sort of … I think."

"Sort of?"

"Well, you see—"

"I'm afraid I do not see," he stated. "You can explain it to me in the morning. Right now I've other urgent affairs to attend to which I cannot be distracted from." Dragging the violet and gold treasure chest, he then headed straight towards the North–West tower.

"Em—Dr. Vant, wait!"

"Now, William," he began, though not lessening his pace. "I said we can discuss in the morning anything that may be of concern to you—"

He stopped to notice a light coming from the library.

"Hell–o!" he declared quietly to himself, as if to say, "What do we have here?"

He continued to advance upon the scene, and as I came up behind him, we witnessed Mrs. McGillian closing the secret entrance behind her. She had been caught leaving his private study.

He stood there, motionless, as she turned around. Though I could not see his face, I could see hers. She gasped at his presence.

"Dr. Vant? I-I-I can explain."

"Out," he said.

"I—"

"Get out!" he yelled, in a voice so dark I'd scarcely believe it came from him.

"Please," she said, as she gently came towards us. "I didn't mean to—"

He then did something I'd never have thought him to be capable of. He attempted to slap Mrs. McGillian in the face with the back of his hand but stopped himself just short of her face, while biting his lower lip.

"Hey now," I said to him. "Just who do you think you are?"

"Escort Mrs. McGillian off my property," he demanded, otherwise ignoring me. He then depressed the continent of Africa on the globe. "And William," he said, as he turning around. "Don't ever question my authority in my own home again."

With that, he descended the secret stone staircase, dragging his cursed treasure chest after him.

"Mrs. McGillian, are you all right?"

"I'm fine, Master William. Be cautious. I've never seen him like this before. Something's up. Keep an eye on him."

"Listen," I said. "As I mentioned in the wire, I've smoothed things out with the Faulky family. You can go and stay there for a few days until I get this straightened out. They won't turn you away. Trust me, Cara wouldn't let that happen."

"Fine. Come by tomorrow with an update. I can't put my finger on it, but there's a reason he's back this early."

True, he had said he'd be gone a year when he'd departed the previous April. It was now scarcely the beginning of February, and here he was. Though it may seem like a minute difference to the average person, a detail like that to someone as precise as Dr. Vant spelled out something much more sinister than I felt prepared to deal with.

After Mrs. McGillian left, I went to the edge of the secret staircase and gazed down. I heard strange sounds coming from the room far below. I decided to see what it was all about. Slowly I descended the stairs, half expecting a delirious Dr. Vant to come rushing up at me, ordering me to go away. But that didn't happen. Instead I was able to reach the bottom of the staircase and look into the room through the open door. An oil trench lamp had been lit and it illuminated the entire chamber. I wondered how difficult it must have been for Mrs. McGillian to find her way to the proper spot where the Morrigan had been while searching in total darkness.

"I trust Mrs. McGillian is safely off the premises?" he asked, as he stretched a piece of rubber over a glass jar and held it in place around the lip with a rubber band.

"Aye, she's gone."

He handed me the jar and hurried over to a cupboard beneath a counter. When he opened it, a surge of cold air blew out like steam from a tea kettle. He removed two glass litre bottles and shut the cupboard. One was empty, but one held an eerie dark liquid that resembled be blood. He then placed each bottle onto an aluminium tray and lit an oil lantern beneath it.

"It occurred to me," he began, "that while I'd planned all along to do this alone, I would, in the end, benefit from someone else's assistance." He then reached up to the wall of crazy masks and removed one in particular. It was yellow and black. "I would, if I could, have my son here with me," he said, as he looked into the mask, which I took to be African. "But his life does not belong in this world."

"And mine does?"

"You'll do. Come, to the North–East tower!"

"I beg your pardon?"

"You heard me. Now, don't drop that jar. It is vitally important to my plans this night. We can take the underground passage." He then pulled out a book from one of his cupboards, and to me own amazed eyes, part of one of the brick walls moved, and inside was a tunnel where more of the oil trenches lit the way. "Do hurry it up a bit."

I followed. I don't know why. Call me crazy. Call it curiosity. Still, I followed.

"When I returned home this evening," he started again. "I couldn't help but notice the way the entrance to the North–East tower looked from my view of it in the foyer."

"Yes, about that—"

"Save it. I know what happened. I know you were overtaken by the same assassins that attacked us in Paris."

"How could you know that?" I asked.

"The female was Langston's wife. She died from snake bite shortly after I installed you here. I put two and two together. Since you learned that, there's no reason to keep the rest from you."

"And why not Mrs. McGillian? Why did you try to strike her?"

"The heat of the moment, I'm afraid. No time for apologies though. But everything will come to light in the fullness of time."

He came to a stop at the end of the tunnel, where a metal grate separated us from the next room. 'Twas then that I became aware of the sound of rushing water.

"The underground river!"

"Yes, the one the well feeds off. Where else would a snake feel most at home, I wonder!"

"Are we looking for the snakes?"

"Only one," he said bluntly. He then took his cane and rattled it across the metal grate. Soon there came a sound, and then I saw them. The anaconda stayed back a ways while the other advanced.

"I've trained the king cobra so he knows to come forth when I make a sound in this fashion. Notice how I've also trained the anaconda to stay back with the same sound."

"What are you going to do?" I asked.

"Hand me that jar, will you?"

I handed him the jar with the rubber stretched across the opening. He then removed a small wooden flute from his inner suit–coat pocket. He played a few notes, and the cobra danced its head through one of the holes in the grate. Dr. Vant then grasped its head, at which it tried to rear back in surprise. Quickly, he forced its mouth open, revealing its protruding fangs. Next he shoved the fangs deep into the rubber atop the glass jar and out he squeezed the poor snake's venom. When he'd finished filling the jar half way, he released the snake, and it retracted its head back through the grate.

"Imagine my surprise," he said. "When I discovered that the anaconda was not a cobra at all and thus had no venom. Ah, well, live and learn, I suppose. Can't be right all the time."

Dr. Vant smiled approvingly and pulled a lever on the wall that brought down yet another brick barrier. This one landed between the grate and us, protecting us from the snakes. Either that or protecting them from him! He then turned around and pressed on back the way we had come.

"Do come along. There is still much to do."

But what *was* he doing, I wondered. I then had an image flash before me mind as I followed him, senselessly, back to the private study. It was the image of Dr. Vant as I had last seen him from the carriage as he departed Vant Manor nearly a year ago. I recalled his words yet again. "There was once a young man who looked in a mirror and realized his entire life had changed before him in the blink of an eye." There was more to that speech that I couldn't seem to remember. When Dr. Vant gave me the next order, I snapped back to reality.

"Help me with this chest," he seemed to command.

He set down the glass jar of venom, as I made me way over to the violet–and–gold trimmed chest. "Violet and gold. Violet and gold," I remember thinking. The chest was long, though not incredibly heavy. From his letter I knew it was the treasure chest he had retrieved from his latest adventure. But why the chest? What did he say in his letter, "The prize was not what was in the box but rather the box itself"? I couldn't fit the pieces together yet.

Together we moved the chest into position atop the four–foot–tall stone platform within the centre of the room. He went for the latch on the chest. I put me hand out to stop him.

"Correct me if I'm wrong, but isn't this the chest you needed that Abbott fellow for?"

"The chest has since been properly cleansed, William," he explained. "All traces of the plague have dissipated." He then opened the chest. I realized that he had to be telling the truth. The crate still stunk of an alcohol solvent.

"Boy," I said, wincing from the odour. "This chest sure has a way of keeping things fresh."

He smiled then, but made no effort to speak his mind. Instead, he hustled over to what I took to be a broom closet, opened it, and removed a strange stick that looked like a tree branch with a deer carved into one end of it.

"Exactly what is it you're preparing for?" I asked , not anticipating any real answer.

"You will learn soon enough, William. Now then," he said to himself. "Where is my checklist?"

"Checklist?" I asked.

"Surely we must have everything assembled before we begin."

"Begin? Begin what? *I'm* beginning to think you've gone daft!"

"Interesting choice of words, William. Did you know that the word daft is related to the term *gedæfte* from Old English, which comes from the early Germanic *gadaftjaz*, which means to put in order or arrange."

"I … did not know that," I gingerly admitted.

"There is a mirror in the second drawer from the top of the cabinet just behind you," he stated. "Please retrieve it and bring it over to this counter where I can work on it."

Work on it? I asked meself, as I opened the drawer and removed an oval shaped object that had been wrapped in cloth. I closed the drawer and took the mirror to him. He unsheathed it and held it up for a good view.

"Bah, I look ghastly," he said. Then he placed it upon the counter in front of him and set to work with the jar of venom. He now wore rubber gloves, which he must have put on when I'd gone to get the mirror. Slowly he poured the thick venom onto the mirror and then he used a small ruler to evenly distribute the vile liquid completely over its surface.

"Come, we've other things to ready while this dries!"

Before I knew it, he was heading out of the study and back up the hidden staircase to the library. I glanced around at the oddities that we'd assembled in the room, then I followed behind. When I reached the top he was nowhere to be seen, but I heard the sliding door of the West End and I knew where to go next. As I entered the inner courtyard, I spotted Dr. Vant . He had taken to the balcony level, which encircled the courtyard, and was rapidly turning a crank.

I heard a peculiar noise and realized it was coming from high overhead. The crank he was turning was bringing a portion of the glass greenhouse roof downward, until it formed a perfect upside–down pyramid of glass with its apex directly over the statue of the late Ristila Vant. The next thing I knew, he was beside the statue and motioning for me to aid him in moving it back some. I don't know why, but I obeyed. As we moved it, I became aware of a four–foot–wide hole in the ground, which allowed a view into the private study below. We were standing directly above the stone platform where the chest was resting.

He stared up at the descending pyramid of glass above him. High above us in the depths of the sky the moon was ever–so–gently creeping forward.

"Finally," he whispered. "After all this time!" Smiling, he sprang back into a frenzied pace, disappearing into the main body of the castle. I was starting to get tired of this endless chase. He was hopping around from place to place quicker than a squirrel that's gone hunting after his nuts!

Somehow I pressed on. It must have been sheer curiosity that drove me. I cannot think of anything else. As I began the trek back to the private study, I found meself thinking of the past again.

There was that violet–and–gold–trimmed chest that I couldn't place. Where, aside from Vant himself, had I heard of such an object? I thought of the utensils we'd gathered. There was the chest, the African mask, the cobra venom, the mirror, the bottle of blood, the deer carved staff, the—. That's it! I thought. The deer staff, of course! Keftiuc, the American Indian who'd come to warn Dr. Vant of a watery doom, had mentioned a staff the Durwaihiccora shaman—what was his name? Sekhettepi, that was it—gave to Dr. Vant. Keftiuc had mentioned a purple–and–gold–trimmed chest that was deliberately destroyed by the chieftess's brother, Asuras, the kid who was jealous of Dr. Vant. That chest, he'd said, had been handed down through the generations of the Durwaihiccora's shamans. Could that have been the reason Dr. Vant sought them out in the first place? But how had he first heard of their tribe?

I thought again of the study as I crept onward. The first time Mrs. McGillian and I had discovered it was when we found Dr. Vant's journal about the Kride. The Kride! He … she … no, *it* was the one who instructed Dr. Vant to travel to America to seek out the Durwaihiccora, who were supposed to have a blood–line to the Atlanteans themselves. Good God! The blood! The blood in the bottle, could it contain that same blood Dr. Vant had collected from the Kride's body all those years ago? How would he keep it fresh? I then remembered the surge of cold air that came from the cupboard where he'd kept it. He'd found a way to generate freezing temperatures in a contained environment. That must have been the reason it was so cold down in that study. But what did it all mean?

When I emerged from the secret corridor, there was Dr. Vant, on top of the platform, connecting two thin rubber hoses to a strange clockwork–pump–contraption beneath which the two glass bottles rested. The one bottle was still empty, and the other still completely full of blood. He brought the hoses over and into the Atlantean chest beside him on the stone platform. From high above, the light of the moon was softly filtering in, yet still a ways off. He fastened the hoses to something inside the chest and released the trigger on the clockwork blood pump. An eerie sloshing sound filled the air, as he set up a saucer of what I assumed must be sage and a pail of water, it suddenly all seemed to fit together. All right, maybe not all, but enough that I got the picture. I then remembered the rest of what he had said to me the night of his departure. "There was once a young man who looked in a mirror and realized his entire life had changed before him in the blink of an eye. But he could never go back to the way things were, because the world had changed around him. He could only look to the future, for what was done could, never be reversed—or could it?"

"You've got the body of your late wife in that chest, haven't you?" I asked him forthright.

He said nothing but only glared at me in astonishment.

"I've learned a lot about you in the course of this last year. What, from the visit of your Durwaihiccora friend Keftiuc to your journal on the Kride and how you've spent years waiting out this chest. It's the reason you've put so many lives in jeopardy. The reason you've no idea what happened to Martin Abbott and, I'm sure, could care less."

"Martin Abbott will be fine," he proclaimed.

"How can you be so sure? You left him to a crazy pirate and his dodgy crew."

"*If* something did happen to Martin Abbott, I would not take his assistance in vain. He was a necessary part of my obtaining the chest."

"And what do you expect that chest to do anyway? How is an ancient Atlantean chest that once kept in the Black Plague going to help you resurrect your dead wife?"

"You don't understand, William. I'll admit, from your limited point of view this must all seem to be fruitless, insane, and morbidly grotesque. But you know not the facts!" he shouted, as he slapped one hand onto his other.

"Then enlighten me once and for all!"

"The Atlanteans were the most advanced race to ever walk the face of this planet. They knew that, whereas religion was concerned, the only deity that existed was the essence of the universe itself, an energy they called *Awen*. Centuries later the word would take on a slightly different meaning with the Welsh, but to the Atlanteans it was the universe's soul and it was that essence that they held above all else. That essence transcends time, space, and the core of every thing and every dimension. As a highly evolved society, they had a profound caste system in which specific humanoid breeds were enlisted to participate at certain levels of this system. The most carefully bred of these people ran the intellectual and spiritual aspects. These thinkers decoded the basic energy field of life and learned how to harness its power. A key ingredient in doing so was their violet crystals."

"Like the Morrigan" I said aloud.

"Exactly," he added. "I see Mrs. McGillian has taken the liberty of filling you in on that little facet. But we digress. Through the knowledge of these intellectual spiritualists, the language of existence was within the Atlantean's fingertips. However, their quest turned to a thirst, which brought down their entire society, as I'm sure you read in my journal entry about my meeting with the Kride.

"With the destruction of Pontus, their capital city, came the downfall of their age. Those that remained were not of the highly evolved strata in the caste system but regardless, certain survivors held onto rituals their counterparts had practised and bestowed upon them. Those people moved on and incorporated those rituals and stories into their own cultures and created new civilizations to populate the world, the closest in terms of spiritual intellect being the Maya and the Egyptians. However, neither would be able to resurrect the true power of their ancestors. A few groups who had retained some of these ancient ways stored them in secrecy within the Library of Alexandria. The library was later destroyed by a rival group and with it its contents.

"As I mentioned, some of these cultures held on to their ancient rituals. The Iboruba of Africa, to which my son Kamahni belongs, held on to the practise of communing with the energies of the dead by taking part in a ritual that summons those energies and materializes them in one set place for a given length of time by the light of the moon. Another such culture was the Durwaihiccora, whose shaman are capable of resuscitating a dead body, so long as the spirit, the energy of the individual, continues to reside within the corpse.

"And so by scouring the globe I have pieced together an age–old recipe for resurrection. For the last twenty years I have kept my wife's body in a suspended state by keeping it cold. With the help of Winston Seadrick I was able to construct an electric generator that runs off the underground river and powers a series of cooling lockers around this room. To warm her body and bring it back to the state she was in at the time of her life, I am pumping in the blood of the Kride itself. With the

Kride's blood comes an added attribute of health benefits, as the Kride's blood was subject to the so–called "fountain of youth" elixir, derived from steeping the Atlantean crystals within hot water, which the Kride drank.

"As the moon rises, within the hour it will come to a focused position directly above this chamber. My inverted pyramid of glass will concentrate that energy and beam it down to a point where I will increase its energetic potential with the Morrigan—"

"The Morrigan?" I parroted, as I felt me legs go numb.

"Yes, the Morrigan," he stated, and he opened the compartment beneath the counter and removed the amethyst Mrs. McGillian had placed within it. "This gem is the key to my entire operation here. Without it I would be doomed to failure."

"Em, doctor—"

"Silence, William. I will continue to explain. So as the moon's energy reacts with the Morrigan" said he, as he motioned towards the pyramid of glass above, "I will use the chants I learned from the Iboruba to summon Ristila's life force. I will then treat the enriched light of the moon with a filter created by the venom–stained mirror." He presented the mirror to me. "You see, a chemical in the venom acts as a diffuser to an otherwise harmful side effect of the crystal energy, which I learned of in some texts I took from the Kride's castle. Judging by the look on your face, I take it you neglected to review such documents in your exposé of my studies.

"Never–the–less, the mirror will then be turned into a position to force the light through the inverted Iboruba ritual mask and onto the face of my beloved. This will instil her spirit, if you will, back into her body just as it temporarily gave the Iboruba spirit possession of the mask wearer. I will then close the chest, which is technologically capable of restraining any known energy force, and I will conclude with the healing ritual of the Durwaihiccora. When I open the chest and pour the water onto her body, she will rise up and embrace me once more."

I stood there, stunned.

"I do not expect you to believe, William. You see, I have an understanding of the world today. Your kind must see something in order to believe in its existence. Whereas I am from an older mindset, the true mindset of the masters of *Awen*, and that mindset states that your belief in something is what makes it possible. Humans, who are a part of that essence, can also wield it."

"You're right," I began, "I don't understand. I don't understand a thing about you and just when I think I do—just when I think I've got you all figured out—I realize that, in truth, I don't know a thing about you. You mean to tell me that you've spent the last twenty years of your life on a global scavenger hunt to figure out the lost secrets of Atlantis, which you hope will bring your wife back from the dead?"

"Not hope, William. *Know* they will."

"Why do *you* care so much? Why couldn't you just let her go? You've spent your entire life searching for a way to return to the way you were before you began your search. You're living in a dream, a dream of the past. Hell, I don't even know how to talk to you! You've let countless people parade you around the world and share their inner most secrets with you.

Keftiuc came here to warn you because he was worried about you. But when I brought him up earlier, you didn't even ask about him! He thought you'd drown while your arms and legs were bound with rope. He cared about you. But you only cared about using him. I might say the same for this African boy you mentioned. You used him too. How many people, Dr. Vant? How many people does it take? How many people died so that your wife might live again? Did you ever stop to think about that?"

"Any casualties would be necessary."

"What right do you have to make that decision?! You're not fate. You're not God. You're just selfish and pathetic, that's what you are. You don't care about any cultures or lost civilizations. Anthropology, me arse! You only care about what you want. You're no different than that Shih–Chieh Ling character you mentioned in your letter! Did you ever think about what your wife would want? How do you know she wants to be born again? What happened to the phrase *'till death do us part?* Why, in God's name, are you doing this to her and to yourself?"

"Because," he blurted.

"Ain't that an end–all answer!" I hollered, getting further and further annoyed with the crazy man in front of me. "'Because' why?" I demanded.

"**Because I killed her!**" he shouted.

XVII
THE SEED OF MADNESS

Dr. Vant's face was red as beetroot, and he was having trouble breathing. I stood there thinking about the rumour Erin had told me she'd heard from Jacob Faulky, that Dr. Vant had murdered his wife. I then thought of Cara's father, Henry Faulky, and how his blood boiled whenever Dr. Vant's name was mentioned in his presence and the accusations he had made at me show in London.

"Then the rumours are true?" I asked.

"It was the night of our one–year anniversary," he began to explain.

* * *

As a resident archaeologist, my work frequently allowed me to work from home. I didn't travel nearly as much back then. At any rate, I closed my books up at three that afternoon and went into town to gather some groceries for a special dinner I was preparing for Ristila.

Ristila worked for Old Man Faulky, as he was known then. She worked as a seamstress in his tailor shop. She would be home later that evening, and I had just enough time to get the necessary provisions and cook the meal. So half an hour later I found myself at the local butcher shop over on Luxembourg Avenue. The shop was relatively busy that day, but I soon found myself second in the line of common folk. It was cold outside, as it was autumn. I'd been forced to wear my black woollen overcoat with my usual matching top hat and spats. I suppose I set myself apart purposefully. I liked being different. I liked the idea of being a nobleman.

I stood there in line behind a huge man, rather obese, I must say. Aside from his size, he was like any other man in Leocadia—average. Back then I did not pay much attention to others, but this man in particular was beginning to agitate me, as he seemed to be ordering up a storm and taking up my precious time—time that I could have spent preparing the feast.

"All right then," sniffed the butcher. "Let's see, we've got two T–bones, three pork loins, one rump roast, one dozen gizzards, and a ham. Anything else, sir?"

"Better make it two hams," replied the obese man.

The butcher nodded and went about with the order.

"Preparing for a long winter?" I asked, not able to help myself.

"Winter?" asked the obese man. "Hardly! I'll be lucky if this lasts a week in my house."

"You must have a large family," I offered.

"You don't want to know," he said. Then he squinted his eye and looked at me for an awkward moment. "Say, you're that new guy in town, ain't ya? I read about you in the paper a few days ago. Some kind of doctor, right?"

"Archaeologist," I said.

"Bless you," offered the butcher, as he bagged up the obese man's order.

"No, I didn't sneeze. It's my title. I'm an archaeologist. I study ancient artefacts," I explained to the butcher. Then I turned back to the heavy fellow. "And I'm not entirely new to Leocadia. I've been living here nine months already and used to visit some summers as a child."

"Well", said the obese man as he gathered his bags. "I'll be seeing you, Dr. Vant. That's your name, right?"

"Yes, Dr. Irel E. Vant, PhD."

"That's a bit irrelevant, ain't it?" he asked, as he stepped aside from the counter.

"I beg your pardon?" I asked. Oh I knew full well what he meant. I've been ridiculed my entire life on account of my name. Regardless, I enjoyed playing right back with them.

"I think he means your name," said the butcher. "Kind of weird. I mean, who names their kid irrelevant?"

"I'm afraid I fail to see your point."

"Never mind. What do you need?" asked the butcher.

"Do you have any quail in stock?" I asked.

"Quail?" asked the obese man rather loudly as he headed for the door. "Who in their right mind eats them things?"

"It's for my anniversary dinner. My wife and I have been married a year this day."

"I'll see what we've got," stated the butcher.

"Quail!" proclaimed the obese man in disbelief as he shook his head and carted his bags off out the door. "Of all things!"

Unfortunately for me, they were out of quail. So I settled on duck instead. After buying the duck, I returned home to Vant Manor. As I mentioned some time ago, I had inherited Vant Manor shortly after receiving my doctorate. The day I inherited the castle I proposed to Ristila, and we were married a short time later. We then moved to Leocadia to start a new life. We were young then. Everything seemed to be working with us. I had written my dissertation on Atlantis, explaining my theory on how the culture populated the world. Still, my work yielded very little capital at first, which was why Ristila was forced to take a job herself. As for my monetary inheritance, it was tied up in legalities and it would take another ten to fifteen months before the entire situation was sorted out.

Ristila never minded working, though. She was in love with life. She adored people and was such the opposite of the hermit I had always been. She was to be home at a quarter past six that evening. She was always fairly punctual, so I knew exactly how much time I had to make the preparations. Upon arriving home, I hastily prepped the duck. While it cooked, I covered the dining room table with an old ivory table cloth, lit what must have been a hundred candles, placed a vase of freshly cut flowers in the centre of the table and surrounded the centre–piece with rose petals. Everything was perfect. I had out–done myself. I opened my pocket watch to monitor my timing. It was six o'clock. Within fifteen minutes the eventful evening would begin.

Eager to see my wife's expression, I cranked up a music box and let it's sweet melody drift into the night. A while later, I checked the time again. It was 6:45, and there was no sign of Ristila.

"Perhaps Old Man Faulky is having her work late," I thought to myself.

When the hands on my watch reached eight, I blew out the candles, closed up the music box, covered the duck, and set off to find her. I followed her usual route to and from work but found no trace of her. When I arrived at Faulky's Tailor Shop, the sign on the door read *CLOSED*. I knocked regardless.

"Coming," I heard a meek old voice call out. Soon Old Man Faulky's face came to the window, and he peered out at me. He opened the door a bit. He was an old man in his early eighties with sagging skin.

"Yes?" he asked as he focused his spectacles. "Oh, Dr. Vant! What brings you out this way tonight?"

"Ristila," I stated, rather out of breath. "Is she here? Has she left yet?"

"Oh, she left the usual time, I would think."

"Well she hasn't come home yet. I'm beginning to get uneasy. Did she mention anything? Leave any clue as to where she might be going?"

"Not that I can recall."

"Thank you anyway. I must be off."

He watched from the door's window as I hustled off into the night fog. The rest of the evening I kept busy, checking every place Ristila might have gone. I left no stone unturned. She was missing, and I knew it. After a long while of endless searching, I sat down on a bench, as freezing rain began to come down. The icy water ricocheted off my coat but cut through my hair and stung my scalp, as I'd left in such a hurry that I'd gone out without my hat. I sighed. Soon my eyes began to well with tears. What was I to do? Where could I turn? The constables in Leocadia would be useless, as there were only three of them ever on duty in the entire village. Then, in my despair, I heard distant footsteps in the icy rain. I glanced up only to see the obese man from the butcher shop running towards me.

"Doctor!" he hollered as he struggled to catch his breath. "Dr. Vant, thank God, there you are." He coughed. "I was just on my way to see you!"

"You're out of breath. Sit down!" I ordered.

"That's your problem, you idiot," he bellowed. "You're too damn courteous!" He then plopped down beside me on the bench.

"Now, what's this all about?" I asked.

"Your wife, man. It's about your wife!"

"Ristila?" I questioned as I sprang to my feet and confronted him eye to eye. "What of her? Where is she?"

"She just left the tailor shop, 'bout ten minutes ago."

"Impossible. I was there scarcely an hour ago. I spoke to Old Man Faulky. He told me she left at her usual time."

"I'm telling you what I saw. You've been tricked, Vant! She's been fooling around with that geezer! I was out on an errand when I came upon the tailor shop and heard them talking about how easy it was to get rid of you earlier. She kissed him, they laughed, and she trotted off."

"*My* wife? Wait, hold everything, you don't even know who my wife is. I only met you this afternoon in the butcher shop!"

"We live in a small town, Vant. I'm telling you, they're having an affair. Old Faulky's bedding your wife!"

"You're probably just jumping to conclusions. I'll go back to Faulky's myself and straighten this whole matter out."

I said nothing more. I left him there on the bench as the icy mixture continued to fall. When I returned to the tailor shop, Faulky was just leaving. He was a frail and bony old man with a balding head.

"Mr. Faulky," I called as I came closer. "It's Dr. Vant. You and I need to talk."

"Oh, have you, um, found Ristila yet?" he asked, as he opened his umbrella.

"I heard that she left the shop only recently. How could that be when you specifically told me she left at her usual time?"

"Yes, yes … about that."

"So it's true?"

"Well, it is, but—"

"But nothing! How dare you, old man? Who do you think you are?" My anger was flaring then, and you might have guessed that I've got something of a temper and I worry about asking questions later, usually when it's too late. "You ever come near my wife again and I swear that I'll kill you with my own two hands. Do you hear me?" I shouted.

A man came upon the scene, as I stepped up to Old Man Faulky's face. He shivered but not from the cold.

"Here now," came the voice of the spectator. "What's going on here?" He grabbed me by the shoulder and I swatted him away.

"Make no mistake old man," I said, as I pointing back to Faulky before walking away. "I'll kill you, in cold blood!"

In hindsight I realized it wasn't the best thing to say. But I was disgusted in the moment. And so I hurried home, where I found Ristila seated in the foyer with the fireplace lit. I stood there with the door open behind me, dripping wet, soaked nearly through to my dinner jacket.

"Where were you?" I asked coldly.

"I was at Betsy's house," she replied.

"On our anniversary?"

"She's very sick, you know." She stood up and closed the door behind me. "She's been having hallucinations again."

"Is that so? Odd, as she seemed rather fit when I stopped in to see her just a short time ago."

"Did she? What were you doing at Betsy's?"

"Looking for you. Only I don't remember seeing you there. Neither did she."

"Poor Betsy," she sighed as she attempted to help me remove my topcoat. "Her mind is going you know."

"Save your lies, Ristila," I snapped, and I pulled away from her. "I want the truth! Where were you?" I tossed off the topcoat myself; it landed in a heap upon the floor.

"All right, I'll tell you. But first, follow me upstairs."

I trailed close behind her and, when reached the top of the staircase, I addressed her once more. "We're upstairs now. So tell me. Where were you?"

"Let's go into the bedroom first."

"No. Tell me here," I said and I grasped her arm. "Tell me *now*."

"Irel, what's come over you? You're hurting my arm."

"Isn't this a good enough place to tell me that you've been unfaithful to me—with your boss?! Hmmm? Is that why you got a bonus after only a few months work?"

"What are you talking about?" she questioned, as she pulled her arm out of my hand. "Are you mad? I didn't do anything with Mr. Faulky. Honestly, Irel! I think you need a holiday. You've been working too hard. Now, if you'll just come with me to the bedroom—"

"First explain."

"Irel, on the bed is—"

"Where you slept with him? On *our* bed?" Hurtful tears streamed down my face but soon they turned into tears of anger. "God have mercy on your sinful soul!"

"Irel!" she begged, grabbing hold of my arm.

"Let go of me, you filthy whore!" I shouted, and I batted her away with such force that she fell clear over the railing and down to the foyer floor below. "My God!" I screamed. "What have I done?" I stared down at her limp body from above and then flew down the staircase to be by her side. "Ristila? Ristila, darling, are you all right? Darling, I apologize. Ristila?" I felt for a pulse. There wasn't one. "***RISTILA!***" I bellowed out into the night in a sorrowful wail that I'm sure could be heard for miles. I stayed there beside her body for hours until a constable showed up at my door.

I was being questioned on a charge of assault on Old Man Faulky. Apparently, after I'd left him that evening, he'd suffered a stroke right there on the street in front of his shop. He lived but never regained consciousness. When the constable saw Ristila, I was taken to the station and imprisoned for murder as well. The university I worked for and schooled at appointed me a lawyer, who joined the police in searching my estate. There they found something resting on my bed, which they brought to me in my cell. It was a gift–wrapped box with a violet ribbon around it. When I opened the box, I took out an enclosed card that read:

My Dearest Husband,

We've only been married for one year and yet it's as if we've known each other a lifetime. Here is my gift to you. Mr. Faulky let me work late some nights to finish it for you. I hope you enjoy it. Happy Anniversary.

Love, Ristila

Tears once more plagued my face, as I placed the card aside and withdrew a plum–coloured top hat with a lavender band accompanied by a matching top–coat."

* * *

"Jaysus Christ," was all I could say to Dr. Vant, my voice coming out in a low whisper.

* * *

She'd known I had loved the colour violet ever since I learned of its connection to the Atlanteans. There's little left to tell, then. At the trial my lawyer was able to clear me of the charge of intended murder, and instead I received a charge of manslaughter and, of course, the assault charge, for what I did to Old Man Faulky. The university had previously posted my bail and my lawyer was so good, I never served a prison sentence. Needless to say, the Faulky family made my stay in Leocadia very miserable thereafter. I was accused of having political connections and paying off the court.

One day I knew I would right my wrong. I had studied the ancient Atlantean resurrections as part of my work and had Ristila's body frozen while Winston Seadrick and his crew made alterations on Vant Manor. We were in agreement that I would pay him after receiving my inheritance, which I did.

I then immersed myself in everything ever written on Atlantis and began travelling the world to piece together a plan to return Ristila to the living."

"And that led you to all this?" I asked, knowing the answer before I'd finished the question.

"Indeed. My chance to alter the course of history, reverse time, and take back what I have done."

"How's that going to help Old Man Faulky, I wonder?"

"He passed away some years ago from natural causes," said Dr. Vant.

"What, you mean you don't want to dig him up and bring him back from the grave as well?"

"Don't be absurd! His body would have to have been frozen. Aside from that, his family would never have let me near his body."

"Do you hear yourself?" I asked dumbfounded. "You're talking nonsense. Even if you were able to bring someone back from the dead, that'd be the work of the Devil himself."

"There is no Devil. No God either, for that matter. Just the essence of *Awen*!"

"You'll pardon me for sticking to me own beliefs."

"William, I'm not asking for your blessing. I've got everything in order now, so you're welcome to leave."

"Leave? Leave you to this? Not a chance. It's time to put away your toys, Dr. Vant. I'm taking you to an asylum."

"An asylum?" he laughed. "My dear boy—"

Then, before I knew it, I found me hands being lassoed by his feckin' pocket–watch chain. Suddenly he was behind me, and he tied me hands behind me back and strung me up to a hook on the wall. Granted, it was only about two feet off the ground, but the chain dug into me wrists almost immediately. I tried to kick at him, but he was instantly out of me range.

"You've lost it. You're absolutely mad!"

"Forgive me, William. I realize how this must all look to you. Still, you don't know what I've been through, and you don't know how close I am."

"I know bloody well more than you give me credit for. I know more about life than you do."

He sighed, then reached into his pocket and removed a handkerchief.

"You understand that I need it absolutely quiet so I can concentrate," he said, as he came closer.

"You're going to gag me?"

"You have a better suggestion?"

"You're honestly asking me if I can think of a better way to silence meself?"

"I see your point," he said, as he shoved the cloth into me mouth. Now I know what you're thinking: that I could just spit it out, right? Wrong. He stuck it in there so deep, I'm surprised I could still breathe. The only way that thing was coming out of me yap was if it were to be taken out by hand. Now me own hands were a bit tied up and so there I *hung*, quiet, in some small amount of pain, and agitated as all hell.

XVIII
THE DESCENT

As the light of the moon reached its zenith, Dr. Vant stood before a podium with a long, wooden arm–like extension that stretched out across the top of the violet and gold Atlantean chest. Stacked upon the arm were three tiers of wood like shelves that held certain valuables in place. Upon the topmost tier was the amethyst that Dr. Vant believed to be the sacred *Morrigan* he had fought so hard to obtain years ago. Below that—on the next tier—the venom–stained mirror was absorbing the moon's light, which ran through the faux–Morrigan. The mirror could be swivelled 360 degrees; however, it was currently facing up towards the amethyst. The last tier was affixed with two wooden arms that held out the yellow and black African tribal mask, which faced inward, towards Dr. Vant at the podium. The idea was to position it as if his wife, who lay below it, were wearing it.

From what I could make out of her body—given me distance and the fact that it was set into a chest atop a platform—it was wrapped tightly in cheesecloth–like bandages. I was surprised at the absence of hoarfrost, given that her body had been frozen for so long. Looking at it made me sick to me stomach and I found meself again thinking about me own recently departed mother and how she looked in her own coffin.

Dr. Vant stood before the podium and took a bite out of some strange tree bark and then made one last trip to the wall of masks and took down one that I'd overlooked. He then lowered it onto his face. It was the mask of the Kride. I knew it by his initial description of it in his journal on that Atlantean high priest. It was elongated, and ivory white, smooth as cream with two large dark eye holes, though I could not see Dr. Vant's eyes. Its appearance was like an abstract interpretation of the Egyptian god, Anubis. The idea is a fitting one because, as I later learned when I first read about Anubis, the god was associated both with the dead and mummification. Dr. Vant looked otherworldly then, even intimidating.

As he returned to the podium, he took up a small drum that rested beside it and started to tap out a hypnotic beat. Rum, bum, bum, bum, bum. *Rum, bum, bum, bum, bum*—something to that effect. Then, suddenly, he broke out into song. I've no recollection of the actual words. Whatever it was, he repeated this chant over and over again while never losing his beat on the drum.

Now I realize this may sound like I was losing me own mind, but after a time there was a different feel to the air around me. The coldness wasn't what it had been. Instead, there came a sense of warmth and vigour, I guess you could say. I don't know if it came from the energy of his late wife or from the trance–inducing sounds he was conjuring up, but it was the most bizarre feeling of humility and peace I'd ever felt. The sounds in that room were lulling. There was the drumbeat, Vant's chanting, and the clockwork blood pump making a strange mechanical sloshing noise as it rocked back and forth drawing blood from one glass bottle, down one hose, into the body of his wife, back through the other hose, and into the other bottle that had once been empty.

Light was now pouring in from the hole in the ceiling above, and the beam was extremely brilliant as it radiated through the amethyst and down to the mirror, then back up and out to the ceiling. It was an eerie purplishy–orange colour. It reminded me of a sunrise I'd once painted during me first few weeks in Leocadia.

Then, quick as lightning, Dr. Vant swivelled the mirror so as to reflect the light through the African mask and onto the bandaged face of his bride. The next thing I heard was the high–pitched tones of a little flute Dr. Vant wore around his neck. He had taken it up in his right hand, put it to his lips beneath the Kride mask, and was blowing on it.

I wondered what this was for. It then came to me as Dr. Vant reached out and tried to adjust the amethyst upon the top tier. He meant for that tune on the whistle he'd whittled to do what he'd hoped that gypsy's song would do, unleash the energy within the gem that he took to be the Morrigan. Only it wasn't the Morrigan. It was nothing more than an amethyst.

Dr. Vant lifted the Kride mask from his face, looking agitated with *this* Morrigan. Not knowing exactly what he was expecting, though, he shrugged and returned the mask to his face. I knew, from all that I'd learned, that he would then close up the chest and light the crushed sage—known as qas'ily—as he had done in the Durwaihiccora village long ago. He would then either smudge the qas'ily onto the lid of the chest or open the chest and place the qas'ily on the forehead of the body itself. He would proceed by placing a solution–soaked cloth on the body or on the casket and pray in the tongue of the Durwaihiccora to their ancestors for divine intervention. He'd then conclude by taking up a handful of cinders from his fireplace upstairs and blow them onto her or it. He'd say a final prayer and baptize the whole mess with the pail of water or whatever it was he had in the bucket next to him. He'd then expect her to sit upright, remove the bandages, and embrace him. They would rekindle their love and live happily ever after. But that was not to be.

It seemed God—the Lord—fate—essence, whatever you want to call it—had other plans that night. As you're aware, the gem that rested upon the top tier of madness was not the Morrigan, it was nothing more than an amethyst. That isn't to say the Morrigan would have done what he'd proposed it would. It's just to say that the amethyst did not.

As the magnified light of the moon began to burn through the bandaged face of Ristila, Dr. Vant realized something was amiss. He tossed off the mask of the Kride, as he'd probably not been able to see well enough through it. He then watched in horror as the bandages caught fire. Not knowing what to do, he slammed the lid of the chest shut, hoping to extinguish the flames by cutting off the oxygen supply. However, the tubes from the blood pump kept the lid open just a crack—just enough to allow fresh oxygen to get in. Smoke was suddenly seeping out from beneath the lip of the lid, and Dr. Vant was forced to open it back up, only to find the entire body of his wife engulfed in flames. Sheer terror swept across that man's face, and he made a dash for the bucket of water beside the podium. When he finally did toss the water onto the body he was too late. Not only did the solution *not* put out the fire, it caused a plume of smoke to billow out into the chamber. Then he truly lost it.

Dr. Vant screamed out into the night at the top of his lungs. I've never heard a more bone–chilling wail in all me existence and hope to never hear such a thing again. He knocked into the podium in a fit of rage, took up the amethyst and pitched it clear across the room, where it crashed into one of the bottles of the Kride's blood. The thick fluid spurted out everywhere, prompting Dr. Vant to collapse in tears onto the floor just before the flaming corpse. The chest, if you're curious, seemed to be fireproof, just as Kamahni mentioned a few chapters back. However, the podium's wooden tiered armature directly above it was not. Soon it too was aflame and the fire danced its ways from one object to the next in the study. A heavy cloud of black smoke began to take form.

It was then that I knew if we were going to get out of there alive, I would have to take matters into me own hands. I searched me surroundings for anything that might give me an idea. Most of the study was now engulfed in flames and I was about fifteen feet away from the worktop that lined the circular chamber where most of his tools and peculiar paraphernalia lay. There was nothing within me reach. We were doomed. I hung there for a moment listening to Dr. Vant's persistent weeping, and I began to think back on me life.

I thought of Cara and the life we'd never know. I thought of me art and how I'd got so close to making a success of it. I thought of Erin and me brothers. Then I thought of me mother and how I'd missed her passing. Monsieur de Croismencer flashed in me memories, and even me father and the fun we shared down at the docks between his shifts came to mind. I'd come such a long way in me life and I was still so young. I felt cursed; robbed of everything I'd fought for just as me life was becoming fruitful. I thought of Dr. Vant. I thought of his wife and his endless quest to revive her and its ending this way. As ghastly as it sounds, there was a tinge of romance in there somewhere. I believe he really did love her. I then prayed for strength. That's when I decided that this man's fate did not have to be me own.

I thought of the hook I was on. Yes, I was hung on it, but it was *just* a hook. I started clawing at the wall with me feet until I was able to get enough traction to push up. I slipped back down, and the chain dug deeper into me wrists. I winced at the pain but fought to walk me feet up the wall once more. Finally, on the third attempt I was able to bring meself up and just over the top of the hook. It had worked—I was free of the hook! Only I fell face forward to the ground just below. Me face felt bruised, but still I pressed on. Once I was able to see what I was doing I pushed meself up then pulled the handkerchief from me mouth. Upon inhaling in the smoky air I coughed profusely but still managed to untie meself, tearing tiny bits of flesh off with the chain but that was a small price to pay for a second chance at life. I kept the cloth close to me mouth and then tied it around me head, using it to filter the air I took in.

Flames and smoke had completely taken over the room now, and it was difficult for me to see where Dr. Vant was lying. However, I was able to follow his unyielding wails and found him just as I'd last seen him. I grabbed him. He made no attempt to do anything. He was dead weight, limp from toe to top, defeated.

"Dr. Vant, for God's sake, you've got to at least try to walk!"

He made no reply but only continued his heart broken lament. I did me best to drag him to the staircase, where I struggled to pull him to a standing position. He was not up long, but long enough for me to hoist him up onto me back. Strange, I never would have given meself credit for being able to lift a man. I guess when your life is hanging on by a mere thread, you find you can do a great many things. Then you think about it later and marvel at the feat.

Shortly thereafter we reached the library, with the smoke following close behind. I temporarily tossed the doctor aside while sealing off the entrance to the secret study. The library was smoke–infested as well, and me main objective was getting the doctor to fresh air far away from Vant Manor. So I pulled the old bugger up onto me back once more and made me way down the hall. As you might have guessed, smoke and flames had overtaken the West End, no doubt having climbed their way up the worktop, cabinets, tapestries, and other artefacts that decorated the walls in his private study far below. The hole in the ground that once held hopes for letting in some mystical light of resurrection now became an outlet for death and destruction. I glanced briefly inside only to see Ristila's statue scorched by the encompassing flames. Suddenly the ground inside gave way, and the flames gobbled up the remains. Down she fell into the heart of hellfire. Needless to say, I wasn't about to wait for it to finish off the rest of the place with us still in it.

Fifteen minutes later, what seemed like an eternity in purgatory, we reached the front gate. I had had to resort to dragging Dr. Vant by the scruff of his topcoat. A snowy sky had since engulfed the moon and it wasn't long before the powdery flakes came sauntering down. I took refuge on the little stone bench just a little ways up the path from the gate. I had a mad fit of coughing and could feel the bruises that covered me face. I stared back up at Vant Manor. Somehow or another the entire castle was glowing red–orange and looked like something in a nightmare.

Suddenly there came an explosion from within, and I figured the flames had either found a stash of paraffin for the oil lamps or the wine cellar, assuming wine can explode. Still, how a stone building can fill with fire so fast was beyond me. I can only presume it was caused by all the books in the library, the oil trench light systems, and all that archaeological junk he had. So there it was, contrasted by the white snow falling around it, which made the blaze that much brighter against the blue–black sky of early morning. I was sure it could be seen from the village. Victor flew high overhead in a continuous circle around the blaze. I was glad to see he had made it out and was sure the snakes would be safe down in their pit or the adjoining river.

* * *

Half an hour later, I heard the sounds of a coach and saw the horses come into view. I remained seated on the bench, now with a sad Victor's head resting upon me lap, and Dr. Vant still lying in the accumulating snow. The carriage stopped at the gate, and Mrs. McGillian, Cara, her brother, and Mr. Faulky emerged from within.

"Thank God you're safe!" Cara declared, and as soon as Mrs. McGillian unlatched the gate between us, she was embracing me.

"Ow, easy love, easy," I said, as she was agitating me ripe wounds.

"Sorry, Billy," said Cara, while taking a good look at me. "My God, look at your wrists!"

"They'll heal," I replied.

"I'm just so thankful you're safe," she cried, as she hugged me once more.

"We all are," added Henry Faulky.

"What happened?" asked Mrs. McGillian, as she made her way over to the pile that was Dr.Vant.

"'Tis a very long story. I'm not even sure I can put such odd events into words. Not yet anyway."

Henry Faulky, Adam, and Mrs. McGillian pulled Dr. Vant up. He had ceased his wailing and merely twittered his lips and twitched nervously; his eyes looked glazed over.

"So this is what became of the man who brought the Faulky family to its knees and ended the life of his own bride," observed Henry Faulky. "Fitting, I guess, but cruel the way fate can balance out a man's actions. I bet he suffers the rest of his life locked up in his own head. Just like my father."

Cara pursed her lips at her father and he raised an apologetic eyebrow for his comment.

"I might be wrong," said I. "But I think Dr. Vant's paid the price for everything he's done."

"I agree," added Mrs. McGillian. "Now the healing can begin."

"What's to become of him, then?" asked Henry Faulky.

"I'm not sure yet," I replied. "But I can't just leave him homeless in his condition."

Henry Faulky sighed. "I've a feeling I'm going to regret this," he said. "But you can bring him to our place until we work out some proper living arrangements."

"*You* would do that for *him*?" asked Cara.

"I don't know what's come over myself lately either, Cara. But look at it this way: I can show off what's become of him to the rest of the family."

"Father!"

"You know I'm just kidding … partly."

They then escorted Dr. Vant and meself back to the Faulky residence. We left Victor to guard the estate.

* * *

At the Faulky's, Mrs. McGillian slept on their sofa, while the doctor was put in the guest bed. Because of me wounds they let me have Adam's bed and he slept in the same room upon the floor. I was incredibly grateful to be alive and to be under the same roof as Cara. Naturally, there was talk in the town over the next few days about all the commotion and the fire up at Vant Manor. Rumours had Dr. Vant dead and buried alongside his wife. But we worked to set the story straight whenever we encountered such tales.

Dr. Vant was most certainly a changed man. He made me think about Erin and how one man permanently scarred her soul in a single evening. Sometimes the people with the strongest character end up being the most susceptible in life. Perhaps they'd always been a little vulnerable at heart and the strength was just a bit of armour to safeguard themselves. Other people wear no emotional armour at all and add a new scar of awareness twice or more daily, chalking it up to a lesson well learned.

One evening, about a week or so after that dark night, Mr. and Mrs. Faulky made an announcement during dinner. They said that as business was good and the season was going well—on account of their being one of the few in–town shops to bring goods in from London on a weekly basis—the time was ripe for a wedding ceremony. They'd even pay for it. I was sure the idea was more the Missus's than the Mister's. So we all discussed it over dinner and decided that the best course of action would be to set a date in March, and we chose the twentieth, not too close to me birthday, which would be on the fifteenth.

There was, of course, another reason to reschedule it a little ways off. I secretly hoped that it would give me brothers a chance to make it in from Ireland. Our falling out was still fresh in me mind and I wanted terribly to make amends with them. Erin would naturally be there and maybe—just maybe—if they came, she might perk up and seem like her old self again. Yet there was one person whom I couldn't see perking up. Dr. Vant had said not so much as one word in the entire time we'd been at the Faulky's. He never joined us at dinner, never moved from the bed, and it was I who had the unnatural job of putting him on the bedpan. He had become a shell. This made me wonder how Mum looked in her last days. Maybe it was better I hadn't been there to see them.

* * *

As the days slowly passed, the question about what to do with Vant Manor came up more than once. We knew Dr. Vant was in no position to deal with it, and it was decided that it'd be best if Mrs. McGillian and I went in to survey the damage alone. We felt Dr. Vant would have wanted it that way, had he been able to speak for himself.

When the fire had been burning that fateful night, and after the others came to pick up meself and Dr. Vant, the local fire brigade arrived on the scene. Their main objective had been to prevent the blaze from spreading, as there was no way their minimal water supply would be capable of putting out Vant Manor itself. Aside from that, their ladders would never have reached the roof. So Vant Manor was left to purge itself of the last two decades in the wee hours that morn. When Mrs. McGillian and I returned to the estate, we came upon a sign affixed to the front gate which we assumed the authorities must have left. It read:

DO NOT ENTER. This zone has been quarantined and is pending police investigation. Trespassers subject to full penalty of the law.

The lock on the front gate was broken and a chain now shackled it closed. Snow covered the grounds.

"How do you like that?" I asked Mrs. McGillian.

"It's out of our hands now," she said. "Best to leave it be."

"Nonsense," I declared and went over to a nearby tree.

"What are you going to do?"

"I just want to take a peek at the damage is all," I explained. "Remember how Keftiuc got in that one night? He said he climbed a tree and shimmied over the fence by clinging to a branch." Next thing you knew I was scraping the snow off the bark with me shoes as I clumsily made me way up the trunk and into the snow–covered limbs.

"What can you see?" she asked, from about six or so feet below me.

"She's all scorched up," said I, as I stared out at the castle's charred carcass. The ominous edifice had been reduced to a ghostly, blackened pile of rubble. Oh, it still held its old form, don't get me wrong on that. But everything that had been made of wood had been completely devoured, leaving black ash to mix with the newly fallen snow, which had partially covered some of the more oppressive wounds. "Dreadful sight," I continued. "No way she'll recoup. Even if she were capable of being rebuilt, you'd never get the smell of the fire out of those stones."

"Any sign of Victor?" she asked, while trying to peer through the front gate herself.

I searched the estate and scoured the skies with me eyes. "'Fraid not," I replied.

"You think the authorities got to him then?"

"Tough call. He's a resourceful old buzzard, though. For all we know he could be sitting inside the castle trying to stay warm."

"He must be freezing."

"I'm freezing," said I.

"Maybe you should go in after him. You're nearly there anyway."

"Och, why not? Watch the gate until I get back. If you notice anything suspicious signal me by pretending you're looking for your dog gone astray. Call out 'Petrie' or something."

"Petrie?"

"Doesn't matter. Call out anything, and I'll get the hint," I answered, as I crawled along one of the branches. When I reached the end I had just cleared the hedge line that extended just beyond the black iron fence. It would be quite a jump down, and I started having second thoughts. "You know I just thought of something."

"What's that?" asked Mrs. McGillian.

"After I get down there, how am I to get out again?"

"Hmmm—"

But before she could finish, the branch I was on snapped off and down I fell into the shrubbery. I cursed on the way down through the prickly brush to the patch of snow on the ground. Still, it wasn't as bad as it most likely would have been had there not been some snow to break me fall.

"Are you all right, Master William?"

"I'm fine, Mrs. McGillian. Just got some of the cockles knocked out of me is all."

"Do be more careful when you get to Vant Manor. I don't want you falling into some hidden pit."

I dusted meself off and walked over to the inner side of the gate and said to Mrs. McGillian, standing on the other side, "Don't worry so much."

"I may not be your mother, but I am still *a* mother, and mothers always worry. It's our lot in life. Now be gone with you."

"Aye, before the coppers come."

And so, although I wasn't able to really see the path in all the snow, I headed deeper onto the estate and slowly came upon the castle. It most definitely appeared to be a castle now, whereas weeks before it might have passed for a grand Victorian mansion. Now she showed her true colours. As I got closer I noticed the blackened stump that was once the fine totem pole given to Dr. Vant by the Durwaihiccora. "Funny," I thought. "Why hadn't they foreseen *this* and come to warn him?"

"Victor!" I called. "Victor, you in there somewhere?" I continued calling as I entered the doorless entrance. All around was scorched debris lightly dusted with snow blown in through the open doorway and windowless windows. The staircase was gone, the furniture disintegrated, and all signs of decor had been charred so that only the cold stonewalls showed through. "Victor!"

I crept onward until I came to the West End, or what remained of it. The entire inner courtyard had been reduced to a circular quarry of rubble and waste. Far below, in the centre of the exposed private study rested the snow–covered statue of Ristila Vant a top what I guessed was the Atlantean chest. I'd know the shape anywhere. For reasons I can't justly explain in words, a tear came to me eye, and I suppose I felt responsible in some way for Dr. Vant's misery. It had been I who had taken the Morrigan from him and possibly stripped him of his chance to rekindle the spirit of his wife. I know it sounds bizarre to think such a feat could be possible, but what do we really know about the world anyway? I also thought about how I'd have to come clean with Cara about the Morrigan. I just wasn't sure how.

Just then, I felt a tap on me back and was momentarily startled until I turned 'round to meet Victor, who dropped Dr. Vant's purple top hat from his beak and snorted a friendly welcome. I bent down and hugged that bag of feathers, despite how much he protested, and took up the doctor's hat. I patted Victor warmly on his noggin. I could tell he was happy to see me once more. But then his mood changed, and I knew the look in his eye. He was listening. Something had caught his attention. I listened closely and heard a distant call.

"Mrs. McGillian!" I said aloud to Victor. "Come on, boy, we've got to get out of here."

Sure enough, as Victor and I made our way back towards the gate, we heard Mrs. McGillian shouting, "Petrie, Petrie? Where could you be?"

Once we got closer, I stood near the gate but out of sight, keeping Victor behind me.

"Look, lady," I heard a man's voice say. "This property is off limits. What are you doing out here?"

"It's my dog, Peatrie. I was taking him for a stroll up the long path, it takes him a while before he'll make, you know, when all of a sudden he goes running off under that gate and onto the private grounds. Now how am I to get him back?"

"Your dog; aye?"

"Yes sir, he's a little terrier named Petrie."

"All, right then," said the man, and I heard the clank of the chain. "I'll go in and look for him. But no funny business. You stay here. Come on, Astor, let's go see if we can't find this ball of fuzz."

"Right then," said another man and soon the gate swung open. I stayed crouched down beside the hedge as the two constables advanced on the castle. When they were a ways farther up, Victor and I made our move and hurried out the gate where Mrs. McGillian awaited us.

"Hey," I heard one of the officers declare. "These are human tracks, I don't see a dog's tracks anywhere."

"Best be off then," said Mrs. McGillian. As we ran off as fast as our legs, and wings, could carry us, we heard the police somewhere back behind us shouting, "Stop in the name of the law."

Well, we didn't.

XIX
REVELATIONS

I stood before the large mirror in the Faulky family lav. Before me stood a young man in a fine black suit who'd aged more in the past year than it seemed he had in all the previous years of his life. The door to the lav stood open, and I heard Mr. Faulky shuffling around in another room.

It was the day of me wedding. Cara, her Mum, Erin, Desiree, Mrs. McGillian, and the rest of the gals were off getting ready at the Faulky Tailor Shop whilst the men maintained dominion over the Faulky home. We did so mostly because Dr. Vant was still laid up in bed deep within the far reaches of his mind and it wouldn't have been fair to leave the ladies to tend to him.

"You all right, boy?" asked Mr. Faulky, as he passed by the open door adjusting his shirt cuffs.

"Just a little nervous, I guess," said I.

He came into the room, gave himself a quick glance in the mirror, and then said: "Good Lord, what's that smell?" Before I could answer, he'd lifted up me arm and me suit coat to view the sweat stain that had polluted me shirt below.

"Just a little nervous?" he asked. "Christ, you could harbour half the Royal Navy in that pool!"

I collapsed me arm in a huff.

"Sorry," he replied. "Still getting used to the nice talk." He paused for a moment, and we looked at each other through the mirror. "Here, I've got an idea." He bent down to a cupboard and took out a canister of sorts.

"What is it?"

"It's talcum powder. I picked some up one day in London 'bout a year ago. It's for use after shaving, I think. I meant to try it out to see if it'd be worth a test in our store but I never got around to it. It's supposed to absorb excess water from the skin. Has a masculine scent to it, too. I think the French invented it or something."

"Okay, I'll try anything," said I, as I removed me jacket.

"Holy mackerel," declared Danny McArthur, Adam's red–haired friend from the hall.

"Go on," ordered Mr. Faulky. "Go about your business. Get out of here. Adam," he called. "What's Danny doing here?"

"Cara said he could come to the wedding," replied Adam, entering the tiny hallway.

"Look at that sweat," Danny pointed out to Adam. "You think that happens to every man on the day of his wedding?"

"If so," declared Adam, "I don't want to ever get married!"

"Go on, out," commanded Mr. Faulky. "Both of you. Get yourselves ready."

When they'd left, I'd already removed me shirt and taken up the canister from Mr. Faulky.

"I can't believe it," I said to him. "You actually stuck up for me. You really are starting to treat me like family."

"I did nothing of the kind," he stated. "I don't know what you're talking about."

"Come off it, man. You know exactly what I'm talking about."

"You want me to get 'em back in here?" he asked in a hardened tone.

"No."

"Then, hush up about it, and let's finish getting you ready."

When it was just about time to leave, I checked in on Dr. Vant, all stiffened up in that bed with his top hat resting on the nightstand beside him. He still looked the exact same way he had when we put him there, a soulless man.

"You about ready?" asked Mr. Faulky, as he shuffled into the room.

"Yeah, I was just checkin' up on the doctor. Think he'll be all right while we're gone?"

"He'll be fine. That bugger's a survivor. Kind of like a cockroach. I don't know how he does it, but he does. Besides, we've got people taking shifts to come in and check on him. Don't let him—of all people—ruin the day. Especially not *this* day!"

"He told me everything that happened between him and your family, you know. Just before he fell off the deep end. Do you really blame him for the death of his wife and the death of your father?"

"All I know is that they'd both still be here, were it not for him. Well, maybe not my father, he was fairly old then, but still."

"I know what it's like to lose a father. I lost mine about six years ago. I wish he could have been here to see this day. And me Mum."

"For what it's worth, you're not so bad, William, not really."

"Thanks."

Just then there was a knock at the front door. "Bound to be the coachman," said I. "I'll go and tell him we're almost ready." I left Mr. Faulky in the room with Dr. Vant and made me way to the front door. Another knock rattled the door, and when I opened it up, there—before me own eyes —stood me brother Arlen dressed in a grey suit. He looked picture perfect, with his dark eyes and hair and that smooth skin, like a baby's bottom. Sure I was a bit jealous, after all, as the groom I was supposed to be the best–looking man in the church. But I was too overjoyed to care.

"I realize I may not match the party," he began and then cleared his throat. "But I'd still like to be there, if you'll have me."

I said nothing at first; I just reached out and hugged him for a long moment. I couldn't believe he had actually shown up. Then I let him go and I looked around for Glenn.

"You know Glenn," he said awkwardly. "He'll never get over his foolish pride."

"It's all right. If he doesn't want to be here, then I don't want him to be."

"Well said, brother," he added. "Oh, here, I almost forgot." Arlen reached into his pocket and removed me mother's diamond wedding ring. It wasn't glamorous, but it was simple and humble, just like our mother. "Mum would have wanted you to have this. Besides, Glenn, Erin, and I got married without it. Maybe it'll bring you luck."

"Thank you, Arlen. 'Tis a fitting present."

"And you should know, I opened up a bank account in your name with your share of the inheritance at your local bank here in town."

"You mean the *only* bank in town," I added, and we both laughed.

Soon we were joined by the Faulky men and Danny.

"And who's this?" asked Mr. Faulky.

"Mr. Faulky, this is me brother and best man, Arlen."

"You mean that?" asked Arlen.

"I do."

"Please to meet you, Arlen," said Mr. Faulky.

"The pleasure is mine, Mr. Faulky," Arlen replied. I then caught a faint smile on Mr. Faulky's face and knew he was up to no good.

"Call me Henry."

* * *

Saint Helena's was a small church–also the *only* church–in Leocadia, situated over on Brookberry Boulevard, near the town's square. Brookberry, if I haven't mentioned, is the main road into Leocadia from the east. The church was constructed to house scarcely a hundred patrons when Catholicism began to regain its foothold in England, but it was enough for the village. It held a number of services to ensure all the town's people could come and worship.

Mr. Faulky ushered the men down a hall and into a back room, where we were greeted by Father Cheris, who presided over the Saturday ceremonies while Father Packard, the more senior of the two, took a day to rest.

"How are you, my son?" Father Cheris asked of me.

"I could never lie to a man of the cloth, father. I'm as nervous as a sinner in Satan's den, excuse the language."

"Excellent, my boy, excellent. Such butterflies comfort a priest, for it means your intentions are true and you will not make light of this union or contribute to the daily scuff of married life."

"He's as ready as he'll ever be," commented Mr. Faulky.

"Then let us take our places," suggested the priest. "The service is about to begin."

Arlen rested a hand on me shoulder to comfort me worries, and we followed Father Cheris further down the hall. As we entered the nave itself, me eyes fell on Mrs. McGillian, who sat beside the Deerings and Mr. Cronley. She gave me a wink, while Adam joined Arlen and me. Danny took a seat, and Mr. Faulky disappeared to fetch his daughter.

The light shone in through the stained–glass image of what I took to be Saint Helena. I knew little of her, I must confess, but I knew she was extremely pious and such was probably the reason they reached out to her for heavenly support. A small choir of about ten or so ladies and gents congregated behind Father Cheris as an elderly gentlemen sat down to an organ. It was a mighty one for such a tiny place, its pipes reaching clear to the ceiling. Its melancholy tune began to fill the air.

All the guests rose. I saw Hector in the back joined by his date, a lovely Oriental gal I had yet to meet, though she seemed somewhat familiar. The great doors opened, and Cara's little cousin, Marcella, Jacob Faulky's five–year–old, appeared first, dropping clumps of daisies along the aisle as she was coaxed forward by her proud mother, who sat in an aisle seat near the front.

Next came Erin, whose face came alive as she saw me for the last time as a bachelor, joined by our brother Arlen. Though she was a changed woman and we changed men, we were still a family. She shed a joyful tear and took her place across from us, to be Cara's matron of honour. Now, as Arlen wasn't really expected there, it was supposed to be just Erin and Adam joining meself and Cara, so it seemed a bit off balance up there in front of everyone, but we ignored it, and the organ reached a new note as Mr. Faulky entered the doorway with me bride–to–be; the lovely Cara Faulky.

I had been surveying the room up until their arrival, but now found me glance glued to me lovely. Before I knew it, she was down the aisle and beside me. Orange blossoms were fixed in her hair, and she wore her best dress, though it was not white. In those days, while white was preferred, you wore the best you could afford and everyone appreciated the effort. She was like a statue come to life, with skin so smooth and eyes dancing so wildly I had to remind meself that we were in a house of God and such ideas as I was having could not be entertained there. We smiled at each other and addressed the priest who stood in front of the altar, where me parents' white onyx unity candleholder rested, bearing the single candle that was to represent our new life together. The guests were then seated.

"Dearly beloved," started Father Cheris, "We are gathered here this afternoon to bear witness to a blessing that strengthens our community and reaffirms our faith. Today we are here to witness William O'Brien and Cara Faulky declare to God, our Father, their devotion to each other and promise a lifetime of servitude both to him and each other as husband and wife. Now then, who here gives Cara's hand to William?"

"I do," declared Mr. Faulky, who stood beside Cara and took up both our hands ready to place them together.

"And who here," Father Cheris continued, "vouches for the honour of William O'Brien?"

The doors to the chapel swung open in the back at that very moment and before Arlen had a chance to say anything, a strong, firm voice from the entrance stated, "I do."

As we all turned in wonderment, there before the assembly, stood Dr. Irel E. Vant, neatly dressed, top hat and all, seemingly in the pink of health. Astonishment swept through the room as he advanced slowly.

"Dear Parishioners, indeed, the entire village, I owe you all a great debt and, if nothing else, an explanation. Truly I beg for your forgiveness for the way I've treated you all these years. The rumours are true. I did kill my wife. Granted it was an accident, but it was *I* who was the cause of it. Likewise, I take responsibility for my actions against the late Senior Mr. Faulky, who too would have had a longer life were it not for knowing me. I've spent a lifetime mourning my wife and trying to find a way to make amends for the damage I caused her, never stopping to live. Perhaps some of you have heard of my recent downfall, my descent into oblivion. This too I take credit for, as I attempted the unthinkable. I tried to revive Ristila in a very unholy act of selfish greed." At this the crowd became uneasy. "Do not worry, I was not successful. It was not meant to be. Who am I to play God? Who are any of us? Since that day—I myself am not sure of exactly how much time has passed —I have been held prisoner within the dark depths of my own soul.

"My body punished me for my sins and left me unable to repent. Indeed, I do not feel I would be here today were it not for one man, Mr. Henry Faulky. Earlier today, I was able to hear a faint voice in my unconscious despair. It was the voice of Henry Faulky. He said to me, 'I forgive you.'"

The room suddenly turned back towards the front where Mr. Faulky became the centre of attention. I stared out into the room at the sea of confused faces, noting that Hector's date was missing from her seat in the back. Still, Dr. Vant ascended the aisle.

"Here is a man, who—despite what I've put him and his family through—became the bigger man by bestowing that forgivene—oh dear. I, I'm doing it again, aren't I? Who am I to interrupt this joyous affair? Please, please excuse me. I, I suppose I'm still regaining my senses. Thank you, Henry. Thank you for giving me a new lease on life, a chance to be reborn into a better man. And you, William: I was wrong when I forbade you to see Cara."

"But you were right when you told me to treasure her," I reminded him.

He thought for a moment, no doubt recalling the day I first arrived at Vant Manor and told him I'd met a fantastic woman. He had not had a prejudice until I mentioned her name. "I suppose I was."

Suddenly there came a clapping of hands farther down the aisle, and as we turned to address the sound, the doors to the church were closed and sealed by Hector. Standing before us, in the back of the room, was a slightly aged Oriental man in a white suit.

"Shih–Chieh?" questioned Dr. Vant in disbelief.

"You must forgive me for not having a bridal gift," remarked the cool, collected voice of the mysterious stranger.

"*You* are Professor Ling?" I asked.

"Ah, so Irel's told you of me. Yes, I suppose it would have been ill–mannered of him not to mention his mentor at some time or another."

"You have never been *my* mentor, Shih–Chieh," declared Dr. Vant.

"I've, I've seen you before," said I. "At the art show in Paris, the night I met Dr. Vant!

"You were there that night?" Dr. Vant asked Shih–Chieh.

"I've always been a part of your life, Irel."

Hector came around from the hall behind us. Although I'd known him a few months now, he still had something of a limp.

"Have all the doors been sealed?" Shih–Chieh asked.

"Everything's locked down, sir," answered Hector.

"Hector?" I asked. "What in God's name are you doing?"

"You know this man as well?" Dr. Vant asked me.

"Aye, he brought some of me paintings up to London a while back. We've been friends since."

"This is low," said Dr. Vant, turning back to Shih–Chieh. "You've robbed young William of a friend he's never had."

"My people have but one mission, Irel. Restore the power of Atlantis to its rightful rulers."

"Those being yourselves."

Shih–Chieh shrugged. "We are a patient people and we continue our quest no matter the cost."

"So—so Hector works for you?" I asked.

Hector said nothing but stood emotionless, like a stone–faced soldier.

"That's the same Hector that I wrote to you about in my letter," stated Dr. Vant. "Tell me Hector, how have those gunshot wounds healed?" Again, Hector remained silent.

"You mean the obese fellow you mentioned when you got off Shih–Chieh's yacht in Spain? The one who later attacked you with that Chinese woman ..." I thought of Hector's Oriental date. My eyes again searched the room for her to no avail.

"Obese fellow?" questioned Dr. Vant to himself.

"Irel, you know why we are here," reminded Shih–Chieh. "You give me the key to the Atlantean crystals, and I'll leave you all to your wedding. You hold that power in your decision, Irel. Haven't you put these poor people through enough in your lifetime?"

"Now hold it right there," began Henry Faulky. At that moment a guest on the Faulky side of the pews stood up and pointed a pistol at Mr. Faulky. Shih–Chieh smiled.

"I'm afraid you do not have permission to speak, Henry," said Shih–Chieh. "You see, Irel? The Yishnalta have successfully infiltrated this town. There's no way of telling who is one of us and who is not."

Irel turned to Hector, eyes blazing like a wild fire. "It was you."

At this even Shih–Chieh became confused and uneasy. "What are you going on about?"

"You were the obese man!"

"He is a bit rotund," admitted Shih–Chieh. "But I wouldn't under—"

"You've greyed since then, but there can be no mistake about it. It was *you*," Dr. Vant continued.

Now Hector seemed nervous and backed up a step.

"It was you who convinced me that Ristila was cheating on me with Old Man Faulky all those years ago!"

"What?" asked Henry Faulky aloud.

Understanding the nature of Dr. Vant's words, Shih–Chieh spoke again. "Your wife was in the way, Irel."

At this Dr. Vant's attention sprang back towards Shih–Chieh.

"It should come as no surprise to you that the Yishnalta have had a hand in your life since you were conceived. Your entire life has been irrelevant. Hence the name we came up with."

"*You* killed my wife," whispered an enraged Dr. Vant.

"Hector merely poisoned her. It was the fall from *your* blow that allowed it to work its magic at an unprecedented rate; but on its own, a fall like that does not kill."

"Everything I've ever thought—"

"Was necessary," proclaimed Shih–Chieh, as he advanced towards Dr. Vant. "For years the Yishnalta moulded you into the prize–winning pupil you became. The foremost figure on Atlantean culture. You think you came up with the idea yourself? If you had it your way, you would've been off learning about trivial world cultures rather than reinstating *the* world's culture." Shih–Chieh was now nearly in Dr. Vant's face. The doctor retreated, one back step at a time, as Shih–Chieh continued to pursue him, slowly, while he patronized him. "The Vant fortune, your parents, everything you've come to know has been a carefully crafted plan of the Yishnalta council with myself at its helm. You were a sharp boy who promised to be a powerful man but when you met Ristila all that changed. Your work began to suffer. You travelled less. You even brought up the idea of a family to me one day back at the university." They had now passed the altar, and Irel's back was right up against the organ. "Those ideas would have been cancerous to the greater power."

"The greater power?" Dr. Vant asked himself.

"Perhaps that coma did more damage to you than I thought," said Shih–Chieh. "No matter. I knew you'd come out of it sooner or later. You see, Irel, everything is just a matter of time."

"Oh, shut up already!" declared Henry Faulky and he hurled his prayer book at Shih–Chieh's head. Shih–Chieh ducked as the man in the Faulky's pews fired his gun. A fight then broke out amongst the congregation between our honourable guests, the shooter, and two other planted Yishnalta spies. As Hector was about to make his move, Hugo and Mr. Cronley lashed out at him, bringing the obese man to the ground.

When Shih–Chieh regained his composure, he found Dr. Vant scaling the organ's pipes towards the ceiling. Arlen tried to grab Shih–Chieh, but he brought Arlen to the ground with one swift knee to the groin. Soon he was trailing behind Dr. Vant, and when Dr. Vant reached the top of the pipes he turned and looked down to Shih–Chieh, who was three–quarters of the way up.

"You know," said Shih–Chieh, "I heard you failed to resurrect your wife—but then I shouldn't have expected you'd be able to decode the key."

"You want the key, Shih–Chieh?" he asked.

We all looked up, waiting to see what was about to unfold. By then the Yishnalta spies had all been overtaken by the congregation.

"Have it your way," said Dr. Vant. "Choirmaster," he shouted from above. "Give me your highest C–sharp!"

"What?" asked Shih–Chieh. It was then I knew: Dr. Vant was hoping the organ's vibration would loosen Shih–Chieh's grip and force him to plummet to his demise. But as the choir singers took in a large breath of air and the organist took to his keys, I knew what was really about to happen, and I had to act. In a blur, I sprinted to me fiancée and, in the blink of an eye, removed the Morrigan from her finger and cast it out into the air just as the music of God, the greater power, filled the air.

A fraction of a second later an ominous burst of violet light erupted from both the Morrigan and Shih–Chieh's small ring. The force of the shockwave severed his finger, and, as Dr. Vant had planned, the vibration of the organ sent him hurtling down towards the ground. The energy of the Morrigan shot through the roof of the chapel and out into the afternoon sky. Shih–Chieh's body slammed into the marble floor below the altar, his bones shattered within him, and his body took on a contorted, inhuman pose. Debris rained down from the ceiling above, covering part of his body.

"Now there's a fall that kills," I heard Mrs. McGillian say from behind me. All eyes were on me as the lifeless Morrigan fell down through the air and crushed into several pieces on the ground at me feet.

I could feel the weight of the situation suddenly shifting onto me own shoulders. Nobody said a word and soon Dr. Vant had descended from the pipes.

"I–I–I" I stuttered. "I tried to tell you," I said, turning to Cara. "I *wanted* to tell you. I, I was *going* to tell you. I just—. When you thought that I was giving you the ring as an act of proposal, I couldn't say I wasn't. I mean, I wanted to marry you. I'd thought about it, but I just wasn't ready to propose at that moment. Not in Dr. Vant's private study."

Cara's eyes began to tear up.

"But I've realized that I *am* ready. Marriage is something that you learn from as you're in it. You never really know what's in store until you're there. Lately it's been as if we were, and I've loved it. I've learned that I am ready, Cara. Honest to God, I love you more than I could ever say. And you, Dr. Vant, I don't know if your wife would have truly been reborn had it not been for me switching the Morrigan with that amethyst. Maybe you would have succeeded and maybe you wouldn't but I just … I'm sorry. I'm sorry for everything I've done to everyone."

The silence that crept in after me speech was broken as Dr. Vant recited:

"Over seas and far away
Live the lands of yesterday
There were no kings
There were no tsars
All were equal beneath their laws
Education reigned on high

Until the day that greed came by
From that day on things weren't the same
Power and slavery became their ways
They conquered nearly all the earth
Until the hand of God set forth
And put an end to their control
Spreading winter ever more
And so their kingdom had been destroyed
But new ones would one day fill their void
The hope was that they would not forget
The greater power that overall sits."

Dr. Vant approached me and gave me an embrace. "My dear William, perhaps Ristila would be here were it not for you, but she wouldn't have deserved to be. She wouldn't have *wanted* to be. I see that now. For better or for worse, this is how it was meant to be. You've given my life back to me, William. So in a way it's as if Ristila were here, in spirit."

Dr. Vant then turned to Cara. "In truth, while I've known William for nearly a year, I've probably actually known him for only a week, but I can tell you that in that time I've seen a boy become a man and I've seen the love he has for you blossom from a simple crush to something eternal. Anyone can see how much he cares for you. Relationships are about growth. Learn from what you've witnessed here today, but don't live in the past as I have. Live in the moment, because sometimes it's all you have."

"Here, here," added Henry Faulky, as he came up behind Dr. Vant and patted the doctor on the shoulder.

"Cara," said I, and I got down on me knee and reached into me pocket. "Will you marry me?" I presented me mother's diamond wedding ring, which Arlen had given me earlier.

She remained silent for a long awkward moment. Then, gingerly, she took the ring from me. She then smiled and placed it on her finger. "I will," she replied through her tears, and I sprang up to embrace her.

Ten minutes later we were pronounced husband and wife. Then I kissed me bride, finally.

EPILOGUE

A little over a week had passed. Hector and the unnamed evil allies from the Faulky's pews were incarcerated. Shih–Chieh Ling's body was burned. The Deerings, Mr. Cronley, and Erin had returned to London. Arlen accompanied them to see how Erin was getting on. Mrs. McGillian gave us all a tearful good–bye as she left to go back to Edinburgh. Change was in the air. There comes a time in life when you've changed so much that you cannot possibly go back to how things were. Whether or not you're ready, life moves on.

Dr. Vant donated his estate to the people of Leocadia. Vant Manor itself was demolished. The grounds were carved up in thirds. One area became a small theatre district with two theatres and a few shops. Another area became the town's zoo, in which, I might add, the snakes and Victor found homes. Victor wasn't chained or even fenced in by bars, so worry not. He was given free reign of the town, but stayed in his new lodgings just the same. He enjoyed the visitors, and the arrangement let him keep an eye on the old estate.

The last bit of land was set aside for the town's first and only park. A tree was planted where Vant Manor had stood. It was dedicated to Dr. Vant and his wife, Ristila. Through the years the tree grew to be an enormous life force. Some say it grew bigger than the castle itself had been. Its branches hung low and touched the ground. I painted it once.

* * *

As for Dr. Vant, it was on the first of April, not long after me wedding, that he asked me to meet him at the estate grounds one last time. I found him standing at the front gate in a light, misty shower gazing into the fog where the flame–scorched edifice that had once been his refuge stood, though he could not see it.

"Evening," I offered as I approached. Dusk had just faded, and a cool breeze set in. He stood there in the muted moonlight with his face concealed in the shadows cast by that familiar plum–coloured top hat.

"Hello, William," he replied without facing me. "How is married life?"

"Em, grand, sir, but it has only been about a week and a half."

"Time is a precious commodity. You've taught me that much." He was still staring off at his estate through the black iron bars.

"You can go in, you know. The place is still yours, for another few days or so anyway."

"No, I think not. I don't suppose it's been my home these last twenty–some years. Not since I lost her. I wouldn't let it be. Now it isn't. Seems appropriate, I suppose."

"How are you getting on at the inn?" I asked.

"Oh, it suited my needs, thank you."

"Suited?"

"Yes. I checked out this afternoon. I'll be leaving Leocadia tonight."

"To go where? This is your home."

"Someone once told me to keep home with you wherever you wander," he said, staring off into the night. Then he faced me and he reached into his pocket. He removed a bundle of money. "For you, William."

"Och, no, Dr. Vant I don't want your money. You've given me enough. Really. I mean look at what you've made possible for me."

"Yes, perhaps you're right," he agreed, repocketing his money.

He smiled briefly, then the smile faded. "If what you said about the day of your wedding was true, then Kien Ling is out there somewhere. Shih–Chieh was no fool, William. For all I know, he could have planted her somewhere knowing, somehow, I'd reveal the secret of the crystals. If she's out there, and has that knowledge, she must be stopped."

"And you're thinking it's up to you to stop her?"

"I never said anything of the kind," he remarked, and his grin returned.

"There's the old Vant spirit we've all been missing," said I.

"Vant?" he asked. "That name has little meaning for me anymore. I am a thousand other people in this world. It just depends on where I am and when."

"And who are you now?" I asked, giving him a cocky look.

"I go by many names, but my title is Kride," said he and with his hand he partially revealed a glimmer of white ivory from under his coat. The fire hadn't even scathed the Kride's mask and it was then I knew he'd already been inside the castle for the last time.

"An honour to meet you, your excellence," I acknowledged with a wink as I extended me hand to his.

He shook it then and surprised me with a great fatherly hug. He then straightened up and began to creep into the nightly fog. As he walked, he quietly recited: "There was once a young man who looked in a mirror and realized his entire life had changed before him in the blink of an eye. But he could never go back to the way things were, because the world had changed around him. He could only look to the future, for what was done could never be reversed …"

"Or could it?" I asked, but he was gone. There on the cobblestones lay his top hat, shed like the skin of a former life.

I never saw him again. I left there that night feeling a renewed sense of vitality. A few months later one of me paintings was bought for five *thousand* pounds by an anonymous collector. It had been priced at only ten.

THE END

ACKNOWLEDGEMENTS

This novel has been for me, as it has for my narrator, the culmination of a number of years of experience shaped by humble small town beginnings and diverse big city influences. I am grateful for those experiences and this novel would not be what it is without them.

Thanks to CreateSpace and Smashwords for providing independent authors a platform to reach an otherwise impenetrable marketplace. Their step by step guidance and invaluable technological tools, is the reason my novel has reached its audience.

For giving my novel a more professional sheen, thanks to Amy, my copyeditor at Kirkus Editorial. Although we've never met, her sage advice has strengthened this novel ten-fold. Thanks also to Kirkus Reviews for helping me realize that I needed more of an editorial overhaul.

To my wife, Kate, thank you for your support during the time it took me to conceive of, write, rewrite, publish, and market this novel. Thank you also for keeping me focused on a marketing strategy and pushing me to pursue independent publishing. You keep me sharp and put my creativity to work. You remind me that there is more to being a successful author than writing a novel. For those and thousands of other reasons, I love you.

Jeremiah Hoehner, thank you for your unwavering belief in me and this novel. As a reader of one of my earliest drafts, your infectious optimism helped keep me going whenever I doubted myself.

Duane Smith, thank you for assistance with the Violet Top Hat advertising project. The photos you took in L.A. were amazing and gave this novel an edge that it needed.

Patricia Bartos, I thank you for encouraging me to add suggested book club questions. They give my readers something else to chew on and provides them more insight into my choices.

Thanks to my Violet Top Hat instagram followers for putting blind faith in a small card. I thoroughly enjoyed travelling around the country to obtain the photos that kept you all in suspense.

Mom and Dad, thank you for providing me the means to take my dreams out of my head and make them something for others to share in. Mom, I take your model of perseverance with me into whatever I embark upon. Dad, I credit your example of hard work and dedication as the blueprint for my success.

Finally, thank you, the reader, for taking time to read William O'Brien's impressionistic collection of Irel E. Vant's tales. Writing it has given me years of enjoyment.

ABOUT THE AUTHOR

Tim-"Othy" Jones has been writing creatively ever since he first learned to write. Having studied English for two years at Detroit, Michigan's Wayne State University, Othy transferred to Brooklyn College in New York City where he graduated with a film degree in screenwriting. Upon graduating, Othy turned his talents to writing novels which he hopes to use to inspire the world to think differently. *The Irrelevant Tales* is Othy's first novel. He and his wife, Kate, still live in the New York Metro area.

CONNECT WITH THE AUTHOR

I greatly appreciate you reading my book! Let's connect online at the following:

Like *The Irrelevant Tales* on Facebook!

Follow me on Twitter: https://twitter.com/othyjones

Favorite my Smashwords author page: http://www.smashwords.com/profile/view/OthyJones

Subscribe to my blog: http://othyjones.blogspot.com/

View the Violet Top Hat instagram page: https://www.instagram.com/violettophat/

Visit the novel's website: http://www.theirrelevanttales.com/

Review *The Irrelevant Tales* on good**reads**!

BOOK CLUB QUESTIONS

The following are suggested book club questions. If your book club is interested in having a live chat with the author, please e-mail him at othyjones@theirrelevanttales.com.

• What do you think is the significance of the novel's title? How does the title relate to Dr. Vant as a character? How does the title relate to the format of the novel? How are the chapters presented?

CHARACTERS

• What is your take on the relationship between Dr. Vant and Billy O'Brien? How do their beliefs influence their actions? How are they alike and how are they different?

• What do you feel Othy Jones meant to convey by frequently referring to Billy as William?

• Many of the characters take on multiple archetypes in "The Irrelevant Tales". In which ways does Dr. Vant take on the role of mentor, hero, herald, shapeshifter, shadowy antagonist, and trickster?

• Most of the characters are given a character arc that leaves them changed by the end of the novel. Pick a character and discuss how that character has changed by the book's end.

• Did your presumptions about the characters and their role in the story change as the novel progressed or did you accurately predict their ultimate role from the very beginning?

• Did you find yourself liking or relating to one character at the beginning only to have it changed to a different character by the end? If so, what do you think drove the change?

SCENES & SETTINGS

• This novel incorporated various countries and locales. Did you enjoy the changes in setting and location? Was it too much, too little, or just enough?

• Scenes and settings play an integral part in explaining a character's origin, story arc, and overall role. Which location or setting provided more insight into a character's background, decision-making, and motives? How did the location or setting do that?

• Locations themselves can often times feel like characters in a novel. Did one location take on that role for you in *The Irrelevant Tales*? If so, how and why?

• Which scene, passage, or chapter stands out most to you and why? What do you feel Othy Jones meant to convey in it?

• Was there a scene, passage, or chapter that surprised you? If so, do think it was intentionally crafted with that purpose in mind?

DIVERSITY

• Othy Jones has expressed that he meant to portray a sense of diversity in "The Irrelevant Tales". Do you think he was successful? Why or why not? How did the representation of each culture make you feel? Most of the cultures represented were given protagonists and antagonists but do you feel any one of those characters were truly "good" or "evil"? Did any of the cultures represented in this story play against a typical stereotype, reaffirm a stereotype, or provide a new perspective to challenge a stereotype?

• Discuss how gender and sex is portrayed in the novel. How are women portrayed? Which is the most memorable female character? What makes them memorable? How are men portrayed in *The Irrelevant Tales*? Which is the most memorable male character? What makes them memorable?

• Discuss the character and role of the Kride in "The Irrelevant Tales. How do you feel about the Kride as a character? Did you feel uncomfortable with any scene or passage containing the Kride? If so, which scene or passage and why? How does the Kride's character address diversity? Was the Kride's character handled appropriately? How would you have written this character differently and why? What is the significance of the term Kride as a title? How does this title relate to Dr. Vant by the end?

• How is religion touched upon?

• What do you think is the significance of the Celtic terminology such as Awen, Morrigan, Sidhe, etc.?

REPRESENTATIONS & THEMES

• How did you feel about the dialects, mannerisms, and vocabulary expressed by each character?

• How do you think the idea of impressionism and painting, in general, relates to the novel?

• Othy Jones refers to himself as an impressionist author. Why do think that is? What is an impressionist author?

• How historically entrenched was the novel? Do you think this was intentional? Why or why not?

• If the novel were made into a film, who do you think would play each character? Who would be best to direct it? How has the writing of the novel influenced your reasoning on these film related questions?

• What other books, films, or stories does *The Irrelevant Tales* make you think of? Why?

• What is the significance of the color violet in the book?

- How are love and lust addressed in the novel?
- The novel was designed to be historical fantasy. How do you think the fantasy element was handled? Was it presented too soon or too late in the story? Was there enough of it or too much?
- What do you make of the symbolisim in the novel?
- What role, if any, did steampunk play?

STRUCTURE

- In a three act play audiences are introduced to characters in their normal life, watch those characters encounter hardships, and survive those hardships to be forever changed. How does this structure relate to the novel as a whole and how is each chapter broken down into this paradigm? Is there a chapter that doesn't fit this model? If so, which and why?
- Describe what you liked or disliked about the writer's style. Have you walked away with a different take on topic, theme, or taboo as a result of reading *The Irrelevant Tales*? How do you feel the novel made you think differently?
- How do you think the dialogue propelled the narrative forward?
- How do you feel about the length of the novel?
- Would you recommend *The Irrelevant Tales* to your friends and family?

Made in the USA
Middletown, DE
21 July 2017